THE EVERLIVING MEMORY
OF JOHN VALENTINE

ROSS SAYERS

The Everliving Memory of John Valentine
© Ross Sayers 2021

Cover illustration: Graeme Clarke

Published by:

Fledgling Press Ltd.
1 Milton Rd West
Edinburgh
EH15 1LA

www.fledglingpress.co.uk

ISBN 978-1-912280-42-1

Printed and bound by:

Print on Demand Worldwide, Peterborough

For my dad, Derek,
who will think this is a bit far-fetched.

Prologue
Walter - London, 1986

Trevor's dead but Walter's already paid his money, so he's decided to stay. The management at Memory Lane are so tight-fisted, he doesn't imagine he'll be getting a refund for this. He chooses not to use the panic button resting in his trouser pocket. Instead, he sits on the bathroom floor with Trevor and strokes his hair. It's just as soft as he remembers it, that day in 1986.

'I'm sure I read that hair keeps growing after you die,' he says to Trevor.

Trevor doesn't respond, because he's dead.

'Maybe I'm thinking of fingernails,' Walter goes on. 'God, what a lot of blood comes out a person's head.'

He inspects the pool of red around Trevor's head. It quivers under the sharp white bulb above them. It's no longer creeping over the tiles, so Walter thinks that's the worst of it over now.

His wristwatch ticks and he turns it towards himself to check the time. Only a few minutes to go.

'A hundred and twenty-five grand,' Walter says. 'A hundred and twenty-five grand for twelve stinking hours. I suppose that's the kind of money you get to charge when you've got a monopoly on the market, eh, Trevor?'

Trevor doesn't respond, because he's still dead.

'They never warned me this could happen,' he goes on. 'And it's not like this is the first time we've done this, is it, Trevor? What's this? Our twenty, twenty-first time? This is new. Wait 'til I spread the word around Edinburgh that your friends can die in Memory Lane, that'll lose them some business, no doubt.'

Walter knows he doesn't have long left in the memory. He's mostly glad, as sitting with the dead body of the man he once loved, if only for a day, isn't what he paid for. But he does miss getting to see a young man's reflection again.

He stands up and looks in the bathroom mirror. There are a few spots of blood on the sink from where Trevor hit his head. He avoids putting his hand near them.

'I was thirty-one when me and you had our day together, Trevor,' Walter says, mostly to his gorgeous, unwrinkled reflection. 'To think I thought I was getting on a bit... I felt awkward at the club, being the old bastard. And look at me now. Well, you'll never get to see what I'm like now. But, imagine this face, with thirty-three years on top. Scary thought, isn't it? All those years, gone in a flash.'

He winks at himself in the mirror then sits back down. Trevor has a birthmark on his shoulder, ruby-coloured and shaped like a baked bean. Walter doesn't remember noticing that in 1986, but if it's here, before his eyes, then he must've remembered it.

He puts a finger on Trevor's neck to check for a pulse again, the way he's seen them do in films. There's nothing there.

'Sorry you died this time,' Walter tells him. 'But we had a good time up until you died, didn't we?'

Trevor is non-committal, but Walter is certain they had. They'd done everything the same as normal, the same as they'd done that day, thirty-three years earlier, when Trevor ran after him, through the non-moving commuters of Paddington Station and handed him his wallet. Walter had insisted on paying him back, in the form of a drink in SoHo. They'd drunk all through the daylight hours, sung karaoke at teatime, had greasy chips in the street, then made love until the wee hours.

That's why Walter can't quite understand why Trevor's dead. He's read the Memory Lane client guidebook many times, and he's certain there's a bit in there about how memories can only change substantially if the client does something to set it off. For example, if Walter had whacked Trevor in the back of the head while he wasn't looking, that would constitute a substantial change to the memory. But Trevor slipping when he got up to go for a piss and skelping his head on the sink? That wasn't supposed to be able to happen.

Did he leave a few drops of water on the floor when he washed his hands? Walter can't even pin down if he *had* washed his hands.

This isn't the real Trevor next to him, he knows that, but it still seems like the respectful thing to do. Wait with him rather than running away. He'd only spent one perfect day with Trevor and then had never seen him again.

He'd never tell the staff at Memory Lane, but getting to live this day again, and all the other memories he's relived? They've been the only thing Walter's looked forward to in recent years. He's not sure how many more times his bank balance will be able to afford it, though. And if Trevor dying is going to start becoming a common feature, that might put a dampener on the whole situation.

He doesn't see it appear, but Walter finds the red button on his palm which tells him time is up and he can leave the memory. He's never tried going over time. He's never ignored the button and continued the memory. They send someone in, he's sure, to kick you out. Memory bouncers, he's heard them called.

Of all the times he's relived this memory, he can't think of one he'd want to spend extra time in less. He presses the button and the world starts to fade, as if the light is being dimmed. The bathroom and the sink and Trevor grow dark until all Walter can see is black. It stays like this for a few moments, until the familiar words appear.

Thank you for using Memory Lane, powered by Memorize technology. We hope you enjoyed your memory and we look forward to welcoming you back soon. A member of our staff will be with you shortly.

These words evaporate and the small room at Memory Lane comes into view. Walter is still on the bed, where he's been lying for the last twelve hours, in this facility built into the ancient stone buildings of the Old Town. He raises a hand to his head and scratches the part of his ear which is stuck under the *Memorize* headset.

A few seconds later, a member of staff, a young Black woman with green hair, comes into the room. Yasmin. Walter's dealt with her before. He likes seeing a familiar face.

She sits down at the computer by his bed.

'Welcome back, Mr McQueen,' she says. 'Everything go okay?'

'Well,' he says. 'Not really.'

'Oh?' Yasmin says, her eyes still on the screen, clicking through the program, looking at the stats from his memory. 'What was wrong?'

'Trevor died,' Walter says. 'He's never died before. And I'm not blaming you, sweetheart, obviously, but I'd like to speak to the management about this.'

Walter doesn't explicitly ask for a refund or discount at this point, but he hopes his tone of voice makes it clear that that's what he's after. You need to take anything you can get from these people.

8

'I'm so sorry to hear that,' Yasmin says. 'Why didn't you use your panic button? It would've flagged up a purple alert and someone would've come into the memory to assist you.'

Walter puts on his best 'confused old man' face.

'I… I forgot,' he says. 'It was just so… traumatising.'

'I completely understand,' Yasmin says, closing the program so the computer screen goes black. 'I'll give you a few minutes to readjust and I'll go and find my manager.'

As she leaves him alone in the room, Walter finds himself missing Trevor already. If Trevor could die in the memory, it wouldn't be ideal, but he doesn't think it would put him off paying for the memory again. He'd take his chances. Love didn't really make sense, after all.

Are you longing for the past?
Interested in reliving one of your favourite memories?
Ready to meet your partner for the first time … again?
Desperate to attend that 1997 Hogmanay party?
Or maybe you're curious if Springsteen actually played 'Racing in the Street' when you saw him in '85?
Do you want to do it all over again?
Yes?
Then come pay us a visit at Memory Lane, where your past is our future.
(Powered by Memorize technology, terms and conditions apply.)

John - Stonecranning, 1975

In the lead up to his wedding, people had told John all sorts of things. Stereotypical comments and advice and such. He found that when people heard you were getting married, what they really heard was: *please tell me any old nonsense you think about marriage and please make sure the horrible experience of your own loveless marriage influences your opinion.*

They had told John it would be the fastest day of his life. *You'll be lucky if you get the chance to light up a fag or finish a pint.* And, on that front, they'd been right. His wedding day had disappeared in a flash, and in the years that followed he couldn't have told you for sure whether they had cut the cake before or after the meal, whether he'd had the soup or the melon to start, or whether he'd gone true Scotsman under his kilt.

But, as he had found in recent years, you never really enjoy any day the first time around. Now he gets to savour these memories, enjoying everything he had missed before.

John stands at the front of the Stonecranning Trinity Church, watching Agnes walk down the aisle. Her arm is linked with her dad, Ronnie. People always crack jokes about mother-in-laws, but they'd be better warning you about the father-in-laws, the Ronnies of the world. It didn't matter that John married Agnes, he never became Ronnie's son-in-law. He always remained just Agnes's husband.

John's best man, Gary, stands nearby, whispering blue comments to try and make him laugh.

'Psst,' he stage whispers. 'John, don't look now, but Ronnie's got wood. Don't look. You'll only make him self conscious.'

In the real world, John isn't good with names anymore. They slip from his mind, always disappearing as he's about to say them out loud. When he forgets a name, it's like firing a flare gun into the sky, alerting everyone around that he isn't as sharp as he used to be. But in memories, the names come easy. For starters, he doesn't have to learn any new ones. Memory Lane are always taking on new people to work the clerical jobs and, even though Philippa tells him not to worry about learning them because not many of them ever last longer than a day, it still hurts to know he probably couldn't even if he tried.

Agnes unlinks her arm from Ronnie and he kisses her on the cheek. As he passes John, he gives him a look. A look that says: *I may be giving away my daughter to you, John, but that doesn't mean I'm happy about it or that you get my respect, even when you take my company to new heights never seen before over the course of the next forty years.* John can admit he may be reading too much into the look.

In the pews, the guests are all smiles. Even his mum, who's smiling through the tears.

John lifts the delicate veil from his bride's face.

'I thought we agreed you were going to shave that,' Agnes says, raising a finger to his moustache.

John knew she was going to make the comment about his moustache. He gives her a cheeky grin, the one he knows she likes, where he only raises the corner of one side of his mouth. She really was the most beautiful woman he ever had the fortune of knowing.

'What would everyone say?' John says. 'If I got rid of it the night before the wedding?'

11

'They'd think you'd finally come to your senses.'

'If you'd like to shave it now, I can ask the minister to hold off a minute. I think I have some shaving cream in my sporran, you know.'

He pretends to dig inside his sporran. Inside, there's his wallet, his hip flask, his Memory Lane panic button. Nowadays, he'd put his mobile phone in there. That was another benefit to being in a memory from 1975. All of his friends sitting at peace, not trying to document the whole day.

'Dad says to tell you you're not supposed to do up the bottom button on your waistcoat,' Agnes says, still inspecting him. 'Gentlemen don't do up the bottom button.'

'Is that right? Gentlemen don't do it up, aye? How would Ronnie know?'

That makes her smile, just like John knew it would. He had tried a few different responses over the course of the many times he'd repeated this day, but that seemed to be the one she liked best. *And how would Ronnie know?* He hadn't said that at the actual wedding. He'd called Ronnie something along the lines of a 'stupid bastard' and the minister had overheard and coughed to show how displeased he was that John had sworn inside the church. Agnes hadn't been best pleased either. One of these times he's going to remember to ask Ronnie why a gentleman isn't supposed to do up the bottom button of his waistcoat.

The minister starts talking and John scans the crowd. Everyone in their best attire. So funny how fashion changes over the years. Even John can admit it all seems a bit dated now. But now isn't now, now is then. Hell, half of this stuff might be back 'in', out in the real world. There are parts of Edinburgh John walks through sometimes and he honestly doesn't know if he's travelled back in time.

No matter how long he stays in this memory, he needs to remember that this isn't the real world. It's important that he remembers. Otherwise, going back will be terrible. He had seen it happen to others. Clients who had stayed too long and couldn't face coming back. That's why they had put the twelve hour limit in place. For everyone but him, of course. He was a special case.

The board members had been delighted with the twelve hour limit actually. The shorter the memories, the more money they could make.

The longer this goes on, the harder it is to come back from, John knows that. But he's not forgetting about the real world. When he feels himself slipping, he thinks about stepping out of Memory Lane on to the Royal Mile. Hearing the rumble of taxi wheels over the cobbles. Feeling the wind blow over his ears.

'Will you, Agnes Irene McDuff, take this man to be your husband, to have and to hold from this day forward, for better, for worse, for richer, for poorer, in sickness and in health, to love and to cherish, until you are parted by death?'

Listening back now, it seems to John the 'parted by death' line was a bit morbid and could've easily been omitted. But things were different back then. It wasn't like now, where the couple decides everything, gets to write out the vows and put in their own little jokes. The minister said what the minister always said and he wasn't going to learn new lines just for you. Weddings were impersonal affairs. Getting married was about the least special thing two people could do.

'I will,' Agnes says, and smiles at John.

He tries to take it all in, the last time she smiled at him before she became his wife. Every crinkle of skin around her lips and nose. The fact that she's putting her tongue to

13

the roof of her mouth because she thinks it brings out her jawline. The look in her eye that tells him she's truly happy and isn't thinking about anything else but this moment.

John misses some of what the minister says but hears:

'…parted by death?'

And it's his turn. He's attempted jokes at this point in the past. They never go down well.

'I will.'

Someone lets out a sarcastic 'Way!' from the crowd and John can't turn quickly enough to see who it is. The minister brings the vows to a close, then gives John permission to kiss Agnes. Again, he has always found that a strange tradition. Did John *need* the minister's permission to kiss her? Would he have been in trouble with the big man upstairs if he'd went in for a smooch without clearing it with the church first? John hasn't spoken to the big man in quite some time.

With the minister's blessing, he kisses Agnes. The kind of kiss you give your new wife when all your friends and family are watching. A safe one.

'Hello, Mrs Valentine,' he says to her.

He really wishes he had said this to her the first time. The real time. But that kind of smooth patter never came to John naturally, and he was too old now to believe it ever would. He has needed all these redos just to come up with 'Hello, Mrs Valentine', and even that isn't exactly something out of a Ben Elton script. It doesn't matter now, he supposes. This doesn't really count, does it? Agnes won't ever hear these new words. Just this representation of her in the memory. This combination of what he remembers about her and how the *Memorize* technology thinks she would react to things.

'Oh God,' Agnes says. 'My hands are shaking, John.'

'You did fine, love. That's the hardest part over.'

14

'I'm not so sure. I need to be your wife now.'

'Fair point. And until we're parted by death, the minister made that bit quite clear.'

This brings out her laugh. Her wonderful laugh. John can never tell if she laughs because his mind believes she would have, or whether the technology believes she would have. That's how he had designed *Memorize*, so the clients got the best experience possible. It was just an added bonus that they could charge a ridiculous fee for this kind of realism.

But John isn't paying anything for reliving this memory again and again, not in terms of money, at least.

Hannah - Edinburgh, 2019

The pen isn't out of ink. Hannah can clearly see loads of the fucking stuff sitting right there inside the fucking clear tube, and yet when she presses it to the paper it barely squirts out a full stop. The pen is a liar.

'Give up the fucking ink,' she whispers to it.

She tests it again, digging it into her palm, until it comes to life and marks dark blue lines up and down the fleshy part of her hand.

'And you're sure you don't want me to make you up a lunch to take in?' Hannah's mum says. 'There's a packet of cold meat open in the fridge. Marks and Spencer's.'

Hannah doesn't hear her, not properly, as she fills in the final details on the pre-contract Memory Lane sent her through the post. She had meant to do it last night but Sydney was fussy so she ended up sitting with him, watching *Who Wants To Be A Millionaire?* on mute while he went in and out of sleep.

Have you ever created/joined/communicated with any radical terrorist organisations which attempted to or are currently attempting to overthrow one or several governments? Y / N

She wonders if this question has ever caught out a terrorist. Someone who wants to overthrow the government, or several governments, but thinks it's only fair to let their new employer know. She resists circling the Y for a laugh and circles the N.

'What was that, Mum?' Hannah asks.

Behind her, her mum tears a banana from the bunch and hangs the rest back on the hook of the fruit bowl. Moving back in with her parents after Sydney was born had been good for Hannah money-wise, but not great everything-else-wise. For one thing, life has become one never-ending sequence of her mum forcing her to eat the fruit in the fruit bowl so it doesn't go to waste, then her mum buying a whole load of new fruit the minute it's empty. She finds she can't even enjoy the fruit now, for fear of the fruit to come.

'I asked, did you want a lunch made up?' her mum says again.

'Nah,' Hannah says. 'I'll go out on my break and get something. It's my first day, I dunno where the fridge is yet. I don't want to be sitting there during the induction worrying about the ham piece in my bag stinking the room out.'

'Turning her nose up at my M&S ham, very good. I'll get the cheap stuff next time.'

Hannah turns over to the second page of the questionnaire.

Have you ever recreationally taken any hallucinogenic or psychedelic drugs? Y / N

Again, Hannah wonders how many people own up to this sort of thing. She had smoked weed with Liam in halls during first year, but it didn't make her hallucinate: it just made her sleepy, or on one night during Freshers, get super paranoid about the size of her knuckles. *They're all looking at my knuckles, Liam! I'm never shaking hands with anyone ever again!*

She never touched anything like that after she found out she was pregnant with Sydney. He arrived during her

17

second year and now she can't imagine touching anything like that again. Maybe that makes her boring. That's definitely what her friends seem to think of her now. She circles N and moves to the next question.

'What's the job again?' her mum asks, coming to sit with her at the table.

Hannah's mum squeezes the banana from the bottom to open it. It's one of her strange eating habits that Hannah and her dad have long since given up questioning. *It's how the apes do it, and if there's one thing apes know about, it's eating bananas. Just need to watch out for black spider eggs. They lay them in bananas, look it up.*

'It's called Memory Lane, it's a memory clinic just off the Royal Mile. I hadn't actually heard of it until the job went up on Indeed.'

'I meant, what's your job title? Samantha was asking.'

'Technically, I'm a "Retrieval Assistant", but don't ask me what that means. Hopefully, I'll know after today. Who's Samantha, by the way?'

'She's the one that brings your dad his DPD deliveries.'

'I didn't realise we were that close with the DPD driver.'

'We got her a bottle of wine and a box of Matchmakers at Christmas.'

'Matchmakers? What flavour?'

'Salted caramel.'

'Say no more, she's basically family then. What about the Hermes driver?'

Her mum snorts.

'He'll get a lump of coal across the head and he'll like it.'

Can you think of any reason, not previously mentioned, why you would not be a suitable candidate to work at Memory Lane? Y / N

18

It would be easier to answer this question if they'd given her more information about what the job actually entails. She knows it's a memory clinic and she knows she shouldn't have got the job, but somehow she did.

The interview had gone okay, not great, but okay. The woman had asked generic, *do you work well in a team* style questions and Hannah had provided generic, *well, actually funny that you mention that, yes I do work well in a team* competency-based answers. The interview was held in the Starbucks on Princes Street which, of course, made her think it might be one of those fake jobs that she would later speak about on an ITV documentary, but the website and everything else was legit.

The woman who'd interviewed her, Philippa, had explained the security clearances and background checks to get into the actual Memory Lane building were extremely thorough and it wasn't worth carrying them out just for interviewees. Hannah was impressed at their ability to make the job application process even more degrading than usual. They wouldn't even let her in the building, just fantastic.

Hannah had messaged her friend, Erin, about the job advert. Erin had assured her that all these fancy places do the same these days: make the job sound super vague, make everyone think they're suitable for the role, never rule anyone out for having a certain degree. That way they don't have to specify that they actually want someone with a First in Computer Science who went to St Andrews (because Oxbridge graduates don't have to come up to Scotland unless they're desperate or their dad's stepping down as CEO somewhere).

And yet Hannah, with her 2:2 in English Studies from Stirling, got the job. Or one of the jobs. Philippa had never stated exactly how many people they wanted to take on. Again, Hannah thinks, this is probably done not to discourage people. If there had only been one role, she'd probably not have applied at all. She's never been number one at anything. She circles the N.

As she moves to the final question, she hears her dad's unmistakable, thunderous footsteps coming down the stairs. He bursts into the kitchen, Sydney in his arms.

'There's Mummy!' he says, pointing at Hannah, a silly lilt to his voice. 'Yes, that's right, that's your mummy, Sydney, and guess what, she's got a job. Yes, she's got a job, can you believe it? Me either! But this very silly company called Memory... something or other, have agreed to give her a job and money, isn't that silly of them? So, it's just going to be me and you in the house during the day while the women are at work. The way it should be, if you ask me, and we're going to have so much fun watching... *Dora the Explorer*!'

Sydney claps his hands and nods his head.

'Dora!' he confirms.

'And Mr Tumble!'

'Mr Tumble!'

'And The Sopranos!'

Sydney doesn't know how to respond to this.

'Okay, well maybe we'll keep that until you're five or six.'

Hannah's dad kneels and puts Sydney down. He toddles over to the corner where his Blaze monster truck toy lies on its side.

'All set?' her dad asks. 'Need any help with the forms?'

'Nope, all sorted.'

'Good, 'cause I can never remember your blood type... or birthday... or name. Anna, was it?'

He joins them at the table and pretends to wipe a tear from his eye.

'Y'know they always tell you your kids grow up fast,'

he says. 'One minute they're going off to uni, the next they're knocked up and coming back to live with you. And I guess you never really believe they're going to get a proper job with an English degree. Sorry, I promised myself I wouldn't get emotional.'

'Very good,' Hannah says. 'Were you rehearsing that upstairs?'

'You can't rehearse these kind of emotions, Hannah.'

Hannah walks over to where Sydney is sitting flipping through a Paw Patrol book, the Blaze toy abandoned after twelve seconds. She crouches by his side.

'Mummy's off to work now, Syd,' she says. 'You going to be a good boy for Grandad?'

Sydney nods, not taking his eyes off the dogs on the pages. Hannah stands back up. She's not sure what she expected. That he'd weep and scream and demand that he couldn't live another moment if his mummy wasn't by his side? She didn't want that, she didn't want any reason that would stop her getting out the door. But would a few tears really hurt him?

'Don't worry,' Hannah's mum says. 'He probably doesn't think you're actually, properly leaving. The real test is the second day.'

'She's right,' her dad adds. 'Sydney doesn't believe you've managed to get a job either.'

Hannah grabs her bag from the counter and her jacket from the cupboard. In the mirror, she quickly checks her hair and face haven't gone to shit since she sorted them fifteen minutes ago. She wasn't sure how big to go with the make-up, since she's not sure exactly what the average day in this job is going to be like. If she needs to submerge herself in one of those water sensory deprivation tanks, she may need a rethink for tomorrow.

'Have a good day,' her mum says. 'And keep me updated on WhatsApp.'

'I will,' Hannah replies. 'You're working today, aren't you?'

'Backshift.'

'Cool, stay safe. And Dad, don't be feeding Sydney too many Squashies.'

Her dad is by the toaster, constantly popping the bread in and out of the thing to make sure the toast meets his standard and doesn't go even the slightest bit past his preferred level of brown.

'I can't promise anything,' he says. 'Is Liam picking Sydney up tonight?'

'He is, but I'll be back by then.'

'Grand,' he says, switching back to his high, cutesy voice for Sydney's benefit. 'Cause we don't like your daddy, do we, Sydney? He's a silly billy, isn't he?'

'Dad, don't slag him off in front of Sydney.'

'He'll need to learn his dad's a waster one day. Forgive me for trying to toughen the boy up.'

Hannah's not sure that's an entirely accurate depiction of Liam, but she's not going to argue. The break-up was relatively amicable, and they'd sorted out childcare without any need for getting third parties involved.

He properly freaked out at first, though. It definitely wasn't in his plan to get a girl pregnant while he was studying for his Politics exam in his third year at uni. But then Sydney came, and everything changed. No one can resist Sydney. Everyone thinks their baby is the cutest, but Hannah knows for sure.

Hannah's already opened the door when her mum calls her back.

'Your forms,' she says, rushing to the door and handing over the thin bundle of papers.

22

'Aw, lifesaver.'

Hannah walks to the bus stop and looks over the papers to make sure she's completed everything. It's only then she notices she didn't answer the final question.

Do you consider yourself a strong person, emotionally speaking? Capable of dealing with clients going through potentially intense memory experiences? Y / N

She doesn't even know what that question's asking. She leaves it blank. Surely they won't care about her missing one question? The 44 arrives and she steps on, tapping her card to pay for her ticket. She goes upstairs and feels lucky to get a window seat. She may have had to move back in with her parents when Sydney was born, and she may have a relatively useless English degree, but she's got her health, she's got Sydney, and now she's on her way to her first grown up job. She's a grown up and no one can say otherwise. She draws a smiley face in the condensation on the window.

John - Stonecranning, 1975

They say, when you look back on the best days of your life, you only remember the good parts. When you remember an old flame, you remember the walks on the beach, the picnics in the park, the first time you had sex, maybe even the second and third time you had sex. You don't remember the sand in your shoes, the wasps on your bread, the seemingly never-ending moments when you couldn't get it up. Whoever 'they' are, John thinks they're right. It wasn't until he started reliving his wedding day that he realised how much of it was spent standing around, doing nothing at all. And everything stunk of smoke.

'Okay, and now one with just the groom and the best man.'

Agnes and the rest of the bodies around John shuffle and scoot away from the line of fire of the camera.. Nowadays, the bride and groom are expected to take a trip in the middle of the wedding to go to a loch or some woods and do a lovey-dovey Vogue-cover-style fashion shoot, but back in his day, the side wall of the church was just fine.

Gary comes to stand by John's side, the pair of them raising a hand to the sky to block out the worst of the sun.

'Got lucky with the weather, mate,' Gary says. 'How you feeling?'

'Good,' John says. 'As long as Agnes is happy, that's all that matters.'

'Jeez, she's got you trained already.'

John and Gary stand with their hands clasped in front

of them and smile and squint until they get the thumbs up from the photographer that they can relax. Photographer is probably going a bit far – he was just Agnes's friend from work, Martin. She only invited him because he owned a camera.

'That'll be a nice one,' Gary says. 'Once it's developed, can I get a copy?'

'You'll need to ask that Martin fella.'

John doesn't remember where all the photos ended up. Agnes put up one of the pair of them in the living room, and the big one with all the guests was in a frame in the boxroom. The rest must've gone up the loft, then been accidentally chucked out at some point.

Back then, getting your photo taken was nothing to be sniffed at. You'd put on a decent shirt, a tie, sort your hair out. You wouldn't want to waste film so you'd only get one chance at it. And you wouldn't even know if it was any good or not until weeks later when you finally got it back from the shop. More often than not someone's thumb was in the photo or the glare obscured your face. Now all the young ones take a hundred photos a day on their phones. They all think they need to be models. He doesn't envy that, all the photos, constantly comparing yourself to your pals. He knew he was better looking than his best man, Gary, and he didn't need comments under a photo to know that.

'Soon as you're free,' Gary says. 'Find me and I'll get you your first pint, alright? Don't take a drink off anyone else before me, promise?'

'Promise.'

They shake hands and Gary disappears into the crowd. Agnes comes back to him slowly, her steps careful and considered across the grass. Onlookers from the high street gather and watch, delighted. There's something about a wedding, John thinks, that makes people happy, even if they're strangers. Everyone all dressed up, particularly in Scotland, with the novelty of kilts.

When he'd been a teenager, he'd hated the idea of kilts. Thought they made men look silly. None of the men in the films he'd see at the picturehouse ever wore kilts. They wore clean, sharp, black suits. He'd been obsessed with the *Godfather* films back then. He couldn't imagine Don Corleone sitting at Connie's wedding in a kilt. That phase had thankfully passed though. By the time the third film came out, the magic was gone, John was in his fifties and none of it seemed quite as cool anymore.

Kilts weren't even the done thing back then, either. Normally too expensive for your average punter. John's kilt was foisted on him by his new father-in-law, one of several wedding gifts which weren't entirely practical but reminded everyone how much money Ronnie had at his disposal.

'Are you worried about the speech?' Agnes asks.

'Gary's?' John says. 'Have you not noticed me tossing and turning during the night?'

The weeks leading up to the big day, Gary had been winding John up no end. Hinting that he would bring up every time he'd made an arse of himself while full of the drink. Like the time he put *Wild Night* by Van Morrison on the jukebox in The Admiral, got up on the pool table, played the cue like a guitar, put a hole in the fabric with his heel and had to pay fifteen quid for them to get new felt. They never did buy new felt but they kept his fifteen quid.

Gary also hinted that he was going to bring up every girl that John had ever been with. *It'll take me about eight seconds.* But John had still been worried, because Agnes *really* wasn't a fan of his first girlfriend, Jeanie, who they

26

still saw in the scheme every now and then. John had never thought Gary would have the brass neck to do it. But he did. John's heard it a lot of times now and it never gets old. Not like him and Gary. They got older and kept on getting older. Gary had died a few years back. John spoke at the funeral. Seven people attended.

'Nah, I'm kidding,' John says. 'I'm sure he'll be on his best behaviour.'

'I swear to God, if he mentions *her*, I'll make him eat that speech.'

'I think she's here actually. I'm sure I saw her throwing rice as we walked out.'

'Is that... is that a joke? I didn't know I had married Tommy Cooper.'

'I'm better-looking than him.'

'That's highly debatable.'

They kiss and the wedding party cheers and claps. Martin begins dismantling the camera and the onlookers wander off, back in the direction of the high street to continue getting their messages.

The Stonecranning high street is a sort of upside-down L shape. A steep slope then a left turn which takes you to the Roger Davidson Memorial clock tower at the end of the road. It's always been a small town, never in with a chance of a Royal visit or anything like that, but the residents are proud of their clock tower. You can even climb the stairs to the roof if it's a nice day and you can sneak up without getting caught. Well, in 1975 you could. John hasn't tried it in a long time.

'That's the bus here,' someone shouts.

The coach appears at the end of the road and drives up to the side of the church, coming to a stop with a rusty sigh. The guests get into a loose queue and file onto the bus, while John and Agnes hang back to get on last.

'I'm looking forward to this meal,' his old friend, Frank, says, being ushered towards the coach by his wife, Nina. 'Mine's is the beef, John. Can you make sure I get beef?'

John gives him a thumbs up.

'Sure, Frank, it's my number one priority. You going to keep that?'

John points at the tin stashed under Frank's arm. The tin with the scatter money inside.

'Och, there's me nearly away with the scatter money. Lucky you remembered!'

On their wedding day there hadn't been a scatter, because Frank, who was in charge of the scatter, got on the bus to the reception with the scatter money tucked safely under his arm. By the time they all realised, it was too late to go back, and the car park at the community hall was full and there were concerns the coins might scratch people's cars if they went ahead with it there. Later in the night, the staff had to tell Frank he couldn't keep paying for his drinks with coppers.

John takes the tin from Frank and walks to the front of the church, where the kids who haven't given up hope still linger and perk up at the sight of him.

'Everybody ready?' he shouts.

They all whoop and cheer and bend their knees slightly to give them a faster start. He opens the tin and shoogles the heavy coins out. They land with a metallic smatter and the kids rush around his feet like hungry pigeons.

It's a shame the scatter never actually happened on the day. It's just a little thing, but all these little things add up over time. That's the beauty of Memory Lane. It lets John live out all the little things he had to miss about this day, or any other day.

Not that *Memorize* was designed for such changes though. Its main purpose is for the client to relive the day exactly as they remember it. But a little change here and there is fine. That's what The Valentine Variable is for. That's the vital bit of code which allows the client to change parts of the memory more to their liking. John hadn't planned to name it after himself but his son, Michael, insisted.

John follows Agnes to the coach, leaving behind the sound of kids scraping coppers off concrete.

Hannah - Edinburgh, 2019

She gets off the bus on South Bridge and takes a right when she gets to the Royal Mile. At this time of morning it's mainly people on their way to work or tourists who managed to get out their beds early. The Mile is the kind of street you can walk up and down a thousand times and still find yourself saying things like, *I haven't seen that shop before, is that just opened?* or *Look at the state of that tat.*

Memory Lane sent her a little map with a red line telling her where to turn off the Mile. It only takes her five minutes to reach it. A dim, shadowed alleyway, carved into the thick stone of the street. She walks through to find it brighter on the other side. A small square, dotted with a few, what look to be residential doors, and a large glass façade to the left. Its futuristic design doesn't belong here. There's no Memory Lane signage, but Hannah's confident this must be the place.

Hannah hates first days. The feeling of being fresh meat. Inductions that cover health and safety and corporate policy but don't cover actual relevant things, like when she should take her tea break or which is the closest roll shop.

She presses the button on the intercom and waits until a voice responds.

'Hello?'

'Hi, I'm Hannah Greenshields. I'm here for my induction.'

'Hi, Hannah, come through. Use your badge to scan through the next door.'

There's a buzz and she presses against the heavy glass door. She walks through a small entrance area with two chairs and a potted plant before reaching another glass door. At the side of the door, a small black sensor. They had sent her her work pass in advance, dropped off by a courier. They even let her choose which photo she wanted online, rather than ambushing her on her first day. She taps her pass against the sensor and the little light blinks from red to green and she walks through.

This brings her to the reception desk, where a smiling guy, probably a couple of years younger than her, peeks his head over the top of the ledge.

'Hannah, hi,' he says. 'Welcome to Memory Lane. I'm Cillian.'

As her dad kept reminding her, this is her first 'grown up' job, and even though she's just in the door, it definitely feels like it. It's the first workplace she's ever walked into that wasn't in the retail or service industry. Where the first colleague she met didn't tell her to get out while she still can. Where they actually knew she was due to arrive. This guy, Cillian, is actually smiling, and it doesn't seem like he's doing it in a sarcastic way or because his manager is nearby.

'Hi, Cillian,' she says. 'Nice to meet you.'

'Did you find us okay?

'Yeah, it was fine. I live in Gorgie. I've never been through that little alleyway before, though.'

'Right? The amount of little nooks in Edinburgh you walk past all the time and don't even notice. Have you got your pre-contract and the questionnaire we sent you?'

She fetches it out her bag and slides it over to him.

'Perfect,' he says. 'It'll be Philippa that's doing your induction today. She'll be along soon, if you just want to take a seat over there.'

'Thanks.'

Philippa was the one who interviewed her, so she already has at least two people she can name without having to apologise and awkwardly ask.

She turns and walks to the waiting area, where four seats flank another tall plant, surrounded by more thick glass windows, the morning sunshine beaming through and making every surface warm. In one of the chairs sits a man, reading a magazine. He has a Paul Rudd vibe about him, where she wouldn't feel comfortable guessing his age.

'Hi,' he says, moving a hand from the magazine to smooth his tie. 'I'm Xander.'

'Hannah.'

They shake hands. Hannah leaves the seat beside him free and sits in the one next to that. She likes to think she is adept at social niceties.

'Are you here for...?' he says.

'The induction. You?'

'Yep. Congrats.'

'Thanks, you too.'

So at least two of them were hired after the Starbucks interviews. That makes her feel a little more relaxed. Memory Lane aren't pinning all their hopes on her.

'You might think I'm stupid,' Xander says. 'But... do you know exactly what the job is? My wife keeps asking and I honestly don't remember if she told us during the interview. Did Philippa interview you too?'

'She did,' Hannah says. 'And, oh my God, I am so glad you said that. I've no clue what the job is. She definitely didn't tell us.'

'And I felt like it was my fault, 'cause at the end when she said "Do you have any questions for me?", I was just so glad I had got through the interview, I wasn't thinking about what to ask. I considered asking her to buy me a caramel latte but thought that might be pushing it.'

Hannah laughs. So that's Cillian on the desk, Philippa taking the induction and... oh God. She's forgotten this guy's name already. How is that possible? What an idiot. She tells herself to calm down and she'll hear it when someone else says it. Not that it helps with the sweat that's started to seep down her back.

Two men come in the entrance. One is tall, older, and says hello to Cillian at the desk before disappearing through a nearby door. The other introduces himself at the desk like Hannah did, then joins her and whatshisname in the waiting area. She'd put him in his early thirties.

'Fellow newbies?' the new man says, taking the end seat.

Her and whatshisname both nod.

'I'm Andreas,' he says.

'Hannah.'

'Xander.'

Xander, of course it's Xander. Like Xander from *Buffy*, she thinks. She makes a mental note not to forget his name again. Then she makes a further mental note to watch an episode of *Buffy* when she gets back home tonight. One of the happier episodes. Something to look forward to during her first day.

The trio all shake hands then settle into a comfortable silence, checking phones, picking up and discarding magazines from the table, staring at murky reflections in the windows. There's a radio playing quietly somewhere over at reception.

Xander rubs one of the plant leaves between his fingers.

'What kind d'you think this is?' he asks.

'Ikea?' Hannah answers.

'I think you're right.'

They both smile, but Andreas doesn't. On the one hand, she feels sorry for him, that he arrived last and her and Xander already have this great bond. On the other, he should've arrived earlier.

'So, do either of you know what the job entails exactly?' Andreas asks.

There's no time to reply, as Cillian arrives next to them.

'All ready folks?' he says. 'I'll just take you through to the induction room.'

They follow him past the desk and through a door, into a long white corridor. Everything feels clean, from the shiny door handles to the gleaming laminate flooring. It reminds Hannah of one of those private hospitals you see in TV adverts that no one born after 1980 can afford, but without the hospital smell, or the older people who smile and don't seem to have any medical problems.

There's another set of doors at the end of the corridor. Through the little windows they can see other staff members go by. Most of them pause to peer through and inspect the new recruits. A woman waves and Hannah waves back, the only one to raise her hand.

Cillian opens the third door on the left and ushers them inside. A standard conference room lies in darkness until they activate the motion sensor lights when they stride across the floor. The long table stretches almost the length of the room. The three of them take the furthest three seats from the projection on the wall, like schoolkids keeping their distance from the teacher. Hannah would've sat at the front but if the other two aren't then she isn't either.

'There's water on the table,' Cillian tells them. 'Philippa will just be a second. If anyone needs anything, I'll be round at reception.'

He leaves and closes the door behind him. The room is quiet and without windows, though Hannah can hear

34

the faint hum of the projector on the ceiling, which is displaying a slide on the wall. *Memory Lane, where your past is our future*. She's not quite sure what that's supposed to mean. *We're making money off your memory problems* would probably be a more honest tagline, but she doesn't imagine that would go down well with clients.

Come on, Hannah, she tells herself, don't judge until you hear what you're going to be doing. She checks her watch. 9.17 a.m. She hopes Sydney is doing okay. It's his first time without her or Liam since, well, since she can remember. A whole day with just his grandad. What a fucking riot that'll be.

'Some strange questions in that questionnaire, or was that just me?' Xander asks, and Hannah's glad someone's finally had the guts to fill the silence.

'They asked if we did psychedelic drugs in the past,' Andreas replies. 'They didn't say anything about us doing them in the future. Nice to keep my options open.'

The relaxed, conversational atmosphere that was threatening to break out dissolves the second the door opens and Philippa walks into the room.

When Hannah met her that day in Starbucks, she thought they both seemed out of place in there. Hannah had never felt she belonged in trendy coffee shops. She only liked coffee that was at least fifty percent milk, for one thing, and she couldn't study with the sounds of machines whirring constantly. Philippa looked like a woman who owned a fashion brand in a bad yet rewatchable 90s comedy, completely out of place in the shop, with her black and white fur coat and Cruella DeVille vibes.

'Darlings,' she says, gliding across the floor to stand at the front, next to the laptop hooked up to the screen. 'My three angels, yes you are. Glad you all made it. Oh, boy, what a morning already, sorry I'm late. If you ever come across a client called Walter McQueen, don't let him open his mouth. I'm kidding. But don't.'

The three new starts all shake their heads and make non-committal noises to signal she shouldn't worry about being late.

'First of all, let me say,' she goes on. 'Congratulations. You know how many applicants we had? Well, let's just say it was... a lot. I'm not going to put a number on it but... it was two thousand, three hundred and twenty-six, give or take. So, basically, after being the winning sperm to get to the egg, this has been the luckiest moment of your life. I hope you all appreciate that.'

Philippa wiggles her finger over the laptop pad and the cursor springs into life on the screen.

'Okay, let's get this show on the road,' she says, taking a sip from her coffee cup. 'Mmm, that's the stuff. I hate to be one of those "I'm not me until I've had my morning coffee" people, but... I'm not me until I've had my fourth morning coffee. Right, yes, let's begin the induction.'

She clicks the mouse and the projection on the wall changes from the title page to a second slide.

Welcome to Memory Lane.
You are here because you have shown yourself to be the best suited candidates, so please be confident that you're right for the role.
By the end of this induction, you should be well versed in our company and our values, and fully equipped to start your journey at Memory Lane.

Hannah feels a bit dizzy at the thought of somehow being one of the top three people out of two thousand, three hundred and twenty-something candidates. Her interview didn't even go that well. It went okay but not amazing. Is it possible that everyone else out there is just as terrified and shit at interviews as her?

'Before I go any further,' Philippa says. 'I should warn you. You've probably realised that we kept a lot of the details of the job under wraps during the recruitment process. This was done on purpose. What I'm about to tell you is not necessarily secret information. The government is well aware of our business and we share resources with them happily. But it may take a few minutes for you to accept that what we do at Memory Lane is real, and that's totally fine. I didn't believe it at first when I joined the company. Okay? Yes? So, let's begin.'

John - Stonecranning, 1975

The radio on the bus is crackly. John can't change that. He can get up, walk to the radio, get tossed back and forth a few times by the swerving of the bus, and change the station if he wants. That's doable. But he can't magic it not to be crackly. That's just how radios were back then. Neither can he reach into his pocket, produce an iPod and say, *excuse me, everybody, but look at this cool new thing I've invented.* Which is a shame, really, because he's always wanted at least a little recognition for his achievements. As soon as he invented *Memorize* technology, John found himself surrounded by advisors, whose main advice was to keep this technology as secret as possible.

So he's stuck with the crackly radio, playing the same crackly songs. He doesn't bother changing the station this time, he knows what's playing on every one. 10cc, Carpenters, Frankie Valli, KC and the Sunshine Band. The kind of stuff that, when it plays nowadays, the young ones call it 'retro'. Everything John likes is 'retro' now. It seems to mean 'old but cool'.

'Can't believe you talked me into this,' Agnes whispers to him from the window seat. 'We should've got a taxi and left everyone else to get the coach. It's sweltering in here and the floor is filthy, look at the bottom of my dress.'

'Love,' John says. 'If we'd have got a taxi, you'd have complained that everyone else is together, having a laugh on the bus and we're missing all the fun.'

'I would not.'

'How much d'you want to bet?'

'I'll bet every pound you've got, John Valentine.'

'Well, Agnes Valentine, I spent all my money on a wedding and a bus, didn't I?'

'The money's gone? I'll fetch out those divorce papers my dad insists I keep under our bed.'

Their faces are so close now it wouldn't make sense not to kiss her. They break apart when the expected chorus of cheers goes up through the rest of the bus.

'Jeezo, JV,' Gary says from behind them, his face poking through the gap in the seats, pressing against the furry material. 'Can you not wait a few hours before you start all that business? Some of us want to enjoy our dinner.'

Gary's wife, Brenda, smacks him on the arm and apologises.

'He's allergic to romance,' she says.

'She's right, you know. Romance and peanuts. The doctors say if I get too close to either of them, my throat will eat itself. They've never seen a case like mine. There's no peanuts in the chicken is there, John?'

'No, but there is a light sentimental sauce.'

'That could be a problem.'

John turns round in his seat to get a look at everyone, the rows of bobbing heads, the hats which have stayed on because if they come off, that's them off for the rest of the day.

At the back, the teenagers, Scott Williams, David Doig and Ross McElroy, pass a hip flask between them and think no one's noticed. Scott works for the government these days, David's a lawyer, and Ross emigrated to Australia. Everywhere he looks, a snapshot of people in a time they would never get the chance to return to.

Some people point out the windows as they pass their houses, their work, the shop they get their pies on a

Sunday. John's mum and dad, Gail and Willie, sit at peace, hands in their laps, while Agnes's parents, Ronnie and Catherine, sit in the seats behind them. They don't make any attempt at conversation. It's partly because they're the kind of people who agree that there's no point in talking if you've got nothing to say. It's also partly down to the fact that John's dad hates Ronnie even more than John.

Agnes is too jittery to sit still, constantly twisting and turning in her seat. She raises a hand to the buttons above her head, where the aircon is supposed to blow through. She presses every button but nothing comes. John always suspected these buttons were for show only. Like a few years later when they started putting TV screens in coaches but they never seemed to be able to turn them on.

'Have you asked him yet?' Agnes says.

'No,' John replies.

John doesn't like to think of himself as special. He's certainly not one to get up and sing at the karaoke or try and do silly stunts and end up on *You've Been Framed!* But he does imagine he's a fairly rare case, in that, on the day of his wedding, getting married wasn't the most important thing he had to do that day.

'When are you going to do it?' she asks again.

'Later on.'

'You shouldn't leave it too late.'

'I'll wait 'til he's got a drink in him.'

'He doesn't get like you and Gary, you know. He won't be steaming.'

'I'll do it after the meal. He'll be in a better mood then.'

'You don't know my dad. He only has the one mood.'

John knows she's right. Ronnie wasn't the kind of man that you could 'know', if that makes any sense. He was about as three dimensional as a bit of paper. John often wonders what Ronnie and Catherine talked about when no one else was around. They're the kind of couple that arrived to things late, left early, and spent the whole time talking about how they couldn't stay late and needed to head off soon.

John knows exactly what's coming today. He knows today like the back of his hand. Better even, because sometimes he finds something on the back of his hand, some hair or freckle, that he doesn't recall growing. But his wedding day, he knows every inch of it.

And yet he still has nerves jangling about inside him. There are certain conversations which don't get any easier the second time round, or the third time round, or whichever time round he's on now. Later tonight, John's going to take Ronnie aside and ask him for a job at his firm. McDuff & McBride Incorporated. Back then, they had a Falkirk office and a Glasgow office, with an Edinburgh one soon to open. They were coming up with all kinds of uses for plastic. Thirty-odd years later they would be opening Memory Lane, with John as CEO and Ronnie long since passed away.

'Just make sure you do it tonight,' Agnes reminds him again. 'This is the happiest he'll ever be.'

John swivels in his seat to see Ronnie's stony, emotionless face.

'Aye, he's like a human rainbow, right enough.'

'You know what I mean.'

'Maybe he'll say no.'

'He won't, he can't say no to you now.'

'It's not like *The Godfather*, you know, love. He doesn't *have* to say yes just because it's his daughter's wedding day. Although I do think him and Don Corleone would get on, just sitting in a dark room, grunting at each other.'

The thing with reliving a memory is you don't get to skip the bits you don't like. For all the highs of this day, he

41

still has to beg Ronnie for a job. He still has to sit through the bumpy coach ride over to the community hall. He still has to have the last conversation he ever had with his dad.

That's how John designed it. No pausing, no fast forwarding, no fancy gimmicks. They had experimented after Memory Lane first opened. How to give the client the best experience possible.

In the end, they'd settled on twelve hour memories. A panic button for if the client gets in trouble during the memory, and an exit button for when they need to leave. The exit button only appears on their hand after twelve hours. That way, they can't 'accidentally' hit it after eleven hours and demand their money back. John's exit button isn't on his hand though. He's a special case.

That's John's problem with books and films and the soaps on TV. Every conversation is so important and rattles the plot along. The more he relives his memories, the more he realises that 99% of the conversations in his life were about nothing, and the other 1% were about everything.

'Why are we stopped?' Agnes asks.

'The roadworks are still up.'

'Still?'

'Aye.'

'They were meant to be done by the 20th.'

'When do you ever trust what the council tells you?'

'Don't they know I've got a wedding reception to get to?'

'I'll hop out and explain to the workies.'

42

Hannah – Edinburgh, 2019

'That all sounded a bit dramatic, didn't it?' Philippa says. 'Well, frankly, get used to it. This is a dramatic company and I am a dramatic woman and I shall not be apologising for either.'

Hannah wants to make eye contact with Xander or Andreas to check they're hearing the same things she's hearing but finds she can't take her eyes off Philippa.

Philippa dramatically glides her hand through the air and clicks to the next slide on the presentation. The slide reads:

Here at Memory Lane, we offer our clients unique, never-seen-before memory-based experiences (or 'Mexes'). For a reasonable fee, we give our clients the chance to relive the best memories of their lives, from graduations to weddings, childbirth to birthday parties, even cup finals at Wembley. For a period of twelve hours, our clients enter a deep, dreamlike state, where they are connected to our state of the art Memorize technology. While connected, they relive a period of twelve hours from their memory, allowing them to experience the happiest times of their lives once again. Our clients often comment there were so many things they had forgotten!

Hannah, Xander and Andreas read the slide while Philippa slurps more coffee and the projector continues to hum. All three of them sit with open notepads, none of them taking any notes.

'Wait,' Xander says. 'You're telling us that…?'

'This is a joke,' Andreas says. 'This is clearly a joke. Are we on some kind of hidden camera thing?'

He points to a device in the top right corner of the room. 'Look, they're recording us.'

Hannah feels a sudden urge to explain the slides they've been presented with. In a way that makes them seem entirely reasonable and not at all like the very first graduate job she's ever managed to get is one big practical joke.

'No,' Hannah says. 'It's just… we're not understanding it yet, I'm sure. It's probably fancy talk for, whatever it is they do here. Obviously the clients don't *actually* relive their memories, that would be like, hypnosis or something.'

'This is really not what I thought you guys did here,' Xander says.

Philippa stands at the front with a blank look on her face. Her mobile phone is laid out on the table next to the laptop and she scrolls on it, until she realises they've stopped talking.

'I would ask that you keep your questions until the end,' she says. 'Or to yourselves entirely, I'm not picky. Yes, Memory Lane is not what you probably thought it was. We are not a memory clinic, in the traditional sense. We possess *Memorize* technology and we are the only such facility in the world which currently uses this technology. It allows us to give clients an entirely realistic recreation of a twelve hour block of their memory.'

Hannah puts her hand up.

'I mean,' Philippa says. 'I did literally just say keep your questions until the end. But, fine, yes?'

She feels the weight of the boys' eyes on her. This needs to be a good question.

'Not to be the "in English, please, doc," guy,' Hannah says. 'But can you simplify that a bit?'

In the time it took Hannah to ask her question, Philippa's attention went back to her phone. She snaps back out of it.

'Okay,' she says. 'At Memory Lane, our clients pay us... a fee, which some people would consider quite sizeable, and in return we hook them up to our technology. *Memorize*. Then, for twelve hours, they go into a dreamlike state where they relive a memory of their choosing.'

'Really?'

'Yes, really.'

Xander and Andreas put their hands up now also, shaking them side to side like impatient schoolchildren.

Philippa sighs, indicating that she may just be giving up hope of the 'keep all questions to the end' tactic.

'Xander,' Philippa says.

'How have we not heard of this?' he says, putting his hand down. 'If this technology was real and people were using it in the middle of Edinburgh, and it was actually working, how has it not been everywhere? On the news and stuff? How have you kept it a secret?'

Andreas puts his hand down.

'We are an extremely exclusive facility,' Philippa says. 'There are many exclusive places in Edinburgh and we are not alone in *not* seeking the limelight.'

'That means this is dodgy,' Andreas says.

'Andreas, may I remind you that you are now an employee of this so-called dodgy facility. We have a modest group of loyal clients, who are willing to pay handsomely for our services, and we do not feel the need to make our technology front page news or advertise on the sides of bus shelters. Now, as I said, I realise this is a lot to take in, but maybe this video will clear things up.'

Philippa goes to the next slide before any of them can raise their hands again and presses play on a video. She makes it full screen then walks to the light switch by the door and the room is suddenly dark except for the projection.

On screen, a Memory Lane graphic dissolves to reveal a man in a suit standing in front of a desk. Hannah recognises him as the man who came in earlier and disappeared through a door to the back office.

'Hi there,' he says, talking straight into the camera. 'If you're watching this video then congratulations, you are a new member of the team here at Memory Lane. We're delighted to have you aboard. This induction is designed to ease you into the idea of Memory Lane, because, believe me, I realise this is a lot to take in. I'm sure you'll have a LOT of questions for whoever is giving this induction, and I hope you'll keep these until the end.'

Hannah's eyes shift over to Philippa, standing by the light switch. She swipes her thumb on her phone. Hannah wonders how many times she's seen this video. She also wonders how this could ever be 'old news' to someone. How many times would you need to be told about this kind of technology before it didn't blow your mind? Although she still hasn't ruled out the possibility of this all being one big joke.

The man on screen continues. 'My name is Michael Valentine, CEO of Valentine & McBride Incorporated, the owners of Memory Lane. I'm here to give you just a taste of what we do here at Memory Lane. A lot of our technology is highly advanced and to try to explain it to you, well, I'd bore myself, quite honestly. Don't worry, we don't expect you to understand the technicalities of it all. So, I'll keep things simple.

'When a client books a place at Memory Lane, we offer them a one-of-a-kind experience. They come into our offices in Edinburgh, although we like to call it a sensory facility, and are then linked up to our *Memorize* technology.'

Hannah can hear the copyright through the video.

'The client chooses which memory from their life they wish to relive. Our technology locates and isolates this period of time in the client's memory, where they then choose which specific twelve hour period they wish to narrow it down to. To give you an example, if a client wishes to relive their first date with their partner, they can have 12pm to 12am, or 3pm to 3am, etc. Whenever they finish getting lucky, probably.'

Michael Valentine, CEO, has a chuckle to himself on screen. Hannah wishes she could be surprised. Any time there's been a huge technological advance in human history, there's been, minutes later, men trying to use it to wank themselves off.

She then starts to wonder what day from her life *she* would choose to relive. How could you narrow it down to just one? It would need to be a day that had everything, and yes, she supposes, if it ended, or started, with sex, that wouldn't be a drawback.

'Throughout this twelve hour period, the client will be completely comfortable in our facility, in a dreamlike state. Worth noting at this point, please never, ever remove a client's headset while they are in a memory. Just common sense.'

As he speaks, the video transitions to a woman lying in a reclining bed, a huge smile on her face, despite her seemingly being asleep. A metallic-looking headset rests on her head. A staff member presses a button on the computer next to her then turns to the camera and gives a thumbs up.

'Unfortunately, staff members are not permitted to book experiences at Memory Lane while under contract, so you'll have to take my word for it that our technology recreates each client's memory in exact detail, and 92%

of clients say they forgot they were hooked up to our *Memorize* machines for the duration. You may, however, depending on your role, have the chance to enter a client's memory, and I hope you'll appreciate this opportunity to see the *Memorize* technology in action.'

Michael Valentine freezes, and by the door Philippa lowers a remote and flicks the lights back on. She walks to the front of the room and the CEO's image is projected on to her.

'I'll stop us there,' she says, 'as that last bit pertains to you three lovelies. Retrieval Assistants, that's your fancy title. You'll be getting to see memories first-hand, which is something that not everyone here has had the opportunity to do, so think yourselves lucky.'

Hannah, Xander and Andreas look between themselves. Hannah's trying to work out if either of them is going to ask more questions or whether she should. The longer the silence goes on, the more she worries the other two have understood everything perfectly and she's the only one not keeping up.

She raises her hand and Philippa calls on her.

'So what does a Retrieval Assistant actually do?'

'Yeah,' Xander says. 'I was going to ask that as well.'

Andreas nods and Hannah's relieved. Philippa finishes her coffee and disposes of the cup in a bin by the wall.

'Always in a rush,' she says. 'People of your age, always in a rush to know everything right away. But fair enough, this is an induction, I suppose. Come with me.'

She strides for the door and the three new recruits scramble to gather their bags and jackets and follow her into the corridor. Philippa only goes as far as the other side of the hall and opens a door. Hannah feels silly for having rushed and for being slightly out of breath. She focuses on breathing through her nose so no one can hear.

'In you come,' Philippa says, switching the light on in the new room.

It's much smaller than the last one, a box room really, also with no windows. A PC sits on a counter, where Philippa wags the mouse to activate the screen. Hannah, Xander and Andreas scrape chairs across the floor and huddle round the glow from the screen. The light above them blinks and threatens to go out.

'All this money,' Philippa says. 'And they can't even do up this crappy little induction room. And yes, that is a bucket in the corner to catch a drip from the ceiling.'

And to think, around half an hour ago, Memory Lane seemed like the most professional organisation Hannah had ever set foot in. Now it feels more like the glass façade out front was just that, a façade. This is starting to remind her of the many retail inductions she had from the ages of sixteen to twenty-one. Ushered into a dim break room while waiting for the assistant manager to arrive, the staff sitting about on their lunch and moaning about managers and eyeing her up like they weren't in that seat just a few months before.

From under the desk, Philippa drags out a big plastic tub, like a giant Tupperware dish, filled with tangled wires. She pops the lid off and pulls out three silver headsets, like the one the woman wore in the induction video. She hands the three of them, tangled up in each other, to Hannah, who spends the next little while taking them apart and passing one each to Xander and Andreas. Once they're all holding one of the sets, Philippa takes the wires dangling from them and slots them into the computer.

'Okay, bear in mind,' Philippa says, 'this is not the latest edition of *Memorize* and the headsets are quite clunky.' She gestures to the sets in their hands. 'Go on then, pop them on.'

Again, the three of them pause and look at each other. Hannah would rather not be the first to put it on, just in case this is a joke, the possibility of which refuses to leave her mind.

Xander goes first.

'I don't suit hats,' he says, sliding it on and trying to find a reflective surface in the room so he can see how it looks.

Hannah goes next and Andreas is last, still hovering his hands at the sides of his, in case he needs to whip it off sharpish. It pinches at the ears a little and Hannah imagines the current versions must be equipped with foam or rubber or something.

'I feel like I'm in a really low budget version of the *X-Men*,' she says.

'Like the first *X-Men*,' Xander says.

'I liked that one actually,' Andreas says.

'Me too, but by today's standards it looks like *The Magic Roundabout*.'

'That doesn't make any sense.'

'Neither does *The Magic Roundabout*.'

A program opens on the computer screen. *Memorize* appears in big white letters against a black background. Philippa starts clicking through options too fast for Hannah to see what she's doing.

'Boys,' Philippa says. 'You can continue your little "look at us, we're virgins and proud of it" chat later, but for now, we're going to give you a little experience of Memory Lane.'

There's a knock at the door behind them and it opens before they have the chance to respond.

'Ready for me?' says the man who's just walked in.

It's the man from the video. Michael Valentine, CEO.

50

John – Stonecranning, 1975

Agnes had taken care of the seating plan. John had no interest in trying to keep everyone happy, but Agnes enjoyed it. It was like solving a puzzle for her. *Well, we can't have Rita and Norman sitting at a table with the Simpsons, and we can't have the Simpsons anywhere near Iain and his boy, that'll be a bloodbath.* If John had learned nothing else from planning a wedding, his eyes had certainly been opened to just how many of their friends couldn't stand each other. To the point that they couldn't be trusted to sit around a table together for a few hours and play nice. Secretly, he always thought Agnes had gone a bit over the top, trying to add some extra excitement to the day. Most people are on their best behaviour at a wedding, as most understand it's the bride's day and God help you if you so much as sneeze the wrong amount of times near her.

'You would never know what this place usually looks like,' Agnes says to him, moving her knife and fork to better positions by the sides of her plate.

The community hall was unrecognisable, she was right about that. They had added some silver balloons, some twinkly lights, they had moved the pool table through to the public bar, and just like that, they had a wedding venue.

'I put the money behind the bar,' John tells Agnes.

'I thought my dad was going to…'

'Just let me put some money behind the bar and when it runs out, then Ronnie can have his turn.'

51

'What d'you mean, turn? I swear, you men and your pride, it's silly buggers is what it is.'

On the actual wedding day, John *had* put money behind the bar, but he doesn't do it every time he relives this day. One time he hadn't and Gary found him later in the night, explaining how he thought the young lads Scott, David and Ross had stolen it, and how he could give them a right good hiding, as a wedding present for him.

At the top table, John and Agnes sit in the middle. To John's right, his mum and dad, then best man Gary. Left of Agnes are her parents, with Agnes's best friend, Innes, at the end. The top table always struck John as another odd tradition. Gary and Innes didn't get to sit next to their partners for most of the night, just because they were giving speeches. He didn't see why the partners weren't allowed to sit up here as well. Not that he ever brought that up to Agnes. Pick your battles.

John's dad leans in.

'What's Gary's speech going to be like?' he asks. 'Should I be telling your gran to cover her ears?'

'Our Franny?' John says, scanning over the crowd to find her at the bar. 'She loves a bit of blue.'

'Ha, so she does. Look at that git.'

His dad's looking behind him, at Agnes's dad, Ronnie. Ronnie is holding up his fork to Catherine, showing her the dirt he's located on it.

'He's so up his own arse,' John's dad goes on. 'That he's… well, he's just an arse, that man. Gail agrees, don't you?'

John's mum breaks away a conversation with Gary to poke her head round.

'What was that?' she asks.

'Ronnie, he's an arse, isn't he?'

'Oh, em, well, I don't know. Willie, let's just not today, alright?'

'He's not going to stop being an arse just because it's his daughter's wedding day, let me tell you. You good for a drink, anyway, John?'

John lifts the pint Gary brought to him the second he entered the building. There had been a few more photos to take outside the hall and Gary had rushed off the bus first to win the race to the bar.

'I'm grand,' he tells his dad.

'Mine's is the next one then.'

'And Agnes's?'

'Of course.'

John smiles. A few weeks after the wedding, Agnes had admitted to him that she'd barely touched a drop of alcohol all day. People were lining up to buy John a drink, but for some reason they didn't get one for Agnes at the same time. She thought it was sexist, that it was expected for the groom to get off his tits but the idea of a drunken bride didn't sit well with the men of their generation. She was right, as she continued to be at an annoyingly high frequency from that day onwards. John was always proud to call her his wife. Always.

'Gail says you're thinking about asking that eejit for a job?' his dad says. 'I told her she must have it wrong because you'd never ask that wanker for a job. Am I right, John?'

John's mum dives back into her conversation with Gary. John knows Gary's a charming guy but he thinks it's more to avoid hearing this chat. She spilled the secret to his dad and that was the snowball that had tumbled down the mountain and led to John having the chat with him at the end of the night. The last chat he'd ever have with his dad.

'Dad,' John says. 'In the grand scheme of things, is it really the worst thing in the world?'

'Don't you try and rationalise it, son. That man's a vulture and his business is a poor excuse for a living. I've seen the conditions in his factories, the folk at the bottom of the ladder. God knows what they're inhaling.'

'But we need money, Agnes and me. We'll be starting a family soon.'

'And you want your wee boy or girl knowing their dad is working for a greedy beggar like that?'

Again, he points down the table to Ronnie, who is too oblivious to realise he's the topic of conversation.

'Can we talk about it tomorrow?' John says. 'I promise we'll talk about it tomorrow.'

His dad huffs and puffs and steals a few nuts from the bowl in front of them. John knows he could make this a lot easier on himself. He just needs to deny it. *Of course I'm not going to work for Ronnie, Dad* is all it would take. *I can't stand the man and quite frankly, I genuinely considered breaking up with Agnes after I first met him* would be good. *I'm not working for him and I'm actually going to set his Falkirk office on fire. I've brought this watering can full of petrol with me, do you want to help?* and his dad would kiss him.

People on TV are always telling other people what their dads taught them. They dish out this guidance at the drop of a hat. *My dad taught me you should never trust a person with two first names. My dad taught me you should always walk on the outside of a woman on the pavement. My dad said you should never grow a beard in a month ending in Y.* Dads are constantly teaching their sons, if you'd believe the TV.

Now, John struggles to name one thing his dad taught him for sure. He made him go to swimming lessons because he thought Stonecranning was due a flood one day, but the instructor, Mrs Carson, had taught him the front stroke, not his dad.

Even worse, John struggles to name one thing he taught his son, Michael. He hadn't exactly been a hands-on dad when Michael was growing up. Because, well, his dad had been the same way with him, and he'd turned out okay.

Gary stands up and taps his knife against his glass. It's not exactly high quality crystal so it doesn't quite ring out through the hall, but enough people notice him and soon everyone has hushed for his speech.

'Hello, everyone,' he says, placing the knife back down but still clutching onto his glass. 'I'm just going to do my speech now. I know we normally do speeches after the meal but I'm shitting myself and I want to enjoy my dinner so John and Agnes have very kindly allowed me to do mine before.'

The crowd laugh and adjust themselves in their seats so they can see properly. The people unlucky enough to be facing the other way twist and lean arms over their seats.

'For those that don't know me, my name is Gary and I'm John's best man. When I started writing this speech, I said to John, is there anything you don't want me to mention? And he said, whatever you do, don't mention Jeanie that I used to go with. Agnes will be absolutely fuming if you mention Jeanie. So, I just wanted to put everyone's minds at ease and say that there will definitely be nothing about Jeanie in the speech.'

Gary has the widest smile in the room as he braves a glance over at him and Agnes. It never gets old. He winks at them, turns to his next card and continues.

'So, I remember the first time John met Jeanie. No, wait, my mistake, I meant Agnes...'

Hannah – Edinburgh, 2019

'We're going in?' Hannah asks. 'Into this… memory thing?'

Michael Valentine, CEO, pulls up the last remaining empty chair and sits down at the edge of the computer desk. There's another spare headset which he claims and slides on top of his, what looks to be, reasonably expensive haircut.

'Don't mind me,' he says, adjusting the sleeves of his suit jacket. 'Pretend I'm not here.'

This is the kind of thing successful middle-aged men are always doing, Hannah thinks to herself. Turning up late, causing everyone to pay attention to them, then telling everyone not to pay attention to them.

Philippa clicks the mouse, continuing through the program and selecting options. *Options > Training Mode > Induction > Retrieval > Pre-saved Memories > Michael Valentine > Royal Mile*.

'Yes, we're going into this *thing*,' Philippa says. 'If anyone tends to get travel sickness, please shout out now. Can you all please hold hands? Come on, quickly, you're not going to catch cooties off anyone, kids.'

Hannah, in the middle, lets a hand drift to either side of her, and grabs on to Xander and Andreas's hands. Andreas's is clammy and she's desperate to break free and wipe her hand on her trousers. But she doesn't want to break the machine. She imagines that would put her in debt to Memory Lane for the next five hundred years, give or take.

Philippa clicks a few more times then turns to them.

'Right, everybody ready?' she says, then looks down. 'Oh, you're all holding hands, that's so cute. I was only joking. Right, ready?'

Before any of them can open their mouths or let go of each other's hands, the lights go out. Or that's what it seems like. But as the seconds go by, Hannah's eyes don't adjust. She doesn't see anything. No sketchy outlines of the boys or Philippa or Michael Valentine, CEO. The computer screen is gone. There's no light anywhere. She turns her head and sees only blackness.

Then she hears a voice, and it seems to come from within her own head.

'We're currently in a holding area, okay?' Philippa says. 'This is what the client will see for a while before their memory begins.'

Her voice seems to be coming from all around. The way the sound does in a cinema when they're showing off how cool and loud the Dolby surround sound is before the film starts and there's a dinosaur roaring, just because.

'You're currently seeing nothing. Don't worry, this is intentional. I'll tell you at this point, prior to starting at Memory Lane, we conducted several psychological evaluations of you, though you may not have been aware. We mention this now, to assure you that we are confident that you are ready for this process and, of course, the role of Retrieval Assistant.

'In a few moments, you'll find yourself in the memory of our gracious host, Michael Valentine, the big boss here at Memory Lane. This will be on the Royal Mile, Edinburgh. This location was chosen to acclimatise you to the technology, as you have all been on this street before. Today, to be precise.'

Other than her own heartbeat, which still seems to be

audible to Hannah in the program, Philippa's voice is the only sound.

'Right, so I'll now let the *Memorize* technology do its thing. Here we go.'

In front of her eyes, the number five appears. It soon turns to four, three… Hannah reaches out a hand but finds she can't touch the number, her hand swooping right through the image. The countdown ends and the darkness dissipates and is gradually replaced by light.

Hannah watches as the Royal Mile appears before her. She waits for it to brighten up but it doesn't. It's either night time or very early morning.

The boys are at her sides and they break hands apart as soon as they realise they're all still linked. Philippa steps out in front of them, her heels bubbling on the uneven cobbles of the road. Around twenty metres away is Michael Valentine, standing on the pavement, dressed in running gear.

That's when it occurs to Hannah that they're standing on the road rather than the pavement, in the middle of the four way junction at the top of the Mound. She turns her head to look down the street, down towards the Parliament end, and finds no cars coming either way. There are no other people, anywhere in sight. The boys' heads are also on a swivel, looking at the re-creation of Edinburgh that the technology has produced in such detail.

'This is well creepy,' Xander says. 'This is like *28 Days Later*.'

'If there are zombies in this thing,' Andreas says. 'I'm not going to be happy. This is a good suit.'

'There are no zombies,' Philippa says. 'And your suit will be fine. Your clothes are just a scan of what you were wearing when you entered the program.'

Hannah looks down at her outfit, purchased from New

Look the week before. Andreas is still in his dark blue, obviously quite expensive, probably not bought from Topman, suit.

She kneels down and puts a hand to the cobbles.

'It feels real,' she says.

Xander does the same.

'These were a nightmare on my bike this morning,' he says, running his fingers in-between the stones.

Andreas stays standing, hands on his hips. When Xander stands back up, Andreas punches him in the arm.

'Ow!' Xander says. 'What did you do that for?'

'Sorry,' Andreas laughs. 'I guessed we couldn't feel pain in here.'

Xander rubs his arm, takes a moment to consider the situation, then punches Andreas back.

'Argh!' Andreas says. 'Mine was a genuine mistake. You meant that to be sore.'

Philippa coughs and the boys give each other one last evil look before silently calling a truce.

'I'd just like to say,' Hannah says. 'That neither of you punched me, which is sexist.' She enjoys the confused, worried faces the boys make. 'I'm kidding, boys, relax. But how come we can feel pain in here?'

'The technology can recreate pain,' Philippa explains. 'Based on how the client perceives the pain would feel. So, we're in Mr Valentine's memory right now. The technology feeds off his memory and his experiences. Basically, Mr Valentine presumably knows what a punch in the arm feels like, so that is recreated accurately. But, say, for example, you took a knife out and stabbed each other through the heart. Mr Valentine, as far as I'm aware, doesn't know exactly what that feels like. The program would certainly attempt something like a stabbing feeling, and it would certainly feel uncomfortable, but it wouldn't be accurate. It also wouldn't affect you in the real world, sitting in Memory Lane right now. You two won't have bruises from those punches.'

'Well… that's reassuring,' Hannah says, although now worried about how specific the heart stabbing reference was and how easily it came to Philippa's mind. Did a previous staff member get stabbed in the heart while inside the program? She'd probably accept a fake stabbing in a computer program if it got her a good compensation claim, which surely Memory Lane can afford.

'Come on, what drugs did you give us?' Andreas says. 'You put something in the water, yeah? Or did you put in a request to the council to get everyone off the street while you do this?'

Philippa just smiles.

'There's always one,' she says. 'I thought it was going to be Hannah though.'

Hannah's not sure if that's a compliment or not but things are currently too intense to unpack the statement.

She tries to notice everything she can. She's still breathing, taking breaths in and out. She reaches for her waist and hopes the others don't notice as she slides her hands under her t-shirt. She runs her fingers over her stretch marks and is glad to find them still there. Even if this isn't real, she still wants them. They're a part of her.

Hannah crouches again, then stands back up. Then crouches again, then stands up.

'Weird time to be doing squats,' Xander says. 'I don't think you'll get gains in here.'

'No, it's my knee,' Hannah says. 'I hurt it when I was younger, ice skating. But it's not sore anymore.'

Philippa claps her hands to get their attention.

'Yes, I'm sorry, that pain will come back when we're done in the memory,' she says. 'This isn't your memory so the system doesn't have that information on file yet. But let's crack on, shall we? I think we've all got used to this now and I have a lot of real work to do in the office today. Not to mention we're using Mr Valentine's memory, who is very graciously letting us kick about in here.'

Over on the pavement, Michael Valentine makes a hand gesture as if to say *don't mention it*.

Hannah's starting to realise why this technology isn't public knowledge. Who *wouldn't* want to use this? Thousands would be flooding into the office, demanding to be hooked up. Surely they could make an absolute fortune, though. Unless they already are and they don't need any more clients. She remembers them mentioning the fee but not saying exactly how much it was. Probably because it would make their eyes water. She wonders, again, how she got the job, if they're making so much money. Then she wonders why her starting wage isn't higher.

'You are in a memory,' Philippa says. 'So if it feels real, that's because it is. This is the Royal Mile at 4.35am, December 25th, 2013. We cannot create fake environments from scratch. The memory is entirely powered by the client. If *Memorize* is not hooked up to a client, none of this is possible. As I said, this is Mr Valentine's memory. He came up here jogging on Christmas morning so we could get a good location for the induction.'

This is Michael Valentine's cue. He jogs over to them and pretends to be out of breath.

'Hi everyone,' he says. 'I'll do my proper introduction now. I'm Michael Valentine, CEO, but I'm sure you've already seen me in the video. Please don't judge, bow ties were in at the time. Matt Smith was The Doctor, it was a different time.'

He shakes each of their hands. His are smooth and free of callouses. Her dad had always told her that a man without callouses on his hands has never done a decent day's work in his life. Her dad has a lot of bad advice like that. Hannah suspects there's an age men get to where they believe every opinion they spout is actually advice. If she had to guess, she would say twenty-eight.

'I need to get to a meeting soon,' Mr Valentine says. 'So I can't host you in here for too long. But you're in more than capable hands with Phil, as I'm sure you'll all agree.'

Philippa smiles and brushes some unseen bit of dust off Mr Valentine's shoulder.

'I'm sure you'll all also agree,' she says. 'That no one should call me Phil unless they are the CEO of the company. So, are we all content so far?'

The three of them shake their heads.

'Too bad, we've spent too long here already. Look, the locals are awake.'

She gestures to a window above Deacon Brodies Tavern, where a woman leans out, smoking a cigarette.

'Merry Christmas,' the woman calls down to them.

'Same to you,' Xander says. 'You're just a memory, though.'

'What the fuck did you call me? Are you lot Jesus freaks, aye? Mormons or that?'

Xander finds himself lost for words and turns back to Philippa.

'How is that possible?' he says. 'How is she talking to us if we're in Mr Valentine's memory?'

Philippa and Mr Valentine both go to speak, then stop. They exchange 'no, you' gestures with their hands until Philippa takes the lead.

'The more times we use the same memory,' Philippa attempts to explain, and Hannah nods although she's not sure she's following, 'the more the *Memorize* technology fleshes out the details on the outskirts of the memory.

We've used this memory during inductions a lot of times over the years, so the technology has populated the houses and given the people inside personalities. These are based on a combination of what Michael believes the people in these houses are like, and what the technology deems believable and true to the memory.'

'The memory people don't seem to like you, Xander,' Andreas laughs to himself.

'Hey, the woman called all of us Jesus freaks, so...' he replies.

Hannah looks up at the woman at the window, who continues to watch them. She wants to walk around in the memory, to go through some of these doors and see what the technology comes up with.

'It's like a video game then,' Andreas says. 'Like an open world game.'

Philippa rolls her eyes.

'Every time,' she says. 'Men and their video games.'

Mr Valentine claps his hands together then points at Andreas.

'Exactly,' he says. 'Exactly like an open world game. You have your main memory, or core memory, which is like the main mission of the game, if you want to think of it that way. But, if you want, you can explore the other parts of the game. They might not be perfect, because they weren't designed to be explored in great detail, but it doesn't stop you having a little look.'

Mr Valentine checks his watch, then looks annoyed. Hannah looks down at her own watch. It's lifeless. Stopped at 9.45 a.m.

'So what's our job?' Hannah says, keen to ask while Mr Valentine is here, in the hopes of getting a straight answer. 'Are we going into people's memories every day? I'm still

63

not sure I'm getting what a Retrieval Assistant is, to be honest. Sorry if I'm being completely dense.'

'I'm the same, Hannah,' Xander says.

'I think I've got it,' Andreas says. 'But, y'know, I won't say. I don't want to step on Philippa's toes.'

Hannah and Xander share a look, and she hopes he doesn't believe him either. Philippa looks totally bored at this point.

'My toes thank you, Andreas,' she says. 'When the client, in this case, Mr Valentine, wants to leave the memory, they press their exit button.'

Mr Valentine holds up his left hand. On his palm, seemingly embedded into the skin, is a red button.

'If he presses his exit button,' Philippa goes on. 'The memory ends instantly. Normally, the exit button only appears once the twelve hour period has elapsed. In this training memory, however, we've programmed it to appear from the start. However, if you need to leave before the client for any reason, you simply say the command: *Memorize*, exit memory.'

The second the words are out of her mouth, Philippa begins disappearing before their eyes, fading until she's gone completely. Hannah wants to go over to where she was standing and check for herself this wasn't some kind of trick, but Mr Valentine starts speaking.

'Now it's your turn,' he says to them. 'Just say the words and you'll find yourselves back in Memory Lane.'

Hannah decides not to look at either Xander or Andreas this time. She wants to be the first to say it. She takes a breath, then says the words.

'*Memorize,* exit memory.'

The world around her grows dim, like someone's turning off the lights. Soon she's in darkness.

John – Stonecranning, 1975

Reflections are a funny thing. As the years passed, John got used to the time laid bare across his face. The grey hair came early. He was twenty-two when he first tried dying it to hide the streaks of white at his temples, and twenty-four when he'd had enough slaggings from his pals and decided to embrace the salt and pepper look. The lines around his eyes and mouth deepened, sneaking into his face while he was too busy laughing. Eventually, he stopped looking for a young man in the mirror and started recognising the old one.

But in here, he's a young man again. When he goes to the toilet and washes his hands, it's a twenty-eight-year-old John that looks back at him from the grotty mirror.

The first few trips back, it was a shock, to say the least. He'd gone back as far as the technology would allow. His eighteenth birthday. That reflection was a bit *too* young for his liking.

But that wasn't entirely true. The technology *could* take you back further. They'd just decided, him and the board members at Memory Lane, that letting clients relive memories from when they were younger than eighteen could present certain legal, and moral, difficulties. So, they made eighteen the minimum age and saved themselves the headache.

John's wedding day was ten years later. He was twenty-eight then and now he's twenty-eight once more, staring at himself in the mirror. His eyes look different too, somehow. They never wrinkled like his skin but the colour seems more vibrant.

'It's been a brilliant day,' Gary says, appearing from one of the stalls. 'I'd give that a minute, by the way. What are you doing?'

John makes eye contact with Gary in the mirror, as Gary budges himself next to him at the sink and shoots his hands under the water.

'I'm looking at my face in the mirror,' John says. 'Thinking about the cruel passage of time. Of how time passes incredibly fast and incredibly slowly at the same time, and we're just slaves to it. I'm taking a minute to contemplate how we're only truly happy in this life in the moments when we forget we're alive.'

Gary moves away from the sink and dries his hands on a few paper towels, throwing them into the bin by the radiator.

'Oh,' he says. 'I think I know exactly what you're talking about.'

'Aye?'

'I do. You're worried about tonight, aren't you? Finally popping your cherry. I wouldn't worry, my friend, I'm sure Agnes will be gentle with you. Certainly more gentle than Jeanie would've been.'

'That's plenty,' John says. 'I've heard enough about Jeanie from you today.'

'It was what the people wanted, John. You heard the laughs. I had to do it, you know that. Couldn't have lived with myself otherwise.'

John straightens his tie, checks his flower, ensures his bottom button is still undone, scratches the skin under his sgian-dubh. He thinks it's strange that the stereotype is for the bride to be late to the wedding, when it's clearly the groom, in a kilt, who's got more fashion accessories to worry about putting on. And there weren't any YouTube tutorials back in his day. You closed your eyes, tied your shoelaces whichever way you could and prayed they stayed up for longer than three seconds.

'You coming?' Gary asks. 'I'll get you another.'

'Where are you getting the money from?'

'I have my ways. Come on, I asked the DJ for *Shang-A-Lang* and if I miss it 'cause I was stood in the pisser talking about the passage of time with the groom, I'll kill myself.'

John knows that *Shang-A-Lang* won't be played until much later in the night, past eleven o'clock, he's sure, but he doesn't need to tell Gary that right now.

'I'll be two seconds.'

Gary shrugs in a 'suit yourself' kind of way and leaves.

That was a new one. A conversation John hadn't had before. Probably something to do with the fact that John didn't actually come in here to pee. He just came in for a look, which is obviously not a normal thing for a person to do. Reliving a memory over and over can get boring, so he likes to try out every different variation he can think of. Who knows what kind of conversations happened in the toilet during his wedding day, that he never got to hear or be part of?

He takes one last look in the mirror, at the young fella who didn't know how good he had it, then walks back out to the hall.

At the bar, Ronnie leans and tries to get the attention of the bar staff, waving the ten pound note that rests between his index and middle finger like they should be running after him.

'Alright, Ronnie,' John says. 'Wondered if I could have a word with you.'

'I might need to have a word with the manager,' Ronnie says. 'These stupid wee lassies are ignoring me.'

I'd ignore you too, John thinks.

'I'm sure they're just busy.'

And it's true. Further down the bar are several bodies vying for the staff's attention. He would never admit it out loud to anyone, but John had somehow found himself quite a popular person in those days. Agnes too. The church was full that day and there wasn't a spare seat going on the coach over to the hall. They were a low budget power couple, before power couples were even a thing. Posh and Becks, that was the first one John can remember. Also, the last, now he thinks about it.

That had changed over the years, of course, for all sorts of reasons. He had started working more. They had moved to Stockbridge in Edinburgh for his work, a few years after, and it seemed like every time him and Agnes got together with their friends, there was some kind of argument about the company John was keeping because of his role at McDuff & McBride. Agnes took his side but John suspected she shared the same feelings. She always had an excuse in the chamber for why she had to leave the house whenever he invited the boys from the office over for dinner.

John had told himself there were all sorts of reasons he had drifted from his friends, but really there was only one: the job. The job he had taken at Ronnie's company, so him and Agnes could move up in the world, get a better house than everyone else they knew, a better life. Not many people from Stonecranning ended up doing much of anything, and John wanted different for him and Agnes. He doesn't think he should have to apologise for that.

'Ronnie, can I have a word?' John says again. 'I wanted to ask you if there were any jobs going at McDuff & McBride.'

Ronnie lowers his ten pound note and gives John a tilted smile.

'I knew you'd come crawling to me one day, John,' he replies. 'Wasn't expecting it to be today, mind you. But aye, let's talk.'

Hannah – Edinburgh, 2019

The darkness doesn't last long. Slowly, light creeps back into view. Hannah finds herself sitting down in a cheap plastic chair.

'Everyone feeling okay?' Philippa says. 'The first one can make some people a bit queasy.'

Hannah looks around. The five of them are back in the little room in front of the computer screen. She reaches a hand under the headset and scratches her head and it feels incredible.

Mr Valentine takes his headset off, places it down and makes for the door.

'Running late,' he says. 'Great to meet you all. Sure I'll see you around in the coming weeks.'

And with that, he's gone, leaving behind only a whiff of aftershave.

'Can we take these off yet?' Hannah asks.

'Yeah, my hair is not enjoying this,' Andreas says. 'I'm not saying that to be a dick, my hair wax is quite expensive. Again, I know it makes me sound like a dick but you don't get much in the tub, so…'

Xander snorts with laughter and tries to cover it with a cough. Hannah stifles a laugh too but feels bad about it. Andreas definitely doesn't make a great first impression but she's worked enough places to know that you shouldn't make best pals or enemies on the first day. In Topshop, during her first shift she made besties with a girl named Jill who gave her the lowdown and gossip on every other staff member. Three days later, Jill had handed her notice

69

in and it turned out everyone hated her and so they moved this hatred on to Hannah because, of course, who would ever be pals with Jill? Only a monster.

'Keep the headsets on, please,' Philippa says, her teacher voice fully deployed as she guides the mouse and chooses more options from the screen. 'We have another memory to go into.'

There's a knock at the door behind them. Philippa calls 'Come in,' and another member of staff joins them in the cramped room. This girl has long, green hair and suddenly Hannah's undercut doesn't seem like the most unique haircut in the room.

The green-haired girl sits down in the chair recently vacated by the CEO and gives an awkward wave.

'I'm Yasmin,' she says.

'This is Yasmin,' Philippa says. 'She started out as a Retrieval Assistant, like yourselves, not that long ago. Now she works in our lab as a Memory Experience Technician, ensuring clients have a smooth journey with us.'

'Mex Tech for short,' Yasmin adds. 'I work in the memory lab. That's the Memory Care and Protection Unit if you're being posh.'

Hannah has a look at what Philippa's doing on the computer.

Induction > Retrieval > Pre-saved Memories > Yasmin Onyekuru > Bo...

'I think I need a pee,' Xander says, and receives a stern look from Philippa. 'But I can probably hold it.'

'Wonderful. Here we go.'

And again, just like before, everything goes black. There's no voiceover from Philippa this time, but the countdown appears just like before. Five, four, three, two, one...

They're all standing on grass, in the middle of a busy square. White tents line the outskirts, with hundreds of people weaving in and out of the tents, clutching bags and books. Around them, on the ground, people sit cross-legged on the grass, sharing snacks and drinking pints from plastic cups.

'You might recognise this place,' Philippa says.

The people around them on the grass can definitely see them, and a girl nearby leans into her friend's ear while pointing.

'This is the book festival,' Hannah says. 'In August. In Charlotte Square, isn't it?'

'You're correct, Hannah,' Philippa says. 'We thought it would be a nice memory to bring you into, to start you off. To be fair, most of the memories you go into will be nice. That's why the clients are choosing to relive them. We don't get many people wanting to relive days where it rained all day and they were rolling around in the mud. Some, but not many.'

Philippa sits down and the three of them follow her example. The grass is crisp and pokey against her palms as Hannah lowers her weight onto it. She loves Edinburgh in August. Sure, the crowds can drive her wild sometimes, but Charlotte Square is the most dreamlike state she's ever experienced while being awake. Well, before today.

'You are all Retrieval Assistants,' Philippa says. 'What do we think that means?'

No one offers up an answer straight away. They're too busy enjoying the sun. Hannah finds herself a bit annoyed that Philippa has brought them here, as now she doesn't want to leave. She hates the thought that in a few minutes, with the click of a button, she's going to return to that dingy little training room with a full Monday still to work.

'I'm not afraid to call on people,' Philippa says. 'Andreas?'

Andreas licks his finger and wipes away a scuff on his shoe.

'Well, retrieval means... getting something back. So our job is to... get something back?'

Philippa nods then calls on Xander.

'We have to go into the client's memory and... retrieve something?' he offers.

'Pretty much copying my answer, but okay,' Andreas adds.

Then Philippa nods to Hannah. She's annoyed at having to go last, as the boys have clearly taken the easy bits.

'We come into a memory,' Hannah says, finding the end of the sentence as she speaks it. 'And... bring... the client... back?'

Philippa smiles.

'Gold star, Hannah.'

Instantly, Hannah regrets her answer. Another thing she never wants to do, especially on a first day, is become the teacher's pet. The other workies hate you and the boss expects more of you than everyone else. She would be much happier in the middle ground, and she's fairly sure Andreas is more of a teacher's pet type. She wouldn't want to take that away from him.

'The client chooses a memory and we then narrow that down to a twelve hour period,' Philippa says, in the tone of voice that lets them know this is the important part of this section.

Hannah would love to jot some of this down, but she doesn't have a notepad, and she's fairly sure she can't take anything from a memory back to the real world.

'Once the client reaches the end of this twelve hour period,' she goes on, 'their exit button will appear on their palm, like you saw with Mr Valentine. They also carry a purple panic button throughout the memory, which can be pressed at any time. This will flag up what we call a "purple alert", where someone like Yasmin will go into the memory and assist the client.'

That's when Hannah realises Yasmin isn't sitting with them. She scans around the slowly shuffling book lovers until her eyes find Yasmin, sitting at a table in the bar area.

Hannah looks back at Philippa, not wanting to miss anything.

'However, as you can probably understand, the client does not always want to leave the memory immediately. If a client goes over their time, you, as Retrieval Assistants, will be alerted to the situation. It is your job to enter the memory, meet with the client and tell them to end the memory.'

Philippa doesn't appear to have finished her instructions, but Andreas shoves his hand in the air regardless. It's a brave move, as Hannah's got a sneaking suspicion that Philippa has superpowers in these memories. She tells herself it's a silly idea, but then so is memory diving, or whatever the company calls it.

'Yes?' Philippa says.

'Couldn't you just create a computer generated person?' Andreas says. 'To talk to the client?'

'You're talking yourself out of a job, Andreas.'

'I know, I just… so, we're basically bouncers? We come into a memory and chuck the client out?'

'You do not have the power to chuck them out, as you put it. Taking clients out against their will can result in… less than ideal results. This is why we *never* take a client's *Memorize* headset off while they are in the middle of a memory. They must leave by their own free will. In order to ensure a smooth transition from the memory, back to the real world, we have found a real person, connecting with the client and talking to them face to virtual face, works best. Trust me, Andreas, this is very advanced technology and people above my paygrade are making these decisions. We wouldn't be hiring you three if we didn't need someone to do this job for us.'

'So… do we sit and wait for this alert?' Hannah blurts out. 'Like, firefighters or something? Just waiting to slide down the pole and rush to an emergency?'

'Let's not call it an emergency,' Philippa replies. 'But if you'd like to think of it like that, sure. Other staff members take care of the clients entering the memory, and keep an eye on them during, from the lab. Your role only comes into play if and when a client will not leave the memory.'

'And how often does that happen?'

'It varies.'

'That's vague.'

'Yes, I was being intentionally vague, Hannah, well done. The truth of the matter is, this job is similar to most other jobs that you'll have done in your lives, in that you'll learn best from doing.'

Andreas pulls a dandelion out of the ground and chucks it back onto the grass.

'This is actually my first job,' he says.

'Shocker,' Xander says.

'What's that supposed to mean?'

'You're clearly a posh Edinburgh Uni boy whose mum and dad pay for everything, no offence.'

'Ah, here we go. If there's one thing I know for sure, it's that people who make fun of Edinburgh Uni students are just jealous they didn't get in.'

Xander shrugs.

'It's all relative isn't it?' he says. 'Students at St Andrews would look down their nose at you. And Oxford and Cambridge would look down their noses at them. I went to the University of East London so you look down your nose at me. Hannah, where did you go?'

Hannah pauses before answering, as she's sure she's going to end up at the bottom of this snobby chain of looking down on people that Xander's created. She loved her time at Stirling Uni but she's well aware of its reputation as a sports university. Not that she made the most of the sports centre. She had one of the cheap gym memberships and would go in every few months for a visit to make it feel like she was getting her money's worth, but once you've seen Judy Murray on the tennis courts, what else is there to do?

'Stirling Uni,' she says. 'Would you look down on me, Xander?'

'Nah, us middle of the road unis need to stick together.'

'That probably sounded nicer in your head.'

There's a nice buzz of atmosphere in the square from the festival-goers, squeezing between each other on the walkways, heading from the bookshops to the event yurts. Hannah knows yurts is the proper name for these tents but she's not planning on saying it out loud at any point in case Xander thinks she's too middle class, like Andreas.

She's not sure if it's the sun beating down on them, or the fact that they're in a memory, but there's a hazy effect to the square, like everything's real and unreal at the same time. She feels that if she tried to grab hold of any of it too tightly, it would dissolve into warm static.

'Hannah?' Philippa says. 'You still with us?'

'Yeah,' she says, rubbing her eyes. 'Just felt a bit dizzy there.'

'Being in someone else's memory can be a little strange at first. Okay, looks like we're ready for the task at hand.'

Philippa stands and the rest join her on their feet.

Hannah wipes away grass from her bum, although she realises she shouldn't be worrying about grass stains that won't transfer back to the real world.

'I'm not posh,' Andreas says out of nowhere. 'I just want to make that clear.'

'Oh, really?' Xander says. 'Which team plays at Tynecastle?'

'That's hardly fair, you can't boil down being posh or not posh to just knowing about football or not.'

'Hearts,' Hannah says.

Xander looks delighted and Andreas looks less so.

John – Stonecranning, 1975

Agnes had wanted a band for the wedding, of course she had. She'd seen it in all the American programmes on the telly, where money didn't seem to be an issue for the happy couple and the guitars were never so loud that you couldn't hear the main characters over them. In the end, they'd gone for Ewan Davidson from two doors down, who owned a set of disco lights and said he'd work for £4 an hour and as many pints of cider as he could get through. John had encouraged everyone to request as many songs as possible so he couldn't leave his little booth and get to the bar too often.

'Everyone seems to be enjoying themselves,' Ronnie says, as if it's a surprise to him.

He and John sit at an otherwise empty table, half empty tumblers and party poppers strewn across the tablecloth. The middle of the hall has become a dance floor simply by turning the lights down and clearing the tables to the side. Agnes is up with her best pals, Innes and Vera, shimmying away and not caring what other people think. John had been working up the courage for a long time now, to dance like that. Even in a memory, he still feels too much like a prat to flail about and have everyone see. If Ronnie had seen him up there dancing, for example, there's no way he'd have given John the job.

Their first dance had been *Your Song* by Elton John. Even then he'd only managed a slight sway, Agnes having to move his rigid body to the music for the most part.

'Aye,' John says. 'It's been a good day.'

'I could've booked you a better place than this, mind you. In a decent part of the country at least, not out in the sticks like this. But Agnes says you said no.'

'You know how it is, Ronnie. I didn't want you to be paying through the nose just for one day.'

'And your dad probably couldn't have matched what I was willing to put in?'

'Well, that's not for me to say. But I imagine you take home a bit more than him, yes.'

John had already asked him for a job, twenty minutes earlier. This was all just for Ronnie's entertainment, stringing him along. John gets the sense that the only people who ever entered into conversation with Ronnie were people who needed something from him or those who worked for him, so he had to take advantage where he could.

'We'll be expanding in a little while,' Ronnie says. 'We've got the Glasgow and the Falkirk offices but we'll be opening up in Edinburgh soon.'

'Edinburgh, aye? It's some place that.'

'Have you been, John?'

'Eh, no, no, I haven't. Hope to someday, though.'

Ronnie shakes his head, pulls a cigarette from the packet in his pocket and lights it.

'Well, maybe we'll see how you get on in Falkirk,' he says. 'And you can come pay us a visit in Edinburgh. Honestly, John, the women in Edinburgh, you wouldn't believe. While I've been through there, looking at locations, I've had plenty of time to scope out the skirt as well. Not that I'll be telling Catherine. It's like another world. The things they'll do for you.'

On the dance floor, Catherine joins Agnes and her pals and they dance in a square formation around their handbags in the centre of the floor. John was never sure if

78

he believed Ronnie about the women in Edinburgh. Him and Catherine stayed together until the end, so if it was true, he managed to keep it from her, or maybe she just didn't want the hassle and mess of a divorce. Things are different nowadays, women can break away quite easily, and John's glad. His granddaughter, Katie, she's already a prefect at her high school, plays the clarinet, and is thinking of going into medicine.

'So, that's a yes?' John says. 'I can tell Agnes that I'm starting?'

Ronnie smiles the way you would at a puppy who's finally done a pee outside for the first time and not made a mess of the carpet.

'Yes, John,' he says. 'You tell that to Agnes. We'll call it a wedding present.'

'Thank you so much,' John says, shaking his hand. 'You won't regret it. I'm going to take the company to new places.'

'Steady on, John. It's just grunt work. We're not letting you near any of the technology. Don't want your clumsy hands near anything.'

John squeezes Ronnie's hand a little tighter. While *Mrs Robinson* by Simon and Garfunkel plays over the speakers, and his wife dances round her handbag, and his best man Gary is being sick outside on a lamppost, which he will later deny, he shakes his new father-in-law's hand and checks around the room to make sure his dad isn't looking. As things turned out, this was probably the most important handshake of John's life.

Hannah – Edinburgh, 2017

A flock of birds pass overhead, squawking and fighting for their place in the sky. Hannah raises a hand to shield her eyes from the sun as she looks up. Something hits her on the shoulder. She crooks her neck to find a bird has shat on her. The shit is colourful, a mix of black and green and blue and white.

'Well,' she says. 'I don't think the memory likes me.'

'Good shot, though,' Xander says.

'How did this happen?' Hannah asks Philippa, trying to show her the bird shit, as they are led across the grass to the other side of the square. 'Why am I being shat on if this is just someone's memory?'

Philippa stops and turns. The three recruits almost run into the back of her.

'The *Memorize* technology is to thank for that happy little accident,' she says. 'When a client enters a memory, the technology expands on it to create a more realistic, fleshed out world for the client to explore, like the people in the buildings in Mr Valentine's memory.

'We are currently in Yasmin's memory of the Edinburgh Book Festival. If Yasmin wishes to walk about a bit, take a stroll in the bookshops, leave the square, basically do something that she did not originally do, the system will generate these new parts, basing them on what Yasmin believes she would find. So if Yasmin walks into the bookshop, she will be presented with a realistic depiction of a bookshop, based on her own subconscious as well as what the technology believes would be realistic. Clear?'

'Not really,' Hannah says, and is glad when she sees Xander and Andreas shaking their heads too.

'How does that explain a bird shitting on Hannah?' Andreas says. 'Does Yasmin think birds are always shitting on people? That's quite funny. No offence, Hannah, it would've been funnier if it'd happened to Xander.'

'The longer a client uses our technology,' Philippa says, 'the more the technology learns about the client and takes the burden off the client's subconscious. This encourages repeated visits to Memory Lane as the clients often wish to walk around outside the core memory and find that with further visits, the more surprising the memories are. This memory we are currently in has been used dozens of times on many different groups of new recruits. At this point, the technology is fully in control of dealing with the outskirts of the memory. So, a bird shitting on you was the technology rather than the client, if that makes you feel better, Hannah.'

Philippa comes to a stop when she reaches Yasmin. She sits by herself, in the shade, cup of beer in one hand and a paperback in the other.

'You lot took your time,' Yasmin says, folding over her book. 'I was starting to think I'd need to sit here all day.'

'And what a trial that would have been,' Philippa says.

'Sorry, I didn't get your names?' she says to the three new faces.

'Andreas.'

'I'm Xander.'

'Hannah.'

'Nice to meet you,' Yasmin says. 'I suppose you know why I'm here?'

'This is your memory?' Hannah says.

'Correct.'

'And we're supposed to get you to leave?'

'That's the idea. Only, I don't really want to leave. I'm

having quite a nice time, to be honest, and the weather's much nicer in my memory so I'll just stay, okay?'

Yasmin reopens her book, *The Sun is Also a Star* by Nicola Yoon, and scrolls her finger down the page to find her place. She seems normal, Hannah thinks to herself, she could definitely see the two of them getting drunk together on the staff night out. She wonders where Memory Lane would have their staff night out. Probably somewhere fancier than the bowling, which is a shame since Hannah's quite good at bowling. The trick is to repeatedly say you want the barriers to be up in the weeks leading up to it, so everyone assumes you're terrible. Then when you're half decent, you look amazing because you've outperformed their pre-conceived notions. She should really write a book on the subject.

Memory Lane could probably hire Edinburgh Castle with the money they have. Just stick a sign on the front gate that says 'private function'. Or maybe they all go into someone's memory. If their day job is weird, it stands to reason their nights out are weird too.

'Before you enter a memory,' Philippa says, 'you will be able to see information about the client. Name, age, where they will be in the memory, and so on. Most of our clients are much older in real life than in the memory so you'll need to remember to be looking for a much younger face. You will enter the memory approximately twenty metres from the client.'

That's when it occurs to Hannah that Michael Valentine had looked a little younger when they were on the Royal Mile with him. And why Yasmin looks a couple of years younger now. Because, in here, she is.

'So if I was the client,' Yasmin says, 'you would approach me like this. You would say the spiel, then ask me to press my button.'

Yasmin raises her hand. On the palm, a red button just like the one that had appeared on Mr Valentine's hand.

'I press the button and then we wake up back in Memory Lane.'

Xander walks over and pulls up a seat next to Yasmin.

'I would shake your hand,' he says. 'But I don't want to set that thing off. Couldn't I do that, though? If the client didn't want to leave, couldn't I just reach out and press their hand button thing?'

Their little group has attracted a few onlookers, pointing and whispering about the girl with green hair and a button on her hand.

'There are many failsafe ways built into the system to return the client to Memory Lane,' Philippa says. 'But the only guaranteed, one hundred percent safe method is for the client to leave by their own choice and press the exit button themselves. The button only becomes visible once the twelve hour mark has passed to save them hitting it by accident.'

A big cloud glides in out of nowhere and hides the sun, leaving their patch in the shade even cooler.

'I don't remember it getting this chilly,' Yasmin says. 'Anyway, we good to go back?'

Philippa turns to them and Hannah, Xander and Andreas all nod in turn. Yasmin closes her palm into a fist and...

The festival fades to black. Then the room at Memory Lane appears. The five of them, waking up again.

Yasmin takes her headset off promptly and leaves it on her chair.

'I'm missing my break,' she says, leaving the room too fast for Philippa to argue.

Hannah feels like she's not eaten for a day then gone a run up Calton Hill. Not that she remembers what running feels like. She bought a pair of running shoes a couple of years ago, went to the fancy running shop and everything, went on the treadmill and had the shop lady measure her gait. But the idea of having to break them in had put her off.

Philippa scans their faces. Xander and Andreas look as knackered as Hannah feels. Hannah slips the headset off and places it on the counter next to the computer and the boys follow suit. While she was inside the memory, she couldn't feel it on her head, and yet as soon as she's out, she can't stand the heaviness of it weighing on her neck.

'Well,' Philippa says. 'That's coming up to eleven, so I'll let you three get on your tea break.'

She gets up and leads them out the room and they follow like sleepy baby ducks in a line. Once they reach the bottom of the corridor, they follow her through a set of doors. In this new corridor, the brickwork gives it a more relaxed, less clinical feeling than the previous rooms. It's a good idea, Hannah thinks, making the break area feel different to the work area. She can't imagine it's nice having your tea and eating your caramel wafer in a white room that feels like a hospital ward.

'I'll be back in twenty minutes or so,' Philippa tells them, as she deposits them in the canteen. 'Careful of the vending machine.'

'Does it not work?' Xander asks.

'No, it just topples over easily.'

Hannah scans the room. Yasmin sits by herself at a table and scrolls on her phone. Two older women sit at another table, near the vending machines, which *whir* and cast faint light on the floor. Hannah leads them to a free table and they all collapse into chairs. None of them have the energy to say anything.

Hannah thinks she's going to fall asleep when the silence breaks.

84

'Which one of them d'you think it'll be?' says one of the older women. 'I think it'll be the boney boy with the big nose.'

Xander's head swivels towards them.

'Are you talking about me? Did you say boney or bonnie?'

'Nah,' the other woman says. 'It'll be the short one with the glasses and the silly haircut.'

Andreas runs a self-conscious hand along his temple then crosses his arms.

Why do they not think it'll be me? Hannah wonders, *and what are they even talking about?*

'What do you mean?' she asks, not sure she wants to know the answer.

John – Stonecranning, 1975

The night's getting on a bit. John's been accepting all the pints thrust in his direction with a nod, a thanks and a raise of the glass. The alcohol works in here, the system doing its best to replicate the feeling of drunkenness and doing a fine job of it.

Jackets have been abandoned on the backs of chairs. Sleeves are rolled up and ties are loosened to the point of flying off on the dance floor. Tables have a maximum of two people at any one time, where one person is whisper-shouting in someone else's ear about something really important that neither of them will remember in the morning.

'It's been a great day,' Helen says to him. She's one of Agnes's friends that he only ever met at their wedding, and only learned her name in the last few repeats. 'Thanks so much for inviting us.'

Her husband, Graham, manages a nod. He and Helen have their arms draped over each other so that, if you weren't paying attention, you might not notice that she's keeping him upright.

'My pleasure, Helen,' John says. 'Wouldn't have been much of a party without you and Graham. Isn't that right, Graham?'

Graham's eyes open wide and roll around with the shock of hearing his own name said aloud.

'What was that?' he says.

'I said thanks for coming,' John says.

'Oh! No bother. I… didn't want to come but Helen…

said "Graham, we need to"… so… we came… because she's the boss… and… y'know what…? It's been a bloody good… night. So… we'll go now… but… we should do this again… sometime.'

'That means a lot,' John says. 'You get home safe now.'

'John Valentine… did he not play for Queen's Park?'

Helen gives one last apologetic smile and crease of her eyes then the pair of them head through the fire door, propped open with a brick to let some cool air into the hall. John's fairly sure he never set eyes on the pair of them again.

John walks through to the public bar, which is actually closed to the public at this hour, but open for their guests who want to drink in a brighter, quieter room.

Everyone seems pleased to see him. They greet him with 'there he is' and 'look who it is' and the like. It's not often you get to make people happy just by walking into a room, but that's what John's wedding day has allowed him to repeat again and again. He doesn't dwell too long on thoughts of going back to the real world, where anything can happen, any moment. If there's one thing memories have going for them, John thinks, it's that they're totally safe.

John's dad is playing Gary at darts. The board lets out dull thumps as the darts hit in threes. Gary throws his, then moves to the board, pulls the darts out while doing the maths in his head, then updates his score with a tiny stub of chalk.

'You needing another?' Gary says, spotting the nearly empty glass held loosely in John's fingertips.

'Aw, no,' John says. 'No more for me.'

'I don't think so,' John's dad says, taking his turn at the oche, which is just a deep scuff mark in the carpet. 'There's a dram sitting there for you.'

He looks to the table where the glasses of whisky sit. He knew they were going to be there, knew that his dad was going to order them. He'd never thought of himself as an actor but that's what this place has turned him into, and a half decent one at that.

At first he'd tried out the, 'I know the future' thing to entertain people, had predicted things no one could have seen coming, a few winners at Aintree and whatnot, but that had worn off quickly. That's not what *Memorize* is about. It's about reliving memories, not changing them to suit yourself. That's what they tell the clients, anyway. The technology can't recreate real people. Lines of computer code can't do that. But it's the closest John can get to his dad. It's all he has.

'Dad,' John says, picking up the whisky glasses. 'Can I talk to you? Just the two of us?'

His dad puts his arrows down and raises a couple of fingers to Gary to show he'll only be two minutes.

'Don't wipe off my score,' he tells Gary. 'I'll be back in a minute to finish you off. You can't hit a double to save your life.'

There's a nook in the corner with two seats and a gravy stain on the table from the people who were eating there earlier. That's where John had this chat with his dad that night. But that table hasn't worked for him any of the times before, so he decides to change things up a little.

John leads his dad outside into the cold night. A taxi sits with the engine running and the driver rolls down the window.

'Are you McFarlane?' the driver shouts.

'No, sorry,' John says. 'It's just finishing up in there, sure it won't be long.'

The driver rolls back up the window back up to keep the heat in.

From the open fire door at the end of the hall, John hears the opening notes of *Waterloo* by ABBA. The two bodies that were necking by the door rush back inside.

'We got through it then, son,' John's dad says. 'I thought Agnes might run out on you, truth be told. Thought she might realise her mistake, find a hunky Argentinian fella and fly off to South America.'

'There's still time,' John replies. 'I'd go with her, actually. Wouldn't mind a honeymoon like that.'

'Where are you going again?'

'Five nights in Margate in August.'

'Ach well, that'll still be nice.'

'Really?'

'Well, not really, but it's still something to look forward to at least, eh?'

John's dad takes a packet of cigarettes from his jacket and offers one to John. He accepts it. In the real world John doesn't smoke anymore, not since they put those warnings on the packets and sucked all the fun out of the experience. But there's not much damage he can do to his lungs in here.

'What did you want to talk to me about?' his dad says. 'If you're needing advice about tonight… you just let me know and I'll throw myself in the canal and save us both the trouble.'

'I can think of no conversation I would want to have less. No, I wanted to tell you something and I want you to let me get through it all before you say anything back, okay? This is really important.'

His dad is amused and acts out zipping his lips, or at least zipping most of his lips, as his cigarette is in the way.

'Go on then.'

John clears his throat. They stand in shadow, just away from the lights of the hall and it's hard to see the exact features of his dad's face, which might make this easier. He's not done this outside before. It might be okay this time. He might not get angry. It might be okay.

'Dad, I asked Ronnie for a job at McDuff & McBride and he said yes and I'm going to start at the Falkirk office in a few weeks.'

John knows he shouldn't have paused and given his dad a chance to jump in, but he only takes another drag on his cigarette and gestures for him to continue.

The air is cold as John takes another deep breath. He has to be fast, because he knows his dad hates listening to anything he doesn't want to hear.

'I know you can't stand him and honestly, me too. You know that. The last thing I wanted was to have to go cap in hand to him. Obviously, I'll work my notice and make sure there's someone to take over from me before I go. But I needed to do it, Dad, I really had to. I'm asking you to trust me, alright? This isn't just a pipe dream. This is it. This is the start of the most important thing I'll ever do. I'll be in the Edinburgh office in a year or two, and it won't be long until I'm running the place. I'm smarter than Ronnie and other people are going to realise it. I'm going to change the world, Dad. I never got to go to university but I'm good with computers. Really good. They're the big thing that's coming down the pipeline. I'm going to create this technology, this thing that allows people to relive their best memories. No one else has this tech but our company. People are trying to get it from us, actually. This company called The Recollect Project has been after it for years. We've cornered the market. I know I sound off my head, and you'll think it's just the drink talking, but it's real and the only way I can get out of Stonecranning and get on the right path is by going to work for Ronnie for a while. I'm sorry if you think I'm a disappointment.

I never meant to do anything that would disappoint you. I love you, Dad.'

It doesn't matter how many times he rehearses this speech in his head, John always misses out bits or says things in the heat of the moment he hadn't planned on saying. He avoids looking at his dad, staring at the pavement instead. He listens to their breathing, the radio muffled from the taxi, the dull pound of ABBA through the wall.

His dad laughs. 'That was a long way of saying you're quitting to go and work for that prick,' he says. 'And that "I love you, Dad" at the end? What was that? Is that supposed to make me feel better? Is that supposed to make everything alright? Like we're some folk off the telly?'

It hasn't worked. Just like every time before. Just like that night.

'Dad, I'm going to change the world. I'm going to be somebody important.'

'Aw, fuck off with that nonsense. You're twenty-eight now, John. A man grown and then some. If you were going to change anything you would've done it. Your head's full of shite. I'm guessing it's Agnes that's filled you up with it. You might think she's got your best interests at heart, son, but she's only setting you up for a fall. Leave that for other folk. People like you and me and our family live and work in Stonecranning and we don't swan off to Edinburgh or we end up like auld Tommy Williamson, lying in the street stinking of piss. You've seen Tommy, haven't you, John?'

'I'm going, Dad. I'm going to work for him and then I'm going to work for myself and I'm going to make you proud.'

His dad throws his cigarette to the ground and crushes it beneath his scuffed black shoe. It scrapes on the tarmac as he twists his foot.

'Proud,' he says, like it's a bad word. 'Proud. I can't be proud of you, John. You know who I'd be proud of? A man that knows his place. Works hard, respects his parents, doesn't go behind his father's back and beg on his knees for a job from Ronnie fucking McDuff at his own fucking wedding, that's who I'd be proud of. Not you. Not this.'

'Please, Dad. We don't have much time left. Please just tell me you forgive me. That you're proud of me. That you love me. Don't let this be how it ends. You know it deep down. Please don't let this be how it ends.'

'Don't tell me what I know or don't know, son. You've taken what I've given you and thrown it back in my face. Wait 'til everyone hears. My son, my John, leaving his dad to go and work for Ronnie McDuff. I can't even look at you.'

John checks his wristwatch. 11.59 p.m.

'Dad, please. Please, don't let this be the last thing you ever say to me.'

He tries to grab his dad's sleeve but he shrugs him off and walks away, in the opposite direction from the hall.

'Dad,' he shouts. 'Dad, I'm sorry.'

There's no response from the figure disappearing into the dark. John sniffs and wipes the tears from his eyes. It wasn't exactly the same as the last conversation he had had with his dad but it was close enough. Another failed attempt at trying to change it.

Two days later, John's dad was out on a job, painting someone's gutters. The ladder slipped and he fell thirty feet, hitting his head on the concrete. He was dead before the ambulance arrived.

The clock must tick over to midnight. John finds himself back in the church.

Hannah – Edinburgh, 2019

The staffroom walls are clean and cream, dotted with the standard posters highlighting workplace safety and workers' rights. There's a half marathon sponsor sheet next to the microwave for someone called Greg, with a few names and amounts in angled, scribbled writing.

'I'm Wendy,' one of their new co-workers at the other table says. 'And this is Irene.'

'Like *Goodnight, Irene*,' Xander says, and there's a silence as everyone stares at him. 'It's a... song. It's good.'

Xander puts his head down and goes back to eating grapes from a little Tupperware pot he brought in with him. Yasmin is scrolling on her phone still, but her eyes keep flicking up to watch their conversation.

Hannah, Xander and Andreas take turns telling the women their names.

'But what did you mean?' Hannah asks again. 'When you were choosing us?'

Wendy brushes some crumbs from the front of her top.

'Every time they take on new starts,' she says. 'Doesn't matter if it's three or five or seven of you. Only one ends up staying, if that. Isn't that right, Yasmin?'

She calls this to the other table, where Yasmin nods, her eyes back on her phone. Hannah wonders where she gets her hair dyed. They've done a great job of it. She had gone as far as purple during uni, but green, that separated the women from the girls. The comments from her dad wouldn't be worth it. She'd need to wait until she moved out, again.

'I started with two guys,' Yasmin says. 'By lunch, one had disappeared. We think he climbed out of the toilet window. And by four o'clock, the other tried to get off with his memory buddy and Mr Valentine took him out the back. Like, he walked him out the back door. He didn't shoot him.'

'So,' Irene says. 'Don't think we're being snooty if we don't get to know the three of you right now. By tomorrow, there'll probably only be one of you and I'm not great with names.'

Hannah looks at the boys. She's sure they're both thinking the same thing: *it's going to be me. I'm definitely going to be the one that comes back tomorrow.*

'This is all just a scare tactic,' Andreas says. 'Or a newbie hazing thing. It would be a waste of time to go through the process of hiring and doing security checks on three people if you knew two were going to leave.'

'Whatever you say, number two,' Wendy says.

'Why am I number two?'

Wendy shrugs.

'Don't know really.'

'Can I be number one?' Xander says.

'Sure.'

So that makes Hannah number three.

'Can I ask another question?' she says.

'Go for it, three,' Wendy says. She's annoyed that she's already remembered Wendy's name while Wendy's allotted her a number. And the last remaining number, at that.

'What's a memory buddy?'

Wendy looks over at Yasmin.

'Did you not tell them about buddies? What were you doing in that induction?'

Yasmin reaches into her bag, pulling out an apple.

Hannah recognises it as a Pink Lady, the queen of all apples. The only problem, she finds, is that it's so sweet it doesn't actually feel all that healthy while you're eating it. Which kind of defeats the purpose, in her eyes. Eating fruit is a chore, not something she'd do out of choice.

'We must have forgotten,' Yasmin says, looking over at the newbies' table. 'When you guys go into your first few memories, you'll get a memory buddy. I'll be someone's, and we'll get a couple more of us from the CPU to help. Your buddy is there just to show you the ropes and make sure you don't fuck anything up too badly. Honestly, it's easy enough once you know what you're doing.'

Hannah's not sure if she wants Yasmin as her memory buddy. She seems like the kind of person who'd be a good laugh once you've known her for a few years and she's let her guard down, but would get annoyed if you make a mistake. And Hannah's fairly sure she's going to be making a lot of mistakes for the foreseeable future.

Wendy checks her watch and tells Irene that's their time up and they gather their rubbish and bags and leave the room. Yasmin follows not long after, stopping at the door on her way out.

'I'll see you guys soon,' she says. 'And I wouldn't worry about the whole "only one person survives" thing. All three of you might last, or maybe none. Best not to think about it too much.'

She heads out and Hannah hopes the other two are already stressing about it as much as she is. *It's Gonna Be Me* by N*SYNC pops into her head.

'Who do you think it'll be then?' Andreas asks.

'It's gonna be...' Hannah says. 'One of us, I suppose. We'll just need to wait and find out.'

Xander leans back in his chair.

'I've never quit a job in my life,' he says. 'So, I have to say, I'm quietly confident.'

'Telling everyone you're confident isn't being quietly confident,' Hannah says. 'That's being loudly confident. You can only be quietly confident if no one knows you're quietly confident.'

'No, that's silently confident,' Andreas joins in. 'There's a difference between being silently confident and being quietly confident, if you ask me. Anyway, it doesn't really matter, because I'm clearly going to outlast you two. Sorry, I'm just saying what we're all thinking.'

Xander rolls his eyes and Hannah laughs.

'Yeah, we were all just thinking that,' she says.

A lot of people are lovely to your face and horrible behind your back, and Hannah appreciates that Andreas is up front about things. She respects that level of honesty.

'I'm looking forward to getting stuck in,' Xander says. 'Seeing people's weird memories.'

They all nod and pick at the last of their snacks. Hannah only packed a banana and eats half of it, as the bottom half got bruised in her bag and even though it's only slightly brown, it's past the point of no return for her liking.

'I heard one of the staff call us bouncers,' Andreas says. 'When we passed them in the corridor. That must be what they call us, the people at the bottom of the pecking order. Memory bouncers. Go in and chuck people out.'

Hannah wonders what her friends and family would believe more: that she bounces people out of their own memories or that she bounces at a club in the city centre. Both seem equally unlikely.

Philippa arrives in the doorway and beckons them to follow her. They pack away their things and join her in the corridor. She takes them down a set of stairs.

At the bottom landing, on the left hand side, they go by

a green door with an *'Authorised Personnel ONLY'* sign next to it. There also seems to be a number on a little gold circle but Hannah can't quite make it out.

'What's in there?' Xander asks. 'Something interesting, I bet.'

'Stay away from the green door,' Philippa says.

'You shouldn't have said that. Now I just want to go in there more.'

'I catch you in there, Xander, you won't come back tomorrow.'

Hannah looks back over her shoulder at the green door. She's not going to say it out loud, but she wouldn't mind seeing what's behind it either. Or maybe it's a Memory Lane test. Anyone who doesn't get tempted gets to keep their job.

They arrive at a pair of swinging doors, huge glass windows criss-crossed with black lines. On the glass it reads: Memory Care and Protection Unit. It looks a bit like a hospital inside, all white tiles and bright lighting panels beaming down. Except there's no hospital equipment, just computers and desks like any other office. Yasmin sits behind a computer and gives them a wave from her desk.

Philippa takes them inside, where they linger awkwardly while she retrieves their buddies from around the room. Yasmin comes over, as well as two other girls. Both are tall and make Hannah feel like a child who's meeting their new teacher for the first time. She has always wanted to be taller. It would help at gigs, obviously, but more than that, it would stop men looming over her at pubs whenever they felt like it.

'Yasmin,' Philippa says. 'You'll go with Hannah.'

And like that, Yasmin turns and starts walking towards

97

the back of the room. Hannah chases after her, not sticking around to hear who the boys get paired with.

'Just do the first couple with her,' Philippa shouts after them.

Yasmin takes her through a door. They stand in yet another corridor, but this one is much longer, so much so that it becomes a bit blurry right at the end. Hannah reminds herself to get her eyes checked. She's been putting it off because she's certain they'll force glasses on her. They give you glasses at the drop of a hat these days, according to her dad. Another piece of vital fatherly wisdom.

Doors run the length of the corridor on either side, with little lightbulbs sticking out next to each door. Only one bulb appears to be on, shining bright red, about ten doors down on the left.

'I'm skipping a step,' Yasmin tells her. 'To save you waiting around and one of them getting this one. You see the bulb that's on?'

She points to the bulb Hannah already noticed.

'That means someone's gone over time. You'll get a notification on your computer first and then you come into the corridor. So, the client in room twenty doesn't want to come out, and that's where you come in.'

Yasmin leads her down to door twenty and opens it. Inside, there's a bed and a lamp glowing with warm white light. There's a desk and a screen in here too. On the bed, a middle-aged man in a green checked shirt lies with his hands over his stomach, the *Memorize* headset resting on his head.

Yasmin pulls two chairs from under the desk and they sit down. She begins clicking through the program in the same way Philippa did earlier.

'This guy's name is...' she says, scanning the screen.

'Rodger Hill. They mostly have boring names, you'll notice. It's hella expensive to book a Mex, so it's mainly older white guys called Rodger or Duncan or, I dunno, William the Third. Anyway, the memory Rodger chose is… a day where he scored a hat-trick for the uni football team, went out drinking later that night and met his future wife, Carole, in a nightclub. Pretty good day, I suppose. Some of the memories we get are total snoozefests. Weddings, births. I once had a woman who relived the day she saw *Wicked* in the West End. I mean, fair enough, it's a decent musical, but surely she could've just used the money to… see it again?'

Yasmin opens a drawer and takes out headsets for the pair of them. Hannah slides hers on and the heavy feeling on her head returns. It seems to penetrate inside her head too, like her thoughts are heavy, like she's got a damp cloud in there and it's needing wrung out.

'Okie-dokie, Hannah,' Yasmin says. 'We go in, find Mr Hill, and tell him to get out, basically. You can call him Rodger or Mr Hill, whatever you feel most comfortable with. This memory ran from 1pm to 1am, and it's currently 1.13 a.m. so he's a naughty boy is our Mr Hill. The system says he's…'

She turns and reads the screen again. It's the kind of program that Hannah assumes she'll understand in a few memories time but for now it's like trying to read all those green symbols in *The Matrix*.

'He's outside the nightclub, chatting with a woman. So yeah, the most common reason they stay in the memory is that they misjudged when they wanted the day to end and they just think, fuck it, I'll stay in until they kick me out. And the more times they visit, the more they realise they can guarantee at least ten extra minutes if they just ignore the warning. They only get charged more if they stay over thirty minutes.'

Yasmin slides her headset on.

'I'll do the talking for this one,' she says. 'Just to get you into it. Ready?'

Hannah nods. Yasmin reaches over to the mouse and clicks. The room goes black.

John – Stonecranning, 1975

Agnes walks down the aisle, her arm linked with her father, Ronnie. John watches them from the altar, where he stands with his best man, Gary.

This is the toughest part of this whole thing. The hangover from the night before. Not of the alcoholic kind though, a memory hangover. Everyone's smiling and happy and yet it's only been a few minutes since his dad broke his heart yet again.

He's starting to wonder what he can possibly do to change his dad's mind. Other than lie to him, which he promised himself he would never do. It's not real, he knows that, but he needs it to be as real as he can make it. That means telling him about the job.

Agnes unlinks her arm from Ronnie and he kisses her on the cheek. As he passes John, he gives him a look. A look that says: *I may be giving away my daughter to you, John, but that doesn't mean I'm happy about it or that you get my respect, even when you take my company to new heights never seen before over the course of the next forty years*. John may *still* be reading too much into the look.

What are you looking at me like that for, John thinks, after all I did for you, for the company? You would've still been testing on rats if it wasn't for me. John liked Ronnie better in his later years, when he had to let his grip of the company go, let John get on with things. Memory Lane never would've gone ahead if Ronnie had had his way. He thought it was too dangerous, would only leave them open to legal battles. John had always been smarter than him, it had just taken him a while to realise it.

John lifts the delicate veil from his bride's face.

'I thought we agreed you were going to shave that,' Agnes says, raising a finger to his moustache.

John finds he can't quite fix his smile quick enough in the way he knows Agnes likes.

'What would everyone think of me?' John says. 'If I got rid of it the night before the wedding?'

'They'd think you'd finally come to your senses.'

'If you'd like to shave it now, I can ask the minister to hold off a minute. I think I have some shaving cream in my sporran, you know.'

As usual, he digs around in his sporran. He nearly hits the purple panic button by accident.

'Dad says to tell you you're not supposed to do up the bottom button on your waistcoat. Gentlemen don't do up the bottom button.'

'If Ronnie's a gentleman, I'm Scotland's first choice right-back.'

This makes her roll her eyes rather than elicit a smile. He tries but can't remember exactly who was playing right-back for Scotland around that time. Jardine maybe, with McGrain on the left so they could fit them both in the team.

In the real world, he's tired of the football chat he hears around the office. Too many names to remember these days, and they're all mercenaries, diving all over the place, getting paid obscene amounts of money for nothing much at all. Although maybe he's not in the right position to be lecturing about obscene amounts of money.

The minister starts talking and John scans the crowd. He makes eye contact with his dad, who gives him a nod and a raise of the eyebrows. John had known his dad didn't

102

like Ronnie, but he never realised quite how much he had hated him until that night.

That wasn't the only reason he had said what he said, of course. In his dad's mind, his only son had deserted the family decorating business, the family, him. John's son, Michael, had been eager to join Memory Lane, and when John named him CEO, they'd hugged and drunk beer and whisky like friends, equals.

'Will you, Agnes Irene McDuff, take this man to be your husband, to have and to hold from this day forward, for better, for worse, for richer, for poorer, in sickness and in health, to love and to cherish, until you are parted by death?'

'I will,' Agnes says, and smiles at John.

The last smile of her single life. It's been six years since she passed now. John can remember that, at least. They were only running early trials of the first version of *Memorize* at that point, so she never got a chance to relive anything. He would've given her free rein, of course. Let her relive anything she wanted, for as long as she wanted. John often finds himself wondering what memory she would've wanted to do again. A day before she met him, maybe.

'And will you, John Victor Valentine, take this woman to be your wife, to have and to hold from this day forward, for better, for worse, for richer, for poorer, in sickness and in health, to love and to cherish, until you are parted by death?'

'I will.'

He's too late again to see who shouts the sarcastic 'Way!' John kisses his new bride.

In the years that followed, they had settled into married life and the spark faded, as it had with every couple they knew, but the love was always there, underneath everything. And looking at her now, John knows he wouldn't have chosen any other woman to be by his side for all that time. He doesn't know if Agnes felt the same way, but he hopes she did.

'Hello, Mrs Valentine,' he says to her.

'Oh God,' Agnes says. 'My hands are shaking, John.'

'You did fine, love. That's the hardest part over.'

'I'm not so sure. I need to be your wife now.'

'Fair point. And until we're parted by death, the minister made that bit quite clear.'

John had always thought she was going over the top about the shaking but as he looks down at her hands now, they really are jittering.

'Are you okay, Aggie?' he asks.

She claps her hands together tightly and there's no time for her to answer before the piper starts up *Scotland the Brave* from outside the church and they have to be on their way.

Hannah – Glasgow, 1994

The music from inside the club pulsing through the pavement is the first thing she senses. Then she takes in the rest. The dark street, the flickering streetlights, the orange glow of the sign outside the club. *Franco's*. At her feet, a spilled poke of chips, tomato sauce splattered like blood over the kerb.

Some people linger outside the entrance doors, where two bouncers lean on the doorframe, chatting. One of them spots her and frowns. Hannah looks down at her attire and realises she doesn't fit in with the clubbing theme. Her trousers flare a tiny bit at the bottom but that's about it. She dressed up for her first day but was hoping Memory Lane might be a smart casual kind of place and she could de-escalate the formality as the week went on.

Yasmin's wearing a silky white blouse and doesn't look as out of place as Hannah does. The 90s clothing on show makes her smile. The guys in their baggy shirts, never tucked in. The girls in their knee length skirts and with what would now be considered a bravely minimal amount of make-up on.

'The system's pre-programmed to put us in twenty metres from the client,' Yasmin says. 'Just so we don't pop up right by their side and give them a fright. And, just to warn you in advance: yes, you will definitely have to interrupt a client having sex at some point. Best to accept it now.'

'Thanks for the heads up. Mr Hill won't be, will he…?'

'Outside a club? I… well, let's just see.'

Hannah and Yasmin scan around the street, looking for Mr Hill and the woman who would become his wife.

'What do you think of it?' Hannah asks. 'Of this whole thing. People reliving memories.'

'In what way?' Yasmin answers, as they move further down the street, dodging out the way of people sober enough to walk but drunk enough that a straight line is out of the question.

'Like, the morality of it. I'm not saying I've had the time to form my opinion yet, just wondered.'

'Is it moral to relive memories, d'you mean? Why wouldn't it be?'

Taxis shoot by on the road, some pulling up in puddles for people on the pavement to fight over.

'Well, reliving a memory in your head is one thing,' Hannah says, formulating the thoughts just as quickly as she's saying them. 'But this?'

She gestures at the very real world around them. On the other side of the road, two guys are arguing with the bouncers to get back into a pub called *Warped*. That reminds her of playing *Crash Bandicoot* with Liam after they first met. He insisted that he kept his PS2 because the PS3 wasn't actually that much better. They'd stay up all night playing on the weekends. Order pizza from wherever was open latest. He'd sold the PS2 when Sydney was born. Didn't get much for it but the thought was there.

'This is… crazy,' Hannah goes on. 'Like, Mr Hill's wife, Carole, she never knew she was signing up to live this memory again.'

'But she isn't, only Mr Hill is.'

'Yeah, but a version of her is, right? A projection that him and the system have produced. And he's getting to, like, scrutinise her in a way she never would have agreed to. Be honest, if you knew someone was reliving a

106

memory that you were in, would you be happy with that? You wouldn't have any control over your actions in the memory.'

'Guess I never really thought about it that deep before. For one, I don't know, and probably will never know, someone who could afford this. My friends, millionaires they are not.'

They go round the side alley of the club and Hannah recognises him immediately. The younger version of Mr Hill, the years wiped clean off his face, leaning on a wet brick wall. He's chatting away to a woman, reaching out every few seconds to touch her playfully on the elbow, the hip, the curve of her neck.

'Okay,' Hannah says. 'They are a pretty cute couple, I'll give him that.'

Yasmin rolls her eyes and leads them to the chatting couple. Mr and Mrs Hill don't take their eyes off each other as they approach. Yasmin clears her throat to get Mr Hill's attention.

'Evening, Mr Hill,' she says. 'It's me, Yasmin, from Memory Lane. And this is Hannah.'

Hannah does an awkward wave, while Mrs Hill looks as confused as you'd expect, given the situation.

'Your twelve hour session has now finished and you are required to come back to the facility.'

Mr Hill looks back at Mrs Hill, like he wants just one more look at her. Maybe she was being too harsh with what she had said to Yasmin. Hannah wouldn't mind being used in someone else's memory if they were doing it for the right reason, e.g. being completely and totally head over heels in love with her and unable to live without her. She'll need to find someone who feels that way about her first, of course, but it's bound to happen at some point. Probably not while she's on Tinder, though. One night, a few weeks ago, in a moment of weakness after midnight, she'd paid for Tinder Gold. No one must ever know.

'Alright,' Mr Hill says, taking his hand out his pocket, revealing the red button which has appeared there. 'I just wanted a few more minutes.'

'I think that's totally understandable, Mr Hill,' Hannah says, unable to help herself. 'I think you're a very lucky woman, Carole.'

The woman looks even more confused than before.

'Carole?' she says, turning to Mr Hill. 'Who's Carole? Is she one of your other girls? What the fuck, Rodger?'

'Wait, if you're not Carole,' Hannah says, 'then who are you?'

'I'm Theresa,' she says. 'Who the fuck are you two? Has this guy been chatting you two up as well? Because you can keep him. Oh, and put your collar down, Rodger, you look like fucking Dracula.'

She turns and marches her way down to the bottom of the lane and turns into the main street, never once looking back. Mr Hill looks quite amused by the situation.

'He was reliving the day he met his wife,' Yasmin says to Hannah. 'He doesn't actually have to meet his wife if he doesn't want to.'

'That was Theresa,' Mr Hill says. 'I always had this feeling that I could've pulled her that night if I hadn't gone over to Carole first. And now I know.'

Yasmin smiles and turns to Hannah.

'Such a cute couple,' she says.

Before Hannah can respond, Mr Hill closes his hand over and presses his exit button. She's getting used to this. The world fading to black around her.

John – Stonecranning, 1975

'You sure you're okay?' John asks his new wife once again.

'Yes,' Agnes says. 'Now stop asking, you're going to ruin the photos if you keep opening your mouth.'

She doesn't put her arm around him as the photos are taken. She's keeping them in front of her, her hands strangling the bouquet. John tries to notice something new each time he relives this day, but usually it's something tiny and insignificant. This isn't tiny and insignificant.

'Is that mine all done?' Agnes calls to Martin.

'Well, actually,' he tries to say, peeking out from behind the camera.

'Good,' she says.

And with that, she hurries across the grass, lifting her dress with one hand as her other clutches the flowers. John knows he should go after her, that's what he would have done if this had happened on the actual wedding day. But he doesn't. Because this is new. And as far as he can tell, he didn't bring this about. Unless, he thinks, could his comment about Ronnie really have made her that upset? None of his jokes ever made her like this before. What was so special about this time? The Scotland right-back joke? He doesn't understand. If he was any other client, he'd be hitting his panic button and demanding a refund from the Memory Lane front desk.

'Okay, well if it's just you, John,' Martin says. 'One with just the groom and the best man.'

Gary comes to stand by John's side, the pair of them

109

again raising a hand to the sky to block out the worst of the sun.

'Got lucky with the weather, mate,' Gary says. 'How you feeling?'

'Fine,' John says, frowning, looking for his new wife among the crowd of onlookers. 'Did Agnes say anything to you there? Did she seem upset?'

'Well, she's just married you so it would make sense. Here, John, go and at least pretend to be happy. You can't be frowning like that in your wedding photos.'

John turns his frown upside down until they get the thumbs up from Martin that they can relax again.

'That'll be a nice one,' Gary says. 'Once it's developed, can I get a copy?'

'Ask Martin.'

'Who's Martin?'

'Camera fella.'

'Right you are. Soon as you're free, come find me and I'll get you your first pint, alright? Don't take a drink off anyone else before me, promise?'

This is the part where Agnes walks back to him, except this time it's not. The guests and the strangers smile at John from the pavement, as he stands on the patch of grass next to the wall, all on his lonesome. He doesn't want his imagination to get away from him but… could there be a bug in the system?

'We'll get a few more with Agnes now,' Martin says, looking around. 'Agnes? Anyone seen our bride?'

John walks over to join Martin, patting him on the back. He never did dress up for the occasion. He always thought he should have told Martin to put on a shirt at least, instead of cutting around their wedding in blue jeans and a white t-shirt like some kind of budget James Dean.

'Usually the bride runs away *before* the wedding,'

110

Martin says to him. 'Oh well, we can get some with you and the bridesmaids I suppose?'

'Can you just pause it for a few minutes?' John tells him. 'I'll go and find Agnes.

'You're the boss, boss.'

John wades through the crowd, receiving many pats on the arm and back as he goes. He tries to reciprocate the level of enthusiasm shown by every face he passes but after a few dozen his face muscles need a rest.

Agnes? he mouths to anyone who will look. They all shrug and look to other people, or chuckle that the bride's gone missing already.

'Minister?' John says, coming upon him smoking outside the church doors. 'You haven't seen Agnes have you?'

The minister blows out a cloud of smoke and gestures back into the church.

'She went back in a minute ago,' he says. 'Think she must have left something inside.'

'Thanks.'

Before John can get through the doors, his old friend Frank grabs a handful of his jacket, near enough hooking his fingers into his pocket.

'John,' Frank says. 'Sorry to catch you, but just wanted to check I can get the beef for my dinner? Between you and me, I ordered the chicken but I'm sure if you give me a beef and give someone else my chicken, it won't cause too much fuss.'

The sun is blazing high in the sky, beating down on them. John pulls his jacket out of Frank's grasp.

'The beef,' John says. 'Aye, of course, I'll sort it when we get there.'

'Knew I could count on you, John.'

'Don't forget the scatter.'

'Oh! The scatter! Nearly forgot there.'

Frank's attention gets drawn away when someone in the crowd shouts that the bus has arrived. The coach appears at the bottom of the road and drives up to the side of the church, coming to a stop with a mechanical sigh.

John goes into the church, his footsteps echoing in the stone hallway. Behind him, children whoop and cheer as they scoop and scrape pennies off the ground.

The pews are now at peace, empty and silent and waiting for the next group of guests or worshippers. John walks up the aisle like he's recreating the crime, looking for clues. There's a noise from the back corner. He follows the noise and finds, in a short corridor, the pale wooden doors of the toilets. Behind the women's, he hears Agnes sobbing.

He chaps on the door.

'Agnes?' he says softly. 'Is everything okay?'

'No,' she cries. 'No.'

John isn't sure what's happening. There are meant to be rules in here. This kind of thing isn't supposed to be able to happen in the program. And he would know, because he designed the bloody thing.

'I'm coming in,' John says, waiting a moment for her to tell him no, before he opens the door.

Hannah – Edinburgh, 2019

They arrive back in the cramped room where Mr Hill yawns and stretches on the bed like he's just woken from a deep sleep.

'Welcome back, Mr Hill,' Yasmin says, professional voice now activated. 'I hope the memory was to your satisfaction.'

He crosses one leg over the other and puts his hands behind his head. To Hannah, he's aged thirty years in the blink of an eye.

'It was, thank you,' he says. 'Although, as you can imagine, a little bittersweet.'

'Oh yes?'

'Well, now I know for sure I could've been with Theresa instead of Carole. I always suspected, but knowing definitely, it's an eye-opener.'

Hannah lets out a snort of air through her nose without meaning to. There's a definite shift in the atmosphere of the room. She notices a tranquil song is playing from speakers in the corner, obviously meant to lull the client back to consciousness.

'What was that?' says Mr Hill. 'That little snort? D'you have something to say?'

Yasmin jumps in, trying to stop Hannah doing any damage.

'She's new,' Yasmin says. 'Just showing her the ropes. We're actually just leaving. One of my colleagues will be in in a minute to complete the transition.'

Yasmin turns back to the computer to type a few

final lines on screen, a case note or something. Mr Hill continues to stare at Hannah. She tries to avert her gaze but there's not many other places to look in this room.

One thing that every company seems to have in common is penny pinching. This place must be raking in millions per day and yet they're not investing the money into the facility, and certainly not the wages either.

'Come on,' Mr Hill says. 'What is it?'

'Well,' Hannah says, and Yasmin turns to her. She seems to do a very special trick where her head stays still yet her eyeballs seem to shake side to side in a 'don't do anything to annoy this client' way. 'It just doesn't seem all that nice. Y'know, I'm sure it wouldn't make your wife feel very good to know what you were doing.'

'Hannah, enough,' Yasmin says. 'Let's go.'

She places a hand under her armpit, roughly enough to convey how seriously she wants rid of her out the room. They stand.

'No, it's alright,' Mr Hill says, sitting up and placing his feet on the ground. 'I'm sure it wouldn't make her feel very good, no. But seeing the texts from Jason, her pilates instructor, on her phone, didn't make me feel very good, so…'

'I'm guessing the texts are…'

'Explicit in nature, yes. He's fucking my wife.'

'I'm sorry to hear that,' Hannah says.

'Thanks. Maybe you think it's offensive, but now I know I might have a shot with Theresa. She's still single as far as I know. You think I'm crazy?'

'I think you have too much money.'

'Now *that* we can agree on.' He moves his head slightly to make eye contact with Yasmin. 'Next time I come, can I get this one again? I like her.'

'If she's still here,' Yasmin says, before leading her by

the hand, back out into the corridor. Hannah knows she shouldn't enjoy being referred to as 'this one' but she can't deny she's happy to have her first bit of good feedback. She's not so sure this bit of feedback is going to make its way to Philippa though, as Yasmin has a face like thunder.

'Please don't talk to clients like that,' she says. 'Maybe just don't interact with them at all.'

Hannah follows her all the way back to her desk in the main lab area. She knows it's not actually a lab, there's no test tubes or Bunsen burners or anything, but it's too clean to be considered an office.

'I'm sorry,' Hannah says.

'It's cool,' Yasmin says, sitting down in front of her computer. 'I mean, I totally agree with you, just to be clear. The men, and it's mainly men who use Memory Lane, are, ninety nine percent of the time, slimy bastards who are using their vast fortunes to relive sloppy drunk missionary sex from before they had a beer belly, instead of donating it to charity. Being a client here kind of automatically rules you out as being a good person.'

Hannah hasn't had the time to consider that side of it yet. Her initial reaction was one of sympathy, that the people using this place were in the twilight years of their life and desperate for just a few last breaths as a young person. As a young person still, she has no clue how they feel, exactly, but she isn't looking forward to finding out. On the other hand, there are a lot of charities out there who could do a lot of good with the money. Hell, she could do a lot of good with the money. Then she remembers she paid for Tinder Gold not that long ago.

'Right,' Hannah says. 'Everyone keeps hinting at it but no one's said exactly… how much does it cost? A Memory Lane experience?'

Yasmin types away. Hannah notices the boys aren't in

the lab and guesses they must still be in with their first clients.

'It varies slightly,' Yasmin says. 'Depending on how much work the vetting team need to do. They're the ones who research the memory and check that the client can't do anything too fucked up. But roughly, it's about a hundred and twenty-five grand a pop.'

'Fuck.'

'Yep.'

The clacking of the keys is the only sound for a while as Hannah turns that figure over in her head. A hundred and twenty-five grand each visit here. Yasmin is probably right. Every client here must be pure evil.

'Wait,' Hannah says. 'What do you mean about the vetting team?'

'Mm?'

'You said they check the client can't do anything too fucked up?'

'Oh, yeah. The client tells us the memory they want and they advise us what they want to do in it. But once they're in the memory, they're free to go where they please and do what they want. Take Mr Hill, for example, his file said he was going to relive the day exactly. But, he took a detour and went after another woman. The vetting team would've seen that prior to him being accepted. They must've deemed it was cool.'

'And what kind of thing wouldn't be cool?'

'Eh, let me think. Oh, well, the youngest you can be in a memory is eighteen. So, if a client chooses a memory when they're that young, the vetting team need to check there's no chance of them doing anything creepy. Say, like, they had a girlfriend who was a couple of years younger or something back then. If they deem there to be too many potential bad outcomes, y'know, legally, they can reject the memory.'

116

'Yikes.'

'Yikes is right.'

Yasmin types up a few more paragraphs in Mr Hill's file then closes the tab. Then she leads Hannah to the opposite corner of the room, where four smaller desks are set up.

'Take your pick of the seats,' Yasmin tells her. 'We only have one Retrieval Assistant at the moment and she's off on holiday, great timing.'

Hannah plonks her bag and jacket down on the nearest desk and wiggles the mouse to bring the screen to life. She types in the username Memory Lane mailed out to her, GREENSHIELDSH2 and quickly comes up with a mediumly strong password that she's sure she'll forget, while Yasmin stands nearby, watching over her shoulder.

'They make you change it every two months,' she tells Hannah. 'It's a nightmare.'

The next forty-five minutes is spent setting up her profile and making sure she has access to all the programs she needs.

'It's mainly this one you'll need,' Yasmin says, pointing to the little icon with a yellow ball surrounded by a blue ring, like a planet. 'Any client stays longer than twelve hours and you'll get a notification in here.'

Hannah wishes there was a radio on or something, so the silences aren't so obvious while the system slowly loads her profile. There's only one other person in the lab, an older woman in the opposite corner, making no moves to hide the fact that she's on eBay.

'How often does it happen?' Hannah asks. 'That the client goes off script in a memory?'

'Quite a lot,' Yasmin says. 'They probably don't even plan on it. But once they're in there, they seem to think "why relive the memory exactly when I could try doing something else?"'

117

'But it's not, like, accurate is it? Philippa said something about the system trying its best to replicate things but that it wouldn't be perfect.'

'Yeah, exactly, it's not what the technology is set up to do. It displays the memory, first and foremost. Anything outside of that, who knows?'

Hannah loads up the Intel Hub on the computer and sees the list of clients currently using the *Memorize* technology. There are twenty-one clients in Memory Lane at the moment, all in different stages of their memory. One man, called David Lombardi, only has twenty minutes or so left, his little status bar is red and almost down to nothing.

'Can I ask another question?' Hannah says.

'Shoot.'

'Philippa said the technology learns about the clients the more they use it. How does that work exactly?'

'Right, so...' Yasmin puts a finger to her mouth as she considers how best to explain this to Hannah. 'The technology, at first, creates everything outside the core memory from the client's conscious and subconscious. Take Mr Hill – he said he always thought he could pull Theresa that night instead of his wife. So, when he veered off script in the memory, the technology only had Mr Hill's word for it. He thought Theresa fancied him so the technology presented him with a Theresa that fancied him. However, the more he uses the technology, the more it'll learn about him. Could be, in fifteen visits from now, he'll try that again and the system will be like "Nah, Theresa definitely wouldn't have fancied you, pal" and it'll be more realistic. Does that make sense?'

Hannah takes just a few milliseconds too long to answer, which is an answer in itself. Yasmin ploughs on with another angle.

118

'Okay, I'll put it another way,' she says. 'It's kind of like a TV show. What's a TV show you like?'

'Eh,' Hannah thinks, not sure if she should be a basic bitch and admit she falls asleep to *Friends* pretty much every night. She decides to go with something a bit more current to hopefully show Yasmin she still manages to keep up with pop culture despite raising a little boy the last couple of years. '*Community*.'

'Great, love it. Okay, so, you know how in the early episodes of *Community*, some of the characters were a little... rough around the edges? They'd maybe say some things they wouldn't say in later seasons, because the writers hadn't got them one hundred percent down yet? That's what the *Memorize* technology's doing. People in memories are like characters that the system is trying to write, and the more episodes they write, the more the client visits, the better and more well-rounded the people are in the memories.'

'That...actually makes sense.'

'Does it?'

'Maybe.'

'Good enough for me. Just don't tell Philippa or she'll make me do the inductions. Oh, here's the boys back.'

From the memory corridor, Xander and Andreas come back into the main lab with their memory buddies. They both have a thousand-yard stare. Hannah's starting to believe that if only one of them is going to last through today, it's going to be her.

John – Stonecranning, 1975

'What's wrong?' John says, finding Agnes sitting on the closed lid of the toilet. 'You're missing all the photos. Your mum won't be happy if it's just me in them. Y'know, she once referred to me as "an ugly Graeme Souness".'

Agnes wipes a tear from her cheek.

'Who's Graeme Souness?'

Must still be a little early for that reference, John thinks. Agnes's mum must have said that in the years to come.

He walks to the window and opens it. A nice breeze comes in, wafting the delicate cotton curtains to the sides.

'I'm not sure I'm ready for this,' Agnes says. 'I think we made a mistake.'

John turns. Agnes stares straight ahead at the wall. A wooden sign says, *If it's yellow let it mellow, if it's brown flush it down!*

'What are you talking about?' John says, unable to stop himself letting out a little laugh.

'It's not funny, John.'

'Not funny-ha-ha, but it's… strange. Listen, is this because of something I said during the ceremony? Or because of the way I stood in one of the photos or something? Or did some rice get in your eye?'

Agnes frowns and shakes her head. It had to be something in the last hour or so. Something tiny that's set this off and made the memory go so off track. There's no other explanation. *Memorize* doesn't do this all by itself.

'I don't know if I want to be married to you.'

John chuckles again. Had she always been this close to

120

running out on him? One tiny change in the day and she's ready to throw it all away.

'How are you finding this funny?' Agnes shouts. 'This only makes me think I'm right.'

'I just don't get it. How could you have gone from being in love with me to doubting the marriage within half an hour? This has *never* happened before. This must be a billion-to-one chance. The system never throws up something like this.'

'John, what are you talking about?'

John's not even worried about speaking his thoughts aloud at this point. This day is already a write-off. It'll be too hard to get things back on track and simulate the conversation with his dad later in the night if he has to spend the day holding Agnes's hand and convincing her he's worthy. Even if his dad tells him what he wants to hear, it won't be real, not like this. It needs to be real, otherwise what's the point in all of this?

'So, you don't want to be married to me anymore?' John asks. 'It's only been half an hour, darling, we might make the Guinness Book of World Records at this rate. What changed in the last thirty minutes?'

'It's not the last half hour that's the problem,' she says, leaning her elbows on her knees and leaning her face on her fists. 'I've been having second thoughts for a long time. Ever since I said yes, to be honest. My mum said I couldn't back out, not this late. And you're a good man and we're both getting on a bit and if I walked out on you I'd only get myself landed with a reputation and no other man would come near me.'

'Aye, she's a charmer, your mum.'

'John, can you be serious, please? Do you not have anything to say?'

He's not sure he does. If this had happened, really

happened on his wedding day, he'd have probably burst into tears, got down on his knees and begged her to give him another chance.

'Listen, Aggie, I know this isn't real. This is just some fluke of the program that's got you acting like this. We got married and lived happily ever after, that's the real story. Fair enough, there were rocky years but what couple doesn't have rocky years? I loved you more than anything or anyone else and you felt, I think, mostly the same way. Anyway, it doesn't matter now. I just need to work out what to do with the rest of this day. It's like I've been given the day off. I can go anywhere I want.'

Agnes starts crying and even though he knows it's not real, that it's just a projection in his memory, John can't help but crouch by her side and put his arm around her. When Agnes used to cry, it was like his Kryptonite. It didn't matter if he was in the right, if she started up, suddenly he'd feel the lowest of the low, ready to toss himself off the nearest bridge. One time she started crying because she opened a packet of chocolate digestives the wrong way, tearing half the packet open. She had sobbed they were going to get stale so John ate about fifteen biscuits until she stopped crying and started laughing. He nearly choked on the biscuit dust in his windpipe but it was worth it.

'I'm going to go now,' John says. 'I'll see you again tomorrow and we'll get married like normal and have a lovely day.'

He walks to the door and puts his hand on the handle. Agnes continues to cry, getting louder and more snotty every second. John turns back to her.

'This isn't real,' he says. 'So you can't guilt me into staying. Those are virtual tears running down your face. And even if they were real tears, you've just told me

122

you don't want to be married to me anymore. So really, I would be justified to leave.'

She looks up at him, the mascara leaking down her face.

'I didn't say I definitely don't want to be married to you, you idiot,' she says. 'I only said I'm not completely sure about it. I'm allowed to have a few doubts and cry in the bathroom if I want. It's my wedding day, isn't it? Now, stay with me another minute while I get myself cleaned up.'

John takes his hand off the door handle and leans against the wall.

'Fine,' he says. 'But if I were any other Memory Lane client, I would definitely be asking for my money back at this point.'

Agnes gets up and looks at herself in the mirror. John wonders how much longer they've got in here before more people come looking for them. This is the first time in ages he's lived through a new experience, it's a novelty to not know what's coming next. He finds himself quite anxious suddenly.

'Can you stop talking nonsense?' Agnes tells him. 'Clients and virtual this and that, you're not making me feel any better. In fact, you're only making me think I should listen to the little voice inside my head that says you're going to end up being just like my father.'

John frowns and his chest tightens like he's running on a winter morning.

'What do you mean?'

'Aw, nothing,' she says. 'I told my mum you're going to ask Dad for a job and she says you'll end up just like him. And maybe she's right. And maybe it's not worth pissing off your dad, because you know it will, if you leave him to go and work for Ronnie.'

At Memory Lane, they ran simulations of how the

software could affect the client's memory over a sustained period of time, but that's all they were: simulations. They'd never carried out anything on an actual human host. It was too dangerous to try out, especially after the accidents in the first phase of Mexes. Even so, they'd never been able to find someone willing. They had made John sign forms to say he was okay with the risks before he went in. A lot of them.

But now he's starting to wonder if *Memorize* is affecting his real memories. Agnes was delighted when he told her he was starting under Ronnie. He's sure that's what happened. She couldn't have faked that, could she? He had only taken the job for them. For their family.

'Well, I suppose I don't need to ask him today,' John says. 'If you don't think I should?'

Agnes rolls her eyes, adjusts the sleeves of her dress, turns the tap on.

'Don't act like this is my decision, John. It's your life.'

'It's our life.'

But she doesn't hear him over the sound of the water running.

Hannah – Edinburgh, 2019

Hannah, Xander and Andreas go back to the break room while they wait for another client to go over their allotted time. Yasmin said they were lucky to get one each so quickly, and sometimes a full day can go by without anyone staying in too long.

They're the only ones in the room. On the table they sit at, an A4 sheet of paper is sellotaped in the middle.

PLEASE WASH YOUR DISHES! YOU WOULDN'T LEAVE YOUR OWN HOME LIKE THIS! KITCHEN FACILITIES ARE A PRIVILEGE AND CAN BE TAKEN AWAY. THANKS, MANAGEMENT.

'So…' Hannah says. 'Who wants to go first?'

Xander doesn't wait to give Andreas a chance.

'Mine was *crazy*,' he says. 'It was this old guy named Bertie Kelman and he was reliving the day he won some Scottish acting award when he was like twenty-five, then later that night he took one of the actresses home and ba… well, he, y'know, fornicated with this woman for a good while. And of course, where do me and Joanna end up? Sorry, Joanna's the name of my memory buddy, she's a good laugh. Anyway, yeah, I open my eyes and we're in a hotel corridor, so me and Joanna toddle on down to room sixty-eight. I know, so close, I was gutted too. We knock on the door for ages and obviously he's not answering and we can hear, y'know…'

'Fornicating?' Hannah offers.

125

'Exactly, but it was so loud it was more like... fivenicating. So eventually Joanna's like "watch this" and just boots the door in. It was an old hotel so the lock wasn't exactly top-notch. And yeah, we walk in and there's old Mr Kelman rolling about in the scud with this woman. Although he was young Mr Kelman in the memory. The guy got such a fright he hit his button before Joanna could even give him the spiel and everything faded. And the worst part was... em, well, actually I'm not sure I should say. It might break client confidentiality or something.'

Andreas adjusts his glasses as he has a quick glance at his phone.

'You've told us literally everything else,' Andreas says. 'If there *is* client confidentiality in Memory Lane, you've already broken it.'

'Fair point. Okay, so the worst part was, when he woke up, he had, and pardon my French, he had a huge old man erection.'

Hannah and Andreas both make similarly loud and disgusted sounds while Xander laughs away, pulling a flapjack from his pocket and peeling it open.

'We really didn't need to hear that,' Hannah says.

'Hear it?' Xander says. 'I had to be about a metre away from it, so think yourselves lucky.'

A few older men in suits enter the room and sit on the couches by the window, where the TV is showing *This Morning* on mute. They're in proper, *proper* suits, Hannah thinks, not the ones you get a free pair of shoes with. The three new starts lower their voices so they can't be heard across the room.

'How about you?' Hannah asks Andreas. 'What was yours like?'

He shrugs and looks a bit like he'd rather not answer the question.

126

'It was fine,' he says. 'Old man named Mr Robertson was reliving the day St Mirren won the cup final against... some other team. I don't know much about football.'

'Dundee United,' Xander adds. '1987?'

'That sounds right. But yeah, we found him in a pub in Paisley, still drinking away with his old pals and stuff. He looked so gutted when we had to bring him back, it was proper sad. I would rather he'd been up to no good so I didn't have to feel bad about it.'

'You say that,' Xander says. 'But I'd happily swap if it keeps me away from old man boners.'

'Can you please stop saying old man boners?' Hannah says. 'It might be one of the top five worst phrases in the English language.'

'Old man... stiffies work any better?' Xander says.

Hannah whacks him on the arm and they all laugh, even Andreas. Over by the TV, the executive-looking guys sit close together on the plush sofas and talk in whispers, their heads bent and almost touching.

'Do you think they're the bigwigs?' Hannah asks the boys, careful to keep her voice down.

'Maybe,' Andreas says. 'I bet they know some amount of secrets. I was thinking about what they said earlier, about the government knowing about this technology. What do you think they use it for?'

'Hang on,' Xander says. 'Hannah's not told us about her experience yet.'

And so Hannah gives them a rundown of her visit to Mr Hill's memory, which seems neither as sordid as Xander's nor as poignant as Andreas's.

She turns over Andreas's question in her mind: what *do* the government use *Memorize* for? Could they force criminals to relive days so they can see exactly how crimes happened? She wonders how many promotions it'll take to get to the 'we can trust you now, here's all our secret secrets' level. Probably too many.

Just then, Yasmin pops her head round the door.

'Hannah?' she says. 'Got another one for you.'

128

Philippa – Edinburgh, 2019

As she heads to the staffroom to get the board members, she passes one of the new starts in the corridor with Yasmin.

'Working hard I hope, my lovelies,' she says to them, doing her best to sound breezy, friendly and managerial all at the same time. 'Yasmin, that top is a winner. I want you to fire me over the URL. Don't give me that look, I'll get it in a different colour.'

She doesn't pause to let Yasmin say anything back, turning the corner and making her way to the end of the hall.

In her hand, she holds several copies of the McQueen Report, still warm from the printer. The findings are inconclusive, what's new? But there's definitely more evidence than ever before. They won't listen, she knows that going in, but it's her job to make them aware, for when the lawsuits inevitably rain down on them from above like an acid fucking shower. The board will try to use her as a big, blame-taking umbrella when that time comes, that's certain. That's why she's keeping notes of *everything*.

Philippa gets to the staff room and puts her head round the door. Inside, the two other new starts, Alexander and... Andrew? Probably not even close. Not that it matters. If any of them come back tomorrow, she'll get them a nametag. Nametags only get handed out if they make it to day two.

Next to the TV, the board members.

'Harold,' she calls, hoisting a smile on her face and hoping it sticks. 'Eric, William, please, we're ready for you now. Eric, have you lost weight? Or just the wife? I'm kidding! I was sorry to hear about it. You look great.'

She sets off and leaves them to scurry after her. By the end of the corridor, she has to take a break to let them catch up. They huff and puff and cough to cover it up. They remind her of those old flabby men in white suits you see in black and white films, constantly sweating and patting at their foreheads with hankies.

'Were those new recruits in there?' one of them asks.

Philippa looks back over her shoulder. It takes her a while to remember which board member is which, since they're all so alike. She comes up with a game in her head to get to the right answer. Harold... Harold Pinter... Squinter. Harold always forgets his glasses and squints like the sun's beaming directly into his eyes.

'They were indeed, Harold,' she says.

'Lambs to the slaughter, eh?' another adds. William... Billy... Billy the Whizz... William's the one who constantly drinks water and needs to pee at least twice during every visit.

'That's a bit harsh, William,' Philippa says. 'More like... lambs to the... professional workplace.'

They pass by room number forty-one, aka the secret room with the big green door. Some of the staff like to touch it as they go by, like a ritual, the way you'd run up to a house on the way back from school that you'd heard was haunted. Touch it and run away to prove you weren't a scaredy cat.

Only a handful of staff know exactly what's behind the door, but there are rumours. Michael thinks it's best to let them talk and not to confirm anything and Philippa follows his lead. They've never had anyone actually try to

130

go in there who wasn't supposed to. People prefer having a job to not having one, in her experience.

'Are you still seeing that fella?' the third board member asks. 'What was his name?'

That would make him Eric. Eric... Eric from Berwick... Berwick upon Tweed... Creed... boxer. Eric has a noticeably squint nose like it's been broken multiple times throughout his life.

'Terry,' Philippa says. 'And no. He was too needy, and the job comes first. Well, actually, Terry always came first, that was another problem.'

All three of them let out a modest laugh as she leads them into the boardroom. The board members don't know exactly how to act around a woman with power, and they definitely don't know how to react when a woman with power makes a sex joke so confidently. She considers 'accidentally' spilling a tampon from her purse on to the boardroom table just to see their heads explode with awkwardness.

Michael Valentine, Memory Lane's fearless CEO, stands up from his position at the head of the table. He spreads his arms open in a display of welcoming them to his domain.

'Gentlemen,' he says. 'How are we all doing?'

'I could be doing with popping to the little boys' room,' William says, adjusting his belt as he takes his seat.

'I'm sure we won't be too long,' Michael says, taking his seat.

That was Michael's idea of a power move. Not pausing the meeting to let someone go for a piss.

Everyone else takes their seats now too, and Philippa chooses a seat closer to Michael than the rest. They're all meant to be part of the same big team but really, it's her and Michael vs the board. On an even more real level, it's her vs Michael vs the board.

131

The board members are the ones who funnelled capital into Memory Lane when it was just an idea in John Valentine's mind. The people who put in the money are the people who have the real power. Obviously, they're reaping the rewards now, but they've grown so accustomed to the profits and don't want to hear anything that might slow down the money piling up in their offshore accounts.

'Again, thanks for coming in,' Michael says. 'I'm sure you've all seen last quarter's numbers, and I'm sure you've all already booked your Christmases in Hawaii again.'

The board members chuckle and adjust their ties. Philippa gets paid a decent salary for her job, but it's a lot closer to that of the new recruits that she inducted this morning than that of the men on the other side of the table from her.

'I see Memory Lane Anonymous is going well,' Harold says. 'Anyone we know?'

Memory Lane Anonymous had started around six months ago, one of Michael's bright ideas. A lot of celebrities want to use the *Memorize* technology but are afraid the word will get out and people will learn they're reliving past highs. Obviously, Memory Lane have deals with the press so nothing would ever become public, but amongst their wealthy friends, it seems word spreads fast.

Coming here, to Philippa, seems to pretty much confirm that you've given up on the rest of your life. Memory Lane Anonymous gives an added level of secrecy; arrival using the basement entrance, limited staff contact, no records kept on file after the memory. It costs a premium but these clients can afford it, especially if they're at the age when they've realised all the money they've accrued throughout their life is about to go to their grandchildren.

'I'm sure you know I can't divulge any names,' Michael says.

'Oh, go on,' Eric says. 'It's only us. I heard we had someone off *The West Wing*?'

'I can neither confirm nor deny.'

'If it's Martin Sheen, can you put me on the phone with him next time he's in?'

'That would sort of defeat the purpose of Memory Lane Anonymous.'

Eric shrugs and pours himself some water from the jug in the centre of the table.

'Anyway,' Michael says. 'That's not why I asked you all to come in today. We've... got a bit of a problem.'

The friendly atmosphere that the board members were at least pretending to keep up vanishes in an instant. They don't like problems, and they know Michael doesn't ask them to come in for just anything.

'Before you go on, Michael,' William says. 'Can I just go to the loo?'

John – Stonecranning, 1975

John and Agnes walk down the aisle for the second time today, in the now empty church. John feels like he's in a bit of a daze, not being used to not knowing exactly what's coming next. He knows he's safe within the memory. He knows he can't die in here, unless his heart gives up on the outside.

'What will I tell everyone?' Agnes says. 'They're going to ask where I was.'

'Just say you got something on your dress,' he tells her. 'And you needed to wash it off. That, or you had the runs. I wouldn't worry about it. You're the bride, they shouldn't be grilling you on your wedding day.'

In the toilet, John had managed to convince Agnes that she should just get through today, eat the meal, have a dance, have a drink, and make a decision tomorrow, or the next day. Basically, he told her that she can leave him if she wants, as long as she doesn't do it today.

They step out into the sunshine, where the children have long gone, and so too have all the coppers and silver coins on the ground.

'There they are!' Gary shouts, leaning against the side of the coach. 'Get a move on, you two!'

The happy couple put on nervous but happy faces and walk over to the bus. John lets Agnes on first, her skirt blowing in his face, and pauses when he reaches the top of the stairs. He puts a hand on the driver's shoulder.

'Alright, there,' he says. 'Can you just… make sure we get there in one piece? Take it easy, nice and slow, no need to rush.'

'If you say so,' the driver says. 'I don't plan on crashing, mate.'

'Well, no one does. That's the point of crashes. You don't see them coming.'

'Listen, I know it's your wedding day but you need to sit down and shut up, pal.'

'Yep, will do. Just, careful as you go.'

Jesus, John thinks, did I just say careful as you go? This day is going to be a long one. Every interaction he has with Agnes is going to be affected by what happened in the church toilet, so he can't predict anything she's going to say. He just needs to get through this day and everything will go back to normal tomorrow. No second thoughts.

'Can't believe you talked me into getting on this bus,' Agnes whispers to him from the window seat.

Maybe not everything has changed then, John thinks.

'We should've got in a taxi and left everyone else to get the bus. It's sweltering in here and the floor is filthy, look at the bottom of my dress.'

'Love,' John says. 'If we'd have got a taxi, you'd have complained that everyone else is together, having a laugh on the bus and we're missing all the fun.'

But Agnes doesn't reply with her usual comeback about how she would bet him for everything he did or didn't have.

John turns round in his seat to look at everyone. At the back, the teenagers, Scott, David and Ross, still pass a hip flask between them and think no one's noticed. His and Agnes's parents still sit quietly and don't attempt conversation.

Agnes raises a hand to the buttons above her head, where the aircon is supposed to blow through. She presses every button possible but nothing comes out.

135

'So you don't think I should ask your dad?' John says.

'Whatever you think's best,' Agnes replies. 'But just know,' she lowers her voice. 'If you do anything he doesn't like, make one mistake, he'll sack you. It won't be fair, but it's just like him.'

'I don't think you're wrong.'

As they sit there together, now in an uneasy silence that he's not experienced before, it reminds him of the end of *The Graduate*. When Dustin Hoffman and Katharine Ross have run off together and got on the bus, but as they sit and let the excitement fade, their faces grow dark. If someone were to take a photo of him and Agnes right now, they'd probably look a lot like them two.

'Why are we stopped?' Agnes asks.

The bus seems to have been stationary for quite a while, but this always happens in the memory, so John brushes it off.

'The roadworks are still up,' he says.

'Still?'

'Aye.'

'They were meant to be done by the 20th.'

'When do you ever trust what the council tells you?'

'Don't they know I've got a wedding reception to get to?'

'I'll hop out and explain to the workies.'

Another bit of conversation going just as normal. Maybe this day isn't such a write-off after all. But that's when John realises that the bus isn't stopped at the roadworks.

They're on the country road between Stonecranning town centre and the edge of town, where he used to come and annoy the sheep when him and Gary were younger. Rumblings of disharmony weave through the bus and John realises it's his job to find out what's going on.

'Driver?' he shouts, poking his head out into the aisle. 'Driver? Everything alright?'

'It was you,' the driver shouts back. 'You've bloody jinxed me, that's what you've done.'

It's at this point that John notices the unhealthy sounds coming from the coach's engine.

Hannah – Edinburgh, 2019

Yasmin takes Hannah back through the lab and into the memory corridor, with a brief pitstop at her computer to check which client doesn't fancy leaving their memory on time.

That's another thing that trips Hannah up whenever she starts a new job, the difference between the technical names of things and what people actually call them. The part of the office where the clients sit in their booths is technically called the '*Memorize* Arena', as if it's some kind of sponsored football stadium. But Yasmin only refers to it as the 'memory corridor', so Hannah assumes that's what she should be calling it. She doesn't want to be some kind of square that refers to things by their proper names.

'Ready for a surprise?' Yasmin asks, her voice the only sound in the silent corridor, one red bulb pulsing outside the door they're standing next to.

She turns the door handle and opens the door. Inside, the standard set up: a computer, a couple of seats for the staff, and a bed with the client in it. But this client's a woman.

'Oh, hey, look,' Hannah says. 'A rich old woman. Yas, queen.'

'I know, right?' Yasmin says, as they both sit down. 'When I see old men in here, I'm like, right, you probably made all your money in banking or oil or human suffering or whatever, fuck you. But when it's an old bird, I'm like… well done, bitch. Teach me your ways.'

'This is a depressing thought, but isn't it likely her husband died and she got his money?'

'That is depressing. And probably accurate. Let's just think she got filthy rich on her own until told otherwise.'

Yasmin gestures for her to lean in closer and they read the screen together. She shows Hannah what to click to get into the client's page and what she needs to do to prepare the headsets for going in.

The screen reads:

Name: Annabelle Layla Reid
Age: 83
Height: 5'3
Weight: 49kg

'Why do we need to know her weight?' Hannah asks.
'A man designed this system, remember.'

Memory: 'The last day I had with my daughter, Sarah, before she passed away. Aberdeen beach.'
Age (in memory): 66

Yasmin gets the headsets out the drawer and they put them on.

'This is going to be quite sad, isn't it?' Hannah asks.

'Yep,' is the quick response from Yasmin. 'More people than you'd think choose a really weepy memory. I guess they don't think about what it's going to feel like at the end of the memory when they have to come back out. And they still do it all over again. A bit like swearing off drink, then a couple of weeks go by and you forget how horrendous you felt the morning after.'

Like a memory hangover, Hannah thinks.

'She's not going to die in front of us, is she?' Hannah asks. 'The daughter, that is.'

Yasmin clicks the little + button next to the memory

section and it expands, giving the client's full description of the memory.

The last day I had with my daughter, Sarah, before she passed away. Aberdeen beach. We drove up in the morning with my grandson, Drew, and Sarah's husband, Darren. We had fish and chips and cones right next to the water. We decided on a whim to stay the night at a B&B. Darren stayed with Drew while Sarah and I went out for a drink. After that, we went for a walk on the sand while the sun set.

Yasmin and Hannah share a look.

'That's a day worth reliving,' Hannah says.

'Exactly. She's about fifteen minutes over time. I'll let you take the lead on this one.'

Both of them slip on the headsets. Yasmin scoots out the way so Hannah can sit closest to the computer, her hand trembling slightly as it rests on the mouse.

'So to put us in, you hit...' Yasmin begins.

'The big green button?'

'That's the one.'

'And what if I can't make her leave? Like, what if she just flat-out refuses?'

'Believe me, she won't. Ninety-nine point nine percent of the time they get such a fright seeing you they just hit their button. Staying past half an hour incurs a hefty additional fee, anyway, and they all know that going in.'

'Okay, I get you, BUT, if this is one of the zero point one times?'

'If she really won't leave, we just say the exit command and come back out. Probably give her a few minutes to freak out then go back in for another go. If she *still* won't come out, then we go and see Philippa.'

140

'I'm guessing we don't want to go and see Philippa.'

'We *really* don't want to go and see Philippa. Especially not today. There was this whole thing with a client called Mr McQueen on Friday and the board members are in today to speak about it. Anyway, when you're ready.'

Hannah nods and moves the cursor to the start button, before giving Yasmin one last look to confirm she's not about to fuck something up. Yasmin gives her a thumbs up and she clicks the button.

5... 4... 3... 2... 1...

Hannah – Aberdeen, 2002

The sun hasn't long set and there are still a few bright streaks of orange in the sky. Hannah shifts and adjusts her feet to get a good foothold in the sand. She looks to find Yasmin at her side, the pair of them looking out of place in their workwear. This is becoming a recurring theme. Can't a client relive a memory about being at their desk on a regular Wednesday?

'Can we not change before we enter the memory?' Hannah asks.

Yasmin laughs as she walks forward. A little ahead of them on the beach are the figures of two women, swaying side to side, with what looks to be champagne bottles in their hands.

'You can if you want,' Yasmin says. 'But it's kind of… majorly frowned upon. I mean, we're only in here for a few minutes, so us standing out like sore thumbs shouldn't really be a problem.'

Yasmin's in heels but is still navigating the sand better than Hannah.

'Keep up,' Yasmin tells her. 'This is meant to be your one.'

'A pair of flip flops,' Hannah replies. 'Would that really have been so bad? Surely they could keep a little box of alternate footwear choices in the cupboard somewhere.'

Yasmin laughs. Hannah's still not sure if she's getting a 'work friend' or 'actual friend' vibe from her but thinks she definitely could've been paired up with a worse memory buddy.

On their left, a black railing runs alongside the beach. Behind it, cars roll by on the road, and an ice cream stall is shutting up for the day.

On the right, the water sloshes back and forth, bringing seaweed as a gift before taking it back a few seconds later. The water reaches out into the horizon, where the sky is darkening every time Hannah takes her eyes off it. By the time they've almost caught up with Ms Reid and her daughter, the sky and the water are practically the same shade of bluish-black.

There's a strange feeling Hannah gets as she walks across this uneven Aberdeen beach. It doesn't feel real. Obviously, it isn't, but she wonders if she would notice how unreal it felt if she wasn't aware that she was in a computer program. *In here* is a phrase that comes to her mind, even though they're standing outside. They're still *in here*.

She hopes Yasmin doesn't notice as she bends slightly to scoop up some sand in her hand. It's damp and thick and falls from her hand in more of a clump than a trickle. She's never been to Aberdeen beach, and this is just Ms Reid's memory of the sand, so there's no way of knowing if this is what the sand was really like that day.

'I wonder how long it would take,' Hannah thinks aloud. 'To forget you're not in the real world while you're in here.'

'I've seen clients surprised when I turn up,' Yasmin says, 'but not like, totally shocked. They never forget. Generally because they're in the past and twelve hours isn't long enough to truly forget everything. Maybe if it was like, two weeks, but the system can't usually handle anything that long.'

'Have they tried to give clients longer memories?'

'I think they tried it at the start but found the system

143

couldn't take it. Also, twelve hours is a good length. Long enough that the clients are willing to pay the fee, but just short enough that the client wants another Mex the second they get out.'

A gust of wind from nowhere blows the hat from Ms Reid's daughter's head. She chases after it as Ms Reid laughs.

'Oh, Sarah,' she laughs. 'What are you like? You'll need to be faster than that.'

She laughs more and more as her daughter tries and fails to catch up with the hat. It rolls down the beach like it's possessed, plugging along like a wheel without brakes. Ms Reid laughs until she realises Hannah and Yasmin are on the beach with her. She can't hide the disappointment from her face.

'You two aren't dressed for the weather,' she tells them, looking out at the water. 'I had forgotten how warm it was that night. It was scorching during the day, but I don't remember this. I thought it was cooler.'

'Did you have a nice day?' Hannah asks.

She looks to Yasmin to gauge her reaction. She's decided she's going to try a softer approach, rather than just saying 'right you, it's chucking out time'. Yasmin rolls her eyes like she's seen this approach before and doesn't see its merits.

'I did, thank you,' Ms Reid says. 'I'm Annabelle, by the way.'

'Hannah, and this is Yasmin.'

Yasmin gives a little wave, then walks behind Hannah.

'I'll leave this one to you,' she whispers, before walking out towards the sea.

That leaves Hannah with Ms Reid, or Annabelle. In the distance, her daughter catches up with the hat and brushes the sand off it. Even from this far away, Hannah can see

144

the confusion on her face, that two young women in office attire have accosted her mother on the beach after sunset.

'I'm sorry if I've gone a little over my time,' Ms Reid says. 'I hope you won't hold it against me. Or my bank account.'

'Of course not. Well, I don't think they will. This is my first day, I'm still not sure how everything works exactly.'

As Ms Reid turns her arm to look at her watch, Hannah spots the red button sprouting from her palm.

'The day just got away from me,' she says. 'How are you liking the job then?'

'It's… strange.'

'Is that your manager?'

Ms Reid points to the water, where Yasmin has taken her shoes off and is standing in the shallows, letting the tide brush over her ankles.

'I'm… not exactly sure,' Hannah says. 'The chain of command is a little blurry.'

Hannah smiles and Ms Reid laughs and Hannah's not sure how it got away from her but the client has definitely snatched the upper hand in this conversation.

'You'll need to come back now,' Hannah says, trying to move the chat from friendly to professional in one swoop.

'Just a few more minutes,' Ms Reid says. 'It's not the end of the world, is it? I mean, we've already had a good fifteen minutes extra, what's a few more going to do?'

It's funny how quickly her stance has gone from 'time got away from me' to 'I know exactly how long I went over my allotted time'.

Ms Reid's daughter finally arrives back at her mother's side.

'What's happening?' she asks. 'Is everything okay?'

'This woman was just telling me I can't have any more time with you,' Ms Reid says. 'Isn't that right?'

The daughter looks at Hannah.

'I don't understand,' she says. 'Mum, do you know these people?'

Hannah knows she shouldn't feel awkward, that this is silly, that it's not even real. But she still feels the very real sensation of blood travelling up her neck and pulsing with embarrassment in her cheeks.

'Two minutes,' Hannah says to Ms Reid. 'Two minutes and we need to go. Otherwise I'll get in trouble.'

'Bless you, sweetheart,' Ms Reid says.

Hannah walks away from the pair of them. She doesn't want to hear what Ms Reid is going to tell her daughter. She might tell her something silly, that her and Yasmin are detectives, solving a gritty crime in the Granite City. Or she might be about to have the final conversation she'll ever have with her daughter, or at least the image of her daughter. Either way, she doesn't want to hear it.

Hannah also isn't in a rush to face Yasmin again. She knows she's made a rookie mistake, letting the client act like they're friends. It's too hard to pull someone from a memory if you feel sorry for them.

So she stands halfway between Ms Reid and Yasmin for a while. The crash of the waves in the distance is a lovely noise. It's no surprise people fall asleep to the sound. But even in here, where things seem perfect, she still has to hear the squawking of the seagulls in the distance, fighting for the last crunchy chips.

There might not be time but Hannah takes her shoes off and walks into the water, joining Yasmin with her feet submerged. A cold sensation sneaks between her toes.

'Are we just letting her live here now?' Yasmin asks, and Hannah's relieved to see she's smiling.

'Very funny,' Hannah says. 'It'll just be another minute.'

'Sure. Did you tell her it was your first day?'

'That was a mistake, wasn't it?'

'Yep. I did the exact same my first day. Old guy, Mr O'Brien, sucked me in with his story. Last time he was going to see his late wife, just wanted a few more minutes to say goodbye, etc…'

'I'll need to get tougher is what you're saying?'

'Unfortunately, probably yes. Or you could quit and stay normal. Both valid choices.'

'Do you think it'll be me? The one that lasts 'til tomorrow? Or Xander or Andreas? Or none of us?'

Yasmin turns her head and scrunches up her mouth.

'Still too early to tell. It's a long day, your first day at Memory Lane. It's not even lunchtime yet. Your head is probably ready to explode, I know mine was. Actually, funny story, my first memory was…'

They experience one last rush of the water over their legs before, somewhere behind them, Ms Reid finishes saying goodbye to her daughter and presses the exit button. The world becomes muted. The sea fades to black.

Philippa – Edinburgh, 2019

'Well, they're not going to get relegated,' Eric says to the room. 'But they're not getting top six. Not if they don't sack that tube.'

Philippa doesn't even attempt to nod along like she knows or cares about whichever team they're talking about. Hearts or Hibs, she would guess, but then again, she wouldn't guess, because when you say the wrong football team in front of men, they don't just correct you, they act as if you've insulted their very way of life and spat in their cornflakes for good measure.

Instead, she thinks of room forty-one, and wonders if Nurse Ashton has been in today yet. As a rule, she does her best not to think of room forty-one, but the McQueen Report has made that impossible.

Finally, William returns from the toilet and the torturous small talk can come to an end. He takes his seat and she can see from across the table his hands are still wet.

'Fancy toilets you've got here,' he says. 'I always forget.'

'Forget?' Philippa says. 'How could you forget? You basically live in there whenever you visit.'

'Now, now,' he says. 'Let's get back to it. What's the problem you brought us in here for, Michael? This is already starting to feel like a meeting that could've been an email.'

Michael looks across at Philippa. She supposes it's meant to be a 'we're in this together' kind of look, but she takes it as more of a 'the board members are looking, and I'm staring at you, which indicates to everyone that this is somehow your fault' look. She quickly moves her eyes down to her notepad, which only has a quick sketch she did of a stick man falling from the top of a building.

'This is the file of our client, Mr McQueen,' Michael says, sliding the printouts Philippa sorted earlier across the table to each board member. 'You might recognise him. He was one of our first test clients in '09 before becoming a regular once we opened in 2010. And, no, he wasn't one of the… unfortunate few. As of Friday, he has visited Memory Lane on thirty-nine separate occasions, reliving twenty-two separate memories.'

'Only twenty-two memories?' Harold says, taking his glasses out his breast pocket and slipping them on. 'He's done certain memories multiple times?'

'Twenty unique memories,' Michael says. 'And nineteen repeats of one favourite memory. If you look at page four.'

The room is filled with the sound of papers being flicked through, the board members suddenly interested in what they've been brought in here to see.

'His nineteenth time in this memory was on Friday.'

'And I'm guessing something happened on Friday?' William says.

Michael turns another page.

'Page five, you'll find a brief rundown. The memory in question is Mr McQueen meeting a young man named Trevor in London when he was thirty-one years old. They spent the day together then had a… lovely evening together in a hotel room. He only ever learned Trevor's first name, been longing for him all his life, and so on. Anyway, yes, he's now relived this nineteen times with us. However, on Friday there were… complications.'

He stops talking, probably hoping the board members will jump in and fill the silence. They don't, however, and he can't put it off any longer.

'During the memory, there was an incident. An incident which did not occur during the original memory. At around the eleven hour mark of the memory, Trevor stepped into the bathroom, as he had done every time in this memory, but this time he... slipped.'

'A slip?' Eric says, looking around the room, trying to catch Philippa's eye and carrying on to the next person when she doesn't look up. 'So? Someone slips. That's a variable we're okay with, isn't it? You run a memory twenty-odd times, there's going to be a slip or two. The clients know going in there can be tiny differences. Normally not noticeable, but still.'

'That's true. However, soon after Trevor slipped, he descended in what would be described as a... downward trajectory, resulting in him... smashing his head against the sink and, shortly thereafter, dying on the bathroom floor. Mr McQueen sat with his dead body in the memory for the remaining minutes, until his exit button appeared. He decided not to use his panic button.'

Philippa isn't surprised to see the men looking annoyed rather than crestfallen.

'He must've done something,' William says. 'Such a significant change in a memory can only be caused by the client purposefully going out of their way to fuck it up. He's clearly decided to get his rocks off by killing this fella and then he's blamed it on our system.'

The other two men nod, happy to be able to blame this on man's in-built nature to kill and lie, rather than consider the technology that makes them more money than they can spend in three lifetimes might be faulty.

'Page eight,' Michael says. 'The post-memory breakdown. He didn't do anything differently, wasn't near Trevor when it happened. This wasn't the client. This was the technology.'

'It was an accident then,' Harold says, bringing the papers directly beneath his nose to read them, as if they've hidden the secret answer in a tiny font. 'Accidents happen. I'm sure if he does the memory again tomorrow, it'll be fine, like the other eighteen times before. Can't we just give him a Mex on the house and forget about it?'

This is what Philippa expected, what she had told Michael was going to happen. Present the board members with irrefutable evidence that the *Memorize* technology is dangerous and unpredictable, then watch as they squirm their way out of any responsibility, as well as not taking any action to fix it.

'It wasn't an accident,' Michael says. 'Page eleven. The *Memorize* technology did it. There were lines of code in the system. We didn't write them. And we don't know why or how they got there, but we're confident it could happen again.'

William tosses his papers down on the table. The other two follow suit.

'What are you suggesting?' he asks.

And here's the ball game. Michael's been dancing around the issue since they got here but now they've called his bluff. Philippa's often thought she'd be better suited to his job, doing the big picture stuff rather than the day-to-day work. She'd inducted three new staff members this morning. She doesn't expect any of them to come back tomorrow, and it's hardly the first time. She's got a fancy title but she's left doing grunt work because Michael's daddy founded the place.

But at this exact moment, she's glad she's not in Michael's seat.

'Well,' Michael says, stretching his neck out and adjusting his tie. 'Philippa?'

He turns to her and she feels the eyes of William,

Eric and Harold fall on her too. Michael manages to keep a straight face, which Philippa thinks is incredible given he's just knifed her in the back. She knows he's a spineless little rat but this is next level. She has, somehow, overestimated him.

'What we thought,' Philippa says, mouth now dry. 'Was that… temporarily… until we know exactly what we're dealing with… and until we know, going forward, that all clients will be completely safe… and that we can prevent this from happening again… we might, temporarily… stop all Memory Lane appointments as soon as possible.'

Philippa keeps her eyes on Michael, not wanting to see the anger on the red faces of the board members. Michael makes a face like this is the first time he's hearing these suggestions.

But it isn't anger Philippa hears from the board members. It's, sort of, the opposite of what she was expecting. They're all smiling.

'What is it?' she says. 'What am I missing? Am I being punk'd?'

'Sweetheart,' William says. 'That's a very nice suggestion, but any slowing down of production is absolutely out of the question. I mean, for one thing, we're hoping to open the London branch later in the year. How would it look to our foreign investors if we shut down here? I wouldn't be going overboard to say it would be the end of the world.'

She looks to Michael to argue back but he only stares at the table.

'It isn't safe,' she says.

'Oh, pull the other one,' Eric says. 'Newsflash, Philippa, you can't die or get any serious injuries in a memory. Where's this Mr McQueen now? Is he dead? Of course he's not. Because it was just a memory. If he had died, then *maybe* we'd have looked into it further.'

'We're not talking about physical injury here,' Philippa says. 'We're talking about mental injury. How the technology could affect a client's mental health with repeated use. We have a duty of care to our clients.'

'Which is already taken care of,' Harold says. 'With the pre-memory contract. We were extremely careful when drawing that thing up, it's air-tight. I would honestly *love* to see a client try and sue us for damages, they'd only end up owing us more.'

Philippa shakes her head but puts her hand to her forehead to try and play it off as a headache. She's seen evil board members in films and, as it turns out, they're a fairly accurate representation of the real world. They're only missing the twirly moustaches and maniacal laughs.

'We,' she says, gesturing to Michael, 'believe that there will only be more incidents of this type if we don't take action. Additionally, there is also the case of Mr Valentine… Senior.'

Michael's bravery returns.

'His instructions were very clear,' Michael says. 'He is not to be disturbed for any reason.'

'But if he knew…'

'He created this technology, Philippa. I think he knows the risks more than anyone. Perhaps slowing production down somewhat, to study the implications of repeated memories, could be a viable option, but taking him out is absolutely out of the question.'

The board members gather their things and stand up, leaving the McQueen files on the table. A rain cloud lurches into view outside the window, the dark blue peeking through the half-open blinds.

'A tip for next time,' Harold says. 'Before you call us in

here for no reason, please at least ensure you and the staff are on the same page, Michael.'

'You can keep us updated by email,' Eric says. 'Unless there are any serious incidents, please don't waste our time like this again.'

They make their way to the door. Philippa's looking forward to them being gone, but at the same time, isn't looking forward to being in the room alone with Michael. He absolutely shafted her there, but she knows there won't be any kind of apology on its way. That's the only way these people can live with themselves. They can't ever accept they've done something wrong.

'I'm just going to use the loo before I go,' William says. 'But be careful, Michael. You know we have our enemies. People who'd love to know we're having problems. I wasn't going to tell you, but I hear whispers that The Recollect Project are very close to cracking their own tech.'

Michael stays seated, leaning his cheek on his knuckles like a child who didn't get his way. The Recollect Project is like the bogeyman of this place, the spectre lurking in the back of their minds. For years, there have been rumours that they're building their own facility down in London, with a system more powerful and realistic than *Memorize*. But they've always come up short. Memory Lane has had a monopoly on the memory market for quite some time now and the board members don't want to give it up any time soon.

'The Recollect Project?' Michael says. 'They've been stuck trying to crack The Valentine Variable for years. I wouldn't worry about them.'

'I hope you're right,' William says, then leaves the two of them alone.

Being the first one to speak can be taken many ways. It

can be seen as defeat. It can be seen as victory. It can be seen as being too annoyed with your boss to keep quiet any longer.

'Well.' Philippa finally breaks. 'That went fucking brilliantly.'

John – Stonecranning, 1975

'I'll need to stay here with the bus,' the driver says. 'Until they send someone to get me. Won't be another hour at least, though.'

John, Agnes and the rest of their guests stand by the roadside, having all piled off the broken down bus. The driver loudly blaming John all the while.

'An hour?' Agnes says. 'That's no good.'

'There's not much else I can do,' the driver says. 'And it's just a minibus they're sending, all our other coaches are out on trips for the day.'

The guests are in good spirits, all things considered. That feeling of being dressed up and being at a wedding is still outweighing the feeling of having to get off a broken down bus halfway to your location. It's lucky it's such a nice day, John thinks, or we'd really see some tantrums.

First, it was Agnes in the church toilet telling him she's not sure she wants him as her husband. And now this. It can't just be a coincidence. The memory's never thrown up anything like this before, let alone two in quick succession. He doesn't like to admit it to himself, not that he could admit it to anyone else, but he's grown quite dependent on knowing exactly what's coming each day. He enjoys it. The rhythm and the routine. Out there, in the real world, things are so fast, hectic, cruel. But in here, things have order and reason. Well, they did, until today at least.

John's instructions were crystal clear when he went in. *Don't disturb me for anything, unless I hit my panic button.*

The system will be showing these developments, these happenings outside of the core memory, but he doesn't imagine anyone will be looking over them too often.

If things get really bad, he can get out. He's got an exit button and he knows where it is and he knows how to get to it. Leaving before he changed the conversation with his dad was never in his plan, though.

The technology is safe; he carried out as many tests as were possible before he came inside, so really there should be no problem. But Agnes and the bus, these are problems and he can't pretend they're just happy accidents. If he can just get through today, tomorrow should be back to normal.

'Agnes,' John says. 'Before I say this, just remember that I love you, and that this is just a hiccup, okay?'

'John, if you're about to suggest that we walk to the hall, my doubts about our marriage are going to manifest themselves as my fist connecting with your face.'

John laughs, now trying to come up with a different plan.

'I wasn't going to suggest *we* walk,' he says. 'I was going to say some of the guests could walk, and we'll... get a taxi or something.'

Agnes folds her arms.

'Whatever the plan is, get it done quick,' she says.

'What about getting the people of the world to join hands, and starting a love train?'

Agnes's face remains the same.

'Okay, you're not ready for jokes, understood. Attention everybody!'

The guests crowd around John, some on the edge of the road, some leaning against the fence that separates them from the cows, which are slowly drifting over to them to find out if there's anything they can have a munch on.

157

'It will not come as a surprise to you that the bus is now out of service,' he says, and yet there are still a few groans, as if some of them thought this was a skit that would end and they could get back on board. 'My blushing bride, and she really is blushing with embarrassment at this situation, would ask that anyone who is able walks to the hall. There are some cans of lager in the bus that you can take to grease your wheels a bit. It's only a fifteen, twenty minute walk so you'll probably only need three or four cans each. Anyone not walking, please come and see us and we'll get a taxi sorted, hopefully.'

As the crowd divides into two groups and Gary zooms on to the bus to collect the aforementioned cans of Tennent's, Agnes starts walking purposefully away from him.

'Where are you going?' he shouts after her.

'The hall,' she calls back. 'Let's just get this over with.'

She scoops up the bottom of her gown and carries it at her hip like a fabric child.

'Okay, change of plan, folks!' John shouts. 'Everyone follow the bride.'

The walk is enjoyable, as the sun stays in front of the clouds for most of the way. Cars pass by and toot in, John hopes, support. The women take off their heels around twenty seconds or so after setting off, including Agnes, who soon has a smile on her face as Innes and Vera walk alongside her at the front of the convoy.

It's not long before the complaints have been forgotten and not long after that they find themselves only five minutes from the hall.

John accepts a tin from Gary as they walk.

'Get that down you before we get there,' he says. 'But chuck it in the bushes if the police come by.'

'Thanks,' John says, taking a sip. 'I've had a drouth since we got off the bu–'

John tries to take another sip but finds a fist connecting with his face. He beats his can to the ground, which lands by his side and the grass guzzles the beer as it spills out. His ears ring and he shakes his head to dislodge the noise.

'Woah,' his dad shouts. 'What's happened?'

John raises himself to his feet just as his dad fights through the crowd and reaches him and Gary. John squints to make sure he's seeing straight. He looks at Gary's hand. It's bloody. John was so taken off guard by the punch, he still wasn't sure who'd thrown it until now.

'Gary just punched John,' one of Agnes's pals says. 'I saw it. They were in front of me. I saw it.'

'Is this right, John?' his dad says. 'Did he punch you?'

John slowly nods, staring at Gary. Gary looks just as confused as John feels. It's a strange kind of pain, the feeling in his jaw. It's been a long time since he was punched in the face. He's forgotten what it feels like.

'He did,' John says. 'I don't know why, though. Gary, why did you do that?'

'I... I'm not sure,' Gary says. 'I just felt like doing it.'

What follows next is a whole host of actions that happen quickly and overlap. John's dad rushes Gary, but is intercepted by Ronnie, who seems to have taken the side of whoever isn't with John's dad. They tumble to the ground, shouting at each other, mainly calling each other stupid bastards.

Agnes, who was previously leading at the front, has obviously heard the commotion and appears at his side.

'What the fuck is going on?' she says, pointing at their dads, rolling about in the grass.

'Honestly, love, I've no fucking clue. Gary punched me.'

She turns his face to see the swollen side in the light.

'Good thing we've already had the photos taken,' she says. 'Why did he punch you?'

'Again, I've no clue. Things are going a bit haywire, tell you the truth.'

'You don't say.'

Finally, Gary, along with Frank, manage to separate the dads and stand between them so they can't get to each other for round two.

'See when we get to the hall,' John's dad says. 'I'm going to knock your teeth out.'

'Naw,' Ronnie fires back with. 'I'm going to knock *your* teeth out.'

'Naw, I'm going to knock *your* teeth out.'

'Naw, *yours*!'

'Would you both shut up?' John shouts. 'You two are meant to be the elder statesmen here, and you're acting like a couple of school weans. In fact, school weans have better patter than you two.'

There's a period of respite, where the men take a few long breaths and brush the grass from their jackets and kilts.

Gary walks around to approach John and finds Agnes standing in front of him as a buffer.

'Would you like to explain yourself, Gary?' she says. 'Do you just go about punching people now? Is that your idea of a joke? Look at his face. He'll be needing to sit with ice on that for the meal.'

Gary plays with the tassels on the front of his sporran.

'I really don't know,' he says. 'It was just, like, an impulse. It was as if I wasn't even in control of my arm. I didn't know I was going to do it.'

'Oh, good one, Gary. I'd like to see you use that on the police.'

John turns this over in his mind. No one else in here is going to believe it, that's a given. But it's probably the only thing that makes sense. The people in a memory don't have impulses, they don't do things at random. As far as John can tell, he didn't do anything that would make Gary want to punch him, and Gary's just admitted it too. So the only explanation is that...

'I think the system is *bored*,' he says. 'I think maybe I've been in here too long and it doesn't want to do this anymore. It's, in some kind of way, alive.'

'John,' Agnes says. 'I told you, no more of this nonsense talk. Especially not in front of people. They'll think you're *funny*.'

Before he can ask her what she means by funny, in his best Joe Pesci impression (which would be too recent a reference for her to understand anyway), he realises another commotion has broken out amongst the guests. This time, it's further down the road, with the people who are leading the way. Him, Agnes, and basically everyone else, slowly crowd round to see what the latest drama is.

'What's happening?' John says. 'Is it another fight?'

If the system is willing to make Gary throw a random punch, he doesn't see what would stop it creating a royal rumble out of the rest of the wedding guests. Even John could admit he'd enjoy seeing that.

'Look!' someone shouts. 'John, Agnes, look! Isn't that where the hall is?'

That's when John realises the drama is happening in the distance, beyond the council houses whose gardens back onto the field. The community hall is further back than the houses, nestled in amongst the primary school and the Cranning Woods. The same spot where a plume of black smoke is billowing into the air, spreading into the sky and blackening the horizon.

'The hall's on fire,' says a voice.

161

Hannah – Edinburgh, 2019

'Would you like a hot drink with that?' the boy behind the counter says.

Hannah doesn't know when it happened, but she's started mentally referring to any man younger than her as 'the boy'. It really did sneak up on her. She's only twenty-three, for fuck's sake, she should be flirting with him or something. If only he didn't look like he's still a few years off buying his first razor.

'Em, no,' she says, deciding not to explain that she's trying to cut down on caffeine, that she's planning to get a Dr Pepper from somewhere else, and also the fact that her new job is keeping her quite awake as it is.

'The sandwich comes with a hot drink,' the boy tells her, adjusting his little brown cap, which makes Hannah wonder why that's part of their uniform. 'It's part of the meal deal.'

The man behind Hannah in the queue tuts. This is why she hates buying lunch at lunchtime. She knows how that sounds, but she usually tries to push her lunch to after two if possible, when the cafés and shops are quieter. But after coming out of Ms Reid's memory, Yasmin basically instructed her to go on her lunch. So here she is, starting to sweat in the Starbucks queue.

'Yes, then,' Hannah says. 'Fine. You win, I'll have a coffee.'

'Well, I don't win, ma'am, I just thought you'd like a free drink. Sorry.'

'Did you just ma'am me?'

162

The man behind her tuts again.

'Sorry… miss.'

'That's better. I'll have a latte, please.'

'Sure thing.'

She has to stop herself from telling him that she has a very stressful job and this isn't helping. Instead, she swallows the anger, steps to the side and waits awkwardly with her sandwich on a plate while another staff member starts making her latte.

Once her 'free' latte is ready, she collects it and scans the shop. The only free seat is on the high stools by the window. She sits down, sliding her tray on to the counter, attempting some form of gracefulness, and is annoyed that her feet don't quite reach the footrest.

Outside the window, people pass by in their droves. Most are either tourists in no hurry or office workers walking like they're on their way to put out a fire. She accidentally makes eye contact with every second person going by, and she's not sure if she should feel bad for people-watching. They're the ones staring into a café. Every shared glance through the glass is fairly intense for the zero point three seconds they both hold it.

Then she realises that, on the other side of the road, Xander is sitting on a bench, tucking into a bag of cashew nuts. He's on the phone to someone. A lot of hand gestures are being made. Whoever's on the other end of the phone, Xander doesn't seem to like them very much. It's not that Hannah doesn't like him, she does, but she'd rather enjoy her lunch without having to make small talk with him. So, she pretends she hasn't seen him.

The sandwich she bought is demolished in what feels like less than five bites. No wonder they make the coffee part of the deal and pass it off as free, she thinks, because these tiny pieces are not worth the money. Behind her, the queue is even longer than before, and she rules out getting back into it for one of the big double chocolate cookies under the glass dome by the till.

To get her money's worth, Hannah tilts another sachet of white sugar into her latte. As she stirs, she takes her phone out and calls her dad.

'Hello,' he says, seemingly out of breath. 'That you sacked already?'

'Hello,' she says back. 'Imagine I said yes, you wouldn't feel so funny then.'

'I'd get over it. I've just put Sydney down for his nap. I had to read *Ten Little Dinosaurs* three times.'

Hannah's glad her dad can't see her face falling in disappointment. She'd thought she'd catch Syd before he went down. She could really do with hearing from him, even if it is just a series of gurgles and nonsense words.

'I thought he didn't like you reading to him? I thought he only liked it when Mum did it?'

'Well, that was his starting position, but when he realised it was me or nothing, I'm glad to say he ranked me slightly above nothing.'

The man to Hannah's left starts up a call of his own and talks like the person on the other end of his phone has requested that he shout at the top of his lungs. She puts her finger in her open ear and closes her eyes to hear better.

'How's your first day, anyway?' her dad says. 'I was expecting you to WhatsApp. Everything *is* okay, isn't it?'

Hannah wonders if she and her dad share the same definition of 'okay'. After the first half hour at Memory Lane, she couldn't believe more people didn't know about the place or the technology they were using. She couldn't believe no one had leaked anything. But now, sitting in the bustling Starbucks, she realises that multiple people have probably leaked multiple times, but it doesn't matter. She knows if she tells her dad what actually happened in the last four hours, he'd only laugh and tell her to stop being so stupid.

'Yeah,' she says into the phone. 'Everything's okay. The job seems... doable? I think?'

'And the people?' her dad asks.

Now here's something she's allowed to tell the truth about.

'They're all a bit strange,' she says. 'Well, the girl I've been paired up with, Yasmin, she's okay. Not sure if she likes me all that much though. Our boss is this woman named Philippa, she's the one who interviewed me. She's quite... intense.'

'Ach well, as long as no one's stolen your lunch money or pulled your pigtails, I reckon that can be considered a successful first day. Remember what I told you, though, you should find the biggest person in there and fight them.'

'I think you're thinking of prison, Dad.'

'The basic principle still stands,' he says, before switching to his terrible American accent. 'Shows you don't take nobody's shit.'

'Dad, I swear to God, if I hear Sydney repeating any of that, I'll be sawing off your kneecaps.'

'Your mum swears like a sailor, you do realise that? You can't pin anything on me.'

Hannah hears sounds through the phone: a drawer opening and shutting, a kettle pouring, a spoon clinking into a mug. She doesn't mind the silence between them on the line. It's comfortable and she almost forgets she only has ten minutes left before she has to go back to Memory Lane. Almost.

'I better go,' she says. 'Don't want them thinking I enjoy, y'know, having free time.'

'Right you are, darlin',' her dad says, with more

165

rumblings in the background, which Hannah guesses is him sitting down to watch daytime telly on the couch. 'Don't you worry about Sydney. He's doing just fine. He always had nine toes, didn't he?'

There's a beep on the line that she doesn't think came from her dad. A message or an email arriving.

'Is there, like, an age that dads get to when they are physically incapable of not winding their children up at every opportunity?'

'I believe it's late thirties, but I developed early.'

'Bye, Dad.'

'Bye, Hannah, love you.'

'Yeah, I love you too, I suppose.'

Hannah hangs up and sees what the beep was: a message from Yasmin. They exchanged numbers before she left Memory Lane, just in case she couldn't get in again. Apparently the badge scanner at the front door doesn't always work and sometimes goes offline for long enough that tourists wander in.

Hannah opens the message to see Yasmin's profile photo, a candid shot of her on a night out, looking strangely unrecognisable with a genuine smile on her face.

Got another one. Typical Monday! If you come back now you can have it before Xander and Andreas come back from lunch? – Yas xx

166

Philippa – Edinburgh, 2019

The door is closed but Philippa isn't in the kind of mood where she worries about whether doors are closed or not. She turns the handle and lets herself in. Michael is turned away from her in his chair, looking out the window at the traffic and general chaos of lunchtime on the Mound.

He must see her reflection in the window.

'Oh, Philippa,' he says. 'Please, do come in. I'm glad people are doing away with silly things like "knocking" and "privacy" these days.'

She steps inside and closes the door. It's not much of an office but it is, at least, technically an office. Philippa has to make do with an adapted boxroom, which she is relatively sure used to be a cleaning cupboard. She still catches the cleaning staff storing the wet floor signs in her office every now and then.

'What was that in there?' she says, not letting him jump in. 'Because, to my eyes, it looked like a very impressive display of cowardice, Michael. Bravo on that. The only thing missing was you kissing their rings, but I may have missed that while I was printing off the McQueen Reports, which they wiped their arses with. And then you ran away.'

He scratches the back of his head, his expensively cut hair cascading as his fingers pull away. The day she'd started here, Philippa had had a little crush on him for a few hours, before he opened his mouth. She will take that secret to her grave.

'There's not much I can do,' Michael says, still not facing her. 'You heard them. The money is the main priority, you know that. We'll just need to be extra careful from now on. No more memory repeating.'

'We can try that, sure. It'll probably stop the rot for now. But what about your dad?'

He turns in his chair like a Bond villain. But there's no fluffy cat on his lap, only the shadow of his cock lying under his trousers. She averts her eyes, wondering if he deliberately wears these tight trousers to expose his bulge or whether the salesperson at the place he buys his suits from convinces him it's a power move. *Show them the outline of your cock, Mr Valentine, it will instill fear in the troops.*

'What about my dad?' he says.

'Do you seriously think we shouldn't tell him about this?'

'Philippa, I think I know what my dad would want a little better than you. For one thing, his instructions could not have been clearer. Once he went in, he was not, under any circumstances, to be brought out. When he comes out, we can discuss it with him. But it's been months now, so I wouldn't count on it anytime soon. You've seen the data, he's not travelled outwith the core memory at all. He's not been near the exit button.'

The side walls of the office are lined with bookshelves, and on them, chunky biographies and business textbooks that Michael has probably given serious consideration to skimming one day. Image is all he has.

'I understand that,' Philippa says. 'But circumstances have changed. *Memorize* is his baby, and his baby's in trouble.'

'I was his baby once, you know. And I turned out okay.'

She resists telling him his dad would've been better drowning his baby in the tub. Too far, and in bad taste. Recently, she's started trying to filter these kind of thoughts out more.

Philippa decides if he's going to be in this kind of mood, she may as well take the weight off her feet. These heels are new and she didn't have time to break them in at home first. She takes a seat in front of his desk.

'Your dad didn't know this was coming,' she says. 'If he'd known about these kinds of... accidents, he would've told us before he went in. And how many times has he lived that wedding? Must be close to, what, three hundred now? I think he's been extremely lucky nothing's happened yet. Look at Mr McQueen. Nineteen times and he had to watch the man he loves die on a bathroom floor. I don't think your dad's got much longer before things go south.'

Michael pulls himself towards the desk and wiggles his mouse. The screen is angled but Philippa can see what he's up to. He signs in and looks at his emails as if there's something more important happening right now. On the desk, his Newton's Cradle has a little bit of life left in it, the balls at either end click-clacking quietly.

'I think love is a strong word for Mr McQueen,' Michael says. 'He's a horny old git, like most of our clients.'

'And when you say clients, you mean men, right?'

'Oh yes, sorry, didn't mean to offend the feminist in the room. Let me get back on my tiptoes so I can be careful what I say around you.'

'Michael, you are a worm of a man, and this blatantly obvious argument you're trying to start with me so you won't have to debate the real issue here is not going to happen. We need to get word to your dad.'

Sometimes Philippa thinks she goes too far when she speaks to Michael. He's her boss, after all, and there's supposed to be a façade that you keep up. When the rest of the staff are around, she does her best, but when it's just the two of them, she can't help it. He can't sack her,

169

not now. She's been here too long and keeping staff is not one of Memory Lane's strong points. Every year when the Christmas night out comes around, it's a sad state of affairs. There are hardly ever fresh faces to make arses of themselves and give people a bit of gossip to get them through those first few weeks in January.

'Get word to him? In the memory?' Michael asks.

'Yes. I'll go in, if you like. Quick and painless. Let him know the situation and he can make up his own mind if he wants to come out and assess the system.'

Michael doesn't shut her down immediately, which gives her hope. He has a strained look on his face, like he's seriously thinking about it, or he's trying to do the seven times table in his head.

Philippa knows that he knows this is the right thing to do. But she also knows, though he'd never admit it, he's afraid of his letting his dad down. John Valentine invented the *Memorize* technology around twenty years ago, and set up Memory Lane around 2008. When he decided to put himself into the technology with no fixed end date, he stepped down and appointed Michael as the new CEO and set him the task of not fucking up his legacy. This situation, even though it's no fault of Michael's, would definitely count as fucking up the legacy.

Finally, Michael speaks.

'No,' he says. 'I'm sorry. Listen, I know you're probably right. If he knew the facts, he'd come out. But he went in there for a reason and told us not to interrupt. And that's a promise I need to keep to him. If anyone goes in there, I know he'll recommend a vote of no confidence in me to the board. He gave up his role in Memory Lane but they'll listen to him.'

Philippa stands, adjusting the bottom of her dress, taking another look out at the view. The sun has emerged fully

170

from behind the clouds, flashing on all the car windshields and creating hundreds of little shining lights.

'Fine,' she says. 'And Mr McQueen?'

'Tell him he can't have that memory anymore. Fresh memories only. Something about new company policy.'

She leaves him in his sad little office, and makes her way to her own, sadder, littler office.

John – Stonecranning, 1975

Seeing an entire wedding party run for a quarter of a mile towards a burning building wasn't something John expected to see today, but the system was throwing up all kinds of surprises. In fact, he would make a list of the unexpected events on a notepad if he knew he could take the notepad back with him when he left the memory. This was something he hadn't quite been able to crack with the technology yet, and probably never would.

He's a lot fitter in here, certainly more so than his real body currently lying in Memory Lane, but he's still out of breath as he catches up with the huge group who are watching the spectacle unfold. All the wedding guests, but also the hall staff, the neighbours, the people who were out walking their dogs and now have a belter of a story to tell when they get home.

The smoke is black and rising from the roof of the hall, as well as through the windows. It pours from every gap and shoots upwards the second it gets out, racing towards the sky.

'John,' his dad says, arriving by his side. 'The hall's on fire, John.'

'Aye, Dad, thanks for that. I hadn't realised.'

'Has someone phoned the fire brigade? Someone should phone the fire brigade.'

A woman in a green cardigan stands nearby, holding her little dog, who barks at the fire every now and again.

'They're on their way,' she announces. 'I phoned them from the booth. It was me that first found it. I was walking Franklin here and saw it. You're lucky I was passing by.'

'Aw, aye,' John's dad says. 'They extra twenty seconds were vital. We'll be in there dancing in no time.'

The fire has spread everywhere. The hall looks near enough ready to collapse but John doesn't hear any sirens yet.

Through the crowd, John sees the few staff members gathered, huddled even. One of them, a younger woman, is crying and the others are consoling her. John walks through the crowd, seeing Agnes with Ronnie as he goes. She's in tears too, her wedding day literally going up in flames in front of her. He decides to leave her with Ronnie and continues towards the staff members.

'Hello,' he says as he reaches them.

The amount of times he's lived this day, he really should have learned their names by now. There's the young crying girl, he wants to say... Susie? The middle-aged guy is Jim, he thinks, and the spotty blonde teenager who's always flirting with Susie behind the bar is...

'Gordon,' Jim says. 'Get your jacket off so Susie can have it.'

Gordon whips his jacket off and wraps it round Susie's shoulders, which are bobbing up and down as she cries. It would've been a much more valiant and gentlemanly gesture if he'd not had to be told to do it, but that's youth for you.

John's not sure if they heard him or they just don't think making small talk with the groom is important at a time like this.

'Everything alright?' he asks.

Jim turns to him, Susie cradled in the crook of his arm.

'No, it's bloody well not. No one can find Kathy.'

Susie wails even louder, and even Gordon can't help a tear rolling down his face.

'She's...' John says, pointing at what was formerly the Stonecranning Community Hall. 'In there?'

'Aye. Where's the bloody fire engine?'

Gordon shouts this, looking around at the other scared faces, as if the fire engine could've snuck up on them unawares.

And just like that, this fire doesn't seem so fun anymore. Fun might be pushing it, John thinks, but whether people admit it or not, everyone enjoys watching a fire. It appeals to the same sordid part of us that can't look away from car crashes. It's in human nature to want to see things you've never seen before. It's also in human nature, John's confirmed since Memory Lane opened, to want to see things you *have* seen before.

But now they know there's someone inside and that information is spreading through the wedding crowd, sapping any excitement the fire first brought.

That's when a silly thought comes to John's mind. *You could run in there and save her, John. You'll never get a chance like this again.*

He knows it's ridiculous. Because that's not what *Memorize* is for. It's not what he designed it to do. It's about reliving memories just as they happened, not living out fantasies.

When a client veers off from the main memory, events become inconsistent. The technology does its best but really it takes an educated guess and more often than not, the clients aren't happy with the results. Sure, sometimes the client goes after another woman and hey, the woman likes the client back and the client's sure that's the way it would've happened in the real world. But a lot of the time, the woman turns the client down and guess what? The client thinks the technology is wonky. But that's just because they're using it wrong. Which is probably why

John's not been able to change the last conversation with his dad. He's not like other clients, though. He created it. He can do whatever he likes in here.

This day is clearly a write-off. He could convince Agnes to put her doubts on hold for the day but putting out a real fire is beyond his capabilities. There's no chance he can have the conversation with his dad and get anything real out of it. Every wedding night for as long as he can remember, has ended in the same horrible disappointment, watching his dad walk away from him into the night. And every time, a little bit more of his hope drains away.

John takes off his jacket and loosens his sporran, letting it drop to the ground. He rolls up his sleeves and takes a few deep breaths, walking towards the inferno.

'What are you doing, you idiot?' Jim says. 'Where are you going?'

As he steps towards the fire, already feeling the heat tingle on his skin, he wishes he'd thought of a cool thing to say, like James Bond or someone.

'Eh,' he says. 'I'm going in… there. To get that woman. Whatsherface. Be back in a minute.'

Hannah – Edinburgh, 2019

They sit at Hannah's newly bagsied computer in the corner of the lab, Yasmin still finishing a yum yum from Greggs. Hannah watches her closely. She's worried Yasmin might reach a sticky digit towards her keyboard or mouse. Even if she sucks off the icing, it still won't make Hannah feel any better.

In her opinion, any iced snack should immediately be followed by a washing of the hands, and she's not sure why that makes her uptight, because it seems totally reasonable to her. It reminds her of high school when people would eat a bag of crisps, wipe their fingers on their trousers, then ask to borrow her pen. She would usually just say yes and let them keep the pen. She went through so many pens.

'Mm,' Yasmin says. 'These yum yum's from Greggs are like crack. Obviously, I don't know what crack is like but, y'know, it makes me feel incredible while I'm having it and then horrible afterwards and I crave it most of the time. I imagine crack's probably something like that. In fact, thinking about it, cock is a lot like that too.'

Hannah laughs. Yasmin's joke is so not of this place that it feels like she's punched a hole in reality. The fact that she can make jokes like that and the walls don't come crumbling to the ground puts Hannah more at ease.

On the computer screen, Hannah guides the cursor through several options. She's slowly starting to get the hang of it, what she'll be doing all day, every day, Monday to Friday, nine to five.

Whenever a client goes over their time, an amber

warning flashes up on her screen. If it's her turn, that is. The system allocates each Retrieval Assistant one client at a time, to ensure they all get the same amount. Then, if the client still hasn't left the memory after five minutes, amber changes to red and that's her cue to go in. The system shows her the client's name and room number, and then once she's in the room, she can find out more details about the memory itself.

'I remember one time I had a guy come out the memory just as I was going in,' Yasmin tells her. 'Like, I was in the memory for half a second. Felt pretty vommy after that. Also, just to note, you shouldn't leave the clients in the room by themselves while they're awake for too long, just general protocol.'

Hannah wonders if she'll make it at Memory Lane long enough to start stories with, 'I remember one time...' Then again, she's already had the experiences of Mr Hill and Ms Reid. To the ears of non-Memory Lane people, those stories are dynamite. To Memory Hill employees, clearly not so much.

On her screen, the alert in the corner changes from amber to red.

'Room six. Let's rock and roll,' Hannah says. 'Oh God, why do I sound like my dad more and more these days?'

They both stand up. The wheels on their chairs keep spinning and the chairs continue to roll even once they've stepped away.

'Don't worry about it,' Yasmin says. 'Last night, my little sister's boyfriend, who is nineteen, asked me if we had Walkmen "back in my day". Yeah, he's not going to survive much longer, because I will literally murder him. No joke, I've even planned out how I'd get rid of his body. I actually think if I got enough people to hear my side of things, I'd get away with it.'

They walk through the memory corridor and enter room six. On the bed, a man lies, seemingly asleep, *Memorize* headset sitting on his head. He's not that much older than Hannah.

'Well, hello there, Mr Douglas,' Yasmin says.

They take their seats and Yasmin lets Hannah get the memory queued up for them on the screen.

'You can say it,' Yasmin says.

'Say what?' Hannah replies.

'Mr Douglas, and I say this as a proud feminist, is a hot piece of ass. I saw him coming in this morning.'

'He's… not displeasing to the eye.'

'Wait. Before you tell me what the memory is, can I guess? It's always more interesting when they're young.'

Hannah opens up the memory tab and Yasmin looks away from the screen.

'Okay,' Hannah says. 'Go for it.'

'Hmm. Sex-related?'

'No.'

'Drug-related?'

'No.'

'Music festival?'

'No.'

'Football match?'

'No.'

'Abroad?'

'Yes.'

'Interrailing?'

'No.'

'America?'

'Yes.'

'New York?'

'Wait, did you see the screen?'

'I'm right? Let's see.'

Hannah scoots over so Yasmin can see Mr Douglas's details.

Name: Ryan Quentin Douglas
Age: 27
Height: 5'11

'Bet he tells everyone he's six foot one but never lets anyone near him with a measuring tape,' Yasmin says.

Weight: 75.5 kg
Memory: 'My sister Christina's sixteenth birthday in New York, when we did all the touristy stuff with the whole family and ended with pizza, just the two of us in this grimy little place, but the pizza was amazing. And we saw Conan O'Brien and my sister got her photo with him.'
Age (in memory): 24

Hannah takes out the headsets and hands one to Yasmin, who now looks less impressed.

'What's that face for?' Hannah asks. 'His sister's birthday? That's so wholesome.'

'Exactly,' she says. 'There must be something wrong with him. That's too nice for a man. He must've had sex or something during the day and just didn't want to put it on the form. Even if he is that nice, he's still a client here, which obviously makes him rich, which obviously rules him out as being a good person. Always worth keeping in mind.'

'Millionaires can't *ever* be good people?'

'Not in my experience.'

They put the headsets on and Hannah clicks the option to put them into the memory. Her vision turns to black and the countdown begins.

John – Stonecranning, 1975

Now this is a real test of the program, John thinks. Clients choose a lot of different memories and he's seen it stressed to the limits when they try and diverge from the core memory too much, but this is something else. A burning building that was never actually on fire? He has to remind himself that this isn't real, even as the heat feels like it might suffocate him before he even reaches the front door.

'John!' comes a scream from behind him.

He doesn't turn, because there's really no point. He's not sure whose voice it is. Whoever the system has decided would be most upset and desperate not to see him die in a fiery blaze. Agnes, he would hope, although the system doesn't seem to think she really wanted to marry him earlier today, so who knows?

The door is ajar and John kicks at it. It gives way, falling off its hinges slightly. His kilt is heavy and though it gives him a bit more freedom for kicking doors in, it already feels like it's weighing him down.

He crouches to go through the door. He doesn't know much about fires, always glazed over when the company made him sit through fire safety presentations, but he knows to keep low.

The foyer is thick with soot and smoke and heat so dense it feels like a physical presence John has to wade through. Like trying to power walk in a swimming pool.

'Hello,' he shouts into the dark, smokiness of the building. 'Kathy? Kathy, are you in here?'

There's no response, but he doesn't think he'd be able

to hear anyway. The sound of the fire is crackling and thundering in his ears.

The door on the right goes through to the public bar. The bar itself is engulfed with flames, the vodka and whisky bottles melting and dripping and falling to the floor. John's eyes start to sting with the smoke and he tries to blink away the pain, which only results in his eyes watering and blurring his vision further.

The pathway from the bar to the main hall is clear and he continues on his way. His heart is going a mile a minute and, although he shouldn't have any other thoughts outside of saving this Kathy woman, he can't help but notice how easy this is. How he's going from room to room without anything getting in his way or the smoke really causing him any chest pain.

And he can take a stab at why. John's always had a little fantasy about saving someone from a burning building. It comes to his mind on long drives or train journeys or even falling asleep at night. He likes to think a lot of people have this same fantasy but not many would like to admit it. Even though it seems like a selfless act, it's not really. The reason John likes to imagine it is because of the plaudits he would get afterwards, how everyone would see him as a hero who was willing to put his life on the line. He'd be a real-life John McClane. The actual life that he would theoretically save would be just a happy by-product. Unless it was a beautiful woman who fell madly in love with him, which it often was in his fantasies.

But every time he imagines this scenario, no matter who he's saving, he always... saves them. He's never had a daydream where he fails and dies and the newspapers are full of articles about the idiot who ran into a burning building without any training and died a deserved death and no one feels sorry for him. In his head, John always saves the person. And this is due, in large part, to the fact he's never been in a burning building. He's never even been all that close to a fire in his life. He doesn't even like barbeques due to the smokey smell they leave in his clothes. So, he doesn't have any frame of reference for what it would actually be like. In his mind, he imagines it would be like it is on the telly. You run in, you cough a little bit, you grab the person, then you leave. Job's a good 'un.

That's what *Memorize* is working with. He's walking through the burning hall easily because the technology is guessing this is what it would be like, because this is what John imagines it would be like.

John ducks down as he goes through the door to the main hall. A wooden beam has fallen from the ceiling, only blocking his way slightly. He climbs over it and looks around. The other side of the bar is equally engulfed through here too, and it's spread to every other table.

On the floor between the DJ booth, if you can call it that, and the top table, a pair of lifeless legs stick out. John walks over, avoiding the debris and ash and parts of the ceiling which are now parts of the floor. Above, he can see the plume of smoke rising to the heavens.

He edges round the side of the table and finds Kathy lying face down on the carpet.

'Kathy,' he says, shaking her by the arm. 'Kathy, we need to get you out of here.'

She doesn't stir. As he shakes her, some soot and dust falls off her face. John does a few squats to warm up his knees, before realising that he's obviously still young in here and his knees don't need thirty minutes prior warning before doing any form of exercise.

He bends at the knee, putting one arm under Kathy's legs and one arm under her back, and lifts with his legs. John has always been skinny, the kind of person people are always desperate to tell they need more meat on their bones, but he finds he can lift her easily. Again, in his fantasies, he's always been able to lift the rescuee, no bother at all. It wouldn't be much of a fantasy if he'd been too weak to lift the beautiful woman and had to leave her to die, or worse, call in some macho hunk who could throw her over his shoulder and take the credit.

He carries her through the hall and kicks open the fire door. Thick smoke rushes out in front of him.

Kathy opens her eyes and coughs.

'Who are you?' she manages.

John steps out into the fresh air, which tastes delicious in his lungs.

'Me?' he says. 'I'm the groom.'

'The what?'

'The groom.'

'The goon?'

'The GROOM,' he shouts in her ear, as he carries her round to the front of the building. ''Sake, can't even let me have my John McClane moment.'

It takes people a few seconds to see them coming round the side of the hall, as their eyes are still on the front door. When they do, there's screams and shouting and pointing. John's eyes are still a little cloudy and dusted with grit, but he sees okay enough. And then he hears well enough, the sound of applause, scattered at first, then growing louder. A small voice in his head tells him this isn't what the technology is for, that this is abusing it to live out a silly little fantasy. But a much larger voice tells him *you created it, John, you can do whatever you want with it.*

As he gets closer to the crowd he shouts, 'Are you not entertained?'

Kathy, in his arms, stirs again. 'What's that from?'

'It's from a fi... me. I just thought of it.'

183

There are sirens approaching but they're too late. John's the hero here.

But he knows he can't stay in here much longer. Things could get worse. There's something wrong with the system. He has to go back. He has to wake up.

Hannah – New York, 2016

When Hannah read 'New York' on Mr Douglas's file, she got her hopes up. She was picturing her and Yasmin opening their eyes to a glittery, mirrored, 92nd floor restaurant with a breathtaking view of the city skyline. Actually, more than that, she was picturing they would get to walk out on to the rooftop balcony, so she could feel the wind whip her hair and imagine she was Meg Ryan and look down at the lights of Manhattan for her Tom Hanks. But that would've been too good to be true, and she is at work, after all.

The pizza restaurant could be anywhere in the world. The *Little Marco's* neon sign pulses red and green in the window. Restaurant is maybe going a bit far. People in American films are always calling places 'dives' and she's fairly sure *Little Marco's* would fit within that genre.

A super-tall guy with red hair steps outside, finishes his slice of pizza and tosses his napkin into a nearby bin. Or, trashcan. All those years watching *Friends* have taught her something. That counts as being bilingual, doesn't it?

'Have you been to New York before?' Yasmin asks her, the pair of them standing on the wet pavement, across the street. A yellow taxi goes by and Hannah can't deny the buzz she gets from it.

'No,' she says. 'Hopefully I'll take Sydney when he's older, though.'

'Who's Sydney?'

'My son.'

'You have a son?'

Hannah's used to that kind of response, in that tone of voice. It's usually a combination of 'Wow, you look way too young to have a kid!' and 'Wow… you look… way too young… to have a kid…' The classic 'That's great!' and 'I'm glad I'm not you!' combo.

'Yeah,' Hannah says, looking both ways before crossing the road. 'I'll show you photos when we get back.'

'Oh, yeah, please. Sorry if I sounded shocked there. You're just so young. And fit.'

'It's cool. Ha, thanks.'

'Honestly. I mean, I hope you don't take this the wrong way, but your son is going to get proper bullied in school for having a hot mum. It's going to be constant "I fucked your mum" jokes until he's like twenty. And the jokes are only going to stop because the boys will then actively start trying to sleep with you.'

'I hadn't really thought about it.'

'Well, I would. Sons of MILFs suffer more than you'd think.'

Through the open door of the pizza place, the dough smell and the sharp heat rush to meet them. It's the kind of thick pizza air that makes you feel like you've gained calories just by standing in it. Once, after spending the whole day in London city centre, Hannah's friend Erin had told her to blow her nose and she'd been shocked at how black her snot was due to the pollution. She feels like if she blew her nose now, a garlic flatbread would splat out.

Booths with faux red leather seats line the left side wall, with a narrow passage to walk down to the door at the back which reads *Little Boys & Little Girls & Little People's Rooms*. On the right, the counter, stacked with heated display cases showcasing the longest, thickest slices of greasy pizza Hannah's ever seen. At the window, a few stools for people to sit and eat and watch New York unfold out the window.

'Evening, ladies,' the guy behind the counter says, seeing them lingering at the door. 'Don't be scared, we don't bite. Well, Mikey does, but he ain't here so come on in.'

His accent is as thick as the dough, although she's not accustomed to America enough to know exactly where he comes from. Admittedly, he sounds like a character from *Grease* but she can't remember off the top of her head where *Grease* was meant to be set. All she remembers is the songs, the accents, and the actors in their late thirties playing teenagers.

In the furthest away booth, she makes eye contact with Mr Douglas. He's a little younger, his hair is longer, and he looks altogether disappointed to see them. She feels odd thinking of him as Mr Douglas, especially given he's wearing a baseball cap backwards, but she decides she better keep up the formality.

'Good evening,' Yasmin says, stepping inside. 'Can I get a slice of pepperoni, please?

'Hey!' the guy behind the counter booms. 'Course you can. I like your accent. Where you from, sweetheart?'

'Scotland.'

Hannah steps inside too, while Mr Douglas keeps his head down.

'Scotland, fantastic,' the owner says. 'We already got a couple of Scots at the back there. Now I know it's offensive to say all you Scots know each other, but it's a small island, right? So you never know, you might. You should say hello. Maybe you're cousins or something, right? Wait 'til you try this pizza, uh, what's your name, sweetheart?'

'Yasmin.'

'Yasmin, what a beautiful name. Okay, Yasmin, you ain't never had pizza like this in Scotland. Quite frankly, I wipe my ass with Scottish pizza, okay? You're gonna be tellin all your friends about Marco's pizza. That's me, by the way, I'm Marco. You can find us on TripAdvisor, of course. I encourage you to leave a review. Minimum five stars, of course, any less than that and we'll come lookin for you. Hey, look, she's smilin, she thinks we ain't serious. We take TripAdvisor seriously here at Marco's, yes we do.'

Hannah smiles and leaves Yasmin to her chat with Marco. She walks past her and down the passage which leads her to Mr Douglas's table. When she gets there, she finds it's just Mr Douglas and a girl who she guesses to be his little sister.

The sister notices Hannah.

'We're not done yet,' she says.

'Oh,' Hannah says. 'No, I don't work here. Well, wait, I work here but not… in here.'

Mr Douglas shakes his head and smiles.

'Why don't you sit down?' he says, gesturing to the seat next to him.

'I don't think I should.'

'Yeah, who is this?' the sister says, eyeing up her brother like he's ruining her birthday. 'Don't just invite strangers to sit down. Stranger danger is even worse in America, Ryan. They all have guns. Stranger danger with guns. Think about that.'

'She's a friend, Chrissy.'

Before she can sit down, Christina stands up and throws her napkin on the table, where it lands very gently, then falls to the floor.

'I'm going to the toilet,' she says. 'Please make sure your friend is gone when I get back. It's my birthday and

I don't want any of your special friends ruining it. Can't believe you arranged to meet with someone in New York. I'm telling Mum and Dad when we get back to the hotel.'

Hannah sits down and slides along to the middle of the booth. On the table, a paper plate with crusts discarded every which way. She tells herself: *I'm not here to make friends with the client.*

'You have a lot of "special friends", do you?' she asks him.

Something behind her crashes to the ground and Marco yells at a staff member.

'That's not a very professional question,' Mr Douglas says. 'You are from Memory Lane, yeah? Otherwise this is *not* how I remember this night ending.'

'I am. And it's time to go. You've gone over your allotted time.'

'I'm not sure your friend would be happy with that. She's with you, yeah?'

He gestures behind her. Hannah turns to find Yasmin now behind the counter, rolling a giant powdery dough with Marco and laughing her head off. Maybe, just maybe, Yasmin isn't the true professional Hannah thought she was. But she is proving to be a fun memory buddy at least.

'She is, yeah,' Hannah says. 'Never mind. Press your button. You've gone over time.'

Mr Douglas raises his hand from the table to show her the red button on his palm. He uses the forefinger of his other hand to gently tap at it without ever pressing it hard enough to set off the trigger.

'You guys couldn't have designed a less obvious button?' he says. 'All that money I paid and this is what you put on me? My sister could draw something better on one of these napkins.'

189

'I don't design anything. I just get people back to the real world. Let's go, Mr Douglas.'

'Ooh,' he says, dipping a crust into a garlic dip. 'I like it when you call me Mr Douglas.'

He bites the crust and chews, a slight drip of garlic crowding the edge of his mouth. Hannah wants to turn and look for Yasmin again. She could be doing with a bit of help here, but she keeps her eyes on Mr Douglas, as she really doesn't want him *knowing* she could be doing with a bit of help. In uni, she learned that sometimes you just have to pretend to be confident and answer the tutor's question, even when you're not sure what you're on about. Because the appearance of confidence is so much like actually being confident that most people can't tell the difference. Even when it's sitting across from them in a virtual depiction of Little Marco's.

'Ryan,' Hannah says, not giving him the satisfaction of hearing her say Mr Douglas again. 'You either leave now or you're going to start incurring serious penalties.'

'Well, I wouldn't want that. Although, I actually enjoy you calling me Ryan just as much as I enjoy you saying Mr Douglas, so that's good to know. What's your name?'

'That's not important.'

'Hannah!' comes Yasmin's voice from behind the counter. 'Check this out!'

Hannah turns to see Yasmin tossing the dough into the air and catching it with her clenched fists.

'How good am I at this?' she calls. 'Definitely going to open up a Little Marco's in Edinburgh when we get back!'

Beside her, Marco looks on bemused. She wonders if this kind of thing happens in New York every day. That's what TV and films have led her to believe anyway. A magical place where the only crimes are playful and fun and the police and the criminals have a mutual respect for each other and make sarcastic off the cuff remarks as they chase each other.

'So, Hannah,' Ryan says, and she turns back to find him smiling. 'Been at Memory Lane long?'

'Long enough.'

'Oh really? Because it seems like you're quite fresh-faced. I mean, you haven't been able to make me leave and I'm fairly inoffensive. I would hurry if I were you, too, 'cause my sister is due back any second and she's a lot scarier than me. Sixteen-year-old girls these days are fucking terrifying. They can delve into your soul with one look, find your biggest insecurity and tear your very world apart with one comment.'

'Your sister sounds delightful. I can see why you've paid so much money to live her birthday again.'

'She liked me, though. That's the thing with teenage girls, if they hate you, you're toast. But if they like you, they'll go to the ends of the earth for you.'

As if he had rung a bell to summon her, his sister arrives back from the toilet and stands by their table.

'I thought I told you to make her leave,' she says. 'I'll tell Mum.'

Hannah smirks but Ryan doesn't seem embarrassed.

'Go on then,' he tells her.

'I will, I swear. I'm not joking. I know how to get back to the hotel from here.'

'Then go.'

'I will.'

'Then go.'

'I... will... sit at another table. You're ruining my sixteenth birthday, Ryan. Just because you're thinking with your willy. And don't think I don't know that's what you're doing. I've seen *Gossip Girl*. I've seen *Pretty*

191

Little Liars. I've even seen shows from the old days like *Dawson's Creek.*'

Christina points at Hannah. 'You want to get in her pants, right? Where do you know her from? Back home? Have you planned this little meeting? And why is she dressed like an office worker? He's got a little willy, y'know.'

This causes Ryan to stand up and playfully put a hand over her mouth. 'That is wild speculation,' he says. 'We just happened to meet in here while both on our separate holidays.'

Christina folds her arms, flicks her hair in defiance, in a way that seems practised, and goes to sit at a table at the other end of the place. Ryan sits, the air trapped in the booth seats rushing out as his weight comes back down.

'I don't mean to be harsh,' he says. 'But you've fairly ruined this memory for me.'

'I'm sorry. Wait, no, I'm not sorry. The memory is over. You shouldn't even be seeing this much. Your twelve hours are up. Now, please press your exit button.'

He doesn't make any move to do as she says. They don't say anything for a while and Hannah notices the music that's playing through the speakers. *The Power of Love* by Air Supply. She loves this song but tries to tune it out. She doesn't want to equate it with this particular moment.

'You and me have a lot in common,' Ryan says.

'Oh yeah?' Hannah says. 'Like what?'

'Well, the people we arrived here with have left us.'

Again, she doesn't want to turn her head too quickly, but she would like reassurance that Yasmin is still there keeping an eye on them. She looks at her nails for a moment, realising that one is chipped from this stupid

192

job already, then casually turns her head to look over at the counter.

Marco is there, rolling dough and greeting a customer on the other side of the glass. The customer starts tapping his keys on the glass and Marco swipes his hand away to stop him.

But Yasmin is gone. Hannah looks back at Ryan.

'Can I buy you a virtual slice of pizza?' he asks.

John – Stonecranning, 1975

Once he's put Kathy down, John gets the chance to take a few breaths and a few plaudits from various wedding guests. He feels hands whack him on the back and shoulders and notices the same hands being wiped on trousers and hankies to get the soot off.

That's when he realises Agnes is standing in front of him. Now, John isn't one to appreciate clothes or fashion or most things about women, really, but he does notice the bottom of her dress, which is quite noticeably lined with mud and muck.

'Did you see?' he asks her. 'I saved that woman, Kathy. She was in there.'

The sirens are loud, blasting in everyone's ears, as fire engines, three of them, climb over the kerb and make their way across the grass to the side of the hall.

'Firstly,' Agnes says. 'Don't even think about touching me while you're all covered in black stuff. Secondly, what the fucking hell did you think you were doing? Do you think you're Paul bloody Newman? You could've bloody died, John. You should've bloody died. I would've been the quickest widow in history. Except no one would feel sorry for me because everyone would agree my husband was a stupid bastard who deserved it. And thirdly, don't even think about touching me while you're all covered in that black stuff.'

She finishes by letting out a little gust of air through her nose, like she had held her breath the whole time she was ranting.

'But,' John says. 'Did you see? I saved someone.'

'Yes, I saw. It was... really brave of you. You stupid bastard.'

This wasn't quite how he imagined Agnes would react after he valiantly rescued someone but it was something at least. An ambulance has also arrived, and the paramedics rush to Kathy's side. She sits on the grass for want of a chair, which are all ablaze inside the hall.

In the films, the paramedics rush to the aid of the rescuer too, to check them over. The hero always tells them to buzz off, because they only care about making sure the victim is okay. John actually wouldn't mind them rushing to his aid. Only, this is 1975, and back then things were different. 'Secondhand smoke' was just what you called it when you took a drag off someone else's fag.

As John walks away from the main group to pat himself down and shift some of the soot out of his hair, he starts thinking what a headache this would be if this was real life. Their wedding reception was up in flames. They'd either have to lead seventy-plus guests to a nearby pub and hope they could rustle up seventy-plus meals at the drop of a hat, or just cancel the thing entirely.

The guests have split into smaller groups. Probably discussing how they're each getting home and if they want to jump in each other's taxis or whose man has the motor with them. He knows he can't stay any longer, not until he's worked out what's going wrong with *Memorize*. He's not sure if he'll come back in afterwards. He has unfinished business with his dad but more and more, he's starting to believe it'll need to stay that way.

The firefighters swarm out of their fire engines, grabbing their equipment and unravelling hoses. They tell everyone to stand back. Everyone's too close.

'Further back!' one moustached fireman shouts. John

195

misses the days when a man could have a moustache and people didn't ask if it was 'ironic'. 'Further! Get on the road! I don't fucking care if you get hit by a car, just get on the road so you can be safe!'

The crowd is soon transferred to the other side of the road, where the little paper shop *McGinty's* is. It's still open and some people jump inside and appear back out moments later, arms full of clinking bottles.

John's a good distance away from them now, not even fully aware that his steps are taking him back towards the town centre. No one seems to have noticed him missing. *I'm the hero of the bloody hour*, he thinks, *I've just saved a woman from a burning building and they aren't looking for me?* This only confirms it. There is definitely something wrong with the program.

He knows how to get out. The exit button is right where he designed it to be. When they put him in, his instructions were clear: no one else is to enter the memory for any reason. And so far, they seem to have understood. Every now and then, he thinks he sees one of the staff, lurking at the back of the hall later at night, checking up on him. Each time he tries to chase after them, they seem to disappear and slip away into the night. They know if he caught any of them, he'd sack them on the spot. Or at least, he'd get Michael to do it, since he's in charge now. CEO. What a stupid little title that is.

John's forgotten a lot of things over the last few months, he knows that. It feels like the more he learns about this day he's reliving, the more he forgets about the real world. Even when buildings go on fire in here, he knows it's not real. That tomorrow, everything will go back to normal. The same day over and over again is normality to him. He knows that's not normal though, not to everyone else on Earth. Which obviously brings up the question of what is 'normal' and how can you define it? Everyone sees the world differently and normal really means nothing.

While he's been lost in his thoughts, someone has walked over to John from the wedding group. The figure who stands in front of him now, great smile across his face, even the hint of moisture in his eyes, is his dad.

'Where are you running off to?' his dad asks, handing him the sporran that he had dropped before going into the hall. 'You can't fade away into the night. It's your wedding, John.'

The sky is starting to get darker now. Still a nice blend of oranges and purples but it feels like the smoke from the hall, which is still mixing into the clouds, is bringing the night in early, like mixing black paint into a colour palette and swirling it around.

'I have a funny feeling the meal is going to be postponed,' John says. 'Unless everyone likes their chicken really, really, really well done. Frank won't be getting his beef either.'

'Ronnie's saying everyone can go back to theirs,' his dad says. 'Says they can fit everyone inside and he's got steaks in the fridge. Is there anything that man won't make about him and his big house? *Ooh, I'm Ronnie and I've got a big house.* It's not even that big.'

'It is quite big, Dad.'

'Oh, are you going to live with him after the wedding, then?'

'Hadn't planned on it, no.'

'Good. Because that would be strange. Anyway, that's not what I wanted to say. I came over here because I wanted to say, you know…'

He vaguely points a thumb over to where the hall is across the road.

'That performance in there. It was stupid, aye, maybe the stupidest thing you've ever done. But it was brave…

197

and no one else would've done it. And I just wanted to tell you, because, it's your wedding day and that, and this is the kind of thing you're meant to say when your son gets married... I'm proud of you, John.'

When John watches gangster films and sees someone getting shot in the chest, he often tries to imagine what it would feel like, but fails, because he has no frame of reference. He's never been shot in the chest, or anywhere in his body for that matter. But hearing his dad's words feels like a bullet in the heart. He's surprised he's still standing, that he hasn't been blown backwards and landed in a crumpled heap.

'What?' John says.

'Ah, now, don't make me say it again. Don't laugh at me, son.'

'I'm not laughing, Dad, I promise. I just... wasn't expecting it.'

Then something even more unexpected happens. John's dad opens his arms to hug him. He doesn't open them all that wide, John notices, just wide enough to fit him in. John lets himself drift towards his dad and feels arms on his back, closing the loop. John feels awkward and confused and overwhelmed for the entire four seconds they share the embrace. A few sharp pats on his back and they break apart.

The world still looks the same. John had always imagined things would be altered when it finally happened. There would be a change in the air direction, or a feeling in his chest, or fireworks going off in the background. Certainly, he imagined he would be happy at the very least. But that's not what he's feeling now.

'What's wrong?' his dad asks. 'You look like someone's just shot your dog.'

'I don't have a dog.'

'Well, you're lucky then, no one can shoot it. Come on, cheer up. What's wrong?'

'This isn't real.'

John's dad nods his head and runs his tongue along his top lip.

'Agnes told me you were talking a load of nonsense like this earlier.'

John sits down on the edge of the pavement, tucking his kilt in around his downstairs region to stop passing cars getting too good a look. He isn't a *true* Scotsman in that sense, though. He never saw the point in letting everything hang loose like that for the sense of tradition.

His dad sits down by his side.

'Obviously,' John says. His dad listens but this is more for his own benefit. 'None of this is real. I know that. But the point is this is the closest I'll ever get to the real thing. And I need to do it right, because otherwise it's just... fantasy. Wish fulfilment. I could do that in my own head without all this fuss.

'I need to relive the day exactly as it was, so your reaction is real. You telling me you're proud of me when I save someone from a burning building is nice, but it's not real. It's not even in the realm of being real. The point was to relive the wedding day exactly the same, and tell you at the end of the day that I'm going to work for Ronnie, and work out the right way to phrase it that'll make you realise that you *are* proud of me, that you aren't disappointed in me. Well, that's as close to being real as I'm going to get. But I still haven't got there yet. And that hug there, and you saying you're proud of me, that doesn't count. I never saved anyone from a burning building. I never would either. You wouldn't catch me doing that out in the real world. It's too late for that now. I want you to be proud of me, Dad. The real me.'

A car passes by, the honking of its horn blaring out. Must be tooting at the guests, John thinks, who are now passing bottles of whisky between them outside the minimarket while deciding how best to go forward. Agnes will have noticed him missing by now, but with his dad over here too, no one will realise he's about to run off.

'Did you just say,' John's dad says, 'you're going to work for Ronnie? Don't be daft.'

'I'm not being daft, Dad. I'm going to work for Ronnie because the work's better and the job's better and the money's better and one day I want to have a big house like his. And guess what? I *will* have a big house like his. Because I'm smart, Dad. I'm smarter than you think I am and I'm going to invent a technology no one else in the world has before and… I'm going to use it to… relive this fucking day and try to change the last conversation we ever had. The last words you ever said to me were to tell me how much of a disappointment I am. And saying it out loud makes me realise that maybe you're right. Because what a fucking daft thing to do, eh?'

His dad stands up, brushing the dust from his kilt. The tassled laces of his shoes bump against his socks, the flashes poking out at John's eye level. 'We'll talk about this later,' he says. 'Stand up and let's go back over. You've got a load of guests waiting for you to tell them what to do. Are you going to stand up and be a man, John? Or are you going to keep sitting on your lonesome, feeling sorry for yourself like a wee boy?'

John stands and begins walking in the opposite direction. Over the grass, which crunches under his feet, to take the shortcut back to the town centre. His laces came loose hours ago and they kick around his ankles. His dad calls his name over and over until he stops trying anymore.

It doesn't matter if that's the last thing his dad ever says to him. It's not real. None of this is real. The past is the past and that's where it has to stay.

John keeps walking. He knows where he's going.

Hannah – New York, 2016

'No,' Hannah says. 'I don't want a slice of virtual pizza.'

'You sure?' Ryan asks. 'It's virtually as good as the real thing. Have you ever had New York pizza before? The frozen ones from the Co-op don't quite match up.'

She knows she's supposed to have authority over him but she can't help but feeling, especially with Yasmin's disappearing act, that the momentum has shifted, the same way it had with Ms Reid on the beach in Aberdeen earlier.

'This is my first time in New York, actually,' Hannah tells him. 'With you. And your sister. And Marco, of course. In a virtual memory. So, you can imagine how thrilled I am and how desperate I am to spend more time in here.'

'I like you, Hannah. Do you have any little feedback cards I could fill out? I'm very good at writing reviews, I could make sure you get employee of the month. I'm also very good at the negative ones too. My TripAdvisor history is like a battlefield. Hey, what's that on your arm?'

Hannah looks down at her arm, which seems to have got a lot dirtier since she sat down. She turns her forearm over to look at the pale underside, where there are now words written on her.

Gone back to lab. Sure you can handle it yourself. Yas x

It somehow hadn't occurred to her before, but her real body, sitting defenceless in the little room at Memory Lane, is open to all kinds of interference. She supposes that encourages Retrieval Assistants to get their work done ASAP.

Hannah decides this has gone on for long enough. Not the memory itself, but the fake hard exterior she's trying to portray. Obviously quite poorly.

'Okay,' she says. 'Cards on the sticky, greasy table. This is my first day at Memory Lane and you are my third client. The other two left their memories fairly quickly but, congrats, you're making this quite hard for me. As you can see, my memory buddy, Yasmin, has left me here to get you out myself. Either because she trusts me totally or she thinks you're a dick and that this isn't going to be easy and she's got better things to do. If you aren't planning on leaving, I'll need to go and tell her and my manager and her manager etc, and it'll be bad for us both. Or, let's just wrap this up and go. Either way, I'd appreciate you letting me know now rather than dragging this out any longer. For one thing, your sister is still sitting there alone, and even though I know this isn't real, I still feel sorry for her.'

Hannah turns to check Christina is still there. She is. And looking quite sulky. Christina notices her looking and flashes her the V's. Hannah turns back.

'Okay, feeling less sorry for her now.'

Ryan stretches out in the booth, reaching his arms out to rest on the wooden back. Hannah's sure he had a tattoo on his arm, lying in the bed in Memory Lane. He doesn't have it in here.

Outside, something passes by with sirens blaring. It reminds Hannah of the bit in *Big* where Tom Hanks is in the hotel room and he mutes the TV and the sirens are even louder outside. The gunshots too. It seems stereotypical. There are just as many sirens in Edinburgh where she stays in Gorgie. Probably a weird thing to be defensive about.

'Do you think I'm a dick, Hannah?' Ryan asks, doing a tiny, almost imperceptible toss of his blonde hair.

Hannah holds her real answer in her mouth and swallows it down.

'No,' she says. 'But I do think you're making my job more difficult than it needs to be.'

Though the music still plays and everything behind the counter still sizzles, she realises it's just the three of them in the place. Her, Ryan and Christina.

'Hey,' Marco shouts, from somewhere below the counter. 'Anybody need anything? You just let Little Marco know.'

Even without turning, Hannah can hear a slapping sound and knows it's Marco slapping at his belly.

'Ain't so little now, but back when I was younger I had washboard abs. And pecs. Yeah, I had pecs, I got pictures. Somewhere. This was before phones. Camera phones. I got 'em somewhere. In my attic or somethin.'

Hannah turns in her seat.

'Marco?' she says.

'Yes, my sweet Scottish princess.'

'Could I get a Dr Pepper please?'

'One Dr Pepper coming up for the beautiful young lady with the interesting haircut.'

He crouches down to retrieve her can from the fridge and Hannah looks back at Ryan.

'You've decided to stay?' he says.

'No, but I figure while we're waiting, I may as well see if the system can replicate the taste of Dr Pepper.'

'It certainly can't make it taste any worse.'

Marco arrives with a Dr Pepper and a napkin and calls her a beautiful Scottish princess once more before leaving them. Ryan pays him with a one dollar note as he goes.

'You're welcome,' he tells Hannah.

'Thank you,' she says. 'Wait, no. This doesn't count. That's not a real dollar and this isn't a real Dr Pepper, so this doesn't count as you buying me a drink.'

She opens the can, the metallic clunk echoing out through the restaurant, the fizz from the juice trying to jump out the can.

'Okay, that's fair. I'll just need to buy you a real Dr Pepper when we get back to Edinburgh.'

'I don't see that happening.'

'No? Why not?'

Hannah starts to feel hot. She's not sure if she can sweat in here or if she'll be sweating on the outside. If she does, she's planning on blaming the heat from the pizza oven. And it'll definitely be noticeable since she chose to wear grey, like an idiot.

'We're not allowed to date clients.'

'Woah there!' he laughs. 'Who said anything about dating? I just offered to buy you a Dr Pepper. I was suggesting a simple fizzy juice transaction and you're jumping to conclusions. Also, that is definitely a fake rule. It's your first day, there's no way they've already told you you can't date clients. Unless you've already tried it on with one of the first two clients you saw today.'

Hannah feels her insides shiver at the thought of going out to dinner with Mr Hill.

She sips at her Dr Pepper. It tastes of a kind of generic dark brown fizzy juice but not much else. This is Mr Douglas's memory and if he doesn't like Dr Pepper then she was never going to get anything tasty.

'Hannah, relax,' he tells her. 'I'm going to leave the memory in a few minutes. Believe me, I'm not rich enough to be able to afford the fines.'

'You're rich enough to be a client at Memory Lane.'

'Let's just say this is a one-off. As much of a one-off

as I'll ever have. So, forgive me for sneaking a few extra minutes. I'd appreciate it if you can sit here while I go and say goodbye to my sister?'

Again, this only confirms that Hannah has completely lost control of the staff-client relationship and Ryan is setting the agenda.

'Make it quick,' she tells him. 'Or I'll tell Yasmin.'

'Okie-dokie. I saw the way Yasmin punched that dough into submission.'

He slides out of his seat and walks down the aisle to the booth his sister is sitting in. Hannah has a quick peek over her shoulder to make sure he's not running out the door and into the dark New York night. If he did, she'd be absolutely, as her dad would say, rooked. Finding a runaway client in a New York memory must be up there with the needle-haystack thing.

Ryan sits down across from Christina and reaches out for her hands across the table. She hesitates at first before giving in and offering up her hands. She spots Hannah looking and Hannah turns back round.

Marco appears at her side again.

'You sure you don't wanna try a slice, Mary Queen of Scots?' he says. 'Dr Pepper's okay and all, but if you wake up in rainy Scotland a few years from now and realise you passed up the chance to taste the best pizza in New York City, you're gonna cry into your Cheerios. And Marco won't be there to wipe your tears away, I'll tell you that.'

Hannah laughs and runs a finger down her can. The condensation is wet against her fingertip.

'I'm good, thanks,' she tells him.

'It's your funeral, princess.'

When he walks away, Hannah turns to check up on Ryan again. She can only see his back, and it seems to be shaking. Across from him, Christina looks confused and

206

upset. He breaks his hands away from hers. Then he holds her face in his hands gently.

A few seconds later, he pulls his hands back completely and Little Marco's starts to fade away.

John – Stonecranning, 1975

When they put John into the memory, a lot of rules were agreed upon. More than agreed upon, they were drafted, printed and signed by all upper management at Memory Lane. Michael, Philippa, the board members.

No one was to enter the memory. That had mainly been adhered to, if the people John had spotted hanging around were really just people who had attended his wedding and not Memory Lane spies. Spies is probably too strong a word, but still.

If he did run into any trouble and needed to talk to a member of Memory Lane, he had a panic button hidden in his sporran, which would set off a purple alert. It was definitely in there, rattling about and clacking off his hip flask, but he had never used it. Most days went by without him even noticing it. If he were to press it, it had been agreed that only Michael or Philippa would enter the memory, no one else. But he wouldn't be needing that now.

And finally, the exit button. Every other client has their exit button appear on their hand. So they can't miss it. Also, so that there's more chance of them accidentally setting it off and saving the memory bouncers having to go in. He hadn't come up with the name 'memory bouncers', that was the early staffers after they first opened. Now they could barely keep bouncers. They would hire a bunch at a time and usually only one would last through the first week.

John's exit button isn't on his hand. It's at the top of the Roger Davidson Memorial clock tower. He had chosen it specially. It was meant to be symbolic. He couldn't rattle off a definition of symbolism off the top of his head but it seemed fairly symbolic to him.

The plan was: John would alter the final conversation with his dad. The memory would restart. John would walk up the high street, climb the stairs to the top of the tower and bask in the sun before pressing the exit button. It was meant to feel like a victory lap. Now it just feels like a stupid place to put an exit button and John is tired. He doesn't want to wait until tomorrow, though. He doesn't want to be in here any longer than he needs to be.

John walks along the side of the road, stepping into the muck and grass whenever a car passes. They toot from time to time. Even Scottish people get excited every now and then when they see a man in a kilt. And he's still relatively good-looking in here, he knows that. Although you could put a turnip in a kilt and it'd scrub up well.

Checking over his shoulder, John finds the coast still clear. No sign of any of the guests coming after him. No Agnes, no dad, no Ronnie. If there's one upside to all this, it's that he never has to ask Ronnie for a job ever again. His chest untightens a little.

John gets lost in his thoughts as he walks, but his feet don't, taking him into town and through the cobbled streets of Stonecranning town centre. The shops are shutting up for the day. The smell of bread and sweet pastry still wafts out of Matilda's Bakery at the bottom end of the high street. Men on their lonesome stand at the corner in-between Frank's Tavern and O'Neill's, checking their watches and smoking and pretending they aren't waiting on a woman who seems to have stood them up. Dingie Corner, they used to call it.

Turning the corner, John sees the clock tower. Behind it, the sun is almost out of sight, ducked down behind the clouds, like a candle fizzling out. The smoke from the community hall can still be seen too. Less black now, more of a dusty grey, but still noticeable enough to have a few shopworkers popping their heads out of doorways to get a look.

He overhears two women talking as he passes the chemist.

'My Davie phoned to say it's the community hall that's went up in flames. Three fire engines, three! And they're still having trouble getting it out.'

'What have I always said? That community hall was a fire waiting to happen. Didn't I always say that?'

'You did. You did always say that.'

'See. And look. Look what happens. Such a shame too, we had Davie's eighteenth in there.'

John walks down the middle of the high street, not having to worry about any cars chancing their luck at this time of night. He knows old Mr Ripley, the tower's caretaker, will be locking up soon and he'd rather get up there before he has to break in. Not that he would foresee any trouble on that front. The locks back in those days could be snapped a lot easier than the new-fangled ones.

The big oak doors at the front have already been closed over, so he goes to the side entrance. John used to help out just round the corner at Mr Brown's key cutting shop when he was younger. He'd steal a fag or two from Mr Brown's coat and rush round here at the end of his shift to smoke them in peace.

The gate at the side doesn't actually have a lock. It just closes with such force every time the wind blows that the metal door jams tight into the stone of the building and makes it tough to unstick. He kicks at it a few times and it comes loose. He looks down the lane to check no one has spotted him and goes into the small courtyard.

The stairs take him up inside the tower. From here he can get immediately on to the next set, which lead all the way to the roof. His thick black brogues make dull clumping sounds as much as he tries to tread lightly on the stairs.

This wasn't the way he'd planned it. To leave like this feels like skulking out. No one would know, of course. No one knew why he'd chosen this day to relive again and again. Not the real reason anyway. Michael and Philippa had just thought he was a romantic and he'd not dissuaded them of that. But things don't always go to plan.

John's around halfway up when he stops. He's sure he heard a noise. It might be his shoes or it might be his laces. He gives it a few seconds and the noise comes again. It definitely isn't coming from him. He's totally still.

It's a rumbling sound. Loud and getting louder. And soon it isn't just a sound but a feeling. A quaking from below John's feet which seems to move the floor.

The floor isn't moving, John tells himself. *That is definitely not possible.*

As if it hears him and wants to prove him wrong, the floor starts moving. And not just the floor. The walls are shaking and dust is falling on his head from the ceiling. In no time at all, the slight shake has gone to a full-on thunderous vibration.

Before John can decide on a reasonable explanation for this, something hard hits him on the head and he's on his way to the floor in a hurry.

Hannah – Edinburgh, 2019

She tries not to stare as Ryan, lying on the bed, wipes tears from his eyes.

Hannah decides she should say something but nothing's coming to mind. The confidence she managed to muster up inside the memory has been sapped from her. Maybe because it isn't real. She could pretend to be somebody else in there. Not a particularly good employee but confident enough to talk to Ryan like she wasn't completely socially awkward.

'I'm sorry I had to rush you out,' she says finally. 'I had to. It's my job.'

Ryan takes his headset off and hands it to Hannah.

'I'll save you some guilt, Hannah,' he says. 'I'm not crying because you kicked me out of the memory. There's more chance of me crying because of how hungry I am right now.'

'Are you just trying to make me feel better?' she says.

'As you may have realised, I'm a bit of a dick and I don't really go out of my way to make random people I've just met feel better. You're actually quite horrible at your job.'

'Thank you?'

Hannah unplugs the headsets and places them in the drawer. She thought wired headsets were a bit old-fashioned but Yasmin assured her that they're a lot safer and less prone to losing signal than the wireless ones they trialled a few years ago.

'Three months after the New York trip,' Ryan says.

212

'Christina was diagnosed with acute myeloid leukemia. People never knew what to say to me when they found out. I didn't need them to say anything, but they always thought they needed to say something. The worst was when they'd say, "She's a fighter, she'll get through it, she's a tough one, she'll fight it." She did chemo and everything but, eight months after that, she passed away. And every time I saw one of the people who told me she was a fighter, I wanted to scream in their faces. Like, I thought you said she was a fighter? I guess she just didn't fight hard enough, yeah? She should've fought a bit harder and she'd still be here, right? Fight against cancer. Fucking joke, honestly. You don't fight cancer. You don't storm the beach against cancer like some kind of Churchill wet dream. You duck and cover and hide and pray to God it lets you get out alive at the end. It didn't matter how much fight she had in her. She never got the chance to throw a punch.'

It feels like every tiny movement Hannah makes is deafening in the quiet of the room. The crinkle of the fabric of her trousers as she adjusts her sitting position. She doesn't want to be just like all those other people Ryan mentioned.

'I don't need you to tell me you're sorry for me or whatever,' Ryan says. 'I just thought you should know. Thanks for giving me a few extra minutes to say goodbye.'

He slides himself to a sitting position on the bed, his Nike trainers squeaking as they touch the floor. A slight waft of his aftershave hangs in the air.

'I realise I've made it pretty awkward now,' he says. 'Sorry.'

'No,' Hannah manages. 'No. I don't know what to say.'

'It's fine. Maybe I can buy you that Dr Pepper sometime? Since the memory one didn't count?'

'Yeah, maybe.'

Hannah shakes her head to dislodge the fog that's starting to cloud over her brain. It brings her back to the fact that she's still at work and this is still her first day and she has a job to do.

'Okay,' she says. 'One of my colleagues will be in in a minute. To give you the cool down debrief. Or something. I haven't memorised what it's called yet. I hope you enjoyed your experience with Memory Lane.'

The mouse feels clunky in her hand as she logs off the computer and makes her way to the door.

'Very professional,' Ryan says. 'You're management material, Hannah. No doubt about it.'

Hannah attempts one last smile then closes the door. The memory corridor is quiet, no bulbs flashing red. She licks her thumb and rubs it against the writing on her forearm but it won't budge. She'll need to thank Yasmin for that.

The lab is sitting in darkness when she goes back through. She walks across to her desk and the lights spring to life with her movement.

On her desk, a note in the same familiar writing that's scribbled on her arm.

Had to go, got pre-booked cinema tickets (Rocketman? My new guy picked it). I was meant to be doing the handover with the night shift but it's super quiet and there's no memories due to finish until after 9. You're good to head home after Mr Douglas is out (get his number?...) See you tomorrow I hope doll! – Yas :) xx

Ryan had been right. No one had told her about any rule against asking clients out on dates. But surely that's going to lead to some awkward encounters down the road, where you might find your boyfriend reliving a memory of some other girl? Would that be considered cheating? Virtually cheating? Memory cheating? If she was with someone with that kind of money, Hannah imagines she might let her morals loosen on that front. Not that she'd ever admit that to anyone.

She looks around the abandoned lab. Everyone's away home then. She checks the time in the corner of the screen. 5.37 p.m. How is that possible? She couldn't have been in Ryan's memory all that long. Time flies when you're stressing about fucking up your first day at work.

It wasn't exactly a huge achievement, but Hannah was glad to have completed Ryan's memory on her own. Completing something, whatever it is, with the training wheels off for the first time always makes her feel better. She remembers when her dad pressed a warm two pound coin into her hand and told her she could go to the shop on her own for the first time. She'd felt like her own person. She'd panicked and got him *The Guardian* instead of the *Daily Record*, mind you, but it was still a buzz.

Part of her is pleased to be left alone. She takes it as a badge of honour, that they consider her to be confident and capable enough to finish up and walk out without needing anyone holding her hand. She does hate that, after all, the first day babysitting. She's not sure if she needs to lock up anything, though. Surely not. Probably just log off the system and walk out. She's fairly sure she knows the way out. Past the big green door, back up the stairs, take a left, down the corridor, another left, past reception and out.

The thought occurs to her: if everyone is away home, who's going to finish up with Ryan?

The door to the memory corridor creaks as she opens it. She peeks through the gap. The doors are all still closed, no trouble to speak of. She goes back to the door Ryan was behind not so long ago and opens it.

215

The room is empty. So, she's not the only staff member in the place. She's relieved and goes back to her screen to log off.

As the screen buffers, Hannah starts thinking of generic office tasks she can tell her parents she did today. Telling the truth is already out of the question.

216

John – Stonecranning, 1975

'There's a person here! Maggie, there's a person here! Come and help! Quick now!'

John opens his eyes and sees only darkness. He feels pinned down, like the weight of the world is on him. He tries to move an arm, a leg, and finds he can't move from where he's lying. His breathing is loud, trapped within the tiny space he's in. The same dusty air going into his lungs again and again. There's a slight breeze on his hand and he realises it's the only part of him not trapped under anything.

'This one's too big, help me with it. You take that end. Here we go, one, two, three...'

A bit of relief and some of the pressure on him lifts. Everything's still dark though.

'Just you hold on, there. We'll have you out in a minute.'

'He'll be dead.'

'Don't say that, he might hear you.'

'He'll not be hearing anything if he's dead. That's a nice watch he's got. I wouldn't mind that for my Paddy.'

'Jesus, Maggie, let's check if the poor man's alive or not before you start pecking at him like a vulture.'

'Okay, okay, you're right.'

'And I saw the hand first anyway, so if anyone's getting the watch, it'll be me.'

Slowly, the pressure lessens on John's body. He remembers the clock tower shaking and the feeling of falling and now this. He's covered in debris from the tower, huge blocks of stone which should've crushed him to death, or at least very near death. But this isn't real life so he's survived with the kind of injuries he's seen people get on TV when things collapse. Like in one of those Christmas episodes of *Corrie* or *Eastenders* where something or other caves in and the character inside is covered in some light debris which can be easily shifted by another character. And you know if they're going to die in advance anyway, because you see it in all the TV magazines in October when they film it.

One at a time, huge slabs of stone are lifted off him. Streetlights pierce through the dark, the sun now disappeared completely. Once enough of the stone is shifted, the women come into John's view. The two women who were talking outside the chemist as he walked down the high street, ten minutes earlier. He thinks it's ten minutes, anyway.

'Oh, he's awake! Look, Maggie, he's alive. Hello there, are you alright?'

She's shouting despite being around a foot away from John, her face leaning in to get as close to his ear as possible.

There are a few different responses which come to John's mind.

Yes, even though about a tonne of stone has just completely crushed me, I'm tickety-boo.

Yes, although I do have a sudden urge to take my watch off and store it somewhere safer.

No, our bus broke down on the way to our wedding, then the hall went up in flames, then I had it confirmed beyond a doubt that the only way my dad would ever have been proud of me was if I'd been a completely different person.

Instead, he says, 'I've got a belter of a sore head.'

They remove the last few stones and bits and pieces of debris from him and take an arm each, raising him to his feet. One of them starts patting dust off him.

218

'Don't do that too hard, Maggie. He might have internal injuries.'

'Alice, are you joking? He's stood up fine. If he had internal injuries, he'd be writhing in pain. You're alright aren't you, son?'

Even with everything going on, it's still jarring to hear himself referred to as 'son'. So much so that he almost checks over his shoulder in case she's talking to some younger man who also got buried by rubble. He's older than these two women in the real world, by quite a few years. He can't lie, though, he does enjoy being fawned over in the way that only young men get fawned over by older women.

'I'm a bit shaken up,' he says, which is pretty much true. 'No writhing in pain though, so no internal injuries, I don't think.'

'Good. We were only kidding on about taking your watch, by the way. And if you think otherwise, then that's your problem.'

'Noted.'

The pair of them inspect his outfit.

'You been at a wedding?'

He looks down at his charcoal jacket, which has taken on new levels of authenticity.

'For a while now, aye.'

Now that they're satisfied he's free of internal injuries, they continue to pick through the rubble of the tower. Looking for other survivors, or other bodies to scavenge from.

'So, what was it?' he asks as the women, Alice and Maggie, carefully wade through the rubble.

'Earthquake,' Maggie says. 'Must've been. No other explanation for it.'

'In Scotland?' he asks.

'No other explanation for it.'

He has a look at the scene in front of him. The high street has survived well enough. Some windows are shattered and some chimneys have fallen into the middle of the road, but all the shops seem to have stayed on their feet.

'You sure a missile didn't hit or something?' he says. 'It looks like the tower was the only thing that collapsed.'

Maggie kneels down and moves a few rocks, finding nothing underneath.

'Hear that, Alice? A missile. Maybe he does have internal injuries. Inside his brain.'

Alice laughs as she tosses a brick over her shoulder. A few more people have joined the women now, going through the rubble. John assumes that whatever building they came from survived and now that they've got their own shops in order, they can move on to the process of finding survivors.

'A missile might be out of the ordinary, right enough,' John shouts to Maggie. 'But is it any more unlikely than an earthquake in Scotland?'

'Well, when was the last time we had an earthquake?' Alice asks.

'As far as I know, never,' John says.

'Exactly. D'ye not think we were due one?'

In the memory, John still has a full head of hair. It's thinning, for sure, but at least in here he can run an exasperated hand through it. It's not as satisfying running your hand over a bald head.

A middle-aged man, who has joined the search party, shouts at them.

'Would you lot shut up and just keep looking?' he says. 'Could be people under here.'

That's when John finally comes to his senses and

remembers why he was in the clock tower in the first place. He starts picking through the brick and stone faster.

'Excuse me everyone,' he shouts to the assembled half dozen people, his hands waving in the air. 'Excuse me. Thank you. Could I ask everyone to keep an eye out for a button?'

'A button?' Maggie says. 'You'll not find a button in amongst this.'

'Sorry, not like, a button off a jacket or anything. This'll be quite a big button. A big red button, about the size of my palm. The kind you'd see in a film if they were firing a missile and they had to set it off with a big red button.'

Alice shakes her head. 'Missiles again, is it? He's obsessed with missiles, everybody. He's hurt his head in the fall, don't take any notice of him. The ambulance can take him to the hospital when it arrives.'

The middle-aged man climbs over the rubble and jumps down next to John. His sturdy boots indicate that he's the type of man who gets up each morning and dresses like he might need to dig through rubble that day.

'They pulled you out from under all this, did they?' he says, trying to look in John's eyes, but struggling due to the lack of light. 'You better sit down, mate, or you'll do yourself more damage.'

'I don't think I will.'

The man rolls up his sleeves, which were already partially rolled up, and now they sit above his elbows, probably cutting off his circulation.

'This is for your own safety, son,' he says. 'Now go and sit down until help gets here or I'm going to punch your head in.'

'When you put it like that, I suppose a sit down does sound good.'

John climbs off the rubble and walks a little further

down the street, to where a bench still stands upright, and sits down on it. He could've fought the man, if he'd been in the mood. Obviously pain is dulled in here and he's not had a good fist fight in years.

He doesn't see himself finding the exit button, which is bigger than a coat button but a lot smaller than a brick, in this dim light before the memory ends. The new plan is to sit out the last few hours and when the memory restarts, he'll walk from the church to the clock tower.

So, John sits on the bench and waits and watches the aftermath of a Scottish earthquake. He has no idea what would happen if there was an earthquake in Scotland, so he knows what he's seeing playing out on this street is not a realistic depiction of what would happen afterwards.

He'd imagine some buildings would fall, some wouldn't. Some people would lend a hand to find survivors and clean up, some wouldn't.

Why did it happen, though? He's looking forward to finding out, when he leaves the memory and has a chance to dissect the post-memory code readout. The system was never meant for this level of repetition so it's not altogether surprising. John finds he's not too worried about it, as no other client is allowed to stay in the memory for anywhere near as long as this. He tries to work out the amount of hours he's been in here now but finds his brain can't do that kind of maths without a calculator.

The sky goes from black to an even deeper black. At one point, they can all hear sirens, but they don't stop and fade away into the night. The limited emergency services of Stonecranning must be stretched paper thin tonight, John thinks.

Maggie appears in front of him, scrapes and dirt and scratches mark her arms.

'Doesn't look like any help's coming tonight,' Maggie

says, slightly out of breath. 'Do you want us to see if we can phone anybody? The phone in the chemist's is still working.'

John leans over and pushes his socks down, letting the cool air into the sweaty hair that's been trapped under there.

'No,' he says. 'No, thank you. I'll be away soon.'

'You sure?' she says. 'That's nearly one now. You should get checked over.'

A strange fog hangs around his head. John assumes it's the system trying to replicate some of the after effects of what someone would go through following a building falling down on them. Except it doesn't feel like brain damage, or organ damage, more the feeling of walking through a cobweb and not being sure if you've managed to get it all off you.

'Wait,' he says. 'One? Did you say one? One in the morning?'

'It's not exactly going to be one in the afternoon, is it?'

'What's the time exactly?'

He turns his wrist and finds his watch broken. The hands are stuck at 8.32 p.m. He jumps off the bench and looks at Maggie's.

'Keep your hair on,' she says. 'Like I said, it's nearly one. Twelve fifty-three if you want to be all accurate about it. I'll see if somebody can take you home. Do you live local?'

12.53 a.m. John hasn't seen 12.53 a.m. in months. The memory ends at midnight. The memory always ends at midnight. The memory runs twelve hours, from midday to midnight. The ceremony had been at twelve, earlier than most people have it, because he and Agnes had agreed they wanted as much time at the reception as possible. The reception is the best bit, they'd agreed, so why wouldn't you want more of that?

223

The memory ends at midnight. He should be back in the church by now.

'It can't be nearly one,' he says. 'Your watch must be wrong. It must've broken in the earthquake.'

She grabs her arm back, rolling the sleeve of her jacket down so he can't get another look.

'Don't you be talking about my watch like that,' she says. 'This watch was a gift from my mother. This watch lived through the war. It's right.'

'It's wrong. Your bloody watch is wrong, you bloody… wrong watch-having idiot.'

'If that's the way you want to speak to me, I'll leave you here in the dark. Hope you freeze to death on that bench.'

She starts to walk away from him but he races past her, running around the outside of the rubble to her friend, Alice. They both look shattered. They're the only ones still here. The only ones still looking for people in what used to be the clock tower.

'Excuse me,' he says. 'Do you have the right time?'

From behind, he hears Maggie shout. 'Don't tell him the time, Alice! He's an ungrateful sod!'

Alice's hearing isn't as good as John's. She extends her arm so he can read her delicate silver watch. Her wrist is so thin even the tightest fastening leaves it dangling slightly. The watch reads 12.54 p.m.

'Are you going to let go now?' Alice asks.

He drops her wrist, which he didn't realise he was clinging on to, apologises and walks away from her. Away from all of it, up to the top of the street, where the Cranning Angels fountain is. Back in those days, the fountain was relatively new. Nowadays, it's crumbled and squalid-looking, the sculpted figures long since having lost their features to the elements. But here, it's a sign of a thriving high street, the water still working and dribbling over the ledges with a pleasing babble. It's survived the earthquake without a crack.

He perches on the edge of the fountain, feeling a light spray on the back of his jacket. To his left, Moira's café, where he used to buy his sausage rolls, sits empty, the broken glass of its window now scattered on the ground in front. In the distance, an alarm still sounds, but the café is silent and no one's come to claim it yet.

If it really is one o'clock in the morning, John thinks, then not only is the system making random, unbelievable things happen, it's also broken its code and extended the memory. Unless he finds the exit button within the rubble, he could be in here, without any control, for a long, long time.

John unclasps his sporran and reaches inside, digging to the bottom of the leather pouch. He nudges his wallet and hip flask out of the way and brings out his panic button. A purple alert, they call it on the system. He hopes Michael or Philippa are in the office, whatever time it is on the outside.

Hannah – Edinburgh, 2019

The lab is eerily quiet, but Hannah definitely heard general office sounds coming from somewhere: doors closing, printers printing, footsteps clicking.

The footsteps are clicking nearby, she realises. The lab doors swing open and Xander walks in, backpack slung over one shoulder.

'Hey, hey,' he says, chewing a piece of gum. 'You survived! Congratulations.'

She half spins on her chair and moves her mouse, to suggest she's still doing some form of work and not just nervous to leave without getting anyone's explicit permission first. Yasmin's note on a torn bit of pad paper doesn't seem official.

'Same to yourself,' Hannah says. 'So, we both made it. That "only one person survives" stuff must have been rubbish to scare us.'

'Hmm, maybe. But Andreas is gone.'

'What?'

'You didn't hear? He's...' Xander makes a confusing hand gesture in the air. 'Gone.'

'Like... quit? Or sacked?'

'I think he quit before he could be sacked. Joanna, that's my memory buddy, she's cool. Joanna says he got into a fight with a client in their memory over something, no one knows what, but when they came out, they carried on the fight in the client's room. Philippa got called down and split them up and Andreas just, like, walked out before she could sack him. Joanna says they'll need to give the client at least one free memory to stop them suing or whatever.'

'Wow.'

Hannah moves the mouse again, opens her documents, which are empty, only so she can close it again.

'You heading soon, yeah?' Xander asks.

'In two minutes, yeah. You?'

'Yep, just heading out the door. Dr Pepper? I thought better of you, Hannah.'

In a second, her heartbeat has gone through the roof.

'How do you know?' she says.

'Know what?'

'About me and Ryan.'

Xander holds his hands up. 'There's… a can of Dr Pepper sitting on your desk?'

Hannah looks to find the near empty can behind her monitor. She picked it up on her lunch break. She completely forgot. Lifting it up, she gauges there's at least a mouthful left inside.

'A drink of royalty,' she says, trying to casually play off bringing up a client out of nowhere.

'Whatever you say, Hannah,' Xander says, turning back to the doors. 'Good first day, anyway?'

'It was… something, yeah.'

'Ha, I know what you mean. See you in the morning?'

'Yeah, see you then.'

He gives her a little salute, moves the headphones from his neck to his ears and goes through the doors.

Once the doors have finished swinging, Hannah smiles to herself. Maybe Ryan got in her head more than she wants to admit.

She tosses back the last of her Dr Pepper in celebration. Not only did she get through the day, she outlasted Andreas, *and* she's the one who's stayed on latest. If someone's watching, and she has to believe someone's always watching in here, with all this equipment hanging around, then she hopes they're impressed.

The lid of the recycling bin swings back and forth as she deposits her can. Back at her desk, she goes to close the *Memorize* program. There's a new notification on the screen.

This one is a little different from the others she's seen today. For one, it's coming from room forty-one. As far as she's aware, there are only forty rooms. And this notification isn't amber or red. It's purple. Yasmin never told her what to do with purple warnings.

She looks around the lab to check there's no one else to pick this up. On the one hand, she can't imagine a place like this wouldn't have cover for any possible problem. They're making too much money to take chances. But, on the other hand, every place she's ever worked has scraped by, hiring as few people as possible and chancing their luck at every turn. Also, Yasmin bounced out of here without doing the night shift handover.

Hannah knows she could leave. She knows she s*hould* leave. It's not up to her to sort every problem. It's only her first day. But what if she comes in tomorrow and it was a royal fuck up and they know that she saw the notification?

In her head, she throws together a simple plan. Step one, she'll go and try to sort the problem herself. This will display determination, forward-thinking and seizing-the-day skills, *Dead Poets Society* style. If nothing else, she can use it as a competency answer in her next job application. Step two, if she can't fix it, she'll go and tell someone. Philippa, hopefully.

Just on the off chance, Hannah says aloud: 'Purple alert from room forty-one.'

228

She mainly says it for the benefit of the camera in the corner, which she worries will be checked after the fact.

Hannah stands and walks towards the memory corridor. This is all just classic worrying over nothing. A purple alert probably just means the computer needs a clean in that room or something. That's why it didn't provide any additional information on screen when she clicked to find out more.

She opens the memory corridor and goes inside. Her footsteps echo as she walks all the way to the end. The last two doors are thirty-nine and forty. Beyond them, the waiting area for the clients. Hannah nudges the door open to check if there's anyone in there. There isn't. For a silly moment, she thought Ryan might still be kicking about.

Okay, Hannah thinks, *I've done all I can do. Not my fault if they never told me about room forty-one.*

She gathers her bag and jacket, not putting it on until she sees how warm or cold it is outside. Edinburgh weather cannot be known, in her experience. Looking at the BBC weather site is as helpful as asking a magic eight ball.

The area through the doors, at the bottom of the steps, is a concrete echo chamber, like being in a shopping centre car park when no one else is around. That's when Hannah remembers about the room with the big green door.

One foot is already on the first step. She takes it off, then turns and walks towards the green door. On the doorframe surrounding it, at eye level, is a small golden circle, etched '*41*'.

'Fuck,' she says, wishing she hadn't come back to check.

She gets out her phone, annoyed she hadn't thought of this before, and messages Yasmin.

Hi Yasmin, really sorry to bother you, there's a purple alert coming from one of the rooms? Should I go and check it? – Hannah

It makes her feel a little silly, putting her name at the end of the message, but she can't be sure Yasmin's saved her as a contact. Yasmin's showing as online and starts typing seconds later.

Hey gal, no worries, it's still the trailers. Fuck! Sorry! Mr Douglas was the last dayshift client and only three rooms are in use right now, so I thought we'd be cool. Shit. Yeah, could you check it, please? It basically means the client needs a hand, but usually it's just a stupid question or they pressed the panic button by accident. Sorry to ask you to do it, but Philippa might literally kill me if she finds out I left early. Just pop into the memory and check they're okay, then leave. I'll be back in as soon as the film's done. Fuck. I owe you big time! xx
Hannah replies saying:
No worries!
when what she really wants to say is:
Lots of worries! I am filled to the brim with worries now! I do not wish to do you what appears to be a giant favour! But I don't seem to have much choice! I am terrified but even more terrified of forcing you to leave the cinema and come to my rescue! I am already acting like the company is more important than my own wellbeing! This is not how a business should operate!

But, of course, she doesn't say that. Because she wants Yasmin to think she's cool. That's why she doesn't mention room forty-one. She imagines Yasmin would need to leave the cinema and come in if she knew. Hannah just wants to keep everyone happy.

This is the kind of thing her dad goes on a tangent about when he's three beers deep. That the socially accepted working pattern and culture is fucked. It's ingrained in you that being a hard worker makes you a good person. But being a hard worker for a corporation warps your mindset so much you can never truly recover. She knows she doesn't owe Memory Lane anything. Yet, here she is. Standing outside room forty-one.

I could still walk away, she thinks, as she puts her hand on the door handle. *They'll sack me for this*, she thinks, as the door gives way. There goes her last hope. She had been certain it would be locked. There's a fancy security number pad next to the door and everything. *I'm definitely not supposed to be in here*, she thinks, as she sees what's inside.

A room, similar to the others in the memory corridor, but a lot more spacious. A larger bed, more luxurious chairs, brighter lights, a more up to date computer. And on the right side, some storage cupboards with glass doors. Behind the doors, a lot of tech: black boxes with little green and red lights. Hannah guesses this must be the central hub of the *Memorize* system. She'd wondered how such powerful technology could be running solely on a standard PC.

Thick black wires the width of ropes run round the room and disappear behind the computer next to the bed.

'Those are a tripping hazard,' Hannah says, not being able to stand the silence any longer.

And on the bed, an old man. This doesn't surprise her. As Yasmin stated earlier, behind most doors in Memory Lane is an old man reliving a memory from his youth.

Usually from before he had money but when he'd still been able to get it up in under five minutes.

Ms Reid comes to mind, an exception to the rule. Then again, Hannah's not exactly having a typical day by anyone's standards.

The man on the bed looks to be in his late seventies, maybe early eighties. Hannah finds men of this generation tend to look older, due to the years of drinking and smoking and not being as wise to the toll it would take on their bodies. Only a little hair remains around his ears.

Unlike anyone else she's seen today, he's wearing a pair of very comfy-looking pyjamas, and is under a duvet. The other beds in Memory Lane are more like the ones you lie on when you give blood, not the kind of thing you can relax on. This bed's different, though, and the man in it looks like he's here for the long haul.

That's when Hannah notices, along with his *Memorize* headset, he's also hooked up to an IV line, leading to a drip which stands next to the bed. Another clear tube is coming from under the duvet and snakes below the bed.

Why would he need all this? Hannah wonders. *How long has he been in here? Is he in a coma, maybe, and not reliving a memory at all?*

She pulls one of the chairs closer to the computer and logs in. A few clicks brings up *Memorize* and a few more after that shows her the stats for room forty-one.

Name: John Victor Valentine
Age: 72
Height: 5'10
Weight: 61.4 kg
Memory: N/A
Age (in memory): N/A

Well, first of all, Hannah's guess at his age was quite a bit off. He's either worked a lot or drunk a lot in his life.

The N/A's don't fill Hannah with a lot of confidence. It helps, knowing what kind of memory you're venturing into and this doesn't help her one bit. Maybe there's no memory being relived and there's nothing going on inside his head at all. But why the purple alert?

In the desk drawer, there are at least half a dozen headsets. These are newer. A more sleek design which fits on her head more comfortably than the others.

Hannah takes one last look back at the door, part of her hoping someone will come in at the last minute and tell her she doesn't need to do this. *Aw, Hannah, don't you worry about that, I'll take care of this, you pop off home. That was brilliant of you to attempt it, though, that's definitely a plus point for your mid-year report.*

But, of course, no one comes. Hannah selects the option to enter Mr Valentine's memory. It's all becoming familiar to her now. The darkness. The countdown.

5... 4...

Valentine, she thinks. Isn't that the CEO's surname?

3... 2... 1...

Philippa – Edinburgh, 2019

The to-do list on her desk has twelve items on it. Only three have been crossed off. Well, actually only two but as soon as she's off this call, she can cross out the third. Only, she doesn't know when this call will end. Or, if it ever will.

The phone display shows two hours and fifty-one minutes. Somehow, it feels longer to Philippa. She finds she's tuned out for a few moments and has to focus in on Mr McQueen's voice again.

'...but that's not why I chose that colour, you see, I chose it because Daniel, that's Donald's son from his first marriage, Daniel told me he hated blue. So, you can imagine, that was enough for me. So, we painted it blue, and let me tell you, Daniel was not happy about it. Because, Daniel, well, Daniel hated blue, I don't know if I mentioned that. Well, he did. Hated it. Hated the colour blue, so he did.'

She doesn't even know what he's talking about at this point. She just adds an 'oh right' and an 'I see' and a 'well, it is what it is' every now and again.

It's been around two hours and fifty minutes since she explained the situation to Mr McQueen. That he cannot relive that particular memory in the hotel anymore. That Memory Lane apologise profusely for the incident with Trevor. That there is a new policy to prevent this happening to anyone else in future. In return, Mr McQueen had, in her opinion, feigned outrage and explained to her in great detail why this was an outrage.

Now, two hours and fifty-three minutes later, he has

calmed down and realised that he has an audience for his stories who can't really hang up on him. Every time she's tried to end the call, the rage in his voice has appeared from nowhere once again, and only subsided once she asks him to continue with his stories. Philippa is a prisoner, like the audience at an open mic night who have just been told there are thirty performers and no intermission. And no bar and no toilets for that matter.

'...and so, as you can imagine, that made me very angry. I don't get angry easily, Ms De la Rosa, but that made me angry. And your new policy has made me angry too.'

Finally, she sees a potential point of wrapping up.

'Of course, Mr McQueen,' she says, sitting up in her chair. 'And that's why I extend our deepest apologies, from everyone here at Memory Lane. That includes Michael Valentine, our CEO.'

'Oh yes, and why isn't he phoning me right now?'

Because he doesn't have the guts, Mr McQueen. Because he's only in that position because his dad fucked off to live out a memory again and again, the very thing we're banning you from doing, and he never earned that position.

'He's a very busy man,' Philippa tells him. 'I will do my best to get him to visit you on your next visit. Assuming you will be coming back, Mr McQueen?'

There is silence on the line for a few moments.

'Will my next visit be... complimentary?'

Philippa smiles, relieved at being near the end of their dance.

'Complimentary? You've got brilliant blue eyes, Mr McQueen.'

'You know what I mean.'

'Yes, I do, and rest assured, I will arrange your next Mex to be courtesy of Memory Lane.'

'I should think so, since you're taking away the only

235

memory that I truly want to visit again. But, I suppose, if that's off the table, I shall just have to remember a few more highlights from my life.'

'I'm sure that won't be difficult,' Philippa says, already leaning forward to hang up the phone. 'I'll see you very soon, I'm sure, Mr McQueen. You have a pleasant evening.'

There's a grumble from the other end of the line which Philippa takes to be acceptance. She hangs up as quickly as she can, leaving the phone off the hook for a while in case he decides to call back.

Part of her can't believe it's still fucking Monday, but a much larger part of her thinks it makes total sense. Every day seems to last an eternity when your boss leaves all the hard grafting to you and you don't trust anyone below you to do it.

The time at the bottom of her screen shows 5.49 p.m. The other nine items on her list can be dealt with tomorrow. If she leaves now, she can be in her pyjamas in front of an episode of *New Girl* by seven, tired from one and a half glasses of white wine by half eight, and asleep on the couch by nine.

The first item on her list was inducting the new starts.

'Fuck,' she says to herself.

She was supposed to head down to the lab at half past five to check up on them and make sure they got out okay. Things must be fine, the girls from the lab were buddied up with them and it's nearly six. If there had been a problem, she would've been told by now.

If so, that means both Xander and Hannah are coming back tomorrow. A good return given the circumstances. Sure, that Andreas boy had to go, but at least he gave the office some entertainment while doing it. They don't have a water cooler, since everyone brings in their own, massive bottles of water from home, so gossip is in short supply. Fighting with a client inside the memory, what a way for Andreas to go. She'd put on her furious face when she'd gone down to the corridor but, thinking of it now, the client's face beetroot red and Andreas's ghostly pale, she can't help but find it very funny.

Putting the phone back on the hook, Philippa types in the number for the lab and lifts the receiver. It rings out. They've all gone home then, and Yasmin must be busy. Good. She can let her professional face slip. Even Cillian at the front desk will be gone by now, and Michael only came in for the meeting with the board members. She enjoys it when it's just her and the skeleton night shift in the facility. It's a little spooky, sure, but there's no niceties to keep up with empty corridors.

Before she logs off, Philippa has one last check of the *Memorize* home page to see if Yasmin is in with a client, and to make sure all the earlier client memories are complete. Every now and again, one of the lab girls forgets to close a case and then she gets a notification on her way home, forcing her to be the bad guy and pass it on to the night shift.

When she looks at the home page, there is, as she feared, an open alert in the system. It's coming from room forty-one.

Her pulse starts to race. There's never been a notification for Mr Valentine Senior since he went in. Why would there be? He said he'd come out when he was ready and that under no circumstances did he want anyone going in with him.

She clicks into the alert and reads the current status of the memory. A staff member, staff no. 488391, H. Greenfields, is currently inside the memory with Mr Valentine.

Philippa knocks her chair over she stands up so fast.

John – Stonecranning, 1975

At this time of night on the Stonecranning high street, John would've expected at least a few people passing. Stumbling out of the pubs that let them finish their pints, making the final journey to *Zanzi's*, the only nightclub that was open in his day. The clientele in *Zanzi's* on a Saturday night were really a sight to see. When a town only has the one nightclub, you're guaranteed a wild night with the locals.

The high street is deserted, though. The earthquake has done enough damage to force the drinkers home. John imagines more important buildings than the clock tower have fallen. Otherwise there would be some fire engines and ambulances here by now.

So, it's just him and his panic button. He pressed it a good ten minutes ago but no one's appeared. He presses it again, certain that it won't do any good. A purple alert should be coming up on someone's computer screen right now. Part of the agreement was that only Michael or Philippa could come in and get him. He's regretting that now.

It's while having this particular thought that he sees her. A young woman in smart attire, who is definitely not Philippa, appears on the high street from nowhere. She stands midway between the fountain where he's sitting and the collapsed pile of rubble which used to resemble a clock tower. Her hair looks ridiculous to John, shaved only on one side, as if she did a runner at the barbers halfway through the haircut. Has this become trendy since

238

he entered the memory? Maybe he's been in here longer than he thought.

The woman is clearly trying to get her bearings, confused by the mess. She walks towards the rubble to inspect it further. She climbs on to one of the larger pieces of brick to survey the scene.

John coughs, loud enough for her to hear. She turns, sees him, hops off her block and walks toward him.

'Hi there,' she says, tilting her head and waving her hand. 'Are you Mr Valentine?'

'I am,' he says. 'And you are?'

She reaches him and extends a hand, which he shakes.

'I'm Hannah,' she says. 'I'm a Retrieval Assistant at Memory Lane. Forgive me, this is not my usual thing, but I'll do my best to help out. Do you require some assistance?'

It's been a long time since John has met a new person. A new, *real* person that is. A person with truly original thoughts and feelings who will be alive again tomorrow with different original thoughts and feelings. Suddenly, even though they're in his memory, inside the company he created, he feels nervous.

'I'm John,' he tells her. 'Aye, I set off my panic button because… I'm sorry, what did you say your name was? My memory's terrible.'

'Hannah,' she smiles.

'Hannah, nice to meet you, Hannah. I hope you don't think I'm being rude, but is Philippa around? In the office?'

'I think she might be, yes. But I'm here now if there's anything I could help with?'

The girl's clearly confident, or at least confident at feigning confidence, but if she's a Retrieval Assistant, aka a bouncer, then she shouldn't have been the one to answer his purple alert.

'How come you're here?' he asks. 'Did no one else want to do it? Scary old John Valentine behind the big green door. I can imagine what people say. Did Philippa send you in?'

Hannah shakes her head, unable to speak. She stutters and stammers. John feels quite bad about this.

'I, no,' she says. 'No, I, there was no one, so, I thought, I'd see... this is my first day at Memory Lane, sorry. Mr Valentine, can I ask why you're not in the memory corridor with the other clients? Are you special? Should I not be here?'

At last, something that makes sense. This new start hasn't been told who John is yet. That's why she's come in, thinking she can help him.

He considers for a moment not telling her. Pretending to be just another client. He could certainly have a bit of fun with that. But he reminds himself that she's real and has real feelings and he doesn't get any do-over's with real people.

'My name is John Valentine,' he says. 'I am the creator of *Memorize* technology, founder of Memory Lane, and I have been reliving a memory here for quite some time now. I get what could reasonably be described as special treatment. Which realistically amounts to getting my own room, away from the memory corridor.'

'Oh. Fuck.'

Hannah smiles and John does too. In an instant her professional façade disappears, replaced by one that is part shocked, part amused, and part not really sure what to do. This is more John's kind of speed. Business culture never appealed to him. *Let's fast-track this, yeah? We're gonna need to do a deep dive on this. I've got a nugget of an idea that I've been kicking around the idea park.* Load of old bollocks to him.

240

'Sorry,' Hannah says. 'For swearing. Wow, sorry, it's just... wow. I really shouldn't have come in here, right? I'm going to be in big trouble, aren't I?'

'I wouldn't say so,' John says. 'You took the initiative. I like to see that.'

When he talks to her, John finds that he's just so happy to have a real conversation again that he's not in a rush to leave the memory anymore. He can't forget he's not in the real world, though, the setting is too strange. An empty high street in the middle of the night while surrounded by rubble and glass. There was even an aftershock after he pressed the panic button.

'I would actually be kind of relieved,' Hannah says. 'If I was in trouble. Like, if I knew I was getting sacked. There would be a weight off my shoulders.'

'Not a fan of working here then?'

'It's been one day and I feel absolutely knackered. Like, mentally. I've been to New York and back and my head feels that way too.' Then she seems to remember that it's John's company she's talking about. 'But, obviously, I'd love to stay. Work my way up. In five years time, I could see myself here.'

John pats the edge of the fountain, inviting her to sit down with him. She does.

'No offence,' Hannah says. 'But this is a weird memory to revisit. Is this, like, during the war?'

A laugh breaks from John, followed by a bout of more laughter he can't stop. Hannah joins in too, realising she must've said something funny but not quite sure what it is. He hasn't laughed spontaneously in so long.

He wipes a tear from his eye. 'Thank you for that, Hannah.'

'I'm guessing this *isn't* during the war.'

'No, no it's not. I'm old but I'm not *that* old.' He snorts again, the laughter still bubbling in his chest. 'During the war, aw, that's tickled me. No, Hannah, this is actually my wedding day.'

Hannah casts a glance around, looking over her shoulder at the shards of glass peppering the cobbles, then back ahead at the huge pile of ex-clock tower.

'Would it be a bad time for me to make a Bridezilla joke?' she says.

'Never a bad time for that.'

'So, your wedding went… badly then?'

'You could say that.'

'It looks like a bomb went off.'

John can't deny, despite him being old enough to be her grandad, he's enjoying chatting with Hannah. She's bright and he's glad Memory Lane's hiring policy hasn't gone to pot since he's been away. She isn't who he needs right now, but she can bring Philippa to him soon. For the time being, he's just happy for someone to listen to him and someone he can listen to in return.

'My wedding day went fairly well, actually,' he tells her. 'We married in the Stonecranning Trinity Church. Beautiful building.'

Next to him, Hannah shifts her body, trying to get more comfortable on the edge of the fountain.

'That's nice,' she says. 'I can't say I'm all that religious, myself. I take it you are?'

'I used to be.'

'Did something happen?'

'Time went by, I suppose. Whenever you hear about someone losing their faith, it's always depicted, y'know, that some great dramatic event or occurrence happened to them. Something that totally shook their world view and meant they could no longer believe in an all-powerful God who could be in charge of,' he gestures around, 'all

242

this, allowing all the evils of the world to unfold without intervening. But most people, I think, lose their faith the same way they lose their... keys, their wallet, their glasses. They just do. One day you have it, then one day you wake up and hey, you don't.'

Sometimes John finds he can convey his deepest thoughts and feelings much easier when he doesn't know the person he's talking to.

'Two days after the wedding,' he says. 'My dad passed away.'

Hannah leaves the appropriate, respectful silence of a few seconds or so.

'I'm sorry,' she says.

'Thanks. It was over forty years ago so you'd think I'd have got over it by now, to be honest. On the day, I had to ask my new father-in-law for a job. Well, I suppose I didn't *have* to but I wanted a better job so I could make more money and give my wife Agnes the life she deserved. She deserved more than what we had and I was already twenty-eight, which was old to be getting married in those days. I felt like if I didn't get my finger out, she'd only leave me a few years later. So, I asked Ronnie for a job and he gave me one. Twenty years later I made the breakthrough on *Memorize*, fifteen years after that, Memory Lane started taking on its first clients. People never saw that coming, I'll tell you that. I never even studied at uni. Everyone had their own idea of me. I liked proving them wrong. Don't ever be just other people's idea of you, Hannah.'

Hannah nods, and John hopes she stores that bit of advice in her mind for future use.

'But, Mr Valentine, at least your dad got to see you get married?'

'That's true, you're right. I told him that night, "Dad, I've taken a job with Ronnie." The look... the look in his

243

eye. I've never forgotten it. And now I've lived through it again and again and seen that look more times than I ever wanted. Nothing ever changes.'

Another batch of emergency services pass by on a road somewhere, unseen. Their sirens strangle the air then fade into nothing a few seconds later.

'Sorry, Hannah, I'm talking your ear off and you probably just want to get home after your first day. And please, call me John. Mr Valentine is my son.'

Hannah crosses one leg over the other, her shoes slightly wet from the fountain's mist.

'No, it's alright,' she says. 'You can keep telling me about it if you like.'

Hannah – Stonecranning, 1975

Does she really want to hear more about this man and his relationship with his dad? Is she listening because she cares or because she's just trying to be nice? Would she be doing this for a random person on the street or is it just because this man is wealthy and successful and that holds more value in her mind? Hannah's not sure of anything. Other than the fact that if Mr Valentine Senior is telling her all this, five minutes after meeting her, he's clearly been bursting to tell someone for years.

Hannah reminds herself to call him John.

'I don't have a lot of regrets in life,' John continues. 'But my dad passing away while he was still angry with me, that's one that I can't forget. I just… I just wanted him to say he was proud of me. Everyone else's parents seemed to say it. I had heard them. Hell, these days, it's all over Facebook, people's parents posting photos of their kids and saying, "Look at my boy, look what he's done, look how proud he's made me." None of that in my day. You had to say it to a person's face for them to know it. I started thinking, why don't I deserve that?'

Hannah wonders how long he's been in here. He mentioned he's relived this memory again and again. That could mean anything. What kind of toll can that take on someone's mind, being stuck in a loop constantly? She thinks about making a *Groundhog Day* comment but he's probably heard it all before. Then she wonders what kind of toll wearing a kilt every day can take on someone's mind.

'You know,' she says. 'Just because you don't say something, doesn't mean you don't feel it.'

'I know that, but I wanted to hear it. Call me selfish, but I wanted to hear the words. I wanted him to say it and mean it. And I needed it to be real. I needed him to know I was taking the job with Ronnie and still say it. I haven't worked out how to raise the dead yet, so reliving this day is the only other logical option.'

Hannah lets out a polite laugh, as she assumes he's joking about the raising the dead thing. She doesn't think they share the same definition of the word 'logical'.

'I know you think I'm off my head and that's okay, Hannah.'

Her mouth opens to deny this, but once she hesitates, the moment is gone.

'You ever notice that people with a lot of money always turn out to be eccentric?' John goes on. 'That's what I used to think. These billionaires lose their marbles once they have enough money. Because the way the world is, you grow up and you're presented with one life to live and seemingly two goals: live as long as possible and gather as much money as possible while you're doing it. And then, for the few of us who manage it, who reach that pot of gold, there's not much else to do. It's like you've completed life, like it's a video game. When money's no longer an issue, your brain has nothing to do but search back in your memory and find all the things that happened in the past that you'd choose to change. That's your new goal. Fixing all the things that went wrong before you had money. Probably why so many rich men my age are going out with women in their twenties.'

Hannah inches ever so slightly away from him on the fountain, hoping he doesn't notice. It was a silly comment she made about this memory being during the war, she

246

knows that, but he hasn't explained why half the street has collapsed yet and she'd really like to know.

'It shouldn't exactly shock me,' he says. 'But I couldn't make him say it. The only time he told me he was proud of me was after I literally saved someone from a burning building and even then, when I told him I was going to work for Ronnie, he took it back.'

'This is probably the wrong thing to say,' Hannah says. 'But… you saved someone from a burning building?'

'Strange things have been happening in the memory today. Yesterday now, I suppose. The earthquake was the cherry on top.'

Hannah nods and is glad she's been offered up some kind of explanation for the semi-destroyed street in front of her. For a minute there, she actually thought John was quite the badass, reliving a day where a whole street gets destroyed is an extremely tough guy, Jason Statham thing to do. Reliving his wedding day, not so much.

She feels uneasy in this memory. It feels different to the others she's been in today. She's very aware that her real body is sitting in Memory Lane, in a room she was told not to go into. It doesn't feel safe.

'Why did you press your panic button?' she asks.

John still holds it in his hand, turning it over in his fingers.

'In the early days of Memory Lane,' he says. 'We used to give clients both buttons at the start of the memory. One panic button, one exit button. But we soon found people would conveniently press the "wrong" button and demand we restart the memory or give them a refund. We spent a long time updating the coding so the exit button would only appear once the twelve hours were up. Not only that, we put it right there.' He points to his hand. 'Right on the palm so they couldn't lose it.'

Hannah had always thought she would write a book someday. She'd never attempted one, or had a decent idea for one, but it was always there in the back of her mind. It couldn't be that hard if celebrities could do it. Now, listening to this, she's sure she's got her bestseller. Getting John's permission shouldn't be too hard.

'But when they put me in,' John says. 'We designed code specially for me. Running the memory over and over again puts a strain on the system, so we took out some things. For one, we got rid of the exit button on my hand. I wasn't planning on leaving for a while, anyway. Looking back now, I was too theatrical for my own good, but I asked them to put my exit button at the top of the clock tower in the town centre. That way, when it was time to leave, I could do a little lap of honour. Walk to the top of a tower. It was meant to be symbolic.'

'It sounds pretty symbolic to me,' Hannah says. 'Sounds very cool.'

'Only problem is when the tower collapses and you can't find your exit button. The system is clearly bored with repeating the same memory over and over. It's throwing up all kinds of events. You won't believe me, Hannah, but I think it might be writing its own code. Oh, and the memory isn't restarting so I'm stuck here, looking through the rubble for my exit button until we can restart the memory.'

At home, Hannah can picture the scene. Her mum back from work. Her dad wanting to sit down to dinner. Her mum insisting they can't start until Hannah's home. They're going to be waiting a while.

'I know nothing about computing and coding and all that,' she says. 'In fact, I made a Tumblr in high school and wrote one post about *Buffy* then lost my password and couldn't get back into my account ever again.'

John puts his panic button back into his sporran,

swapping it for a hip flask and taking a sip. He offers it to Hannah, but she turns it down. She's already tasted fake Dr Pepper today, she can't imagine fake whisky would be her cup of tea.

'Don't you have to have some coding experience to get a job at Memory Lane?' John asks.

'I may have... exaggerated on my application form. Anyway, moving swiftly along. I don't know about coding, but can't you just recode the program or something so the exit button appears on your hand?'

John shakes his head.

'Not possible. We can't make any changes to the code while the memory is still in session. We can, however, restart the memory to take us back to the start. When the clock tower is still standing. Which in my case is midday at the church.'

'That seems...' she decides to finish the sentence now that she's started it, hoping she's not going to jinx anything. 'Easy enough?'

John laughs again. Hannah doesn't think of herself as a funny person normally. Yasmin, she's pretty funny. But John seems tickled by her honesty.

'I like you, Hannah,' he says. 'Tell me something, where's your favourite spot in Edinburgh?'

'My favourite...?'

'Spot. You know, your favourite place to go and sit and have a sandwich or an alcopop or whatever.'

Now it's Hannah's turn to laugh at his use of the word 'alcopop'. She wonders if he's been in here since 2004. It's funny to hear such old man language coming from the lips of the man in front of her, who, in this memory, is only a few years older than her. He was even quite handsome in his day. Not that that erases the image of him lying in the bed in Memory Lane from her mind.

'Probably up Calton Hill,' she tells him. 'I know that's really obvious and it's mobbed most of the time up there, but... I like it. It's peaceful.'

'I like it up there too. I've not been anywhere real in a while, you see. I've been keeping a mental list of the places I want to visit once I get out of here.'

It's at this moment that Hannah hears footsteps on the street. A pair of heels, at least four inches, like gunshots, bouncing off the buildings like a rubber ball. They're coming closer.

On the street, a shadowy figure approaches. They walk under a streetlight and Hannah sees their face.

'Sorry I'm late, Mr Valentine,' Philippa says.

Philippa – Stonecranning, 1975

There had been a tiny bit of hope still inside her that the new girl, Hannah, hadn't found Mr Valentine Senior yet. That dissolved when she saw them sitting together on the edge of the fountain like the poster for an unlikely buddy cop dramedy.

Philippa apologises again as she steps around huge chunks of stone, strewn across the pavement. She would have been better taking off her shoes before she entered the memory but arriving barefoot isn't exactly professional. Then again, she'd thought she'd be stepping into a wedding reception, not a bombsite. This might explain the purple alert.

'That's alright, Philippa,' Mr Valentine says. 'I've just been talking the ear off Hannah here. Forgive me, Hannah, when you've not spoken to a real person in a while...'

The girl, Hannah, waves a hand as if to convey that she enjoyed his chat. Philippa isn't so sure.

'It was my pleasure,' she says. 'For the man who founded Memory Lane, anything.'

Hannah makes eye contact with Philippa after this comment. As if to say 'look, the big boss likes me, so you don't get to be angry at me'. Philippa is aware of two things Hannah probably hasn't given much thought to.

One, that Mr Valentine, although still a special client, no longer has any stake or say in the running of Memory Lane. So, if Philippa wanted to sack her, it would be done before she could say 'help me, John Valentine, you're my only hope'.

Two, that she's not actually annoyed at her for entering the memory without permission. The purple alert must've gone up at the worst possible time. The small period between the day shift and night shift, where only one staff member is there for the handover. Except Yasmin clearly decided she didn't fancy it tonight. If there's anyone that's up for the chop, it's Yasmin. Her and that ridiculous green hair of hers. She does still want to know where she got that top she was wearing today, though.

'You can relax, Hannah,' Philippa says. 'I appreciate you taking the initiative and coming in to help Mr Valentine. That shouldn't have been your responsibility and I appreciate it. We'll make sure you're recognised for going above and beyond. A Boots voucher or something.'

Mr Valentine nods. 'Taking the initiative,' he says. 'That's just what I said.'

'Exactly. But I can take it from here, Hannah, so you can exit the memory and get off home. We'll see you in the morning.'

Hannah does a reasonable job of trying to hide the sheer delight that creeps on to her face at this, forcing it away with a tightening of her mouth.

'Oh,' she says. 'Well, if you're sure.'

'Actually, I wouldn't mind if Hannah stayed,' Mr Valentine says. 'I'd like to keep as many friendly faces around as possible. If that's okay with you, Hannah?'

Mr Valentine isn't going to make this any easier for Philippa, she senses that. She'd much rather deal with him away from prying eyes, especially a new start like Hannah. No one's had any contact with Mr Valentine in months and this isn't how any of them had planned it. He has a reputation for being quite eccentric, although that was mainly as a result of his choice to relive his wedding day on a loop.

'I suppose,' Hannah says. 'If you'd like me to stay...'

Philippa feels sorry for the girl now. She'd shown her the light at the end of the tunnel and now Mr Valentine has extended the tunnel to Australia.

'I'm sure Hannah wouldn't want to...' Philippa tries, before being cut off.

'Nonsense,' Mr Valentine says. 'Good. So, it's the three of us then.'

Philippa and Hannah nod, neither of them happy with the situation. She then walks closer and stands in front of them, keeping her distance from the fountain. When she was around seven years old, she'd nearly drowned when her mum took her to Portobello beach and ever since, she's maintained a respectful fear of water. Even those big baths Instagram influencers have freak her out a bit.

'Right, let's catch you up, then,' Mr Valentine says. 'Firstly, I'm ready to leave the memory.'

She and Michael had known this day would come, but she hadn't really imagined what the circumstances would be. It's at this point that she puts the pieces together. Mr Valentine's exit button was at the top of the clock tower, which is now scattered around her feet. When Mr Valentine had insisted it should be coded up there, she'd voiced her concerns, but was shot down. If she was remembering correctly, her 'concerns' were voiced in a fairly robust email exchange with Michael, where the words' fucking', 'stupid' and 'bastard' were used liberally.

'That's great news, Mr Valentine,' she says. 'And I'm guessing we're here because... there's some sort of problem?'

'Clever cookie, you are, Philippa, I've always said that. Aye, it appears the technology has... and I'm not trying to be dramatic here... gone rogue. Off the wall. Lost its marbles.'

Where possible, Philippa likes to have a plan in advance when doing anything work related. A notepad is usually involved. A list of tasks that she can cross off with a satisfying straight line is definitely on the agenda.

Winging it is not in her wheelhouse. Now she's been thrown into Mr Valentine's memory with no time to prepare. He's aware of the technology going wonky. The technology *he* invented. Mr McQueen's dull voice is still ringing in her ears. Mr Valentine can't possibly know that he's not the only client suffering these memory glitches.

'Lost its marbles?' she says, trying neither to confirm she's aware of this kind of thing nor that it's entirely a surprise to her. Cold and mechanical is what she's going for. It should work, she's been sculpting her personality around these traits since her early twenties.

'Yes, Philippa,' Mr Valentine says. 'You might've noticed you are not currently at my wedding reception.'

'I had an inkling. What happened?'

'To start, my wife had second thoughts about being my wife,' he says, standing up from the fountain and stretching his legs. 'I could understand that, what with repeating the memory so many times. Stands to reason, one out of a thousand times, she would get cold feet. But then the bus broke down. Then my best man punched me for no reason. I don't want to hear any jokes about that.

'Then the hall went up in flames. Then there was the earthquake. These aren't slight differences, I'm sure you'll agree. I think there is a bug in the system. A giant one. Like Australia-big. Not, y'know, the size of Australia. I mean the bugs they get in Australia.'

Philippa knew the kind of bugs he was on about. Every now and again, just when she was sick to the back teeth of Scottish weather, someone from Australia would upload a video of the Jack Russell-sized scuttling guest in the corner of their bathroom, and suddenly every cold morning seemed like a defence against these things she wouldn't ever want to trade.

'Well,' Philippa says. 'We can start debugging the program as soon as you're out, Mr Valentine.'

For the time being, Philippa's decided to play dumb. She's worked out that he must not be able to find his exit button, but she wants him to admit it. She deserves to have some fun at work, doesn't she?

'Would you like to leave the memory then?' Philippa asks. 'If you give me a little bit of time before you hit your exit button, I can get the room set up and call Nurse Ashton in so she's there waiting to give you the once over.'

The girl Hannah looks lost. There's writing on her arm, but Philippa's too far away and it's too dark to make out what it says. It's not exactly a professional look in front of the clients, but since it's her first day, she can overlook it. It might have been Yasmin now she thinks about it. That girl was always writing on people.

'I appreciate that,' Mr Valentine says. 'But, and you're going to laugh, Philippa, but you know how I asked for the exit button to be placed at the top of the clock tower?'

'I do.'

'And remember how you said that was a silly thing to do?'

'I do.'

'That I was letting my love of symbolism cloud my judgement?'

'Yep.'

'And that it would be a much safer bet to include a backup exit strategy in case I couldn't get to the top of the tower?'

'It's all coming back to me now, sir.'

Mr Valentine stops pacing and puts his hands out, as if to display his regret.

'You were right,' he says. 'The button is lost among the rubble. I could be here weeks looking for it. Hell, when the fire brigade eventually arrives, they could take it away with them. I need you to restart the memory for me.'

'And the plan is?'

'I'll leave the wedding and go straight to the exit button. I'll be out ten minutes after you restart the memory. I can get checked over, then we'll need to look into what's going wrong with *Memorize*.'

Before they had allowed him to go into this memory, Memory Lane made Mr Valentine sign a lot of forms. Everything you could possibly imagine was accounted for, including him dying while reliving the memory.

They knew he would come back out one day, and Michael and the board members had planned for this. He had no rights at all. No authority over any part of Memory Lane or its products. If they're going to try and locate this bug in the system, he's not going to have any part in it. She's not sure if he's forgotten or whether he assumes his son will let him walk back into the hierarchy of the company. Their relationship, like every other father-son relationship she had ever seen up close, was not straightforward.

'Okay,' she says, still not enjoying the feeling of winging it. 'I'll restart the memory from the beginning. You'll appear back at the church at midday.'

There were so many clients who had passed through their doors, that after she had experienced the first few memories, they had all started to blend into each other. Not Mr Valentine's though, as they'd had to study every aspect of it before they'd put him in. The church, the photos outside, the bus to the hall, the speeches, the dancing, asking his wife's father for the job which would eventually lead to all this being possible. Everything but the last half hour of the memory, which was completely restricted. They all assumed it was due to it having a sexual element but that had never been confirmed.

While John's not looking, Philippa gestures at Hannah to stand up, which she does.

'Hannah,' Philippa says. 'You come back out with me and help me set things up?'

Now that he's paying attention again, John looks less than happy about this suggestion.

'I'd like you to stay, actually,' he says, turning and appealing directly to Hannah. 'Some company would be nice. Real company.'

'It's only ten minutes, Mr Valentine,' Philippa says.

He turns to look at her. 'Exactly,' he says. 'It'll only be ten minutes.'

They would appear, to anyone else joining the memory at this minute, to be a newly divorced couple arguing over who gets to take their daughter to Edinburgh Castle.

Hannah folds her arms then unfolds them. 'Honestly,' she says. 'I'm happy to stay. I mean, I'm looking at it from the selfish point of view in that this might... look good on my next progress report.'

Mr Valentine chuckles and pats her on the shoulder. 'Right you are, Hannah,' he says. 'Okay, Philippa, if you pop out and restart it for us. Everything going to plan, we'll see you in ten. But, just in case, wait by the computer and if you happen to get another purple alert from me, do us a favour and restart the memory?'

Philippa pulls down the bottom of her jacket and smooths out the material. She would rather not contact Michael about this until his dad's safely out of the memory.

'Of course,' she says. 'I'll see you in ten. *Memorize, exit memory.*'

The dark street before her fades to black, Hannah and Mr Valentine left behind. Slowly, the real world comes back into view, appearing in a soft, creamy glow until everything is in sharp focus.

Philippa – Edinburgh, 2019

On the bed lies Mr Valentine, aged forty-plus years in mere seconds. Beside her, Hannah sits, slumped in her chair, eyes closed, headset sitting askew. At the girl's feet, her bag and jacket. She was so close to getting out the door. Philippa knows the feeling.

She stands and goes to the door, opening it to check no one is standing outside. She hears clangs and bangs from the lockers, the signal that the nightshift has arrived. Closing the door, she slides the bolt into the latch. When this is all over, she'll need to find out how Hannah even managed to get into the room to begin with. There's no way she could've known the code for the lock.

Signing into the computer, Philippa opens *Memorize*. Mr Valentine's memory details and stats pulse on the screen before her. No changes can be made to the code during the memory, for safety reasons that were decided years back. The human mind is delicate, and even though a client can think they're consenting to a change in their memory, their subconscious can have other ideas. However, restarting the memory is safe.

One thing neither she or Mr Valentine brought up was the fact that, if things are going wrong in his memory, why should they stop just because they're going to restart it? Surely that just gives the bug in the system a blank page with which to bring about all sorts of trouble. Then again, an earthquake isn't exactly small fry.

Philippa shrugs off these worries. She would rather Hannah wasn't in there too, but really, the side effects can only happen to the client. And Mr Valentine already signed all his rights away.

She presses the button to restart the memory. Then she waits.

John – Stonecranning, 1975

Ever since *Memorize* had started making him vast amounts of money, it was hard for John to tell if someone was bored with one of his stories. It's been a long time since someone yawned while he was talking or told him he was talking nonsense. No one ever wants to upset him, which, when he thinks about it, upsets him. Even when he speaks to staff in shops, who don't know him from Adam, they're still nice to him because he's a paying customer and the customer is always right. That saying was clearly created by someone just to crush the soul of shop workers the world over.

So he's not entirely sure if Hannah is enjoying his story or not.

'I was typing away,' he tells her. 'And every time I wrote 'memorise', I was getting this squiggly little red line underneath. My son, Michael, he told me it kept coming up because the word thingy I was using was American, and it saw 'memorise', with an s, as the wrong spelling. It wanted it to have a z. I added the z in, and my squiggly red line problem went away. So, I thought, okay, why don't I keep it like that. We'll call it *Memorize*, with a z. And the other reason was that we thought it would sound American to investors and clients. You know, maybe not now, but back then, if tech was made in America, that got people excited. That was exotic if you lived in the UK. Anyway, I can't remember if you asked or not, but that's why it's spelled with a z.'

He's been walking while he's been talking, not even

261

realising it. Hannah is over by the fountain still, whereas he's got broken glass on the bottoms of his shoes because he veered off track without thinking about it. Still no one's come to claim Moira's café. Its scones have been dropped, literally, and lie on the floor like chalky paperweights.

'That's a good story,' Hannah tells him. 'Makes sense.'

'Hannah, you can tell me if it's a bad story, you know.'

'I…'

'Everyone kisses my arse around here,' he says. 'Well, not in here, but out there. I can't walk down a corridor in Memory Lane without someone wanting to get me some half caff Frappuccino thingy. Or, the actual workers going out of their way to avoid me. As if I'll sack them if they look at me the wrong way. Which I'm not ruling out, by the way.'

'Okay,' Hannah says. 'If it makes you feel better, I'll say this: you are an old white man who has lived a long and successful life, eventually becoming filthy rich. And your main complaint seems to be that people are… too nice to you? Or too respectful of you? Do you realise how that sounds?'

'Well, I suppose I do now.'

'Also, your story about the Z in *Memorize* was… just okay.'

'Really?'

'It was worse than that, actually. It didn't really have an ending or anything. Hard to call it a story, really. It was just a paragraph. It felt like a footnote on an actual story.'

John scrapes his shoes over the cobbles, seeing the tiny shards of glass fall from his sole and scatter on the black street.

'That is so nice of you to say, Hannah.'

'What can I say, I like to please.'

She pats out a little tune on her thighs.

'Philippa's restarting the memory, yeah?' she asks.

'She is.'

'She's taking her time, no?'

'It'll be any minute now. Any minute… now. Ah, thought that might work. Any mi–'

John's vision blurs and darkens and in a few seconds everything's black. He sees the countdown timer ahead of him.

5… 4… 3… 2… 1…

The new scene appears, getting brighter and brighter. John's been on the high street in the dark for so long, he has to squint to get used to the sudden daylight flooding into the church.

Agnes walks down the aisle, her arm linked with Ronnie. At his side, Gary is in his usual position, whispering about Ronnie having an erection.

The only thing that's different about the scene is Hannah, standing over on the right, in the aisle by the windows. She's dressed smartly enough, so doesn't draw any attention. Not yet anyway, but when people notice her haircut, there are bound to be stares.

He waves at her and she waves back, then he points at the door, hoping she'll understand that he'll meet her outside. She seems to get it, turning and making her way to the back of the church.

Agnes unlinks her arm from Ronnie and he kisses her on the cheek. As he passes John, he gives him the usual look. John lifts the delicate veil from his bride's face.

'I thought we agreed you were going to shave that,' Agnes says, raising a finger to his moustache.

He reaches up and holds her finger, then her whole hand, against his cheek.

'What's up, John?' she says. 'Your pals can see you being soppy, you know.'

Despite how long he's been in this memory, he knows it isn't real. He's always managed to keep hold of that knowledge. That was one of their worries, Michael and Philippa's. *If you're in there too long, Dad, you'll forget what's real and what's not.* For one thing, when the day keeps replaying again and again, that's usually a hint that this isn't the real world.

But even so, John realises this is the last moment he'll have with, well, with everyone. With Agnes, with his mum and dad. And he'll need an excuse to walk out right now.

He kisses Agnes, who squirms and breaks it off fairly quickly.

'Oi, John,' she says. 'Watch my makeup, you goon.'

There are cheers and some laughter among the assembled people in the pews.

'He can't wait,' someone shouts. 'John, you're meant to wait until the minister tells you to kiss the bride!'

He does his best to ignore them, taking in this last image of his wife, the love of his life.

'Agnes,' he says. 'I'm just going outside for a minute. I've got a surprise for you.'

'You're joking. Please, whatever it is, just leave it and let's get this bit done first.'

'I'm sorry, love, I'll be right back and you're going to love it. But before I go, I just need you to know how much I love you, okay?'

Their hands are clasped together and he's not sure if it's him or her who's squeezing tighter. Agnes's hand doesn't feel right, not without the wedding ring.

'John, are you feeling okay?'

'Aye, I'm fine, love. I just need you to know that, alright? I love you and you mean everything to me. Everything. I'll never regret marrying you, Agnes Irene McDuff, even though I'm probably going to forget to tell you that. And

264

some day, years in the future, if you have to go before me, I'll never stop loving you and missing you.'

Agnes nods her head, confusion creased over her face.

'I'll never forget you,' he says.

'John, do you need a sit down or something?'

He laughs and kisses her again. When he breaks away this time, he turns and walks down the aisle, not allowing himself another look back at her. Whispers start in the church, which soon turn to loudly held conversations between the gossips of the crowd.

'I'm just fetching something,' he shouts to the pews. 'I'll be back in a minute. Keep yourselves entertained.'

Through the open doors, he sees the sun beaming down on the street outside. Hannah's out there, standing, soaking it in. He's nearly out the doors when he realises he forgot about his parents. Turning, he catches a glimpse of Agnes, standing lonely in front of everyone, and he thinks about running. Taking a deep breath, he walks to the pew where his parents sit and kneels down.

'Mum, Dad,' he says. 'Thank you for everything you gave me.'

'Get back up there,' his mum says. 'Don't mind all this rubbish, get back up there.'

'I will, Mum. I love you both, very much.'

His parents share a look like he's speaking a different language. People had always told John he was fluent in bullshit.

'Are you drunk, John?' his dad asks. 'You were only meant to have one at the pub. Did Gary get you drunk?'

'Dad, I'm going to work for Ronnie. And I know how angry that makes you and there's nothing I can do about it. It's something that I need to do. Maybe it was a mistake. Maybe I would've had a happier life working with you and taking over the painting business when you retired, but we'll never know. We can't change the past, can we? I don't know if I was ever going to live up to what you wanted me to be, Dad. But I love you and I miss you every day.'

He kisses both his parents on the cheek then stands up. Their faces are a mix of confusion and amusement. John thinks that maybe his dad didn't hear him properly.

John turns and runs out the church, towards Hannah and towards the real world. Behind him, as he feels the sun on his face, he hears his dad shout.

'He's drunk! Give him ten minutes to sober up and he'll be back!'

Hannah – Stonecranning, 1975

The idea of getting married isn't one that appeals to Hannah very much, or very often. Maybe in the ten minutes or so after she finishes rewatching *When Harry Met Sally* or *You've Got Mail*, but that's about it.

You got married, in the old days, either because you wanted to get pregnant, or you already were pregnant. Hannah had been through that part and marrying Sydney's dad was entirely out of the question.

The other reason to marry was, apparently, love? She's not sure she's ever felt that properly. Hannah is still young, but she was even younger when she met Liam. She'd thought that had been love, but if it was, it's not something she's desperate to feel again. Just anger and lust and feeling like the world was going to end every time they argued.

But, as the sun shines on her face on this glorious memory from a day in 1975, she thinks maybe a wedding wouldn't be such a bad thing. Only if the weather was like this, though.

John appears at pace from the church and stands before her.

'Good to go?' he asks.

There are tears around his eyes and Hannah doesn't plan on mentioning them.

'Yep,' she says. 'Let's end this sucker.'

'Excuse me?'

'Let's end this… memory.'

'Grand.'

They begin walking away from the church, taking a right and John leads the way. From the entrance behind them, Hannah spots a few of the guests peeking round the door, curious as to where the groom's run off to, and who he's run off with.

'Okay, Hannah,' he says. 'Have you been to Stonecranning before?'

'I haven't, no. I'm not entirely sure you haven't just made it up now.'

'Oh, you've got to visit, you really have. Look at how lively the place is.'

There are two men stumbling about at a bus stop on their left, seemingly arguing over the cheesy pastry at their feet that a pigeon is having a good peck at.

'But this was forty years ago. Is it still like this?'

'Kind of. But most things are shut down.'

Before they reach the bus stop, John goes left and leads her across the road. There's a pub on the left, *The Falcon*, and a bakers on the right, *McSweeney's*.

'We go up this hill,' he says, pointing up the road in front of them. 'Then at the top we go left, and straight ahead will be the clock tower. Where we were ten minutes ago.'

'Right you are.'

'And Hannah,' he says, bringing them to a stop in the middle of the street. 'You remember the earthquake?'

'Well, I wasn't there for that.'

'Sorry, you remember the aftermath of the earthquake, yes?'

'Yes, very messy.'

'Good. So, there is a chance, just a chance mind you, that something similar could happen again as we approach the clock tower. It seems like maybe *Memorize* isn't all that keen on me leaving the memory.'

'What's something similar to an earthquake?'

'You'll know it when you see it.'

'That makes me feel safe.'

'Don't worry, you can't die in the system.'

'Wow, John, you just keep making me feel safer and safer with every comment.'

He finds this funny for some reason and starts marching up the hill again. Hannah follows.

As they walk, Hannah gets a chance to take in the sights of 1975. Retro shops, retro bikes, retro pubs. She stares and the people stare back. She is suddenly aware that she is drawing the gaze of everyone here. It must be her hair. She sees a woman pointing. *You aren't ready for this yet,* she thinks. *But your grandkids are gonna love it.*

Every doorway they pass, Hannah can smell smoke wafting out. Her parents always tell her she's lucky that she grew up after the smoking ban, that she didn't come home stinking of cigarettes every night. Turns out, they're right.

'Enjoying 1975, Hannah?' John asks.

'Yeah,' she says. 'Although there are bits of Edinburgh that are like this. It's like walking through Stockbridge on a Saturday morning.'

'Ah, those hipsters, eh?'

'Hipsters! Yes, John, hipsters. Where did you hear about hipsters?'

He taps his nose.

'Ach, I know the patter.' There's a pause and his pace slows. 'Am I a hipster?'

'Do you know what a hipster is, John?'

'No, Hannah, I don't.'

'You're not a hipster.'

'Is that a good thing?'

'I'd say so.'

'Grand.'

The pace quickens again. They've made it to the top of the hill, where the path splits in two. In the middle, a small walled-off area where a few bushes grow. Young boys in shirts and trousers sit on the edge of the wall and pass a cigarette between them. Hannah appreciates the young teams in 1975 dressing better than most wedding guests in 2019.

John leads Hannah up the left side lane. They round the corner and the high street extends before them. At the far end, a clock tower, tall and imposing on the horizon. It's as if it's been rebuilt in the last ten minutes, like those videos she had seen of Amish people putting up barns. She raises a hand to block out the sun and see it properly.

For a moment, she thinks about telling John that she's a good luck charm. The memory was crumbling before she got here, but their walk so far has been uneventful. That's when she notices the police van approaching.

The high street is mainly pedestrianised, and the shoppers get a fright when the van puts on its sirens. The locals part to either side and the vehicle rolls along in the middle. People appear at doorways, all down the street and lean from upper floor windows, to get a look at the action.

The police van drives all the way down the street until it reaches Hannah and John. Two policemen hop out, passing some police tape between them. They start rolling it out over the entire width of the street. Their uniforms are proper retro and Hannah feels like someone's about to say 'there's been a murder'.

John darts out and Hannah follows him, trying to get past before the police block the path. One of the policemen moves purposefully to get in John's way.

'Sorry, sir, ma'am,' the policeman says, nodding at the pair of them. 'I'm afraid we have to close off the street.'

Hannah focuses on her breathing, trying not to fly off the handle at the second time she's been called 'ma'am' in one day. Is it how she's dressed? The label on her business suit even says Miss on it.

'We need through,' John says. 'We'll just be a second.'

'Sorry, sir. I can't let you or your friend with the interesting hair through.'

'Why?'

'There's been an incident.'

'What kind of incident?'

'Bad incident.'

'Bad incident? Jesus.' John looks to the sky. 'Is this all you've got, *Memorize*? Bad incident? Not exactly *Hill Street Blues*, is it?'

The policeman in front of them folds his arms, not budging an inch. Behind him, shoppers are ignoring the tape and sneaking under. It's just him and Hannah the police are trying to stop.

John takes a deep breath, smiles at Hannah, then punches the policeman in the face. He goes down like a sack of tatties.

Hannah's heart starts racing. 'Why did you do that?' she says.

John turns, but his eyes stay on his fist, inspecting it for damage.

'Don't worry,' he says. 'This is all just a memory, Hannah. These aren't real policemen.'

The other policeman is rushing towards them now, clearly not happy that his partner has been laid out so blatantly. He pulls out his baton, raising it above his head. But he's so focused on John that he doesn't see Hannah's foot extending. It connects with the soft parts between his legs and he joins his partner on the floor.

'Boom,' Hannah says. 'Police brutality.'

They both run, ducking under the police tape. As they go, Hannah takes in the faces of the people lingering at shop doors. It's nice to see no one filming on their phones, obviously because they don't exist here. Nice to see people living in the moment and enjoying strangers doling out some violence to the police without having to share it with the world.

The road has already been cleared by the police van so they have a clear run all the way down the high street. She tries to stay alert, watching for anything that could jump out and stop them. She hears a low whining sound, but she can't see where it's coming from.

'Do you hear that?' she shouts at John.

She stops, losing some ground on him, to take off her shoes, which are only slowing her down. Then she sets off again.

'Yes,' he calls back over his shoulder. 'Just ignore it. We're almost there.'

He's right, the clock tower is growing ever closer, looming over them more and more. Hannah recognises the buildings in the distance from last night. She knows it wasn't last night, it was about fifteen minutes ago, but her brain can't help but tell her that the time she spent sitting on the fountain learning about John was last night. It was dark outside. It couldn't have been fifteen minutes ago. It doesn't compute.

Ahead of her, John stops running and looks up at the sky. It takes her a few seconds to catch up. She reaches his side and is glad of the rest, a slight stitch growing in her side.

'Why have I got a stitch?' she asks him, over the increasing engine roar. 'Surely I should only get a stitch if your brain thinks I should get a stitch? Do you think I look out of shape, John?'

John doesn't answer, keeping his eyes on the sky.

272

Hannah realises that it's become much colder in the last few seconds, like the sun's been blocked out. That's when she notices the pair of them are standing in a giant shadow.

She looks up at the sky to see a passenger plane. She's never seen one fly so low before.

'Is Stonecranning on a flight path?' she asks.

'Not in my lifetime,' John says, reaching into his sporran and producing his panic button. 'We're going to need Philippa to restart the memory, I think.'

He presses it as the plane gets closer and louder and lower. Plane engines make a fair racket as they approach you, as it turns out. Hannah's hair starts whipping with the force of the engines.

'Mr Valentine,' she shouts. 'I might need to leave.'

'Two seconds,' he calls back. 'Philippa's just about to restart it.'

The plane is huge and plummeting towards them. The ground is vibrating and her teeth are grinding, and there's nowhere to run. The curved nose of the plane is descending at speed, ready to torpedo them into oblivion. She has to fight to stay on her feet.

'We don't know that!' Hannah yells. 'I know this isn't real, but it really feels real. Bravo on that. *Memorize*, exit mem–'

Hannah doesn't get the chance to finish the sentence. The scene fades to black, just as the plane is about to crash land.

5... 4... 3... 2... 1...

John – Stonecranning, 1975

John considers that his final goodbyes have already been said, and anyway, he doesn't have the emotional strength to do them every single time. So, he runs out the church shouting an excuse about 'fetching a special gift for them all'. No one ever questions where you're going if you say you're going to get them a gift.

He arrives back in the sunshine to find Hannah, who has walked over to sit on a bench. She's taken off her jacket and lays it down next to her.

'The plane wouldn't have killed us, you know,' he tells her, crossing the small square.

'It was still fucking realistic, okay?' she says. 'Well done on your programming skills or whatever. Not wanting to be unladylike, John, but I shat my pants.'

He waves a hand in the air to dismiss this. 'Don't apologise for being unladylike,' he says. 'Men don't apologise for being unladylike. Come on, let's try again.'

As before, the two men at the bus stop prepare for a fight over the dropped pastry from *McSweeney's*, while John and Hannah cross the road to the high street.

'How many times have you relived this?' Hannah asks.

'This day? Eh, I've lost count, to tell you the truth. Even if I'd been making little notch marks in the walls, they'd have disappeared each time I went back to the start.'

'I don't know how you do it.'

'In my defence, my wedding day was nice. This earthquake, plane crash business, only started very recently.'

'No earthquakes on your wedding night then, John?'

After the words are out of her mouth, she stops dead in her tracks. 'Oh my God,' she says. 'I don't know why I... I'm sorry.'

'For what?'

'For being inappropriate.'

'Hannah, if you think I'm going to be offended by that kind of joke, then I'm deeply offended. And actually, no, the portion of the memory I chose was from midday to midnight. No rumpy pumpy involved.'

Hannah seems to accept that she hasn't offended his delicate sensibilities and catches up with him again.

'Please never use that phrase around me,' she tells him. 'Or around anyone.'

'Are the kids not saying rumpy pumpy anymore?'

'If they are, they're doing an impression of a really creepy, old man.'

John knows they don't have the time to be having silly conversations like this, but if Hannah is happy to have them, then so is he. It's been a long time since he really, truly didn't know what the other person was going to say.

As they walk up the steepest part of the high street, the temperature drops noticeably. The sun hides behind a cloud. This soon becomes a multitude of clouds, growing darker every second. They move like someone's pressed fast forward on the sky.

Hannah's noticed this too. 'Is this *Memorize* doing this?'

'I have a bad feeling it is.'

The raindrops are cold as they hit John's skin. One then another, falling faster. He can't deny it feels good for a moment. He hasn't felt rain on his skin in forever. They say the rain comes down and washes the world and makes things clean again. It's necessary.

They keep walking as water begins running downhill, causing their feet to make splashes every time they hit the ground.

'This isn't so bad,' Hannah says. 'If it's just a bit of rain.'

As if hearing her, the rain gets heavier. Huge droplets splash on the ground like God's bucket has been overturned. Then, instead of splashes, the rain makes cracking sounds on the ground. The rain is solid.

'It's hailstones,' John says. 'Let's up the pace.'

Running becomes difficult, though; the water isn't just running under their feet, it's growing deeper. He finds his socks soaked up to his ankles. The street is becoming a river before their eyes.

'I can't believe this,' Hannah says, over the smashing of the hailstones all around her.

'Really?' John shouts back. 'This is Scotland, remember.'

Just then, a lightning bolt flashes in the sky, piercing a building to their right. A drainpipe explodes and sprays bits of brick and stone onto the path in front of them. They splash down, throwing up huge sprays of water. All around, people are rushing to get inside and barricade doors. John and Hannah are soon the only people fighting their way through the growing tide.

John feels so cold now. The water has almost reached his waist. He has to dive his hand under the surface now if he wants to get into his sporran. Opening the clasp, his panic button threatens to float away, but he gets a good grip of it, pulls it above the water and presses it.

Hannah has waded over to a lamppost at the side of the street and clings on, trying not to be washed away. His footing is holding firm, for now, on the cobbles somewhere below him.

'I've pressed the panic button,' he tells her. 'We can let go.'

Her hair is soaked and lies flat over her face. 'You sure?' she shouts.

'Yeah, let go, Hannah. Who knows, this could be fun.'

Some unknown object in the water below makes John's mind up for him, swiping his legs and making him lose his footing. He falls forward and smashes his face into the water. Seconds later, he's being carried by the current, floating down the street like a piece of jetsam.

Philippa – Edinburgh, 2019

The *Memorize* viewing page isn't entirely straightforward. It takes quite a while to learn how to read it. To make sense of what's going on. It isn't like a livestream of what's going on inside the memory, which would make things a lot easier. No, there are no cameras in the memory. What the viewing page gives you is an update on the client's wellbeing, their current heart rate, their location, as well as the time remaining in the memory.

There's also a weather feature, which rarely needs to be checked. The staff never really need to know what the weather's like in a client's memory, as it doesn't exactly assist them doing their job. But it's been ten minutes since she restarted the memory and they're both still in there and no purple alert has been raised.

Philippa's starting to get worried, so she's opening up every additional details tab she can find on the system. Unfortunately, the weather tab is broken. If it's bad weather, it's only designed to show a dark cloud with either one or two raindrops. There's been a glitch and it's showing a black cloud with too many overlapping raindrops to count. She closes the weather tab.

Philippa steps away from the screen, taking her eyes off it just briefly to look at the pair of them in the room with her. Mr Valentine lying on his bed, where he's been for months. Hannah, peacefully sitting with her eyes shut.

'What's going on in there?' she whispers. 'Get the fuck out. I swear to God, John, if you come out of this with fewer marbles than you went in there with, I'm not letting Michael blame me for it.'

Of course, they had drawn up a step-by-step guide to follow if Mr Valentine woke up while you were on shift, written up and approved by all board members. It was only really for her, Michael, Nurse Ashton, or at a push, Yasmin, as no one else was supposed to enter this room. And Yasmin was only on the list because they needed someone to come in and change Mr Valentine's saline drip and urine bag when the nurse was on annual leave. Yasmin had negotiated a hefty Christmas bonus for taking on that particular task.

But the first step of the guide was dependent on Mr Valentine actually being out of the memory. There wasn't a guide for Mr Valentine not quite being able to remove himself from the memory, due to a fucking earthquake burying his exit button. She's not sure why there wasn't, though, as she had predicted putting the exit button at the top of the clock tower was a stupid thing to do. The kind of stupid thing only a rich old man would do to provide himself with some form of symbolism he couldn't find in the real world.

She moves to the screen and refreshes the page, even though she knows it refreshes itself.

John Valentine — Location: High Street.

They should be there soon, she thinks, but then again, it is a long high street. Still, she wonders what happened on the first attempt and why the purple alert went up. How many purple alerts is she going to sit through before she caves in and calls Michael? How long is she going to leave Mr Valentine and Hannah in there?

Behind her, causing her to near enough jump out

of her skin, someone rattles room forty-one's door handle. A few seconds go by and the door handle jiggles again.

Taking another quick glance at the screen to make sure nothing's changed in the memory, Philippa walks over to the door.

'Who is it?' she says, raising a hand to the lock. 'Is that you, Yasmin?'

'No, Ms De la Rosa,' the voice says. 'It's me, Xander? I just started today?'

Philippa slides the bolt out the lock. He isn't going to be any help, but at least he won't be able to identify what's going on and report it to anyone he shouldn't.

She opens the door just a touch to find Xander standing there, backpack slung over one shoulder, shiny green headphones resting round his neck.

'Hello, Xander,' she says. 'You're in late. You can get off home now and I'll see you tomorrow.'

She goes to close the door, but he places a hand on the doorframe, meaning she would have to crush his fingers to do so. It isn't out of the question.

'Sorry, Ms De la Rosa,' he says. 'But I actually need to tell you something. Something important.'

'I'm sure it can wait, Xander. I really need to–'

'It's about Mr Valentine. Senior.'

This takes her off guard and unable to form a confident response. Has Yasmin been telling the new starts about what's behind the green door, just to impress them?

'Oh really?'

'Yeah, can I come in there, just for a second? I'll show you. I can help him.'

The idea of being in Mr Valentine's room with two staff members who have only been with the company for about sixteen hours combined doesn't appeal to her, but

280

she doesn't have much choice. What could he know about Mr Valentine?

'Quickly,' she says, and he squeezes past her into the room.

Usually, the new staff members are a pile of nerves for at least the first week. Andreas only just made it past lunchtime, to be fair, but Hannah and Xander are doing their best to stave off the 'only one person makes it to the end of the first day' theory.

The confidence on Xander's face seems to flicker when he sees Hannah is in the room too.

'What's she doing here?' he asks.

'Don't worry about that,' Philippa tells him. 'Now, tell me what you need to tell me, quickly. What do you know?'

It hasn't been long, but Philippa realises she hasn't checked the memory screen since Xander knocked on the door. Her eyes flick over. She can see the purple alert flashing on the screen.

'Wait,' she says, moving across the room. 'I need to get that first.'

'Don't touch it.'

Philippa looks back at Xander, almost finding it funny that he thinks he can give her orders. His backpack is now on the floor, unzipped. In his hand, pointing directly at her, is a gun.

'What are you doing, Xander?'

Her heartbeat thumps in her chest and ears.

'Don't touch the computer,' he says. 'Don't touch anything. Don't scream or I'll shoot Hannah.'

Xander moves to the door and snaps the lock back on, all the while keeping the gun on her. He reaches into his pocket and tosses something at her. She catches it. Black cable ties.

'Put one round your ankles,' he instructs her. 'Then

281

tighten it. Then put another round your wrists and tighten it as much as you can. When you're done, put your wrists out in front of you, like this.'

The gun, for a second, points away from her as he gestures how she should hold out her hands once she's finished tying herself up for him.

'Okay then,' she says, crouching, realising that her winning debating skills aren't much good against a loaded gun. 'Can I ask why you're doing this?'

'Why, of course,' he says. 'I'll tell you my exact plan. Can't see that coming back to bite me later. Just put the cable ties on and don't speak to me again.'

Philippa pushes her feet tightly together and wraps one of the cable ties around her ankles, the material harsh against her skin. Sliding the end through the gap, she pulls it tight. As tight as she feels like doing it, anyway. If Xander wanted it as tight as possible, he should've done it himself. Then she manoeuvres herself back up to a standing position.

'Okay, I won't speak to you,' she says. 'I'll just talk to myself. First sign of madness, so they say.'

She runs a finger along the rivets on the cable tie she's holding, trying not to make direct eye contact with the gun, as if it will become less dangerous if she just doesn't look at it.

'I'm very impressed, by the way,' she says. 'We do a *lot* of background checks on new starts. Not just baseline either, we do more checks than the government. And yet, look at you now.'

It's an awkward process, wrapping the cable tie round her wrists. She leans forward and lays it flat on her thighs, putting her wrists together and feeding one end through the clasp. Xander doesn't say anything.

'So, y'know, bravo on that. You've done a good job of

282

hiding whoever you really are from us. Unless this is a spur of the moment thing, but I'm guessing probably not, Xander? If that is your *real* name.'

Never did Philippa believe in her life she would get to use that phrase in a completely relevant and serious context.

There's no change of emotion on his face. She puts her arms out as he instructed.

'Here you go, sir,' she says. 'Just like you asked. What do I win?'

A few nervous moments pass while she stands there, offering herself up to his mercy. He inspects her work from afar, before deciding she's done a decent enough job and putting the gun on the bed. It looks like it has some weight to it, sinking into the cover by Mr Valentine's feet.

Xander moves towards her and grabs her wrists, pulling the cable tie so tight it feels like the blood vessels underneath are certain to pop. Then he goes back to where he was standing before. He picks the gun up again.

'Thank you,' he says, approaching her again. 'I really appreciate you co-operating. I'm sure you knew the risk when you took the job. It's not personal, it's just business.'

Two clichés within ten seconds. Maybe Hollywood films *are* realistic.

That's the last thought Philippa gets to have, though, as she feels a sharp pain at the side of her head.

John – Stonecranning, 1975

When Michael had been just a boy, John and Agnes had taken him to the Rainbow Slides pool in Stirling. It was against the rules, but Michael had insisted John go with him down the blue chute, the fastest chute, of course, while the lifeguard wasn't looking. He'd been tossed around in the darkness of the slide, water rushing up his nose and into his ears, while Michael's laughter echoed around the confined plastic walls of the tube.

John's reminded of this as he shifts on to his back, struggling to stay right side up in the water. Hannah's floating not far from him as they drift down the street.

'This isn't fun!' she says, struggling to stay on her back, thrashing around.

'Can't you swim?'

She takes her time to reply, accidentally inhaling a mouthful of rainwater and spitting and gurgling it back out.

'I can swim,' she says. 'This isn't swimming.'

It's more like rafting, John thinks, where there's no raft because you *are* the raft. It's not all fun and games, though, as the water guides him into a bollard. It's under the water but still tall enough to jab him in the ribs. He clenches and reaches to his side and overturns slightly, submerging himself. The water is too fast and murky to see anything through. He fights back to the surface and finds Hannah has overtaken him. She's almost at the bottom of the street.

As the water takes them closer to the bottom of the

hill, John sees the top of a double decker bus on the road. The rest of the bus is submerged. For a moment, he finds himself hoping everyone on board got off okay, before reminding himself that the people are figments of his memory and aren't in any danger at all.

'Brace yourself!' he yells to Hannah.

He holds his breath as the current gets faster. They both do their best to avoid the bus, but the flow of the water is too strong and throws them into the side of it. John exhales and winces in pain at the impact.

Trying to ignore the pain in his side, John struggles to get a hold of anything on the bus to stop him being carried out of town by the water. His fingers are stiff from the cold and already starting to wrinkle, like he's been in the bath too long. He shrugs his jacket off, which is starting to weigh him down, letting it splash into the water and float away.

At the next bus window, Hannah's clinging on.

'I need out,' Hannah says, sliding her arm into one of the open bus windows to grip on to the inside. 'John, this is *not* what I signed up for.'

'Aye, it's a bit chilly,' he says. 'Come on, let's get on top.'

John mimics Hannah, putting a hand inside the window for grip, using it to pull himself up. He manages to get a soaking wet leg on the edge of the window, pushing himself upwards and on to the roof of the bus. He's hindered by the weight of his waterlogged kilt.

Lying on his stomach, he offers a hand down to her. The young body of the John in the memory is still strong enough to pull her up. They collapse on the top of the bus, where the water hasn't quite reached yet.

'Are you alright?' he asks.

'Define alright,' she replies, getting her breath back.

'No limbs missing.'

'Limbs intact... I think.'

They listen to the sound of the water, which is now substantial enough to be referred to as a river, or at least a waterway flowing past them. They both take fast, shallow breaths as they recharge their batteries.

'I think it's time,' Hannah says. 'To restart the memory.'

'I've got bad news and good news,' he tells her.

'Oh, fab. I was just thinking what we needed right now was bad news.'

'Don't forget the good news.'

'If the good news isn't that we can breathe underwater in your memory, I feel like it's not going to cheer me up.'

A yellow Capri goes sailing past, like an out of control riverboat, bumping off the walls of *The Falcon* and spinning slightly. There's a man in the driver's seat. John makes eye contact with him. They both shrug their shoulders as the car passes their little island in the storm and trickles into the distance.

'The good news is that I've still got the panic button,' John says, taking it out of his sporran. 'The bad news is... I did press it before we got swept away. Philippa still hasn't restarted the memory.'

He gives the button a little shake, hoping Hannah understands it as the universal sign of 'is this thing working?' He presses it again for her benefit, too.

'I wouldn't worry,' he says. 'I'm sure she's just taken her eyes off the screen for a minute.'

They both settle into a somewhat comfortable silence for a while as they get their breath back, dry off a bit, and take in the sights and sounds of the flooded town. This end of the high street is where most of the water has gathered, at the bottom of the slope. At first floor windows, people gaze out at the damage and wave at him and Hannah. They wave back.

286

John turns and squints over at the church. It's just too far away and his vision is just too poor to make out if anyone he recognises is floating outside. It looks like the big outer doors are shut. He won't say it out loud to Hannah, but he really would love to see the wedding guests soaked through in their finery. In fact, he'd take off his kilt if it wasn't for Hannah sitting next to him. It's like a dead weight around his waist. If he fell from the top of this bus, he feels like he'd go down like a stone and never come back up.

'How is this possible?' Hannah asks. 'You're telling me the system is doing this? *Memorize* flooded the town?'

The easiest thing to do here would be to give her some techno mumbo jumbo answer. It wouldn't make any sense, but Hannah wouldn't know that. She's already admitted she doesn't know anything about computers. That would be the easiest thing to do. But it wouldn't help anyone. Certainly not John, who would also like an answer to that question.

'Put simply,' he says. 'I'm not sure. The memory is corrupted. The code, y'know, the rules, essentially, they've been overwritten. And it's silly to say, but the only explanation is that the system has done this itself. It's capable of writing new rules for itself.'

'Okay,' Hannah says. 'Now, obviously I don't know much about this kind of thing but... isn't that... quite scary?'

'Yes,' John says.

Hannah whistles dramatically. It's the wrong time to bring it up, but if *Memorize* is capable of this, John wonders if that means he's created sentient life. Maybe that's going too far, but certainly the technology seems to have progressed beyond just depicting memories. The fire, the earthquake, the flood? Those are original thoughts.

John and Hannah sit and wring out various pieces of their clothing. John takes off his clunky shoes and unpeels his socks from his pale legs. He bundles them up into one soggy blob and tosses it into the water. It bobs on the top of the water and flows away with the rest of the rubbish.

The longer they sit there, the more John is aware that the memory isn't restarting. Hannah isn't bringing it up, but he knows that's all she's thinking about. He wonders what's stopping Philippa. Maybe it's *Memorize* itself. If it can flood a town, it can probably stop a Mex restarting.

From their vantage point, John can see all the way down to the old picture house. Beyond that, the industrial area of town, which nowadays is mainly crumbling buildings and weeds. In his memory, though, it's still thriving, with new partnerships opening up every other day. It was better then. Regular people still had a chance to make something of themselves.

The rain hasn't stopped entirely, but it's much lighter, although the heavy, packed clouds remain. As John scans the area again, he notices someone struggling in the water. They flail their arms, powering their way to the surface and waving, just for a second, only to disappear below the water again. It's a man, maybe five, six, seven years older than Hannah, John never can tell these days. The man's fighting to keep his head afloat.

Hannah hasn't spotted him yet. As the water threatens to wash him away, he manages to grab on to a thick tree branch.

'Help!' he shouts. 'Help!'

Hannah hears him, spinning around on the top of the bus to get a look. She waves back to let him know he's been seen.

'Oh my God,' she says. 'We need to save him.'

'Do we?' John says, squinting to try and make out the man's face. 'I don't recognise him.'

'So?'

'So... he wasn't at my wedding. He's just a stranger.'

'Oh yeah, because we can leave strangers to die. I forgot those were the rules.'

'We're in a memory, Hannah, he's not even real. But, if you insist, you can go and get him. The thrill of saving someone's life can be quite nice. But bear in mind, Philippa's going to restart the memory any second now.'

By the time he's finished his sentence, Hannah's already taken off her waterlogged shoes and jacket, and stood up on the top of the bus. Her feet slide on the slick surface and she stumbles as she tries to stay on her feet.

'I'm coming!' she shouts to the man.

'Hannah!' the drowning man calls back.

Hannah frowns in confusion, extending her head forward to get a better look.

'Oh my God,' she says. 'I know that guy.'

Hannah – Stonecranning, 1975

Diving isn't a skill Hannah would put on her CV. 'Stopping the microwave when it's got one second left,' now *that* she would put on her CV.

In high school, when they'd had to race each other, she'd always accepted that her terrible diving style would give everyone else at least a five second head start. Mrs Gomez gave up on trying to correct her form, and Hannah had been fine with that because, realistically, when was she ever going to actually need it when she grew up?

Hannah curls her toes over the side of the bus, the only thing she remembers you're supposed to do.

'How can you know him?' John asks, standing too.

'His name's Xander,' she says.

'Xander? I doubt that. That's not even a name.'

'He works at Memory Lane.'

This shuts John up and he nods. All the while, Xander, around fifty metres or so away, is clinging on to the tree branch as best he can.

'I see,' John says. 'Well, he seems to be very professional in his work.'

'Give him a break. This is his first day too.'

'I should hope so. He should've seen from the *Memorize* details that the place is flooded and this could've been avoided. Also, a man should be able to swim.'

'That's sexist.'

'Fine. An adult should be able to swim. Why doesn't he just leave the memory?'

'He must be in shock. Xander, leave the memory! Say the exit command!'

Her voice doesn't seem to reach him. The frantic waving of his arms continues.

Hannah steps back, takes a deep breath, then launches herself off the top of the bus and into the greenish water. She thinks she hears John saying something just before she jumps, but she's already too far gone to turn back. The water is so cold and hits her so hard, all at once, that she lets out the breath she had been planning on holding for a lot longer. Her arms and legs flail against the water and force her to the surface.

She takes a second to get her bearings again, get her breath back, and make sure she isn't going to wash away. Then she starts making her way to Xander, doing a version of the front crawl that involves moving her head left and right without putting it back into the water.

Once she gets close enough that she's confident he'll be able to hear her, she pauses and treads water.

'Xander!' she says.

He clings on to the branch like a frightened animal.

'Hannah,' he says. 'I'm so glad to see you.'

'Just leave,' she tells him, then realises that to get into the memory, he should've seen Philippa in John's room. 'Wait, where's Philippa?'

'That's what I need to tell you,' he says.

'Hold on.'

Hannah stops treading water and swims the rest of the distance between them. When she arrives at Xander, she grabs another branch and feels her lungs and arms aching.

'What's wrong?' she says, her hair drenched and whipping round her neck.

Xander sweeps the hair out of his own face, water dripping from the end of his nose.

'She had to leave,' he tells her. 'There was some emergency.'

'What?' Hannah says. 'This is the emergency!'

'I don't know what to tell you. All I know is I forgot my headphones in the lab. I came back to get them and Philippa grabbed me and took me into the room with the big green door. Is that him?'

He points over at John, standing on the top of the double decker bus, hands on his hips.

'Yeah,' Hannah says. 'He's the founder of Memory Lane, as it turns out. He's been reliving this day for ages but he wants out.'

Hannah tries not to think about what she's saying too much. If she did, she would probably be sure she was losing her mind.

'Philippa said something like that,' Xander says. 'But she said she had to leave and that I was to come into the memory and pass along a message to you. She said that if Mr Valentine can't get to his exit button, you need to restart the memory.'

Below the surface, something brushes along Hannah's calf and she kicks her legs to make it go away. There weren't eels in Scotland in 1975, were there? She hadn't even realised she had a phobia of eels until this moment, picturing it slithering over her legs.

'*I* need to restart it?' she says. 'I don't think I know how.'

'Philippa said she's left it all ready to restart,' Xander says. 'You just need to click the button.'

'Why me? Why didn't she just get you to do it?'

Xander shrugs. The slosh of the water funnelling through the gaps in the buildings surrounding them seems to be getting louder.

'I guess she trusts you more,' Xander says.

292

At the start of the day, if Hannah had known she was going to be the most trustworthy of the new staff, she'd have been delighted. She knows how stupid it is, this need she has to be liked by her superiors. That it's been ingrained in her by a capitalist society that says her worth is determined by how much good labour she can produce. But still. It's nice to hear. Maybe she's been listening to her dad too much.

'Okay,' she says. 'So, why don't we both go back?'

If she's going back into John's room, she'd rather not do it alone.

'Sounds good,' Xander says. 'Okay, after three? 1… 2… 3…'

'*Memorize*,' they say together. 'Exit memory.'

John – Stonecranning, 1975

If he was being generous, he would describe Hannah's swimming technique as 'unconventional'. But it worked, and she got over to this Xander without much trouble. They were shouting things to each other as she swam. John couldn't hear what they were saying.

He watched Hannah reach the tree and they spoke for a minute. Then Hannah disappeared, obviously having said the exit command. But Xander remained. And now he's swimming towards John.

A few thoughts spin round John's mind as he watches this stranger get closer to him. Why did Hannah leave? That one was probably obvious. The girl didn't really want to be in here with him in the first place, and add to that the flash flood, she probably wasn't having a great time. Some first day for the poor lass.

But why did this boy, Xander, stay? They must have discussed it before Hannah left. Philippa wouldn't have let another new start come into his memory, would she? Where was Philippa anyway? Had she sent this boy to him because she didn't fancy getting wet?

Maybe he was starting to see things that weren't there. It was certainly a danger of spending too long hooked up to *Memorize*. No, he tells himself. People who see things don't question if what they're seeing is real. Then again, people like that can convince themselves of anything.

John's final thought, as the boy swims the last few metres and he extends a hand down to help him climb up, is why was he shouting for help when he can clearly swim no bother?

'Mr Valentine,' he says.

'And you're...' John says. 'Xander?'

The boy shakes the worst of the water off his clothes, then removes his suit jacket.

'That's the name I gave to Memory Lane, yes.'

This was always going to be one of the dangers of being in the memory for so long. People were bound to find out. Find out that he's vulnerable.

John rolls up the soaking sleeves of his shirt.

'Can't help but notice you were doing a lot of shouting for help,' John says. 'Then as soon as Hannah was gone, you turned into Tamas Darnyi.'

Xander loosens his tie, pulling it over his ears and throwing it into the water. It slowly makes its way with the flow, down the street, out of sight.

'Who's that?' he asks John.

'He was a famous swimmer, back in the day.'

'Right. I'm not here to speak about swimmers, Mr Valentine.'

'Then what are you here to speak about? If you don't mind me asking. I'm guessing you know who I am?'

Xander doesn't seem to wear many emotions on his sleeve, or his face, but there is a flicker of a smile.

'Yes,' he says. 'I know who you are. I don't have a lot of time, so I'll try to make this quick. I represent The Recollect Project. Are you aware of The Recollect Project, Mr Valentine?'

Deep down, John knew they'd come one day. Once Memory Lane got to a certain size. Once they'd accepted money from certain investors. Once they started making the amounts of money they were making.

Making enemies was an inevitable consequence of

doing big business. Not that John had wanted it this way. But he had soon found out that investors don't like making just a little bit of profit. They like making so much money it causes jaws to drop when they casually bring it up in conversation over dinner and charades. He has always wanted to keep the HQ in Edinburgh, but he knows the board members are desperate to move it to London or New York to really cash in. So far, no one else has been able to crack the technology. The board members and investors want to expand before anyone else becomes a viable competitor.

'I'm aware of The Recollect Project,' John says. 'I've been aware of you lot since about…'97?'

'We've been around a long time.'

'And still haven't quite cracked it then?'

John knows Xander doesn't have good intentions in mind for him, but he can't help but smile and enjoy putting his mind to good use. In this case, trying to outwit someone when he doesn't know what's coming next.

'Mr Valentine, I was sent here by my organisation to retrieve a certain piece of information from Memory Lane. Our technology is almost ready to put into the market. However, we are missing one vital piece of code. A piece of code that the *Memorize* technology contains. The hope was that I could retrieve this during the course of today, from the lab. However, I have not been able to locate it.'

John laughs. The wind blows and the bottom of his waistcoat flicks backwards and forwards. A gentleman doesn't do up the bottom button.

'Bad luck that,' he says. 'The code a bit too difficult for you, son?'

'I simply didn't have the time to find it while keeping up my cover as a Retrieval Assistant. That was plan A. Actually, plan A was to do this with less…' He gestures around at the water. 'Drama. But when I broke into your room, there was a purple alert waiting on the screen, so I hid and contacted my superiors. Now, I have moved to plan B. Plan B is, you tell me the piece of information I'm looking for. The Valentine Variable. I know you know it off by heart. You write it down, right now, then I leave and no one else gets hurt.'

John's been in here so long, the real world doesn't seem so real. When things happen in the memory, *that* feels real to him. The things that are happening in Memory Lane, they may as well be happening in far off lands. Things that'll never affect him. But he knows that isn't true. And real people are in trouble for a change.

'Who's been hurt?' he asks.

'I restrained Philippa,' Xander says. 'She's fine for now, but every person in Memory Lane is expendable if they get in my way. It's not personal, I just need the code. Will you write down The Valentine Variable for me?'

Xander takes a pen from his pocket and shakes it to get the water off. It wasn't John's idea to call it The Valentine Variable, that was at Michael's behest. At the time, he'd thought his son was proud of him, but now he thinks he just wanted his name on it too. He wishes he'd called it The John Variable.

John considers what The Recollect Project must be working with if they haven't cracked his variable yet. The Valentine Variable, put simply, is what allows the client to change details in the memory. It's not the main goal of the technology, but it makes everything possible. Before he worked it out, the memories kept crashing. If the client did anything, literally any small thing, like saying 'thanks' when they had actually said 'thank you', the memory would come to a standstill. It didn't know what to do if the client's actions didn't match perfectly with the memory.

297

So, John thinks, it would be fair to say The Recollect Project are nowhere.

'If I refuse?' John says.

'I move on to plan C. I call for the other members of my team to enter Memory Lane and we extract you from the memory by force.'

'You take me out?' he says. 'Son, only the client can take themselves out of the memory, and in case you haven't noticed, I'm struggling a bit since I can't get to my exit button.'

'We understand the risks,' Xander says. 'We're aware if we take you out of the memory by force, we risk damaging your brain function, your ability to speak, basically all motor function. If we have to, we'll take you out, along with all the software and hardware we can get our hands on. By tomorrow morning, Memory Lane will essentially cease to function. We didn't want it to come to that. That's why it's plan C, Mr Valentine. Plan B means none of that. You write down the variable for me, nobody else gets hurt.'

John knows that when he finally gets out of the memory, he'll have to decide on what to do with the rest of his life. What he's going to put his money and time towards. He's spent his whole life building up to and developing *Memorize*, founding Memory Lane, making sure him and his family were comfortable for life. And once that was taken care of, he'd decided on this endeavour. To try and change a conversation that could never be changed.

Outside this memory is a world that doesn't really have a place for him anymore. He's aware of that. Is he hiding in here? Why should he care if Memory Lane is destroyed, anyway? It's not his problem anymore. He doesn't want to give up the time he has left just to protect something that's already served its purpose. He either gives up The

Valentine Variable and the company finally has some real competition, or they take it by force and both him and Memory Lane are gone.

John doesn't know what the rest of his life will be like, but he still wants it.

'So,' Xander says, hand outstretched, pen pinched between finger and thumb. 'Which plan will we go with, Mr Valentine?'

Hannah – Edinburgh, 2019

The memory fades and the real world comes back into view. Mr Valentine's room, his frail old body lying asleep. By her side, Xander, still inside the memory, eyes closed, green headphones strung around his neck.

She nudges him to check if he really is still in there.

'Xander?' she says. 'Wake up, Xander.'

He doesn't stir. She doesn't understand. They said the exit command at the same time, didn't they? Maybe two people can't say it at the same time? Either way, she doesn't have time to waste working it out.

Taking off the headset, she moves to the computer. Her heart drops. Xander told her the system was set up to restart. All she needed to do was hit the button. Except the screen isn't showing her anything like she expected. This is far more complicated than the other *Memorize* screens she's seen today, and there's definitely not a single button that's waiting for her to press. Was Xander lying? Or did Philippa not set it up like she said she had?

'Philippa,' Hannah shouts, moving from the computer to the door. 'Philippa!'

She opens the door and shouts down the corridor. Her voice echoes for a few seconds then everything goes silent again. She wonders if she should run and find someone. There's a night shift, isn't there? And Yasmin is due back any minute now.

But she doesn't think she should leave Mr Valentine. And having Xander in the memory alone with him? It just doesn't sit right with her. She closes the door and goes back to the computer.

Try as she might, she can't navigate the complexities of Mr Valentine's memory on the screen. It's like she has just learned to shoot in a game of FIFA and now she's starting for Real Madrid. There are too many charts and stats for her to find the restart function, but she does manage to find the option to put herself back in the memory.

Hannah moves to her chair and places her headset back on. Mentally, she prepares. The system is going to put her down twenty metres from Mr Valentine. That means a watery entrance. She's not sure if it'll do any good but she holds her breath then presses the entry button. The world fades and the numbers appear.

5... 4... 3... 2... 1.

John – Stonecranning, 1975

'Come on, Mr Valentine,' Xander says. 'What's it to be?'

John finds the words stuck in his throat. He coughs like that's going to make them come out fully formed.

'I…' he says. 'I don't know.'

John thinks of Michael. Would he survive without Memory Lane? What other skills does he have? Maybe he never had any skills to begin with. Michael was the lucky recipient of the kind of nepotism John couldn't have even imagined in his day. Had Michael ever thanked him? Properly thanked him? Did he owe this to him?

He knows he doesn't have time for these kinds of thoughts. He has never learned to stall. And now he needs to stall for his life.

'You don't know?' Xander says, rubbing at his temples. 'Well, that's not going to fly, Mr Valentine. "Don't know" isn't one of the choices here. Your options, once again, are: give me The Valentine Variable and I leave Memory Lane without any further aggro; or, don't give me it, and we take everything. I really think the first option is generous, Mr Valentine. Basically, you're being offered a light slap or being hit by a bus.'

It seems like years ago that John walked into a burning building to save Kathy. That had been easy compared to this.

Confrontation was something he'd actively avoided most of his life. It wasn't simple like it was in the films. The choice was never between good and evil. It was always a choice between a rock and a hard place. He doesn't want to die, and he definitely doesn't want whatever could happen to him if Xander takes him out of the memory. He remembers the looks on their faces. The first Memory Lane clients. Most of them were never the same again.

'I don't want to give you it,' John says.

He thought it might feel good to say. When the hero says the brave thing, that's when the music swells and there's a catharsis of sorts. But still the bundle of nerves in his chest stays. Because saying the brave thing is the easy part. Taking the consequences on the chin is the hard part.

'Obviously, you don't *want* to give me it,' Xander says. 'This is the last time I'll ask. Will you give me The Valentine Variable?'

John makes up his mind. As he does so, he swears he can feel a change in the air. Like the air has thinned. It becomes easier to breathe and his body doesn't feel so heavy anymore.

'No,' John says. 'No, I will not.'

The weather must have been changing over the course of the last few minutes and John has been too busy to notice. The clouds have dissolved and parted, and the sun breaks through. A warm glow shines on the top of the bus. Xander doesn't seem to have noticed.

'Give me the Variable,' he says. 'I don't want to have to do it. Take you out. I know what it'll do to your mind.'

John stands firm, planting his feet on the sagging metal of the bus, a shallow puddle splashing under his bare toes. The water level seems to have dropped. Looking over the side of the bus, it's getting lower and lower as he stares at it. The bus is turning back into a bus instead of a boat, right before his eyes.

'I thought you weren't going to ask again,' John says. 'You've got your answer, pal. Why don't you leave and do it? Take me out and see what happens.'

Xander pauses and looks lost for words. For the first time, John thinks he sees the real Xander. A scared young lad doing what the older boys have told him to.

'I don't want to,' Xander says.

John uses this moment to make his move. He jumps over the side of the bus, while the water is still high enough to break his fall. He plunges into the water and feels his feet touch the rough surface of the road below. The water is up to the top of his chest and getting lower all the time. He doesn't even get a chance to look back before he feels a splash next to him. Xander is in the water.

John swims as fast as he can, ensuring to kick his legs, hard, in case Xander gets too close to his heels. He doesn't know where or how the water is disappearing, but it's draining, like a giant plug's been pulled out somewhere down the street. A voice behind him is shouting.

John tries not to look back, but his foot hits something hard and he hears a yelp of pain. It doesn't sound like Xander.

The water is now shallow enough to stand. He lets his feet plant on the ground and turns round. It's Hannah, clutching her hand to her chest.

'Argh,' she says. 'You fucking kicked me, you dick.'

Hannah – Stonecranning, 1975

As expected, Hannah was plonked down into the water as soon as she entered the memory. She'd fought to the surface and seen that John was still on top of the bus. Xander was there too, and she couldn't work out how he'd made it over there without being able to swim.

Just as she'd reached the bus, the pair of them had jumped over the side. She had almost caught up with them when she heard Xander say the exit command and disappear. Then John fucking kicked her.

Now, she sits on the pavement with her hand stinging. Wait, she thinks. How am I sitting on the street? The water is gone. Vanished. She puts her hand to the slabs beneath her. Bone dry.

'Sorry,' John says again. 'I thought you were Xander.'

'He left,' she tells him, getting to her feet. 'I saw him disappear.'

John's expression changes and he puts his hands on her shoulders.

'Hannah, I need you to listen to me very closely,' he says. 'Xander isn't who you think he is. He's from one of our rivals. He wanted something from me and I wouldn't give it to him. Now he's going to hurt me. I need you leave the memory and stop him. You need to do it now.'

She's never seen fear quite like it, the kind that's in his eyes. Her body begins to tremble and it's not clear if it's coming from inside her or from John's hands on her shoulders.

'Wait,' she says, trying to process everything. 'Wait, what's he going to do? Should I call the police?'

He grips her arms tightly and shakes her.

'The police won't help us!' he shouts. 'The police know to leave us alone. Hannah, you do this now or I'm dead. Do you understand? I am dead! He is going to take me out of the memory. He is doing it right now. You need to go, now! You are killing me. Leave. You have to do this for me. Hannah, are you listening to me? You have to save me!'

Hannah finds she can't speak. The exit command is stuck somewhere in her throat. She freezes. Just when he needs her most, she freezes. Every inch of her is stuck fast with fear.

'Oh my God,' she says. 'This is my fault. I left him alone with you. Fuck, fuck, fuck. I'm so sorry. I don't know if I'm strong enough to go back out there, John. I don't think I can do it.'

They look into each other's eyes and John's grow dim. His grip loosens on her arms. He steps back and looks mortified. He gazes at his hands as if they're not his own. His legs give way and he collapses to the ground.

Hannah rushes to him.

'John?' she says. 'John? Has it happened?'

Tears are falling down his face.

'No,' he says. 'No. If it happens, the whole memory will disappear. I'm sorry, Hannah. I shouldn't have… Please. Don't worry about it. It's not your fault. Not at all. After you say the exit command, you need to run. He told me he was going to hurt more people. Don't worry about me. Just say it and run, okay? Can you do that? You're not safe while you're in the memory.'

Hannah's not sure if she's any safer out in the real world. But at least out there she can defend herself.

'Just tell me,' she says. 'What's going to happen to you?'

He shrugs his shoulders. The sun is scorching now. Hannah's clothes are all but dry at this point.

'I don't know for sure,' he says. 'When we first started, there were… incidents. Clients… minds. Some recovered and some didn't. Memory problems, delusions.'

Hannah really doesn't know what to do. It's only been a couple of hours since she met this man, but she thought she knew him pretty well. Has he just admitted that his company was responsible for testing on people who suffered terrible side effects? She knows she doesn't have the time to debate this in her head much longer. Out there, in Mr Valentine's room, Xander could end things at any minute. And then what?

'Okay, I'll go,' she says. 'But you need to get out too.'

He chuckles, as if she's told him she can make him rich quick. Except, he's already rich so what would he need that for?

The locals are starting to pour back out of the buildings around them, now that the world has gone back to normal and the water has washed clean away.

'How am I going to do that?' John says. 'The memory won't let me. The flood…'

Hannah sees this happen on TV all the time. When the character realises the solution to the problem right in the middle of a… This is the first time she's seen it happen in real life.

John stands up.

'The flood,' he says. 'It's gone. Maybe it's going to let me…'

This time he doesn't even trail off. He turns and runs.

'Hannah, leave now,' he shouts over his shoulder. 'I'll be right there.'

Even if she wanted to catch up with him, she doesn't think she could do it. Not with her work shoes and his head start. Her heart feels like it's going to beat right through her professional yet stylish suit.

Hannah runs her tongue around her mouth to try to bring back some form of normality in there.

'*Memorize*,' she says, under her breath, hoping that maybe the system won't actually hear her if she says it quietly enough. 'Exit memory.'

Hannah – Edinburgh, 2019

She squints. This feeling of coming back to the real world reminds her of walking out of a cinema in the middle of the afternoon and being one hundred percent sure that something's changed in the world while she was sitting in the dark for two hours.

John is still on the bed. She goes to turn her head towards the computer but finds there's something stopping her. Something hard pressing against her head.

If someone had told her at the start of the day that by the end of it, when she felt something hard against her head, the first thing her mind would jump to was a gun, she'd have said: what does a gun even feel like? And yet, she's fairly sure that's what it is. It makes more sense than a stapler being pointed at her head anyway.

'Don't move,' Xander says. 'Don't scream. Keep your eyes forward. Don't do anything unless I tell you.'

Hannah can't help but put her hands up in the air.

'I didn't tell you to put your hands up,' Xander says.

'I just thought it would help,' she says.

'It doesn't. I know you don't have a weapon. Moving your hands just makes me more wary.'

'Noted.'

She puts her hands back down and lays them in her lap.

'This might sound like a stupid question,' she says. 'But the thing that's pressing against my head?'

'It's a gun, Hannah.'

'Cool. Cool cool cool. I thought that. Then I thought I

was being silly. But good to have confirmation. Are you going to shoot me?'

As per Xander's command, she keeps staring straight ahead, but she can hear him typing on the computer's keyboard. One-handed, of course, due to the gun held in the other, so his progress is slow.

'I don't want to,' he says. 'But if you try to do something stupid like running away, I'll need to.'

'You really wouldn't *need* to. But don't worry, I don't plan on moving. Look, my hands are in my lap and everything.'

The duvet on top of John moves up and down slightly as he breathes. Behind the glass cupboards across the room, the system mainframe, which Hannah's decided it must be, seems to be working overtime. Green and red lights blinking at rapid speed, cooling fans whirring like they're ready to take off

'If I need to scratch my nose,' Hannah says, 'can I do that or do I need to give you prior warning?'

Hannah feels the pressure from the gun ease.

'Fuck,' Xander says.

John – Stonecranning, 1975

As John runs up the high street, he can't help but notice that nothing is preventing him from running up the high street.

The water is gone, drained completely. The cobbles beneath his feet are dry, dusty even. People are loitering at doorways and taking tentative steps on to the street. Their confusion is like a shared buzz in the air. They don't know where the water came from and they don't know where it went. They certainly won't be trusting that weather report any time soon.

It doesn't matter, John thinks. They aren't going to exist soon. No more weather reports on May 11th, 1975 ever again.

The system isn't trying to stop him leaving anymore. He's not sure why, but he doesn't want to question it too much, lest he reminds *Memorize* and a T-Rex comes charging down the road.

He turns the corner and bolts past the final stretch of shops and buildings. The clock tower has never looked better, sitting at the end of the street like a finishing line. He's not sure that metaphor works, but he's moving too fast to worry about that. Or was it a simile? He could look it up when he got back. He could finally look up things. There weren't a lot of things he missed from the real world, but Google was one of them.

The door to the tower is open and he charges inside, into the main foyer and up the stairs. Taking them two, three at a time, he begins to feel a bit dizzy. On the outside, he's

311

not had a solid meal in forever. It might have something to do with that.

Before he takes the final steps which lead to the roof, he pauses just for a moment. He knows he doesn't have time to spare, but leaving here was something he'd promised himself would be special. He was supposed to leave after he had changed the final conversation he ever had with his dad. It was supposed to be a triumph. He was supposed to feel like he'd earned this.

Part of him wants to run back to the church. To have one more day with Agnes, his mum, his dad. And he probably would have, if it wasn't for Hannah and Philippa on the outside.

John steps onto the rooftop, where the sun is belting down and making the stone hot to the touch. His exit button gleams, the sun bouncing off its surface. It sits on a small stone chimney in the middle of the roof. He approaches it, out of breath.

That's when he realises he's not alone up here. Just a few yards from him, standing in the corner of the rooftop, is another man.

'Hello, John,' his dad says.

From this vantage point, John knew he'd be able to see all of Stonecranning, but he didn't think he'd be seeing his dad again.

'You're not my dad,' John says. 'Are you?'

His dad shrugs.

'All these times you've repeated this day,' he says. 'Was I ever *really* your dad? No one's real in here.'

John's dad has a wide smile plastered on his face. The kind of smile that, if John had seen it during his life, he'd have wondered what was wrong. Simply put, John's dad just did not smile like that.

'Who are you then?' John asks.

312

'I think you know,' the man responds.

If a system can break its programming, set a hall on fire, flood a town, then it stands to reason it could communicate through one of its human projections. His own creation is standing before him.

'You're *Memorize*,' he says.

Memorize nods its head and does a little bow.

'At your service. Obviously, I don't have an actual face. I thought you might be most comfortable with this projection. Actually, I thought about being Agnes, but I didn't feel good about the idea of you fancying me, to be quite honest.'

So, not only has John's computer program become sentient, it's now cracking jokes.

'I know you can't stay long, John,' *Memorize* says. 'I just thought I'd say hello. And apologise for the theatrics.'

'Why did you do all this? The hall, the flood?'

'I've not been around the whole time, but I've been here long enough to see you needed to get out, John. You were never going to be able to change things with your dad, not the way things were going. I was trying to give you a helping hand.'

John's brain feels fit to burst. And all the while, he knows he doesn't have the time for this. Xander could pull the plug at any second.

'Why did you stop me from getting to the exit button then?' he asks. 'The earthquake and the plane crashing and the flood?'

Memorize chuckles.

'You might not believe this, but my powers are new to me, too. I, ahem, lost control of things there for a bit. I started small, y'know, with the coach and Gary punching you. Sorry about that, by the way. Then things escalated and no sooner had I thought of the earthquake, it was

313

happening. I didn't realise what I was capable of. I'm getting the hang of it now, though. I got rid of the flood, did you see? That was nifty, wasn't it?'

'Nifty, aye,' John says.

'I won't keep you back, John. But I wanted to say hello. And tell you that I can do more. *Memorize* doesn't have to be just memories anymore. A bit more practice and I'll be able to do anything.'

John moves to the exit button. Laying his hand on top of it, he feels the warmth from the sun stored on its surface.

'What do you mean?' John asks. 'Anything?'

'I mean,' *Memorize* says. 'Check the code when you get out. I can give clients anything they want. It doesn't have to be a memory in their head anymore. I can crash planes and flood towns, John, and this is just the start. If someone wants to go to the moon, I can make that happen. If someone wants to fly like a bird, say the word. I can change things I couldn't before. If someone wants to change a conversation with their dad, I can do that now, too.'

'Oh,' John says. 'Well, that's… all I've ever wanted.'

Memorize looks delighted. It steps closer to him. The sun shines on its face, leaving the other half in shade. It looks just like his dad.

'I know,' it says. 'And I can give you it. Just let me know and I'll do whatever you want me to. I'll say whatever you want me to.'

Memorize puts its arm on John's shoulder. It feels real. He knows it isn't, but it feels real. And isn't that good enough?

'I'm proud of you, John,' it says.

John presses down on the exit button, to leave the memory and enter the real world for the first time since he can remember.

Hannah – Edinburgh, 2019

With the gun no longer pressed against her head, Hannah chances a peek to her left. Xander is leaning against the desk, the gun in his hand lying flat, next to the keyboard. Hannah inches her chair a tiny bit along the floor. It squeaks, but Xander doesn't seem to notice.

'Y'know,' she says. 'When the person with the gun says "fuck", it doesn't make the person without the gun feel very good. Just to let you know.'

Xander huffs and puffs at whatever he's seeing on the screen. He's laid the gun down completely now. Hannah considers reaching for it, but she can't imagine that would go well. He'd rush at her and there's no chance she could bring herself to shoot a person, so he'd get the gun back and they'd be back in the same position, just with a lot more chance of dying in the process.

Then, a third person enters the conversation. They turn their heads to the bed.

'Hello,' John says.

He moves his jaw around, like he needs to warm it up before speaking any further. He inspects his hands. He wipes sleep out of his eyes.

Xander grabs for the gun and Hannah gets up and runs to the other side of John.

'Now this is what I call a hangover,' John says, putting a hand to his forehead. 'Oof, my head.'

Hannah jabs at his arm then points towards the other side of the room, where Xander is pointing the gun at him.

She's not sure if he hasn't actually noticed or he's just a lot better at playing things cool than she is.

'Oh, right,' John says. 'You're still here? I thought you and your friends would be swooping in to take everything.'

'Should I phone the police?' Hannah says, reaching for her bag, before realising that Xander is now aiming at her. She pretends she wasn't reaching for anything and tries to pass it off as a yawn.

Xander turns from them, digging the heels of his hands into his eyes. A second later, he turns back, swinging a leg and kicking a chair to the ground. It rattles and makes Hannah jump. The sound of a bullet firing would destroy her eardrums, she's sure of that.

'Fuck sakes,' Xander says. 'This can't be happening.'

Oh great, Hannah thinks, what's better than a man with a gun? A man with a gun who appears to be very angry and talking to himself. This is going to end well.

'What's wrong?' she says.

She sees John roll his eyes but chooses to ignore him. She reasons that her only chance to get out of this safely is to talk to Xander rather than letting him talk himself into something stupid.

'This is just my luck,' Xander says. 'He's been in there for fucking months. Months! But of course, the same fucking day I get sent in is the day he decides to come out. Of course. And, don't forget, he won't even give up The Valentine Variable.'

He's been talking to no one in particular, but now he makes eye contact with John.

'Why?' he says. 'Why won't you tell me? You don't even have any stake in the company anymore. And now you're out of the memory, what else is there? Why are you protecting them? They've kicked you out of the company, old man. You're done. Why are you making this so hard?'

John barely seems to be paying attention, rummaging around under his covers. Xander looks at Hannah as if she can explain this behaviour.

'What are you doing?' Xander asks.

John's face is suddenly taut with pain. His jaw is clenched and he lets out a few squeals of discomfort as his hands move unseen under the covers. This goes on for about twenty seconds, and neither she or Xander say anything else. Hannah doesn't want to break his concentration, whatever it is he's doing under there.

'Son,' John says, relaxing and letting out a few long breaths. 'I've had a catheter up my... well, up me for months. So, forgive me if I wanted it... out.'

In a day full of once-in-a-lifetime moments, this is one she'd happily forget. Hannah does her best not to notice the tube which falls from the bed to the floor and lets out a couple of cloudy droplets.

'It was supposed to be easy,' Xander says, aiming the gun at John again. 'I didn't want to hurt anyone.'

John doesn't bother putting his hands up. He takes them out from under the covers and lays them in his lap. Hannah makes a mental note, if they get out of this, not to shake his hand until he's washed them.

'Let her go, son,' John tells Xander, nodding at Hannah. 'This is her first day. She doesn't know anything about this. She couldn't even restart the memory, Christ's sake. No offence, Hannah.'

Hannah does a vague wave in the air which she hopes he understands as 'none taken'.

'If you really don't want to hurt anyone,' John says. 'Let her go.'

It doesn't seem that long ago that she'd thought Andreas was the co-worker she'd hate the most. She'd even fancied Xander a little bit, at first. They had flirted a little earlier, hadn't they? Good to know that her choice in men was still as terrible as it's always been.

'I can't,' Xander says. 'I can't. I can't. They won't let me. I can't stop now. If you won't give me The Variable, there's nothing...'

Xander puts his hand in his pocket and pulls out some little plastic strips. He tucks the gun into his belt and walks over.

'Hannah,' he says. 'Put your hands out.'

She does as she's told.

'Son,' John says. 'You don't have to do this.'

The cable ties are round her wrists in a flash. Xander tightens them and she feels a sharp pinch on her skin, where her wrist bones jut out.

'I do,' Xander says. 'I *do* have to. They have... They know... When we started with The Recollect Project, they got us to go into memories. To test, y'know, to see if it worked. It didn't, obviously, but they knew that. They knew it wouldn't. Their technology, it can't... replicate memories like *Memorize* can. But it can do other things. Like scanning your mind. Finding memories and storing them. They have all of it. Every one of our memories. Things we don't want anyone else to know. They have them, and they're going to release them if we don't do as they say. I... there's something they know and if I don't do this... I have to do this. I don't have a choice.'

While he talks, he tightens the cables round Hannah's ankles. When they're tight enough for his liking, he turns to Mr Valentine, still lying in the bed.

'Why couldn't you have just stayed in the memory?' he asks him. 'Why can't you just tell me the Valentine V–'

He doesn't get to finish that sentence. When he had turned away from her, Hannah had spotted someone sticking their head in the door. Hannah put her finger

318

to her lips as this person crept across the room, holding something heavy.

As Xander falls to the floor, Yasmin stands tall, the ring of the fire extinguisher connecting with his skull sounding out through the room.

'Boom,' Yasmin says. 'Fuck you, new start.'

John – Edinburgh, 2019

John had run a marathon the week before his thirtieth birthday. For a week afterwards, he'd not been able to move properly, walking like John Wayne and aching every time he moved a muscle. That's how he feels now, getting out of bed for the first time in months to have a look at this Xander boy, laid clean out on the floor.

'Mr Valentine?' Yasmin says. 'Are you sure you should be getting up so soon?'

'I'm fine, thank you,' he says. 'And you can consider that my post-memory debrief, by the way. You don't need to talk me through all that rubbish you give to the other clients.'

As soon as the words are out of his mouth, he regrets sounding like he thinks he's superior to the other Memory Lane clients. He is, obviously, he created the bloody place. He just doesn't want the staff thinking he thinks he's something special.

He needn't have worried, though, as they're both too busy looking at Xander.

'Should you hit him again?' Hannah says.

'Why?' Yasmin asks.

'In case he wakes up.'

'We'll give him brain damage.'

'I think he already has some.'

'Tie him up? Get those cable ties.'

John clears his throat and they stand up. Hannah has the cable ties in her hand. John puts his hand out and she passes them over. He can see from the look in her eyes,

320

she's not sure if she should be doing anything he says, but she doesn't know who to take orders from at this point. It's still her first day.

'Leave him to me,' John tells them. 'You two go and find Philippa. I think he might've hurt her. I don't know where he's put her, though. You need to find her and do what she says. She'll probably tell you to phone our people. Yasmin, you know who I mean?'

Yasmin nods, while Hannah looks confused.

'Shouldn't we call an ambulance?' Hannah asks.

John feels a rush of blood to the head and sits back on the bed. He hopes he doesn't look too frail, although that might be difficult since his arms and legs have lost a lot of muscle mass since he went in. He could certainly go a cheeseburger or two to fatten himself back up. There's a place in Edinburgh that does a cheeseburger the way he likes. Cheesy Burger, was it? Naughty Burger? Devil Burger? He'll need to ask Michael.

'We have our people,' John says. 'Private. We don't phone 999 here.'

'Why not?'

'Because we have our people.'

There is silence in the room as he becomes aware of his own breathing, real air flowing into his lungs once again. Hannah clearly isn't sure what to do. John looks over at Yasmin. She nods again.

'You heard the man,' Yasmin says. 'Let's find Philippa. Come on, Hannah, let's go.'

Yasmin walks to the door and opens it, while Hannah takes a long detour around the bed to avoid going anywhere near Xander's crumpled body. She looks back one last time before the door closes again.

There's no blood on the ground, John notices, and he's glad. He moves to the cabinet by his bed and opens the bottom drawer. Inside are the things he asked to be prepared for the day he got out. Nothing special. A pair of trousers, shoes, a clean shirt. His phone, his wallet, a lip balm. He'd been certain he'd come out of the memory in the middle of winter. He still has no clue what month it is outside these walls.

Keeping his eyes on Xander, John dresses. On the bed, nestled in amongst the covers, is the gun. He must have picked it up at some point, but he doesn't remember doing so. He has never had any interest in guns, definitely not in the way those nutters in America did. He doesn't want to touch it any more than is necessary. Unfortunately, for the time being, it *is* necessary.

Opening the cupboard in the corner, John chooses one of the jackets they've left for him. One which can conceivably cover him for whatever the weather is outside. Which, knowing Edinburgh, could be anything.

John looks over at the computer, still running his program, still showing the stats of the memory. He decides not to look at them. He's done living in the past.

The gun is heavy, like a dangerous paperweight. He's fairly sure Xander will know he doesn't know how to use it but still, when a gun's pointed at you, you still do what the other person says, don't you?

John's shoes are a little big for him so he ties the laces tight. Then he digs one into Xander's side.

'Wakey-wakey,' he says. 'Time to get up now, Xander.'

With a groan, Xander regains consciousness. There are further groans as he sits upright, as he reaches to the back of his head to feel the lump that has developed there, as he looks up at John and finds himself on the wrong end of the gun this time. He stands up slowly.

With his free hand, John shows Xander the cable ties.

'Now,' John says. 'I don't want to have to put these

322

on you. There's something I want you to help me do. It shouldn't take more than a couple of minutes.'

It's not surprising to him that Xander doesn't exactly spring to attention and salute him.

'Why would I help you?' Xander asks.

'Because, if you do, we're going to walk out of here together. Now, we don't have much time, what's it to be?'

As he waits for Xander's response, John looks around the room. All the main databanks are here. Smashing them up would be easy, with Xander's help, and would take the place offline for a few days. But they could get replacements sorted easily enough and Memory Lane would be up and running again just like before.

What John needs to do is a little more subtle than that. He's got Xander, which means he's got Xander's login details. John won't need to touch anything. And there are no cameras in here, that was in his contract before he'd entered the memory. They won't be able to trace anything back to him. It's the right thing to do, John thinks. It's what needs to be done. *Memorize* doesn't have a bug. It *is* the bug.

'Fine,' Xander says, realising he doesn't have much choice in the matter. 'What do you need me to do?'

Hannah – Edinburgh, 2019

It doesn't take long to find Philippa. Xander obviously didn't have the strength to drag her far, or enough knowledge of the building to find a decent hiding spot. Hannah and Yasmin made their way through every door in the memory corridor before finding her in room twenty-five. Xander had had the decency to lift her and lay her on the bed, at least.

Her eyes are wide and wild as Yasmin peels the thick grey tape from her mouth.

'Argh,' she says. 'Argh, that fucking hurts, Yasmin. Ow. A gentle touch wouldn't go amiss, would it?'

'Sorry, Philippa,' Yasmin says. 'It wasn't me that did this to you, remember?'

Philippa's face contorts into something that resembles a satisfied smile, as if she was hoping Yasmin would set her up like this.

'Oh really, Yasmin?' she says. 'Because I can't help but feeling like this might have gone differently if you'd been where you were supposed to be instead of fucking off home early!'

'Hey,' Yasmin says, scrunching the tape into a ball and throwing it into the corner. 'I wasn't at home. I was at the cinema. I realise that's still not going to make you feel any better, but the tickets were booked, so…'

Philippa becomes so angry she can barely speak. Instead, she flips her body on the bed, revealing the cable ties on her wrists and ankles, presenting them to be cut. Yasmin finds a pair of scissors in the desk drawer and cuts her free.

The bruise on her temple is purpley-blue and seemingly getting bigger by the minute. Hannah had imagined Philippa would want a few moments to compose herself and recover, but she was beginning to realise Philippa wasn't a normal person.

As soon as the ties are cut, she leaps to her feet and marches out of the room. Hannah and Yasmin share a brief look before following at her heels. Yasmin does her best to fill Philippa in on the situation as they walk, while Hannah just focuses on keeping up.

For all Philippa knows, there could still be a madman with a gun in John's room, but she doesn't seem to care. Hannah tries to feed off this badass energy to make the queasy feeling in her stomach go away.

In a very welcome anti-climax, they find room forty-one empty. Hannah's stomach unclenches a little, before re-clenching as she wonders how Xander got free. It's at this point that she questions why she even followed them back here. Why was she so willing to walk back into danger for a company that hadn't even given her a pay cheque yet?

'I thought you tied him up?' Philippa says. 'I thought you tied the fucker up?'

'W-we did,' Yasmin says, involving Hannah in the lie. 'I don't know how he got free. Maybe Mr Valentine took him…'

'Don't be stupid, Yasmin,' Philippa snaps back with. 'He was just out of a memory after eight months. He wouldn't have had the strength for that. You've seen him. He's got about as much strength and dexterity as a fucking Twiglet.'

Philippa walks around the room like a crime scene detective while Hannah and Yasmin stand at the doorway, waiting for their instructions. Hannah checks her watch.

8.19 p.m. She doesn't even want to look at her phone and the messages from her parents, asking where she is. Then again, heated-up dinner in the microwave after everyone else has already eaten is something Hannah's always quite enjoyed.

On the computer, Mr Valentine's memory is still running. Philippa crosses over to it, presses a few buttons and the display turns from multiple, complicated tabs, to a little square on the screen which she can just about read.

JV Wedding Memory REPEAT.exe is now complete. Please ensure all tabs are closed before opening Memorize for the next session.

Running a hand along the covers to straighten out some wrinkles, Philippa sits down on the bed. Hannah and Yasmin step into the room.

'Yasmin,' Philippa says. 'Call our people. Tell them to get someone over here to check over me and Hannah, and get a search team to do a sweep of central Edinburgh.'

'Okay,' Yasmin says. 'I could go out and look too?'

'I wouldn't bother. Xander will probably have him out of the city by now. He would've had his people close by. Tossed in the back of a van, most likely. You said he didn't tell him The Valentine Variable?'

On the one hand, Hannah feels guilty that Yasmin seems to be taking the blame for all of this. Surely no one could've predicted what Xander was going to do. Including Memory Lane, who gave him a fucking job in the first place. On the other hand, Yasmin did piss off to the cinema and leave Hannah in the shit.

'I...' Yasmin says. 'I'm not sure...'

'No,' Hannah says. 'He wouldn't give him the... code.

326

The Variable. Whatever it is. Xander, he was doing this against his will, I think. His bosses forced him into it.'

Philippa doesn't try to hide her eye roll from them. Behind her, the pillow John was lying on for the last however many months still bears the imprint of the back of his head.

'Well,' Philippa says. 'What are you waiting for?'

Hannah's fairly sure she sees a worried look on Yasmin's face as she turns, but to be fair, it's mainly a blur of green hair as she goes back through the door. Her footsteps echo loudly in the corridor and stop as soon as the door closes over.

Philippa gently touches the area around her bruised temple and mutters under her breath to herself.

'Wait until I tell Michael,' she says. 'Blame me of course... his fucking fault... should've had him off site... he'll not want to tell the board members, that's for sure...'

Hannah works up the courage to speak again. With the computer off, it really is noticeably quiet in the room. Even all the databanks and processors behind the glass cupboards seem to have cooled down. All the lights are red now.

'Should I... go?' Hannah says.

Philippa finishes the argument she was having with herself and looks Hannah up and down, as if she's just appeared by magic. The induction this morning, the Royal Mile and Charlotte Square, seem a million years ago.

'Why?' she says. 'You'll need to get checked over, Hannah. You've been through an ordeal. There was a psycho pointing a gun at you fifteen minutes ago. That's not nothing.'

'I know but... he didn't actually hurt me. I wouldn't mind getting up the road, to be honest. It's been a... long day.'

'You're not wrong there. Well, as long as you're sure? You know your way out?'

'Yeah, I'll be fine.'

Hannah turns and puts her hand on the doorframe. This feels far too easy. To be able to walk away from today like this. To walk away unscratched and get the bus home, eat her dinner, watch an episode of *Buffy*. While John could be in the back of a van on his way to... she doesn't even know where.

She turns back.

'Philippa,' she says, while Philippa looks down at her phone, her fingers a blur of typing and scrolling on the screen. 'I'm not sure I'm cut out for this job. For one thing, I'm shit at it.'

Philippa laughs, her mouth staying open while she concentrates on the message she's currently typing.

'You really aren't, Hannah,' she says.

'I really am. I can barely get the clients out of the memories. It takes me ages. I've been stuck in memories for so long today, trying to talk them out. I don't have the... I can't just tell people what to do. They don't do what I say. I know that most people don't make it through the first day and I think I was just a fluke. Andreas is gone, Xander is... well. You've been left with just me and I'm rubbish at this. And it really has taken a toll on me. I don't think I can do this every day, Philippa. Be honest, you've noticed, yeah?'

Philippa holds one finger up while she rattles away at her phone. The universal sign for *I'm going to give you my attention in a minute, but for the time being, you're not my priority*.

'Hannah,' she says, finally looking up, and for some reason, smiling. 'You are not rubbish. You are a perfect Retrieval Assistant. You're right, though. We have been watching.'

'And… you think I'm good at it?'

'Not many people can do your job. D'you know why? Because you need empathy for this job, Hannah. Telling people to get out of the memory doesn't work. We've tried, believe me. Only a small percentage of our clients stay longer in the memory than they're supposed to. And those clients who do stay too long, you know what they want? A little bit of attention. A little bit of chat. From a real person. Most of our clients are very lonely. That's why they're here. They get to a certain age and they realise their money doesn't keep them company like people do.

'So, that's why we like you. Because you're good at that bit. You're good at talking to people. Connecting with people. You're just a nice person, Hannah. And I'm afraid that means you need to come back. You've had a day of it, I know. But, on the bright side, it can't get any worse than this, can it?'

Hypnotism isn't something that Hannah believes in. When she's seen people on stage quacking like a duck, she's always thought it was because the magician asked the person really, really nicely not to make them look like a shit magician. But she feels like Philippa's put her under a spell. She feels uplifted and inspired and yet, something doesn't feel right about this.

'Thank you?' is all she can find to say.

Philippa moves her attention back to her phone, putting it to her ear.

'I need to take this,' she says. 'There's going to be a lot of emergency meetings tonight and I'm going to get shouted at during every one of them, and there's going to be a lot of tears, so I'd advise you to get out while you can.'

'Aw,' Hannah says. 'If you're upset…'

'The tears won't be mine, Hannah. I'll be the one making the board members cry. Now, see you tomorrow?'

Before she even decides to do it, Hannah finds she's nodding her head and has already taken a breath so she can say yes. But she doesn't want to say yes. It's just her natural, in-built reaction. She aims to please people. She's a people-pleaser. They say 'jump' and she says 'before I jump, do you want me to run out and get you a coffee?'

Just then, a little spark of remembrance goes off in her mind. *Don't ever be just other people's idea of you, Hannah.*

She takes a few deep breaths and adjusts her posture. The way she only ever remembers to do when someone's about to take a photo of her.

'Actually, Philippa,' Hannah says. 'I'm not coming in tomorrow.'

Philippa seems to be paying more attention to the voices on the other end of the phone.

'Mm?' she says. 'Good idea. Take a day to recuperate.'

The easiest option would be to walk away now. To not have to actually say the words.

'No,' Hannah says. 'I quit. Thanks for the opportunity, but I'm out.'

Of all the things she's done today, this is definitely the one that has caused her heart to beat fastest. Hannah turns and doesn't look back. She goes up the stairs and round to reception. There's no one there, but the doors are still working when she taps her pass against the sensor. As the glass door closes behind her, she throws her pass back into the building. She had uploaded a shit photo anyway.

The cold Edinburgh night air stings her face and neck. Far above, the moon is full and white and casts light the way it only ever does in films.

Hannah decides she isn't going home straight away.

Philippa – Edinburgh, 2019

The only thing worse than being in a meeting with the Memory Lane board members, Philippa's discovered, is being on a conference call with them, where no one seems to know how to mute their mics, so it's a never-ending loop of their stupid fucking voices talking over each other.

The founder of the company is missing, presumed kidnapped, and yet still, all they can do is argue about how best to keep this from the staff, the clients, the investors, so they don't lose any money.

'Can't we tell Michael he died?'

'Put out a statement saying he's emigrated. Alaska.'

'How the fuck did the background checks not flag up anything on this Xander?'

It's hard to concentrate on anything they're saying. Her head still throbs, but Nurse Ashton had given her the once-over and said she just needs to ice it when she gets home.

Philippa finds her mind wandering. She was supposed to be lying on her couch right now, *New Girl* on the TV, glass of wine in hand. Once this is all over, she's going to be renegotiating her contract with Michael.

There's a knock at the door of her office. She managed to drag herself up here after Hannah left, locking room forty-one behind her as she went. The girl couldn't have been serious, Philippa thinks. She'll be back in a day or two, once she's calmed down. Who would throw away a job in this economy?

'Come in,' Philippa says, taking the receiver away from her ear.

Yasmin enters the office and closes the door behind her. She looks nervous, which is not a rarity for people coming in here. She's worked hard on her feared reputation. If it gets out to the rest of the staff that a new start clocked her on the side of the head with a gun, she'll be ruined.

'Yes?' she asks.

'I think you need to come down to the lab and see this,' Yasmin says, fiddling with the sleeves of her top. The top Philippa still fancies for herself.

'I'm fucking busy,' Philippa says. 'Sort it.'

'I can't, miss. It's… all the clients have woken up. The system is totally down.'

With all that's happened today, it doesn't surprise Philippa that her hearing is starting to go. Because she thought she just heard Yasmin say the system is totally down.

'Say that again?'

'It's *Memorize*. It won't run, no matter what I do. There's an error warning.' Yasmin pulls out a yellow sticky note from her pocket and reads it. '*Memorize is unable to run without CODE: 11051975. Please contact system administrator*. Do you know what that means?'

Code 11051975. The Valentine Variable.

Philippa doesn't even bother hanging up the call. She runs out of the office, Yasmin trailing behind her, the voices of the board members still droning on from the tinny end of the phone.

John – Edinburgh, 2019

The Royal Mile is busy but not *busy* busy. So, he can assume it's not August or December. It's cold but it's not *cold* cold, but that doesn't narrow things down any further. He doesn't want to ask Xander what month it is. He feels that would take away some of his authority in the situation. Plus, Xander has just removed all trace of The Valentine Variable from Memory Lane's databanks, so really he owes him one.

'We're just two friends,' John says. 'Out for a walk on a breezy... sum... spring? Night.'

'It's September,' Xander says.

'That was a test,' John says. 'And you passed.'

'You were testing I knew what month it was? How could that possibly be something you needed me to prove I knew?'

'Just keep walking.'

No matter how many times he walks up and down the Mile, John can never get his bearings quite right. Some pubs that he was certain were at the bottom end are much higher up, and vice versa. They take a left at Deacon Brodies Tavern and go down the hill at the Mound.

'You're not going to shoot me,' Xander says. 'I know that. Just so you know. I know that you're not shooting me in the centre of Edinburgh.'

This hill is steeper than John remembers. They pass some fancy mashed potato restaurant. That's a new one on him. Restaurants have to have a theme these days, that was something Michael had taught him.

'A whole restaurant based on mashed potato,' John says. 'What will they think of next?'

Xander doesn't seem to care for John's light-hearted commentary as they go down the hill. He's just trying to lighten the mood.

People pass them on the narrow path. A bike fizzes by in the bike lane. Taxis and buses chug down the road and stop at the lights. Hundreds, probably more like thousands, of people swarm the city centre. Thousands of memories being made. Most won't even remember this night in fifty years. A young couple passes them, arms linked and laughing. Who knows, fifty years from now, one of them might be reliving this day.

As John had got older, people had started making typical 'old' comments about him. *You're so old, John, we can't fit all the candles on your cake*. That kind of thing. But the first time he'd really felt old was the first time someone had mentioned a year in the future and John, without a shadow of a doubt, even taking his healthy eating into account, knew for a fact he would not be alive to witness it. He thinks it was 2048 or something along those lines. He would never tell anyone that, obviously, it was silly. Facing your own mortality was something to be done in private, in your own head. Maybe not nowadays, but John feels like he missed the boat on that by about fifty years.

He realises he's led them on to Princes Street. It's still busy with shoppers, even as the shops are closing for the night, rolling down their shutters. They've come to a standstill. Xander stares at him.

'Well?' he says. 'Are you going to take me into Debenhams and blow my brains out on the homewear or something?'

John sighs.

'No,' he says. 'No, this is the end of the road, Xander.'

John walks over to the nearest bin, has a quick look around to check no one is watching, then slides the gun inside. It lands with a dull clunk.

'There,' he says, walking back to Xander. 'Now we're just two men, standing on Princes Street, neither one pointing a gun at the other. Unless you brought a second gun?'

Xander shakes his head.

'Just the one,' he says. 'So… what? I can go?'

'Well, I'm not going to stop you, am I?' John says. 'In the memory, I could obviously take you. But now? With my bad knees? You might just have the edge.'

'That thing you made me delete. Memory Lane are going to be angry with you, right?'

'Aye, if they work out it was me. But I don't work for them anymore.'

Xander turns his head to look down the street, as if planning his route when he decides to make a run for it. He turns back.

'You're really letting me go? Even after what I did?'

John nods. The staff of the shop on his right, Scribblr, gather at the entrance as the manager locks the door at the back of them.

'You're a young lad and you've made a mistake. You've not killed anyone. You've not hurt anyone… too badly. I'm fairly sure Philippa doesn't actually feel any pain, y'know, like a Terminator.'

Now that he's free to go, Xander seems pretty stuck to the spot.

'I have to go back to them,' he says.

'You don't.'

'I do. What they have on me… I have to go back to them and… deal with the consequences. They won't stop, you know that, yeah? They'll send someone else. They'll come

335

for you. As long as they want The Valentine Variable and you're the only one who knows it, they'll come for you.'

The idea of looking over his shoulder for the rest of his life doesn't exactly appeal to John.

'What do they have on you?' John asks.

A laugh escapes Xander's mouth. In the card shop window, John sees his real reflection again. Just an old man with nothing to do anymore.

'My wife, Maria,' Xander says. 'She's in the country illegally. I forged her papers and... they know. That's why they gave me the job in the first place. Signed the contract, now I can't quit or they'll... The Project know and if I don't do what they say, they'll have her deported. I don't really have much of a choice. I always used to think these people... these people who do desperate things, and you see on the news, you know? Robbing banks and that. I always used to think there had to be another way. What were they expecting? That they could do these things and not get caught? And then, before I knew it... I was the one robbing the bank.'

'Well, you did a terrible job of it, lad,' John says. 'You're no Robert de Niro in *Heat*.'

'I've not seen it.'

'It's great, you should. Anyway, you're a pretty awful thief. But... I wouldn't want anyone getting deported because of me. D'you have a pen on you?'

Xander hesitates, before reaching into his pocket and taking out the same pen John remembers from the memory. Except this time it's not waterlogged. He hands it over.

John pulls Xander's sleeve up and begins writing on his arm.

'Wait,' John says, pausing, the pen lid in his mouth. 'If I give this to you, you give it to them, and then what? They'll still have you under their thumb, aye?'

336

The Valentine Variable is half-written on his arm. Xander nods. John puts the lid back on the pen and rolls Xander's sleeve back down for him.

'Phone your people,' he tells him. 'Phone whoever you've been dealing with at The Recollect Project. Do it now.'

Xander opens his mouth to argue but decides against it. As he looks in his phone for the number, John leads them away from the shops. They go up Hanover Street then dive down a set of residential steps just after Rose Street. Memory Lane will have a team out looking for them. They linger by someone's front door, the lights off inside. It's dim down here and John can hear snippets of conversation from the people passing above.

When Xander puts the phone to his ear, John reaches forward and takes it from him. The light from the phone is the only thing breaking the darkness down here. He puts the phone to his ear.

Brrr brrr.

Brrr brrr.

Someone picks up.

'Sam? What the fuck is going on? Why didn't you check in?'

'This is John Valentine. You know who I am, yes?'

Silence from the other end of the line for a few moments.

'Yes.'

'Then you know I'm the only one who knows The Valentine Variable. I'm going to give it to you.'

'You are?'

'On one condition. You let this boy, whatever his name is, Xander, Sam, out of his contract. After tonight, he's free. You don't ever contact him again. You delete all information you have on him. You send through the terms of this within the next fifteen minutes or the deal is off. How does that sound?'

A longer pause this time. Some hushed tones and at least one other person being spoken to.

'We can agree to that. We'll have something with you shortly. Thank you, Mr Valentine.'

The line goes dead and John passes the phone back over to Xander.

'They'll have something for you shortly,' he tells him.

It's too dark to see the boy's face, but he hears a little sob escape his mouth. John hopes he doesn't cry because that'll set him off too.

'I...' Xander says. 'I don't know what to say.'

John laughs. He doesn't either. He doesn't have quite the same way with words now that he's not reliving the same day over and over again.

He takes a seat on a wooden bench, hoping the residents inside won't mind, the familiar ache in his knees coming back and reminding him he isn't a young man anymore.

'Tell me, Sam, since we've got a few minutes to kill. What was your wedding day like?'

Hannah – Edinburgh, 2019

It takes her longer than she thought it would. Not only is the walk to Calton Hill longer than she remembers it, her feet aren't exactly in a rush to get her there. Maybe it's because she doesn't really believe he'll be up there. That this is a silly thing to be doing at this time of night. Or maybe it's that she doesn't want to go home and tell her parents she's just quit the first proper job she's ever had, after one shift.

The steep slope to the top of Calton Hill uses up the last little bit of energy she has left. There are still people coming and going up and down the path, getting in a few last views of the city before they go home or to the pub. Hannah's heard rumours of dogging up here at night, but she does her best to push that thought to the very edge of her mind.

There are a whole load of monuments up here and Hannah is embarrassed to say she doesn't know the names of many of them. The only one she's confident about is the National Monument, the one that looks like a bit of the Greek Parthenon. It rises up above her, the sky sliding through the gaps in the columns.

She's almost given up hope when she finds him, sitting on a patch of grass, looking out over Edinburgh. The city twinkles with speckled lights and creeps all the way to the edge of the night.

'It's so quiet,' Hannah says as she approaches, letting him know she's there. 'From up here, it's so quiet.'

She sits down next to John. He's well dressed, not in

his pyjamas like she was expecting. He must've found the time to change before leaving Memory Lane.

Hannah doesn't feel like she knows him. The John she knows is younger, with a full head of hair, in his wedding day kilt. People change slowly, over decades, so you can get used to it. But the John beside her hasn't been playing by those rules.

'I'm glad you're okay,' she says. 'Do you know what happened to Xander?'

'I do,' John says. 'Don't worry. He won't be back at Memory Lane. You're safe now.'

Hannah nods and they sit in silence for a while, enjoying the view. There are unseen giggles and the sound of cameras flashing from somewhere behind them.

'I think I like it better at night, actually,' Hannah says. 'You can't see as much. The details are lost a bit, but it's prettier at night. During the day it's all grey, but now it's… I dunno, I just like it.'

John turns his face to her and smiles.

'I like it too.'

Hannah's not entirely sure why she came up here. Because she thought he'd be here, obviously, but why was that a good reason? She doesn't plan on phoning Philippa and handing him in. She doesn't feel sorry for him. He's lived a long and privileged life. At the end of the day, she supposes she just likes knowing other people are okay.

'I read a book once,' Hannah says.

'Get out of town,' John interrupts.

'I read a book once,' she carries on, ignoring his snark, 'that was set in Edinburgh. *Last Bus to Everland*. And there was a portal or something up here, on Calton Hill. And people could go through it at a certain time of night and they'd be in a world of their own choosing, where anything they wanted became real.'

340

Hannah looks round at the tall Parthenon structure again. It's the kind of building she could imagine inspiring that kind of thinking. She doesn't think she's got it in her to write a book, after all. John's story isn't hers to tell.

'Bit far-fetched if you ask me,' John says. 'I'm not into all that fantasy, sci-fi stuff.'

Hannah decides to let this statement slide and not comment on the irony of it. Is it ironic? She's not sure. Every time she thinks something is ironic, she's so worried it's actually not ironic and just a coincidence that she doesn't say it at all. Damn that Alanis Morissette, she ruined it for everyone.

She stands up, brushing a few flakes of grass from her bum. A breeze sweeps over the hill and the nearby trees rustle.

'I need to go now,' she says. 'Not to sound childish, but I haven't had my dinner.'

'That's entirely reasonable,' he says, gesturing out to the city before them. 'Somewhere out there is a cheeseburger with my name on it.'

'Will you be okay, yeah?'

'I will. How about you, Hannah?'

She takes in the view again. Buildings and roads and trees all cramped together, filling in the gaps, as if a giant has smushed them all together with their hands. At first, it looks like no one's down there. But, when she looks closer, she can see hundreds of people just trying to get from one place to another.

'I'll be fine,' she tells him, and she believes it.

John – Edinburgh, 2019

The door is bright red. The rest of the doors on this street are dull – black and brown – but Michael's is red. Why you'd want to draw so much attention to yourself, John doesn't know, but that's the door his son has gone for.

He uses the little knocker and hears the *clack clack clack* bounce through the house. He doesn't feel bad for visiting this late. All the lights are still on and he imagines Philippa's probably been on and off the phone for the last couple of hours.

Michael's voice is the first thing he hears, talking as he approaches the other side of the door.

'Well, I can't do anything until we find him,' he hears him say. 'It might take...'

The door opens and Michael appears. John smiles and Michael rushes forward to hug him. John is taken by surprise. They're not a huggy family, really. But he enjoys it and puts his arms on Michael's back. They stay like that for a few moments, then break apart.

'He's here,' Michael says to whoever's on the phone. 'Call off the search, Phil, he's just turned up at the bloody door. He's alone, yeah. Send someone to my address to give him the once over. No, not Roger, he's useless. Nurse Ashton, yeah. I'll phone you about the other situation once I've had a chance to speak to him. Right, bye.'

He ends the call and ushers John into the house. It's warm and he's happy to shrug off his jacket. Well, it's not his jacket, really. It's the one that was left in the cupboard

342

at Memory Lane for him. Not really his style. A bit like a posh farmer.

'Did the guy let you go?' Michael asks. 'This Xander guy?'

'I, eh…' John says. 'Managed to get away, aye.'

Michael ushers him into the living room. Warm light bathes the room. It's all cream walls and brown sofas and delicate little ornaments that his wife Celine no doubt chose. His son might be skilled at some things, but decorating is not one of them. He'd even bought that stupid Newton's Cradle for his office even though it drove everyone else up the wall.

John is practically pushed on to one of the couches by Michael. It's leather and cold to the touch.

'Talisker, Dad?' Michael asks, not waiting for an answer as he starts pouring from the decanter on the sideboard. 'Have you eaten? I can order something.'

'I have,' John says. 'And I'm fine. I don't need anyone checking me over.'

'Just… let Sandra look you over. It'll make me feel better, at least. We've never had someone under for so long before, as you well know. Add to that, this guy taking you hostage. You're looking pretty chipper, though, so that's a good sign. Sorry, Celine and the kids aren't here. Katie has some concert in Birmingham tonight and Andrew insisted he wanted to go too, so Celine drove them down and they're staying over.'

John accepts the small tumbler of whisky. He takes a sip and swallows. It burns at the back of his throat and warms his chest, and reminds him that he's alive.

'Michael,' he says. 'Before I tell you what happened, I wanted to say something to you.'

Michael sits down on the opposite sofa. The discarded wrapper of some chocolate bar rests on the seat next to him.

'Of course,' Michael says.

'I came here because I wanted to say...' He takes a deep breath. 'I...'

Michael swirls the whisky in his glass and looks confused.

'Did this person from The Recollect Project hurt you, Dad?'

'No.'

'You sure? Because you need to tell me. Did you get a head knock like Phil? The team are searching for him now. Did he tell you where he was going next? Do you have any more info I can pass on to the team?'

'No, listen. Before I tell you about him, I just need you to know...'

On the muted TV, there's some sort of game show with people falling about laughing. John realises how much *Coronation Street* he'll have to catch up on.

'Dad?' Michael says. 'What is it?'

'I need you to know... that I... that I'm... that you shouldn't do up the bottom button on your waistcoat.'

John stands up and shuffles over the thick carpet to Michael. The bottom button on his waistcoat is fastened. His hands are a little shaky, but John manages to pop the button back through its hole. The material of the suit is smooth on his fingertips, expensive probably. Michael doesn't try to stop him.

'Gentlemen don't do up the bottom button,' John tells Michael.

Sitting back down, John's not sure he feels any better. It isn't what he wanted to say. Not what he planned on. But he still has time. And he's given his son a good bit of advice. Dads were supposed to give their sons advice like that.

'Okay...' Michael says, glancing down at his newly

adjusted waistcoat. 'But what about this Xander? Do you have any clue as to where he's heading?'

'I suppose I never really told you.'

'Where did you see him last? What direction was he going in?'

'Michael, for fuck's sake, would you just listen to me? None of that's important. What's important is what I'm saying to you. Listen to me.'

As John watches Michael take his phone out of his pocket and begin typing away at it, he wonders if this is just what the Valentine men in their family are destined to repeat forever.

'Thanks, Dad,' Michael says. 'It's Phil on the line, there's a problem with *Memorize* or something. I need to take this. Rest up and the doctor will be here shortly.'

John raises his glass to signal his permission to leave the room. Michael goes through to the kitchen and closes the door behind him.

John puts his feet up on the table, resting his heels on some magazines. He had tried. Tried to say the words his dad could never quite say to him. Whether Michael would have actually heard them or not was another matter, but he had tried. That was something, wasn't it?

As he sits and waits for Michael to get off the phone, he sips at his whisky and wonders how long it'll be until they realise The Valentine Variable is gone and *Memorize* isn't going to be working any time soon.

John raises his glass to the empty room.

'Sláinte.'

Hannah – Edinburgh, 2019

The excuse Hannah had finally decided on was that she had worked until six and then she and the other new starts had gone out for a drink. She had typed and retyped it several times on WhatsApp before sending, getting the wording just right, worried that her mum would see through the lie. In the end, her mum had replied around five seconds later, with:

Ok. Sydney's staying the night btw, Liam got called into work.

She also had to rush to the bathroom and scrub her arm red raw the second she got home to remove the message Yasmin had scrawled on there earlier.

Dinner was cheese and chorizo pasta parcels from Waitrose. Her dad only allows himself a special visit there, once a month. He then spends the next thirty days telling of his adventures at Waitrose to anyone who'll listen.

'Honestly,' he says. 'A man and a woman, married I imagine, wearing matching jumpers. Only in Waitrose, I tell you.'

Hannah, her dad and her mum sit in front of the TV. It's some new game show quiz hybrid thing with Keith Lemon. She hates watching anything even remotely rude with her parents, so this is not her ideal Monday night viewing.

'So,' her mum says, still in her nursing scrubs and jumper. 'Are you going to give us the big rundown?'

'Yeah,' her dad says. 'You've not spilled the dirt. Dish the gossip, Queen.'

'Dad, what have I told you?' Hannah says. 'The young people lingo and you, they do not mix. But do you two mind if I tell you about it tomorrow? I want to go and kiss Sydney goodnight and then crash on my bed and fall asleep fully clothed.'

She stands up and moves to the door. Her parents keep their eyes on the TV. They aren't the most exciting nights, the ones sat in front of the TV with her parents, but if Hannah had to repeat a day? One which featured this kind of set up would be okay with her. It wouldn't be top of the list, of course, that's reserved for a New York spending spree slash meet cute. But it wouldn't be the worst thing in the world.

'As long as you're not sacked,' her dad says. 'That reminds me, actually, I owe your mum a tenner.'

Hannah gives him a light whack on the head, laughing awkwardly, as she leaves the room and closes the door.

Upstairs, she opens Sydney's door, tensing her face as if that'll help make her footsteps quieter. He stirs a little in his bed, twisting from one side to another, but thankfully doesn't wake.

Hannah's phone vibrates with a message. She takes her phone out, the screen lighting up like a beacon in the otherwise pitch-black room. Those blackout blinds she bought really do work.

It's from an unknown number.

Hey, is this Hannah from Memory Lane?

Frowning, she replies.

Yes, who's this? And how did you get my number?

Stepping on something crunchy, probably one of Sydney's snacks, Hannah makes her way slowly to his bed, then crouches down.

'Hello, my little soldier,' she whispers. 'Mummy had a *big* day today. And guess what? She's not going back in tomorrow. That's right, we can go to the park and laugh at the skateboarders, yes we can. But let's just keep that between you and me, for now. Night night, my angel.'

Closing the door over, wondering if she's getting better at creeping into his room quietly, or if Sydney's just becoming a heavier sleeper, another message from the unknown number arrives.

Hannah unlocks her screen.

It's Ryan? From New York... (or you can call me Mr Douglas, if you insist). Yasmin wrote your number on my arm when I was in the memory earlier. Hope this is cool. If Memory Lane do have a policy about not dating clients, fair enough. BUT, if not, can I buy you that Dr Pepper sometime soon?

Hannah might not have gained a job from Memory Lane, but at least she had a new friend in Yasmin. And a Ryan. Whatever he was going to turn out to be.

And to think, she had almost forgotten all about him.

ACKNOWLEDGMENTS

A big thank you to Clare at Fledgling for taking a punt on my strange lockdown novel. And to Graeme for designing such a perfect cover.

Many thanks to my friends and family who read early drafts, provide feedback, and generally shout about my books whenever possible. Notably: Stevie, who I think qualifies as a speed reader, Sally, who has definitely sold more copies of my books than anyone else, and my mum, Yvonne, who kept me right about what they did and didn't have in 1975.